THE DIRE DAYS OF WILLOWWEEP MANOR

For Andrew, my parents, and Daniel Pinkwater
—Shaenon

For Cedra
—Christopher

MARGARET K. McELDERRY BOOKS · An imprint of Simon & Schuster Children's Publishing Division · 1230 Avenue of the Americas, New York, New York 10020 · This book is a work of fiction. Any references to historical events, real people, or real places are used fictitiously. Other names, characters, places, and events are products of the author's imagination, and any resemblance to actual events or places or persons, living or dead, is entirely coincidental. · Text © 2021 by Shaenon K. Garrity · Illustrations © 2021 by Christopher John Baldwin · Cover design by Karyn Lee © 2021 by Simon & Schuster, Inc. · All rights reserved, including the right of reproduction in whole or in part in any form. · MARGARET K. McELDERRY BOOKS is a trademark of Simon & Schuster, Inc. · For information about special discounts for bulk purchases, please contact Simon & Schuster Special Sales at 1-866-506-1949 or business@simonandschuster.com. · The Simon & Schuster Speakers Bureau can bring authors to your live event. For more information or to book an event, contact the Simon & Schuster Speakers Bureau at 1-866-248-3049 or visit our website at www.simonspeakers.com. · Also available in a Margaret K. McElderry Books hardcover edition · Interior design by Christopher John Baldwin and Karyn Lee · The text for this book was set in Baldwin. · The illustrations for this book were rendered digitally. · Manufactured in China · First Margaret K. McElderry Books paperback edition July 2021 · 2 4 6 8 10 9 7 5 3 1 · Library of Congress Cataloging-in-Publication Data · Names: Garrity, Shaenon K., author. | Baldwin, Christopher, 1973– illustrator. · Title: The dire days of Willowweep manor / Shaenon K. Garrity ; illustrated by Christopher John Baldwin. · Description: First Margaret K. McElderry Books paperback edition. | New York : Margaret K. McElderry Books, 2021. | Audience: Ages 14 up. | Audience: Grades 10–12. | Summary: After she saves a man from drowning, Haley wakes up in a pocket universe that appears as a gothic estate and helps three brothers whose job it is to protect her world against a penultimate evil. · Identifiers: LCCN 2020042104 (print) | ISBN 9781534460874 (hardcover) | ISBN 9781534460867 (paperback) | ISBN 9781534460881 (ebook) · Subjects: LCSH: Graphic novels. | CYAC: Graphic novels. | Multiverse—Fiction. | Good and evil—Fiction. · Classification: LCC PZ7.7.G394 Di 2021 (print) | DDC 741.5/973—dc23 · LC record available at https://lccn.loc.gov/2020042104

THE DIRE DAYS OF WILLOWWEEP MANOR

Shaenon K. Garrity
Christopher Baldwin

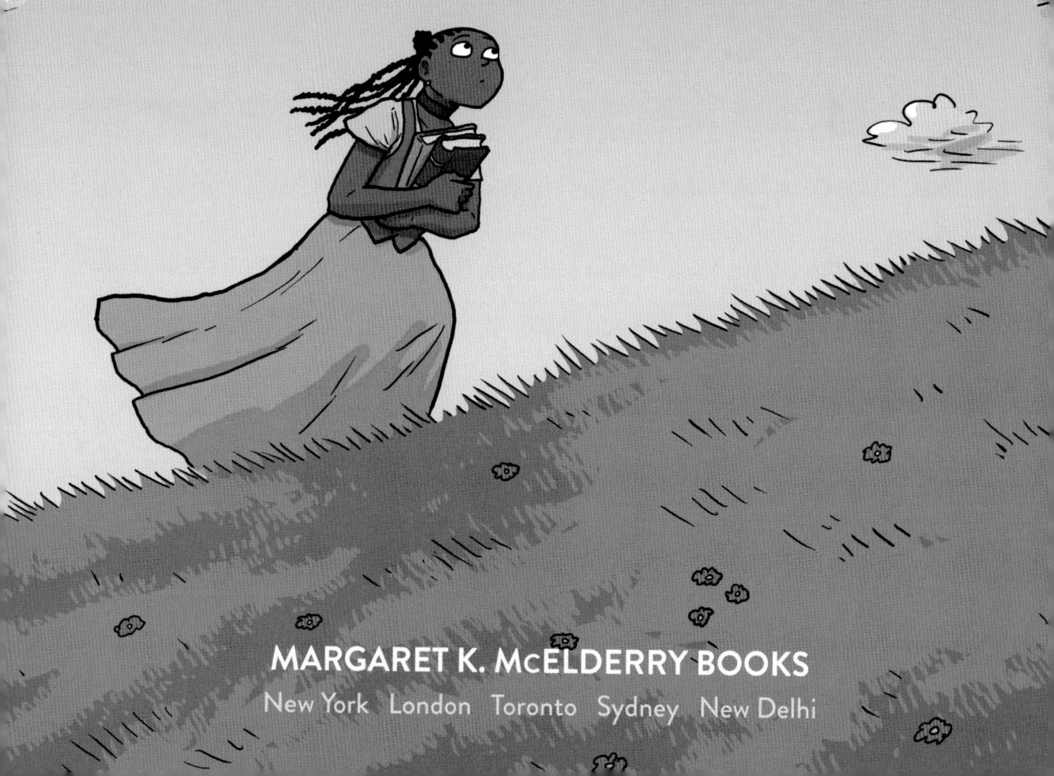

MARGARET K. McELDERRY BOOKS
New York London Toronto Sydney New Delhi

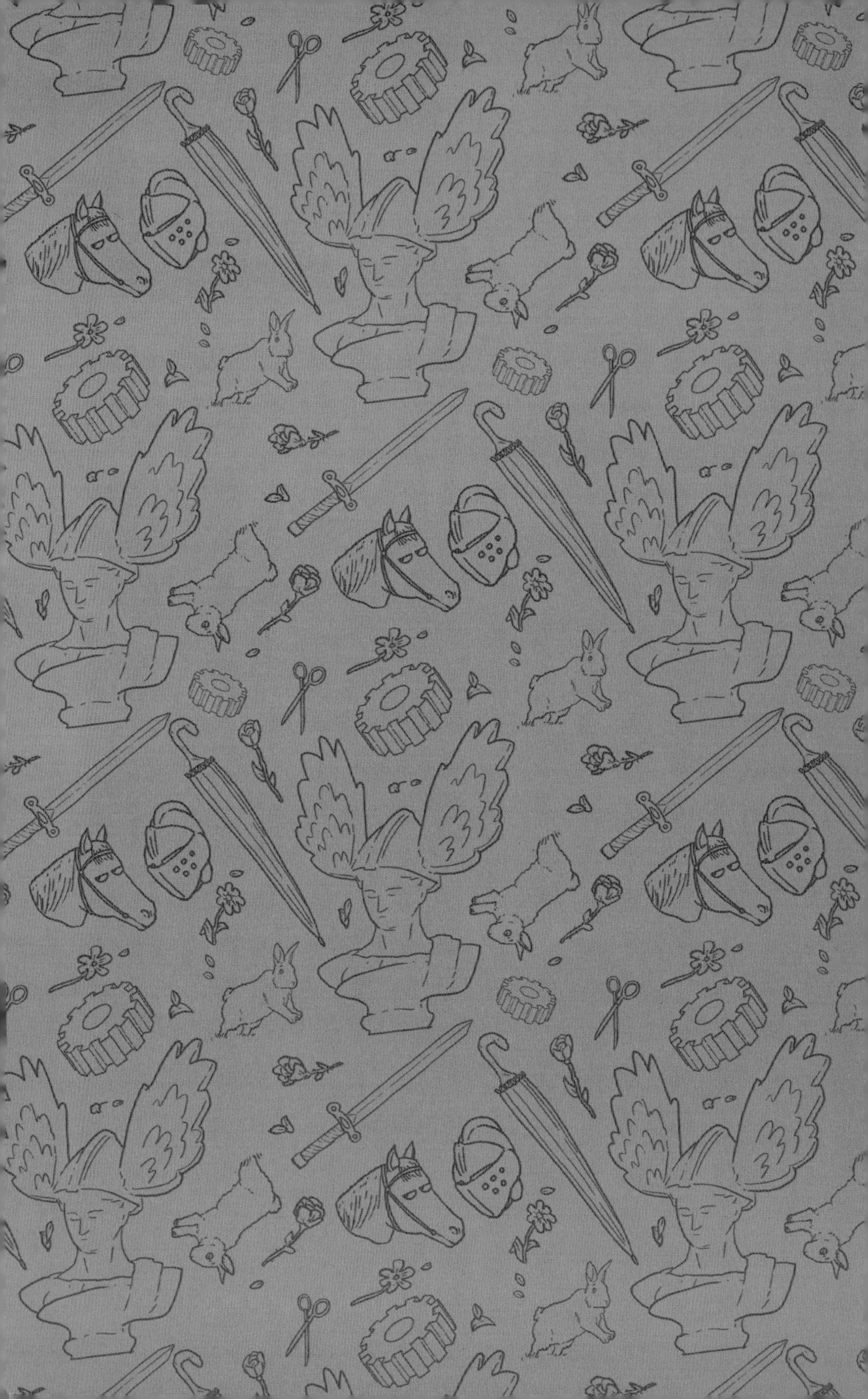

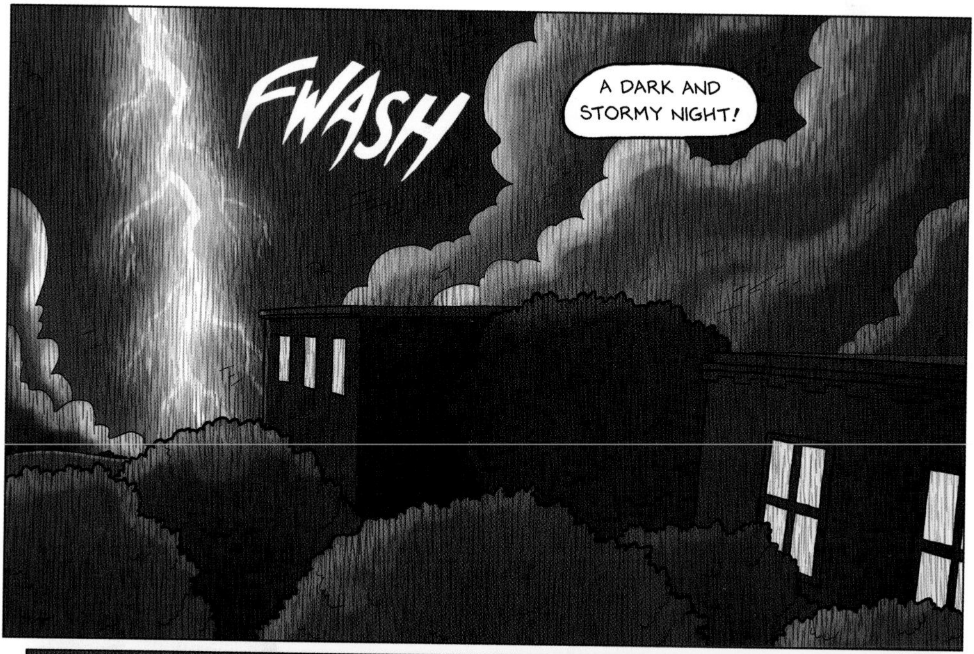
FWASH
A DARK AND STORMY NIGHT!

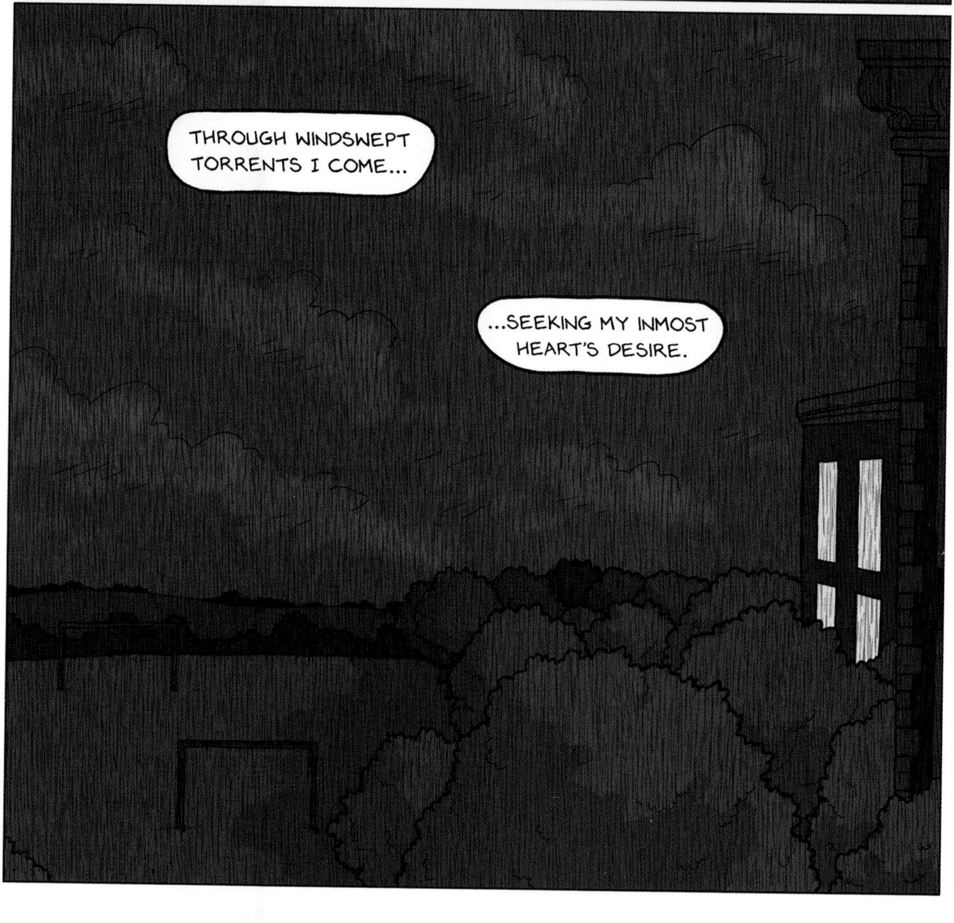
THROUGH WINDSWEPT TORRENTS I COME...
...SEEKING MY INMOST HEART'S DESIRE.

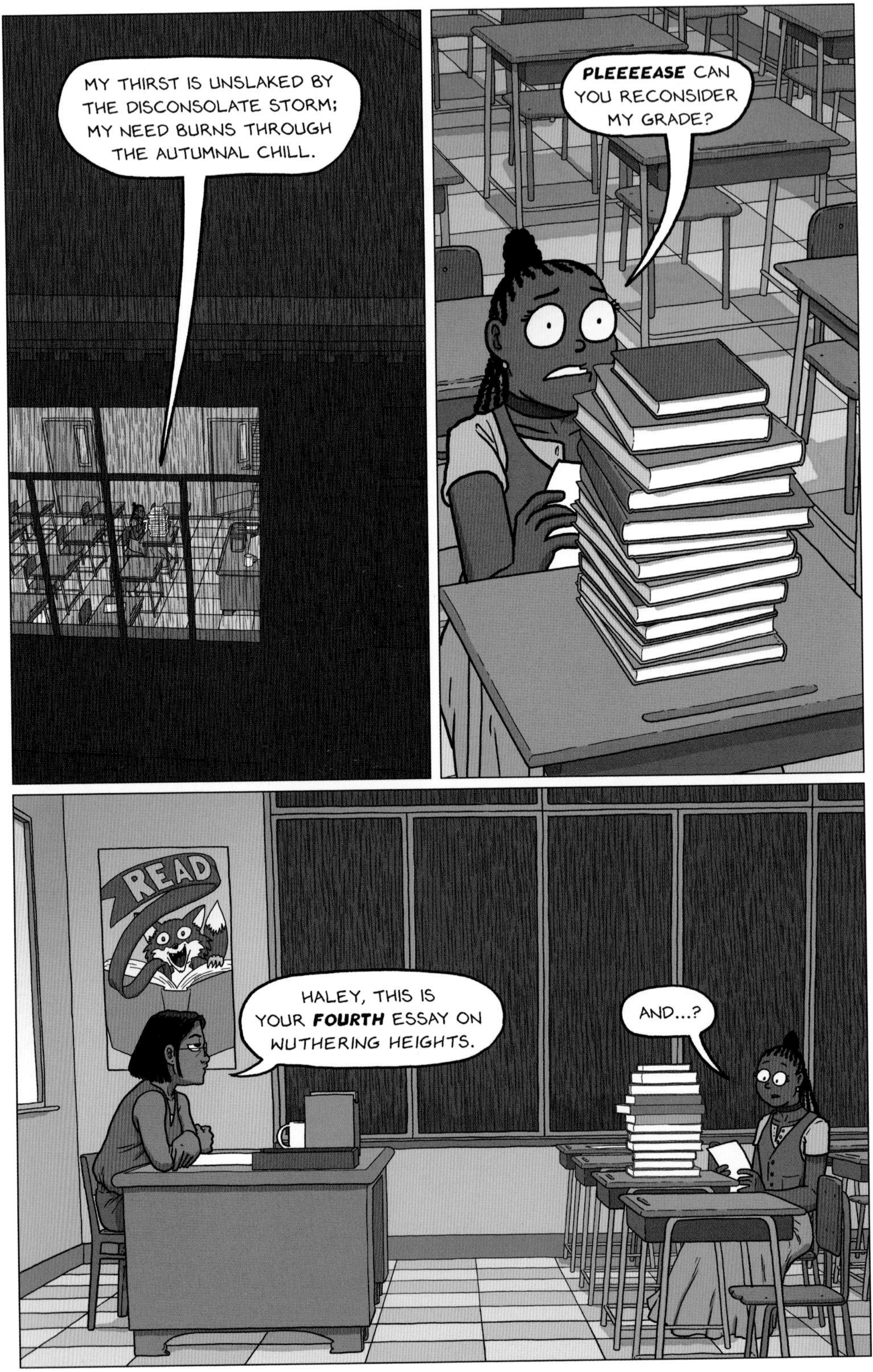
MY THIRST IS UNSLAKED BY THE DISCONSOLATE STORM; MY NEED BURNS THROUGH THE AUTUMNAL CHILL.
PLEEEEASE CAN YOU RECONSIDER MY GRADE?
READ
HALEY, THIS IS YOUR **FOURTH** ESSAY ON WUTHERING HEIGHTS.
AND...?

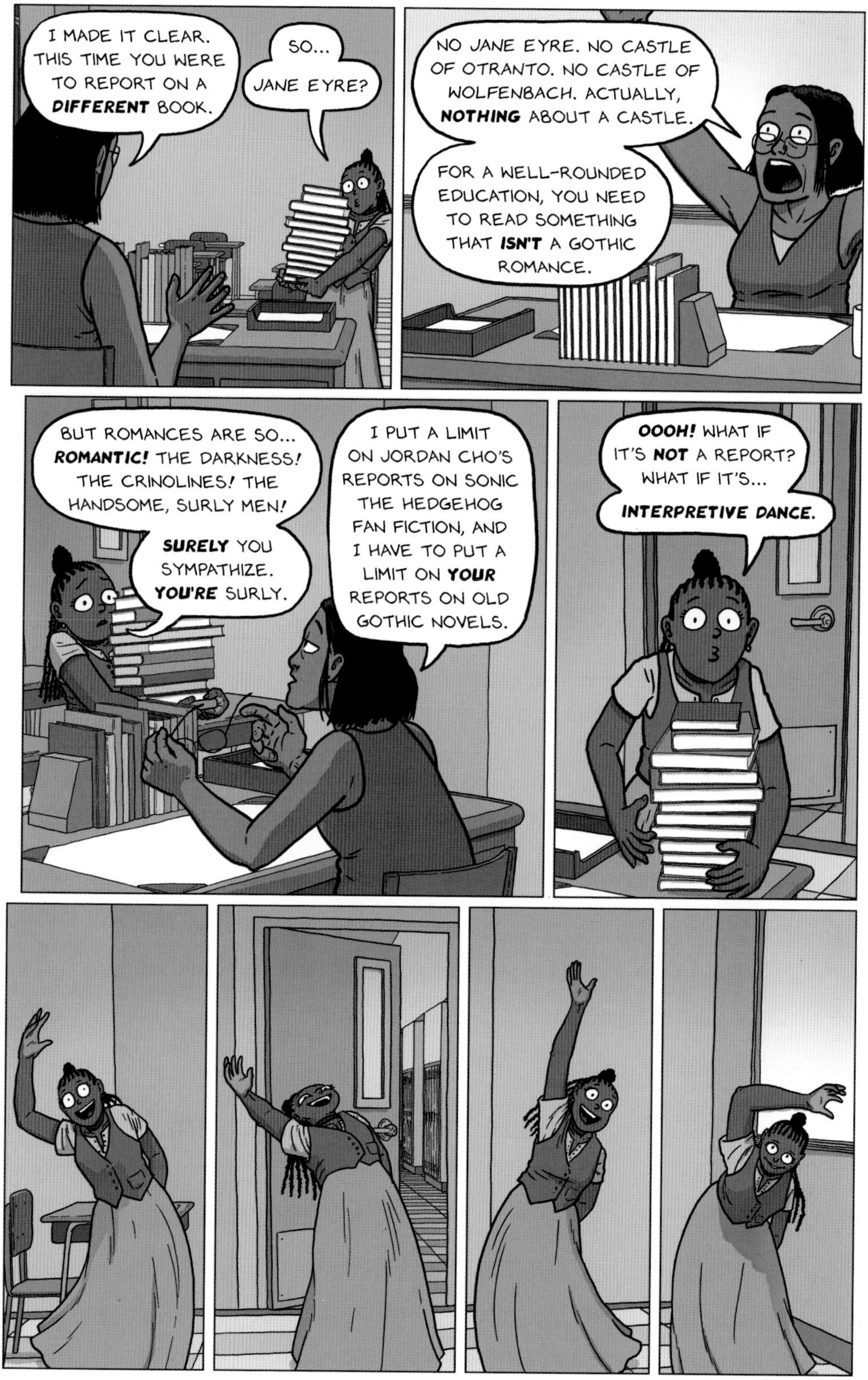
I MADE IT CLEAR. THIS TIME YOU WERE TO REPORT ON A **DIFFERENT** BOOK.
SO... JANE EYRE?
NO JANE EYRE. NO CASTLE OF OTRANTO. NO CASTLE OF WOLFENBACH. ACTUALLY, **NOTHING** ABOUT A CASTLE.
FOR A WELL-ROUNDED EDUCATION, YOU NEED TO READ SOMETHING THAT **ISN'T** A GOTHIC ROMANCE.
BUT ROMANCES ARE SO... **ROMANTIC!** THE DARKNESS! THE CRINOLINES! THE HANDSOME, SURLY MEN!
SURELY YOU SYMPATHIZE. **YOU'RE** SURLY.
I PUT A LIMIT ON JORDAN CHO'S REPORTS ON SONIC THE HEDGEHOG FAN FICTION, AND I HAVE TO PUT A LIMIT ON **YOUR** REPORTS ON OLD GOTHIC NOVELS.
OOOH! WHAT IF IT'S **NOT** A REPORT? WHAT IF IT'S...
INTERPRETIVE DANCE.

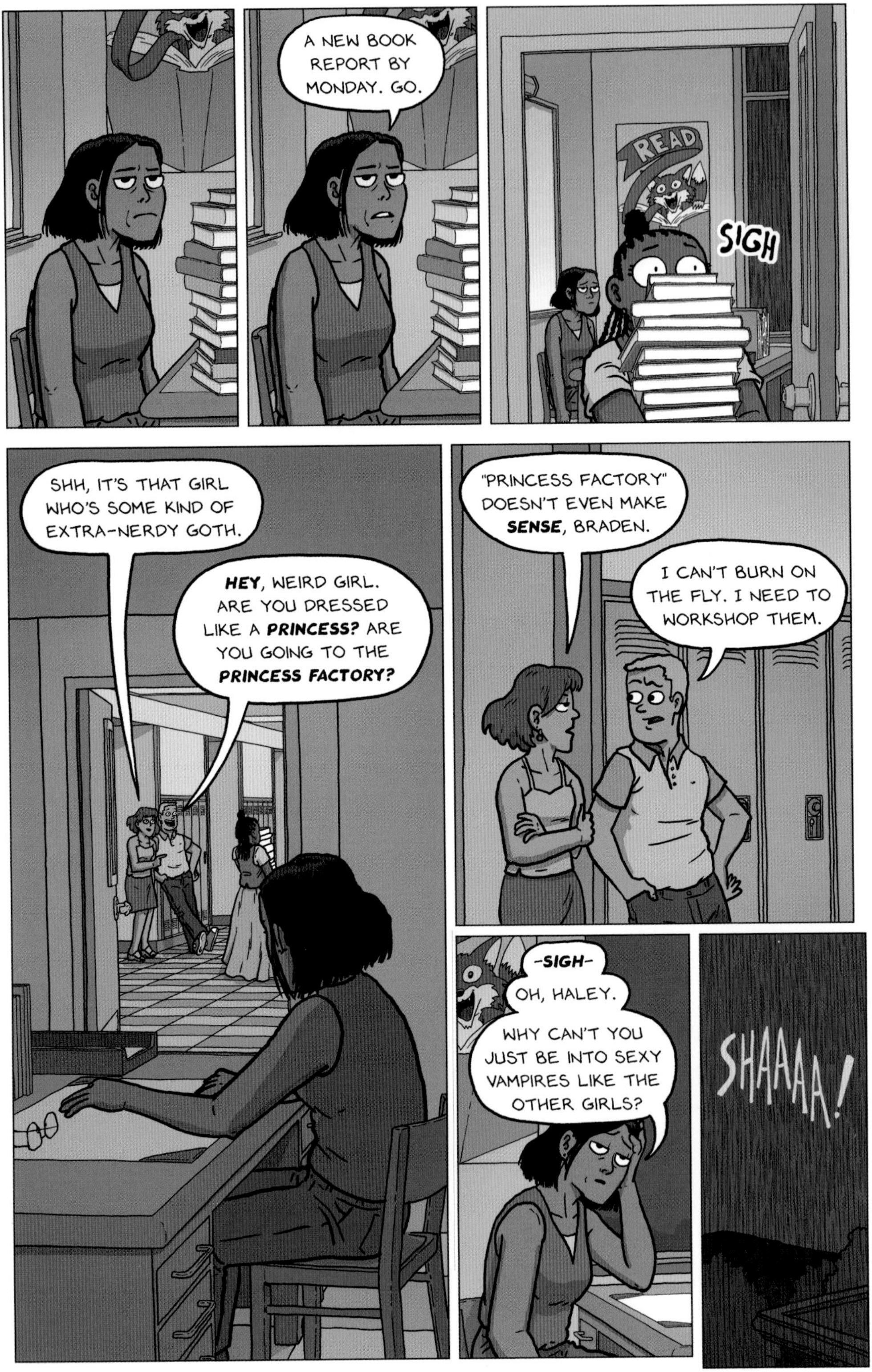
A NEW BOOK REPORT BY MONDAY. GO.
READ
SIGH
SHH, IT'S THAT GIRL WHO'S SOME KIND OF EXTRA-NERDY GOTH.
HEY, WEIRD GIRL. ARE YOU DRESSED LIKE A **PRINCESS?** ARE YOU GOING TO THE **PRINCESS FACTORY?**
"PRINCESS FACTORY" DOESN'T EVEN MAKE **SENSE**, BRADEN.
I CAN'T BURN ON THE FLY. I NEED TO WORKSHOP THEM.
-SIGH-
OH, HALEY.
WHY CAN'T YOU JUST BE INTO SEXY VAMPIRES LIKE THE OTHER GIRLS?
SHAAAA!

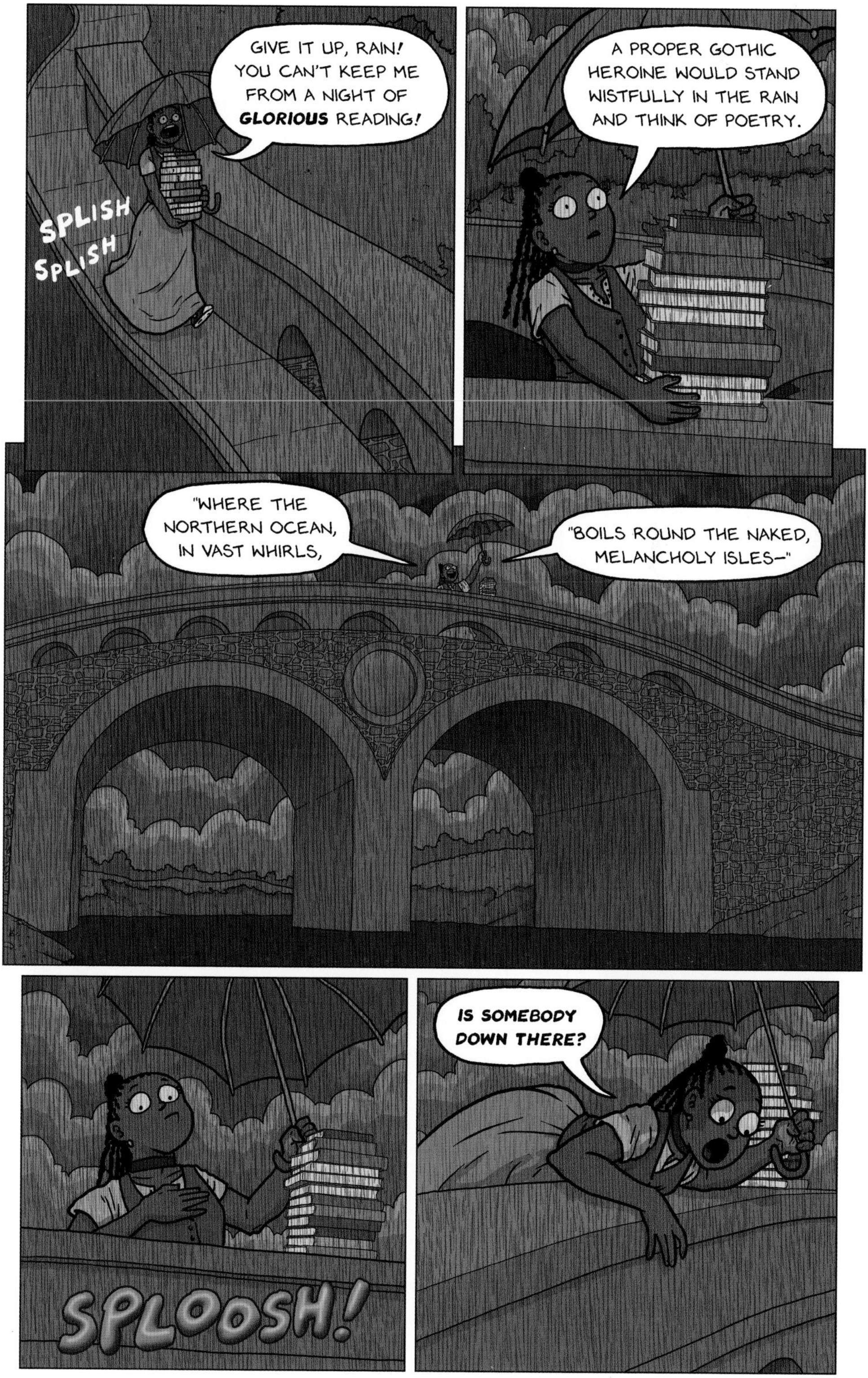
GIVE IT UP, RAIN! YOU CAN'T KEEP ME FROM A NIGHT OF GLORIOUS READING!
SPLISH SPLISH
A PROPER GOTHIC HEROINE WOULD STAND WISTFULLY IN THE RAIN AND THINK OF POETRY.
"WHERE THE NORTHERN OCEAN, IN VAST WHIRLS,
"BOILS ROUND THE NAKED, MELANCHOLY ISLES—"
SPLOOSH!
IS SOMEBODY DOWN THERE?

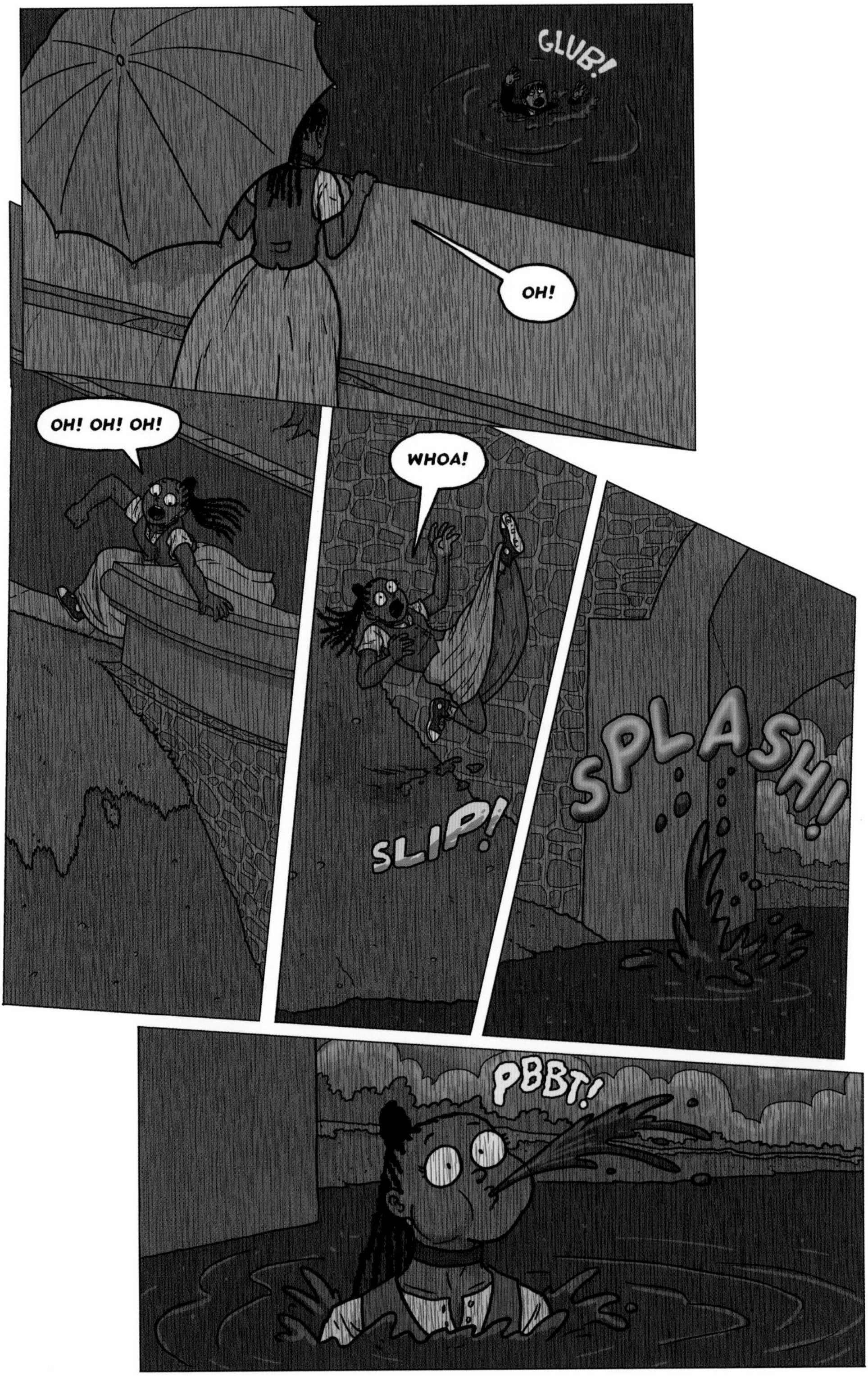
GLUB!
OH!
OH! OH! OH!
WHOA!
SLIP!
SPLASH!
PBBT!

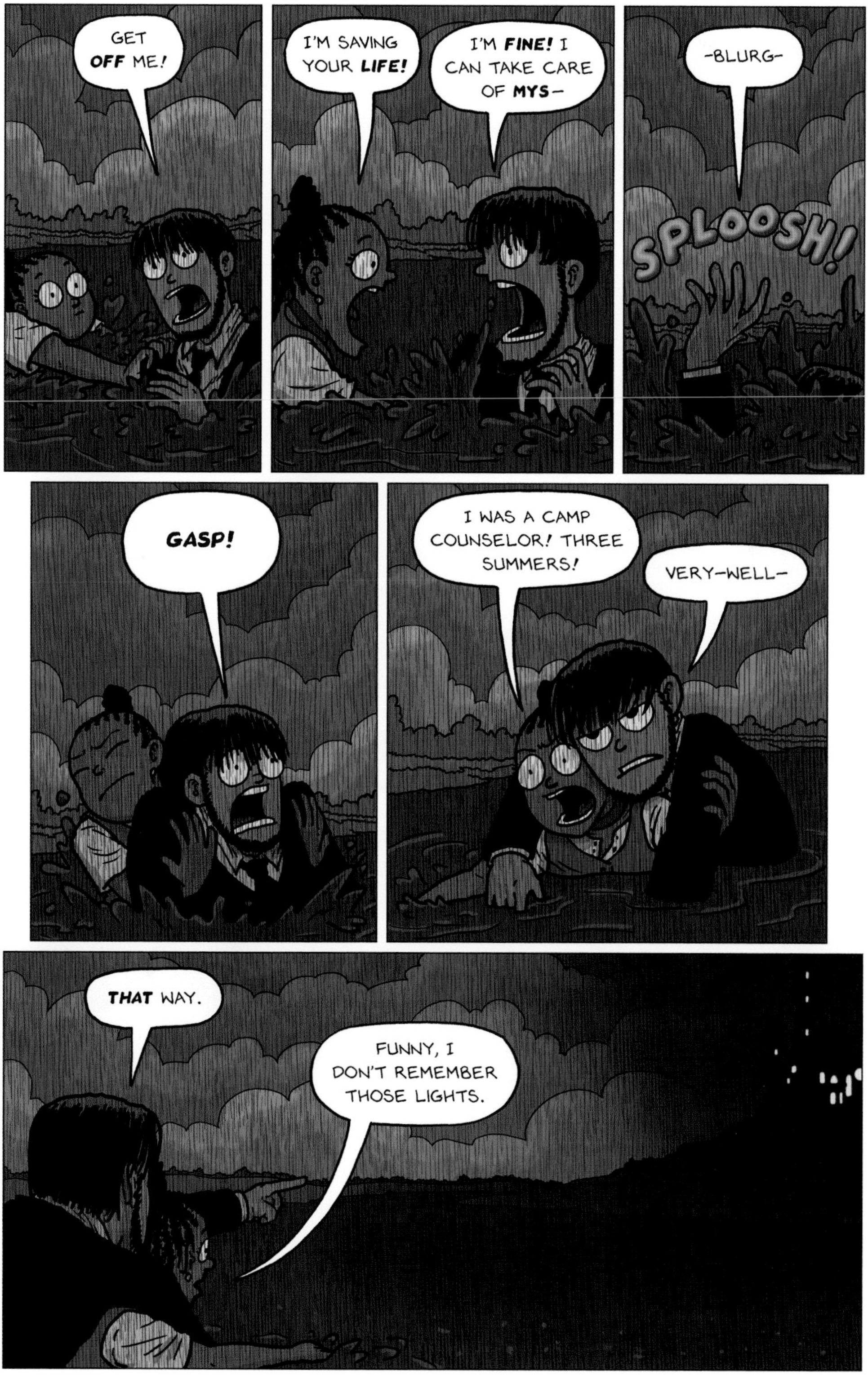
GET OFF ME!
I'M SAVING YOUR LIFE!
I'M FINE! I CAN TAKE CARE OF MYS—
-BLURG-
SPLOOSH!
GASP!
I WAS A CAMP COUNSELOR! THREE SUMMERS!
VERY—WELL—
THAT WAY.
FUNNY, I DON'T REMEMBER THOSE LIGHTS.

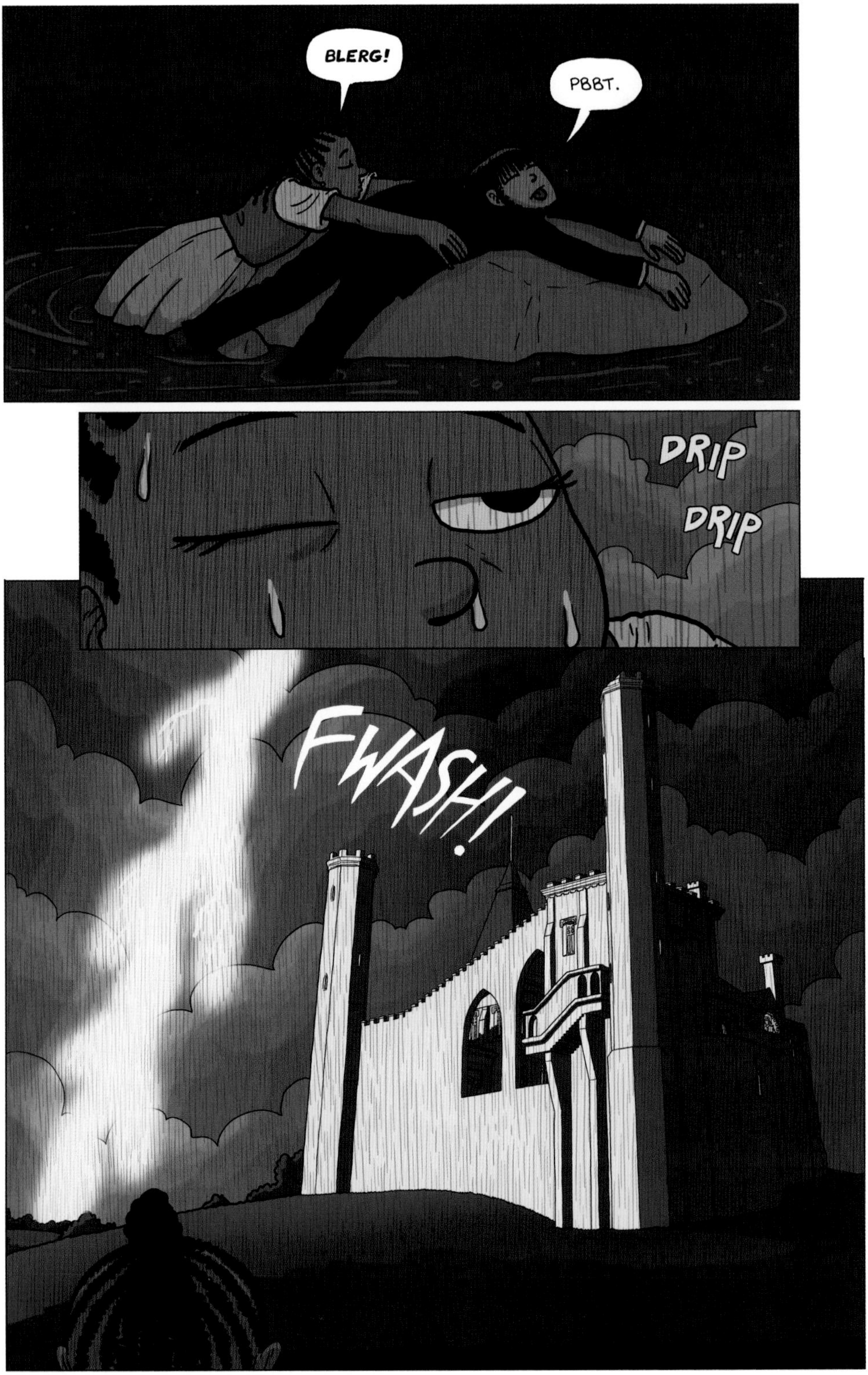
BLERG!
PBBT.
DRIP
DRIP
FWASH!

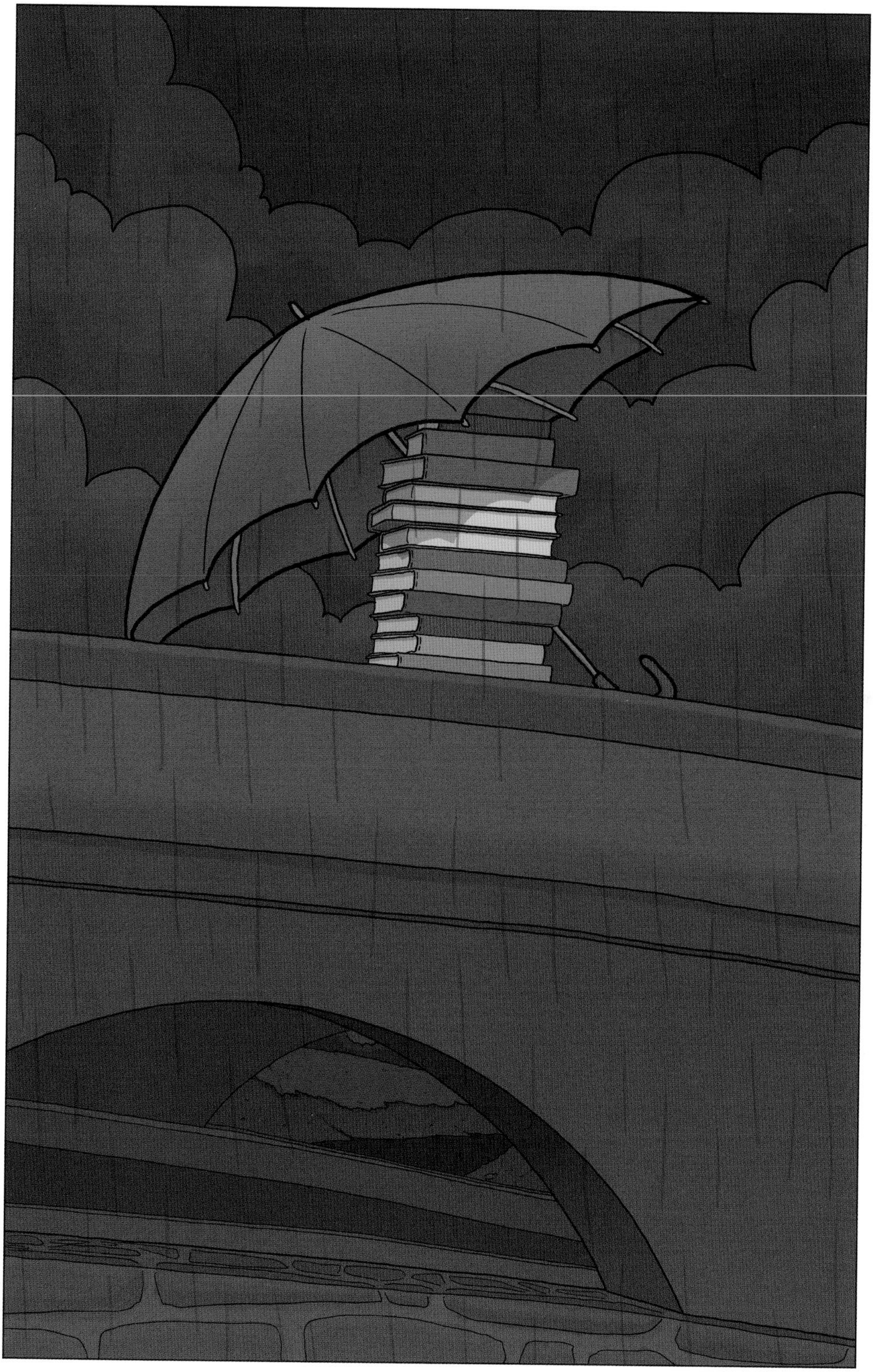

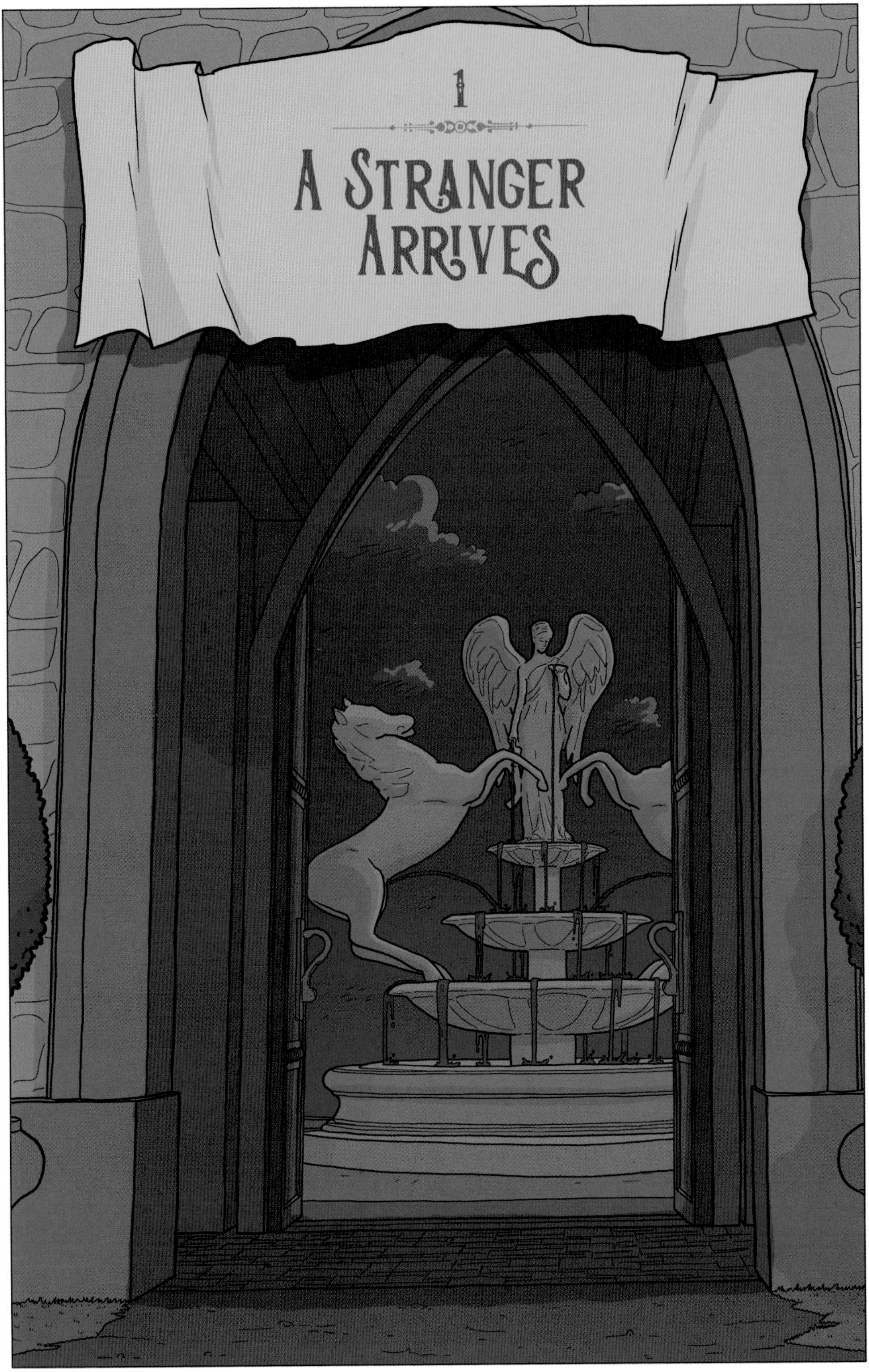
1
A Stranger Arrives

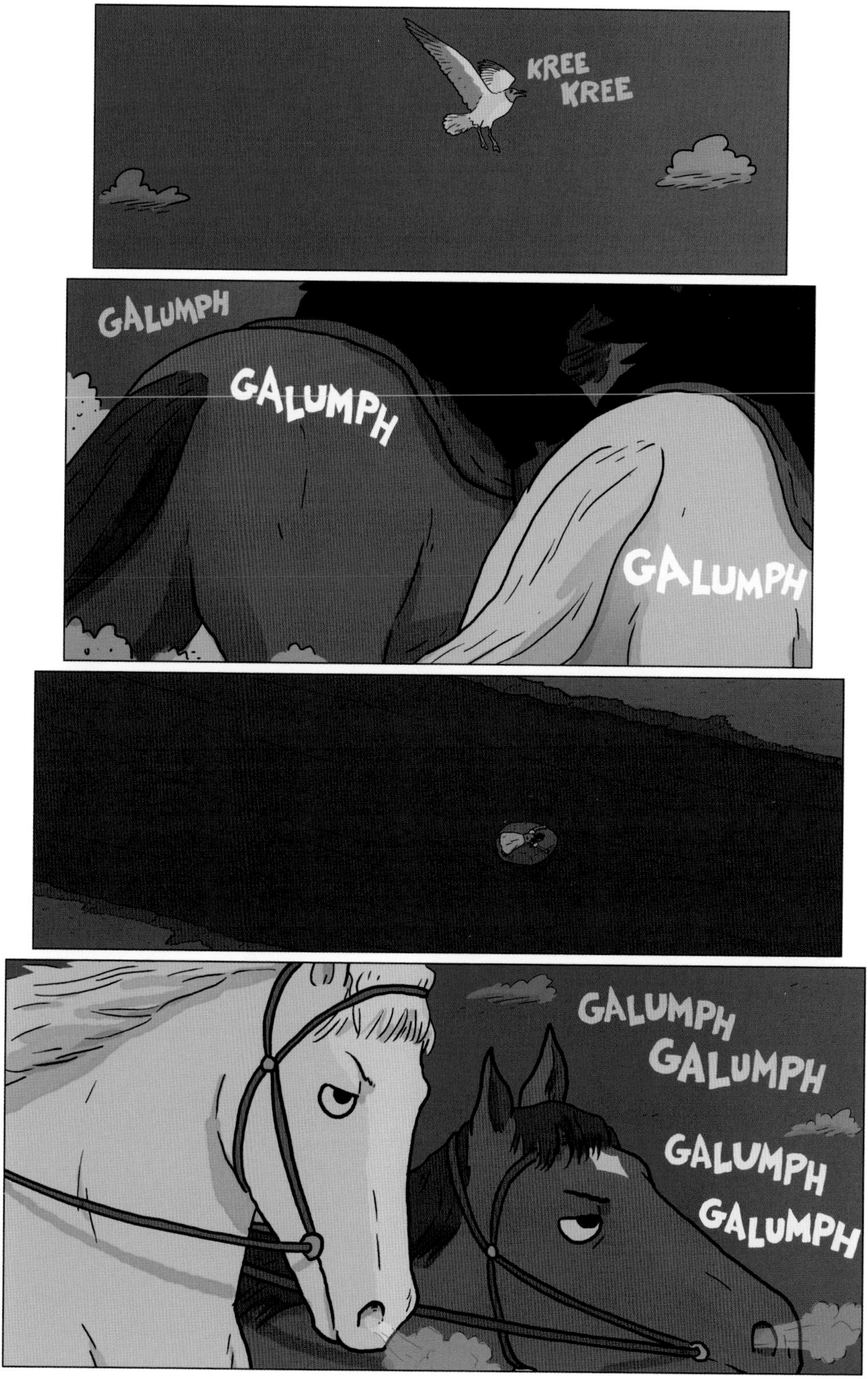
KREE
KREE
GALUMPH
GALUMPH
GALUMPH
GALUMPH
GALUMPH
GALUMPH
GALUMPH

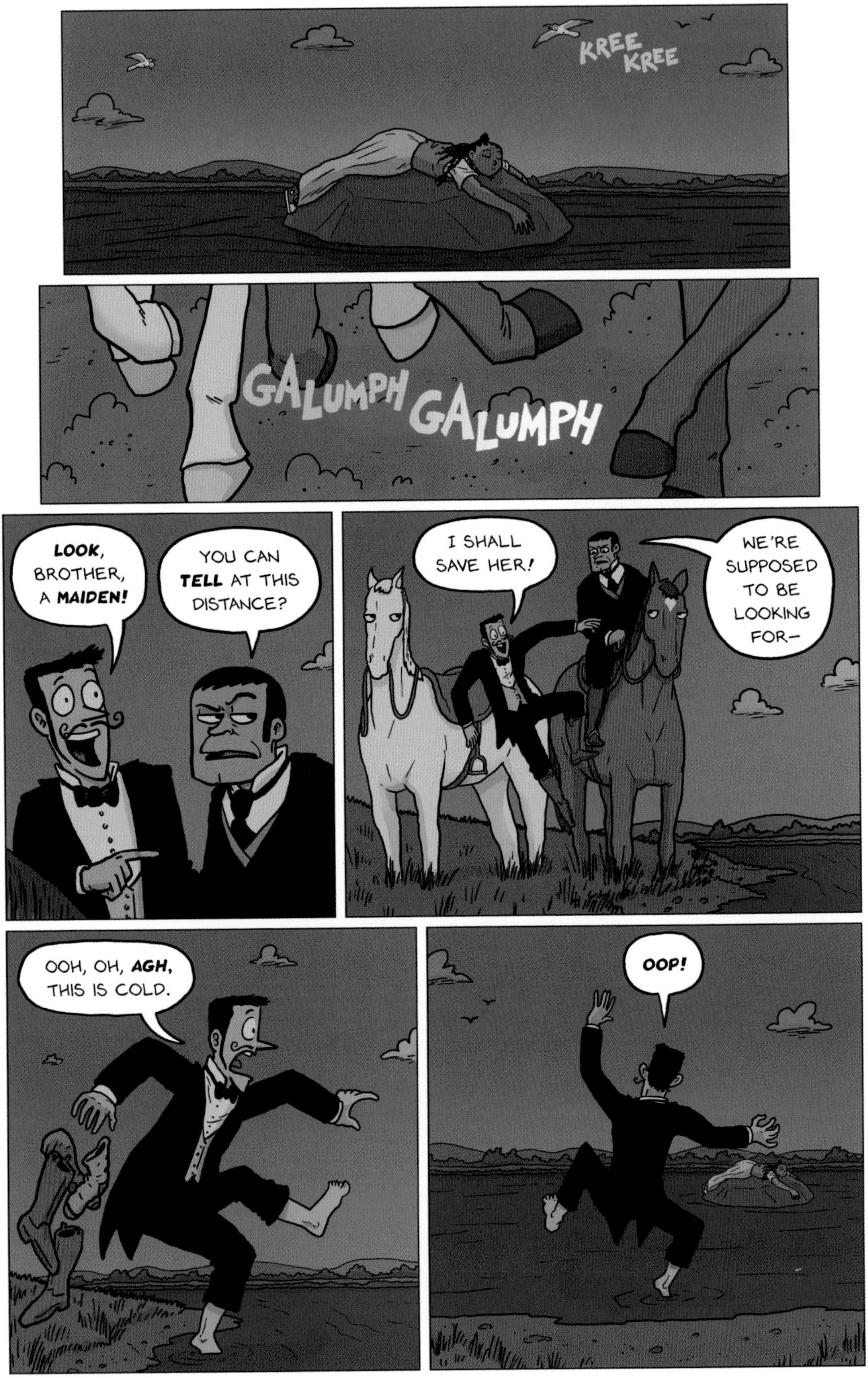
KREE KREE
GALUMPH GALUMPH
LOOK, BROTHER, A MAIDEN!
YOU CAN TELL AT THIS DISTANCE?
I SHALL SAVE HER!
WE'RE SUPPOSED TO BE LOOKING FOR—
OOH, OH, AGH, THIS IS COLD.
OOP!

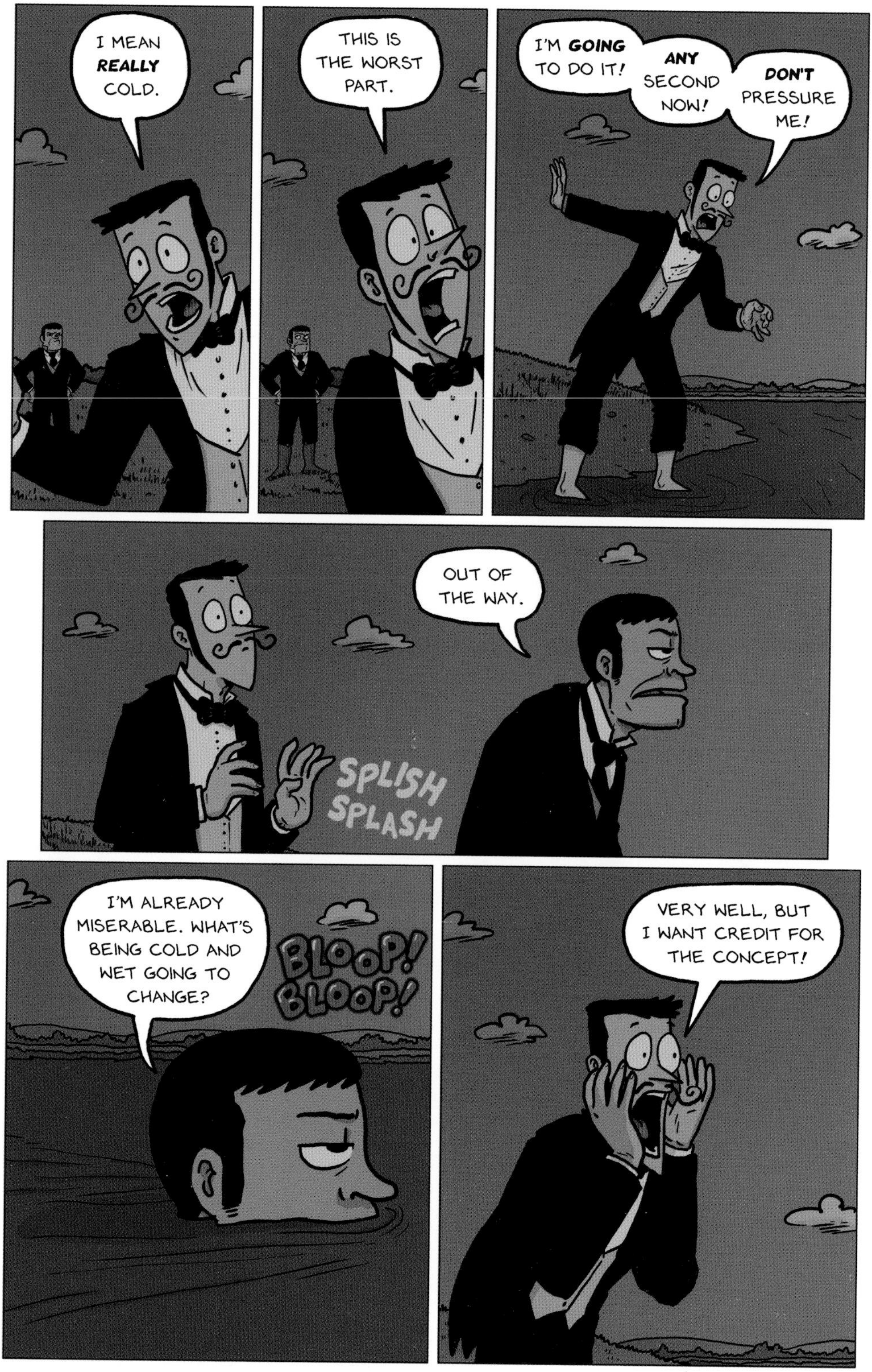

I MEAN **REALLY** COLD.
THIS IS THE WORST PART.
I'M **GOING** TO DO IT!
ANY SECOND NOW!
DON'T PRESSURE ME!
OUT OF THE WAY.
SPLISH SPLASH
I'M ALREADY MISERABLE. WHAT'S BEING COLD AND WET GOING TO CHANGE?
BLOOP! BLOOP!
VERY WELL, BUT I WANT CREDIT FOR THE CONCEPT!

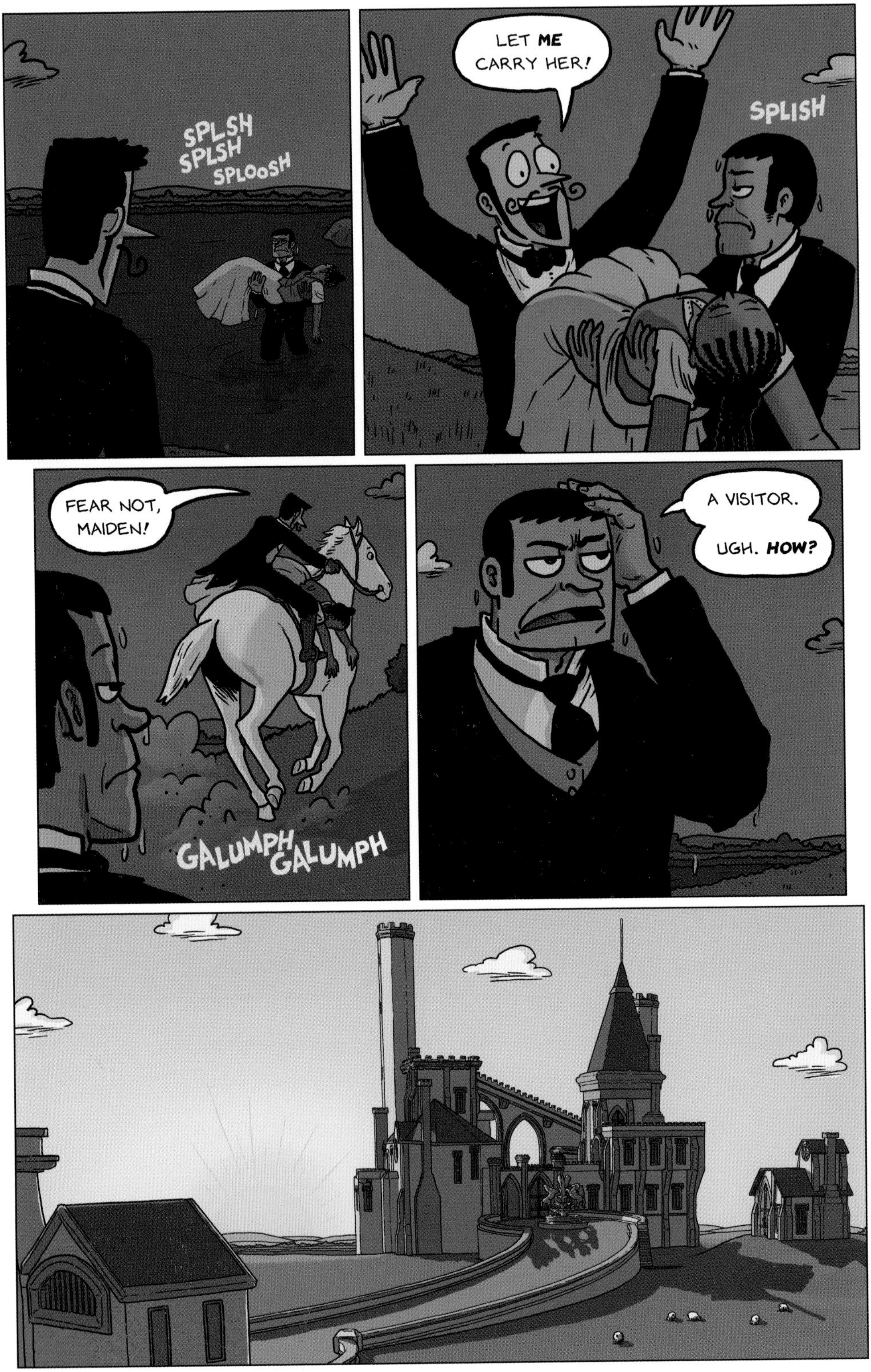
SPLSH
SPLSH
SPLOOSH
LET ME CARRY HER!
SPLISH
FEAR NOT, MAIDEN!
GALUMPH GALUMPH
A VISITOR.
UGH. HOW?

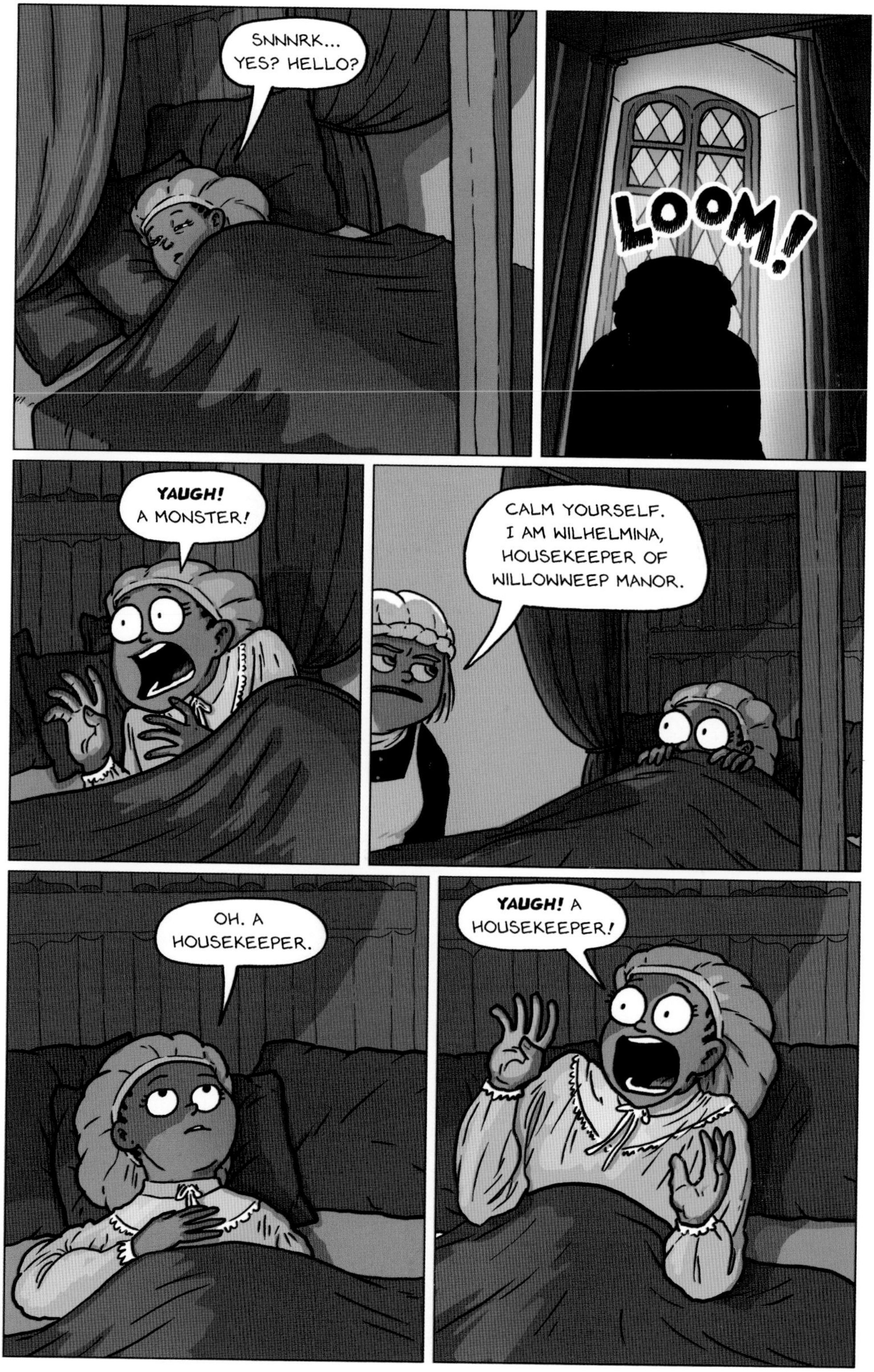
SNNNRK...
YES? HELLO?
LOOM!
YAUGH!
A MONSTER!
CALM YOURSELF.
I AM WILHELMINA,
HOUSEKEEPER OF
WILLOWWEEP MANOR.
OH. A
HOUSEKEEPER.
YAUGH! A
HOUSEKEEPER!

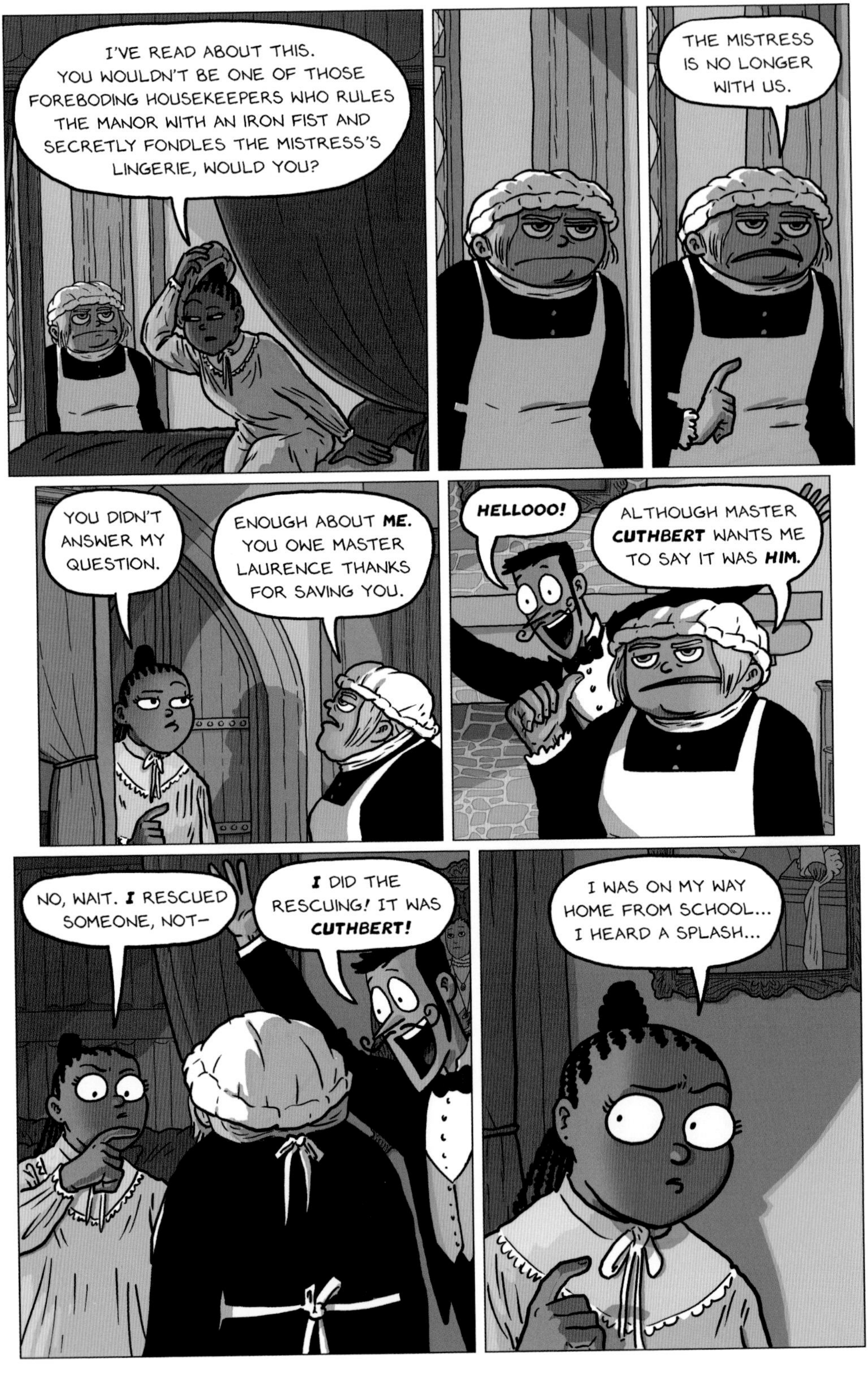
I'VE READ ABOUT THIS. YOU WOULDN'T BE ONE OF THOSE FOREBODING HOUSEKEEPERS WHO RULES THE MANOR WITH AN IRON FIST AND SECRETLY FONDLES THE MISTRESS'S LINGERIE, WOULD YOU?
THE MISTRESS IS NO LONGER WITH US.
YOU DIDN'T ANSWER MY QUESTION.
ENOUGH ABOUT **ME.** YOU OWE MASTER LAURENCE THANKS FOR SAVING YOU.
HELLOOO!
ALTHOUGH MASTER **CUTHBERT** WANTS ME TO SAY IT WAS **HIM.**
NO, WAIT. ***I*** RESCUED SOMEONE, NOT—
I DID THE RESCUING! IT WAS **CUTHBERT!**
I WAS ON MY WAY HOME FROM SCHOOL... I HEARD A SPLASH...

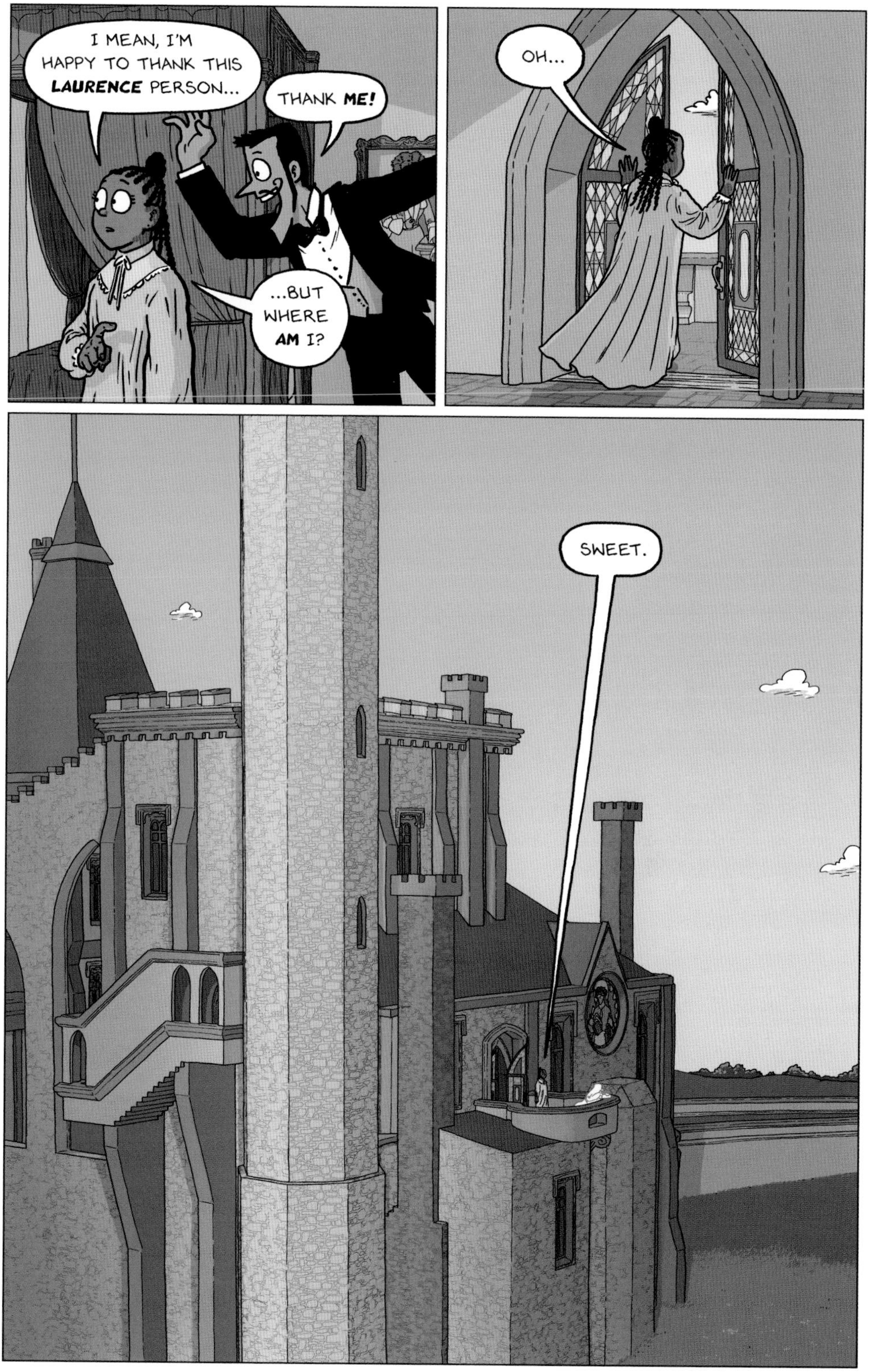
I MEAN, I'M HAPPY TO THANK THIS **LAURENCE** PERSON...
THANK **ME!**
...BUT WHERE **AM** I?
OH...
SWEET.

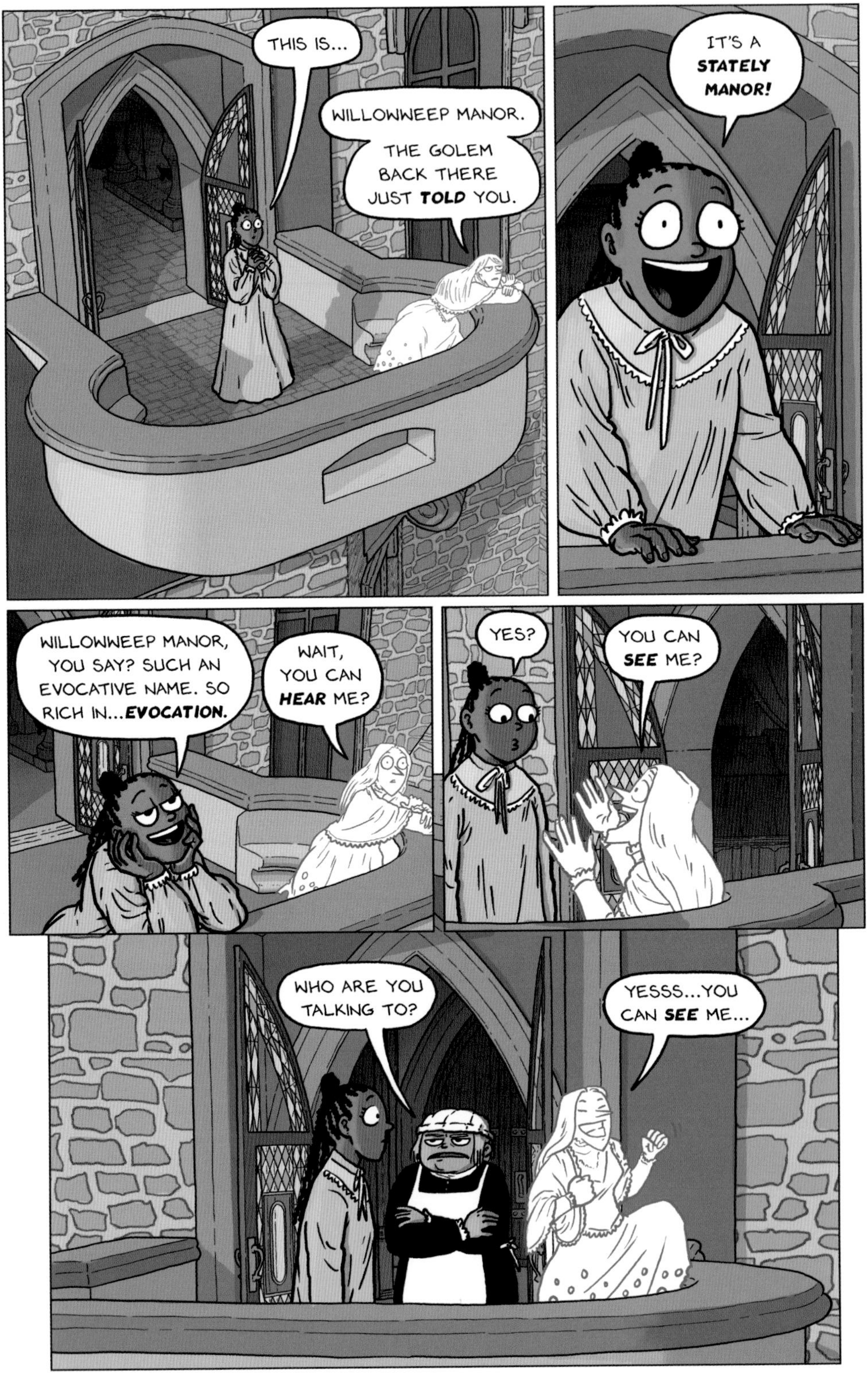
THIS IS...
WILLOWWEEP MANOR.
THE GOLEM BACK THERE JUST **TOLD** YOU.
IT'S A **STATELY MANOR!**
WILLOWWEEP MANOR, YOU SAY? SUCH AN EVOCATIVE NAME. SO RICH IN...**EVOCATION.**
WAIT, YOU CAN **HEAR** ME?
YES?
YOU CAN **SEE** ME?
WHO ARE YOU TALKING TO?
YESSS...YOU CAN **SEE** ME...

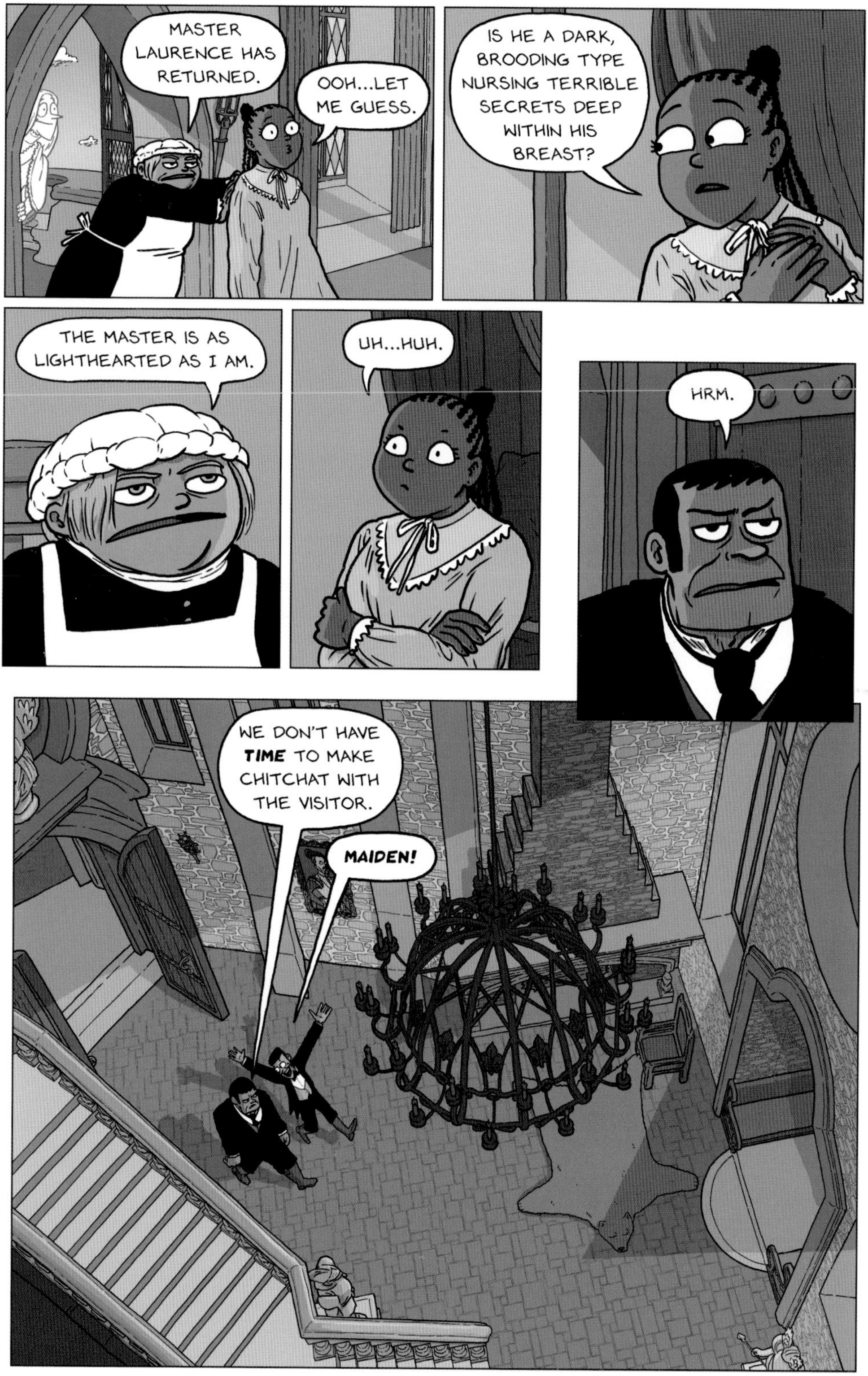
MASTER LAURENCE HAS RETURNED.
OOH...LET ME GUESS.
IS HE A DARK, BROODING TYPE NURSING TERRIBLE SECRETS DEEP WITHIN HIS BREAST?
THE MASTER IS AS LIGHTHEARTED AS I AM.
UH...HUH.
HRM.
WE DON'T HAVE **TIME** TO MAKE CHITCHAT WITH THE VISITOR.
MAIDEN!

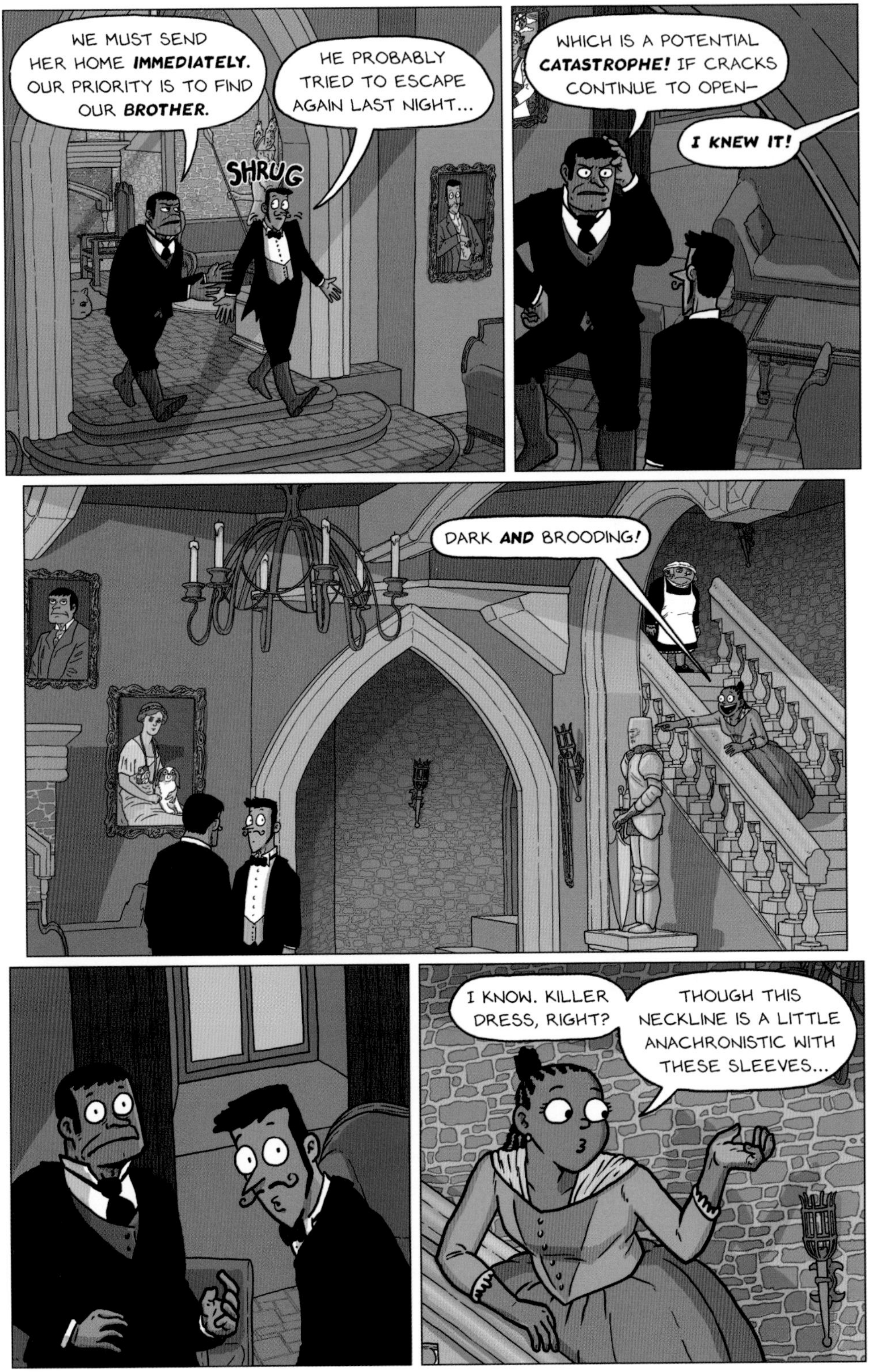
WE MUST SEND HER HOME **IMMEDIATELY.** OUR PRIORITY IS TO FIND OUR **BROTHER.**
SHRUG
HE PROBABLY TRIED TO ESCAPE AGAIN LAST NIGHT...
WHICH IS A POTENTIAL **CATASTROPHE!** IF CRACKS CONTINUE TO OPEN—
I KNEW IT!
DARK **AND** BROODING!
I KNOW. KILLER DRESS, RIGHT?
THOUGH THIS NECKLINE IS A LITTLE ANACHRONISTIC WITH THESE SLEEVES...

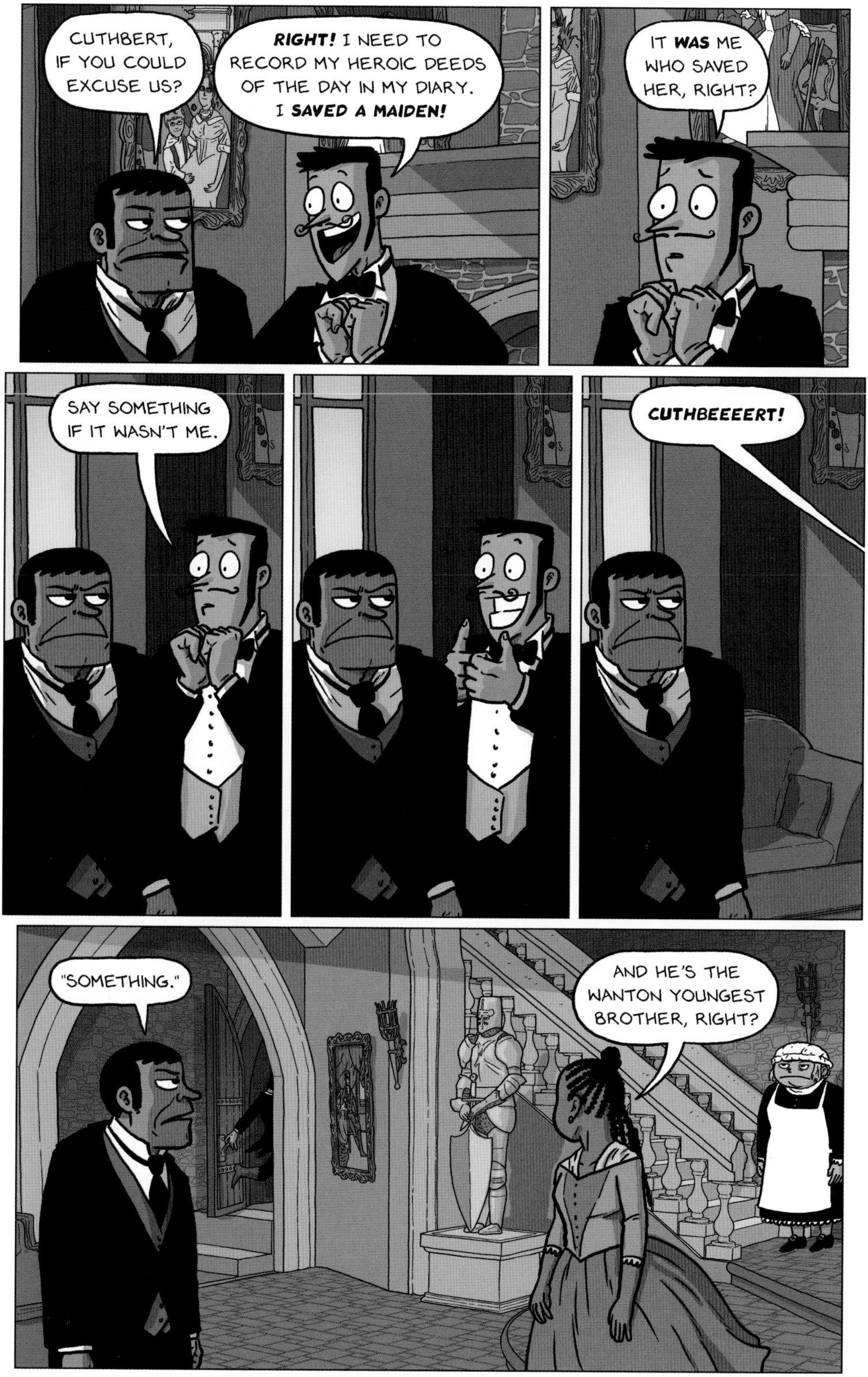
CUTHBERT, IF YOU COULD EXCUSE US?
RIGHT! I NEED TO RECORD MY HEROIC DEEDS OF THE DAY IN MY DIARY. I SAVED A MAIDEN!
IT WAS ME WHO SAVED HER, RIGHT?
SAY SOMETHING IF IT WASN'T ME.
CUTHBEEEERT!
"SOMETHING."
AND HE'S THE WANTON YOUNGEST BROTHER, RIGHT?

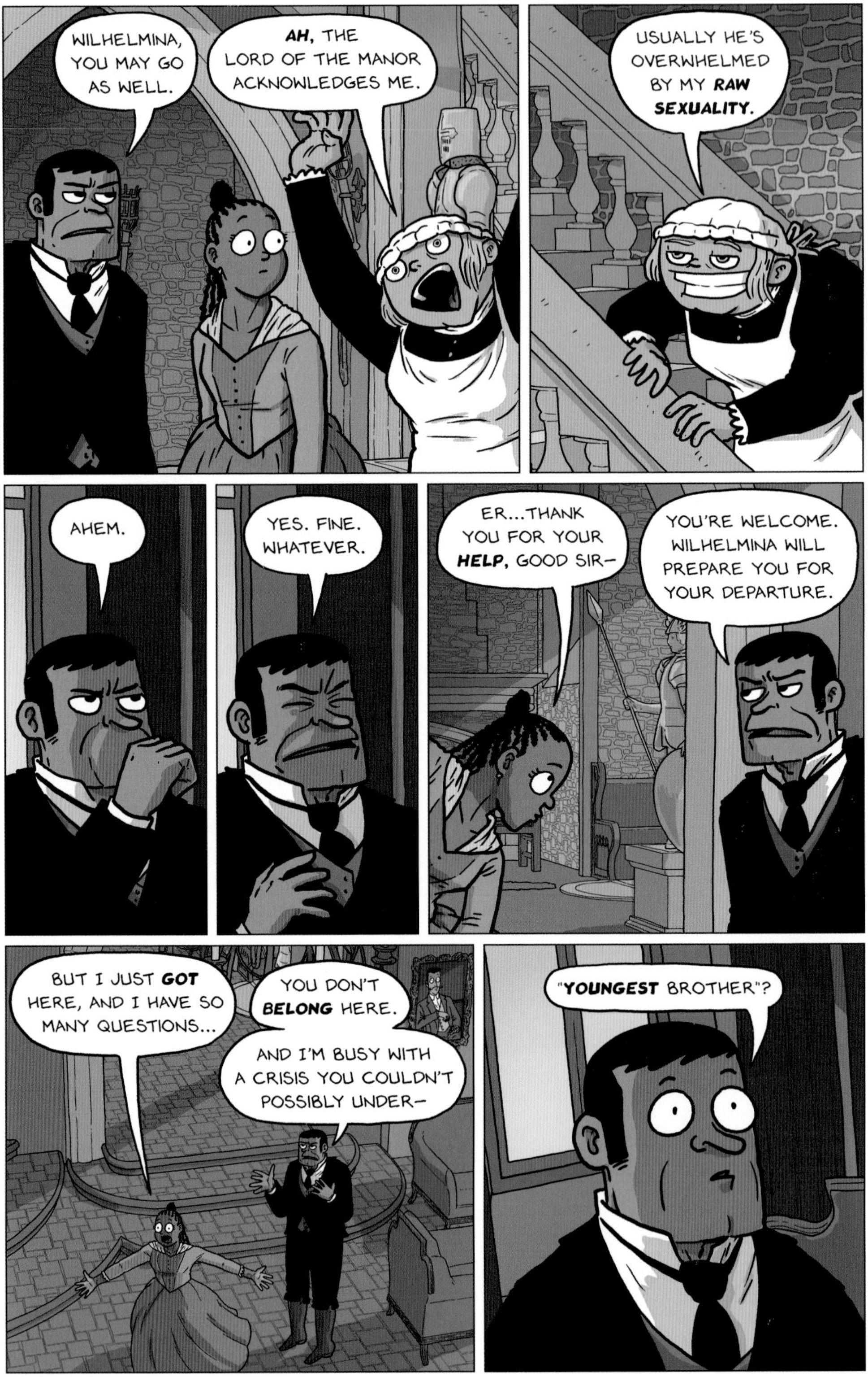
WILHELMINA, YOU MAY GO AS WELL.
AH, THE LORD OF THE MANOR ACKNOWLEDGES ME.
USUALLY HE'S OVERWHELMED BY MY **RAW SEXUALITY**.
AHEM.
YES. FINE. WHATEVER.
ER...THANK YOU FOR YOUR **HELP**, GOOD SIR—
YOU'RE WELCOME. WILHELMINA WILL PREPARE YOU FOR YOUR DEPARTURE.
BUT I JUST **GOT** HERE, AND I HAVE SO MANY QUESTIONS...
YOU DON'T **BELONG** HERE.
AND I'M BUSY WITH A CRISIS YOU COULDN'T POSSIBLY UNDER—
"**YOUNGEST** BROTHER"?

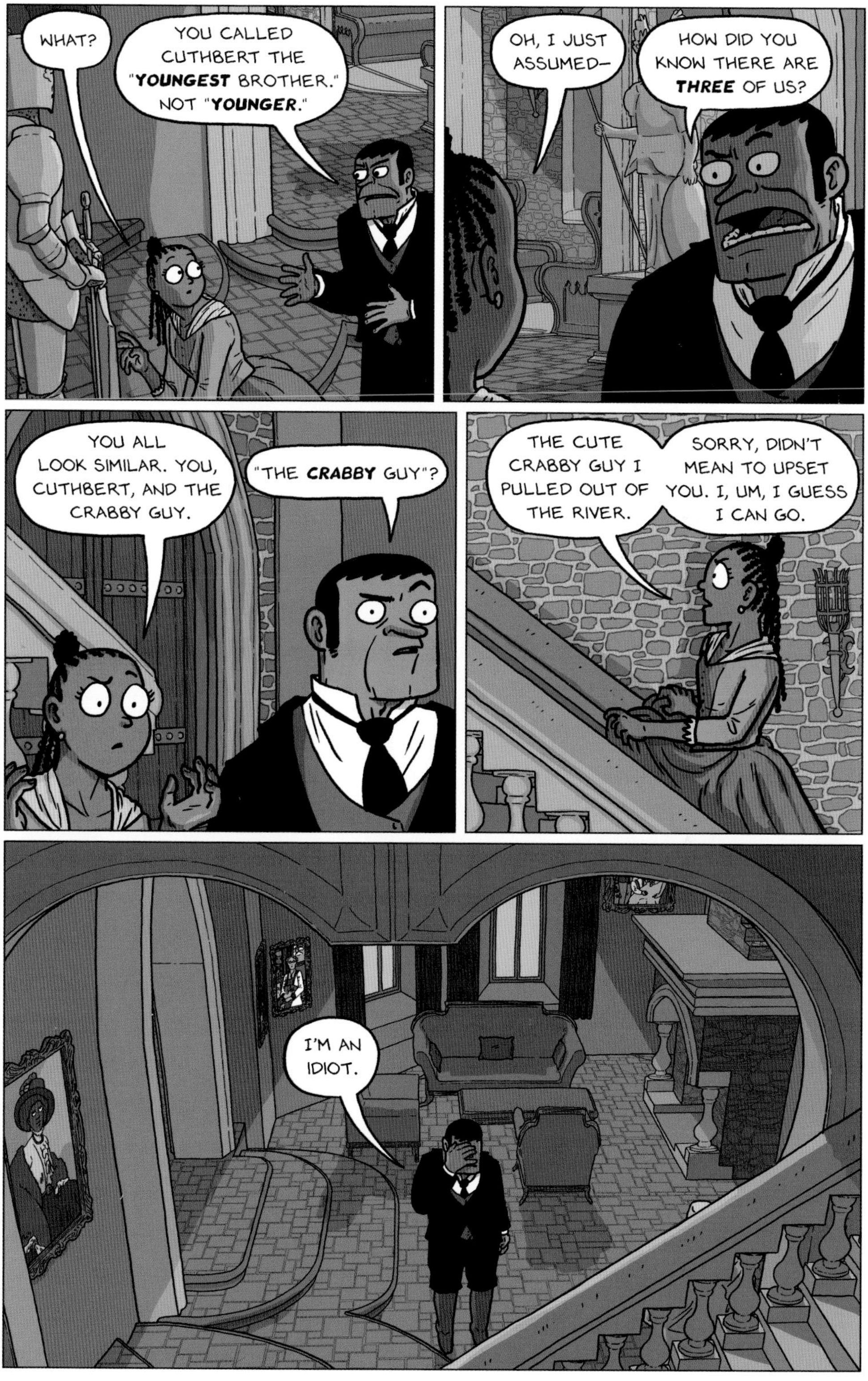
WHAT?
YOU CALLED CUTHBERT THE "**YOUNGEST** BROTHER." NOT "**YOUNGER**."
OH, I JUST ASSUMED—
HOW DID YOU KNOW THERE ARE **THREE** OF US?
YOU ALL LOOK SIMILAR. YOU, CUTHBERT, AND THE CRABBY GUY.
"THE **CRABBY** GUY"?
THE CUTE CRABBY GUY I PULLED OUT OF THE RIVER.
SORRY, DIDN'T MEAN TO UPSET YOU. I, UM, I GUESS I CAN GO.
I'M AN IDIOT.

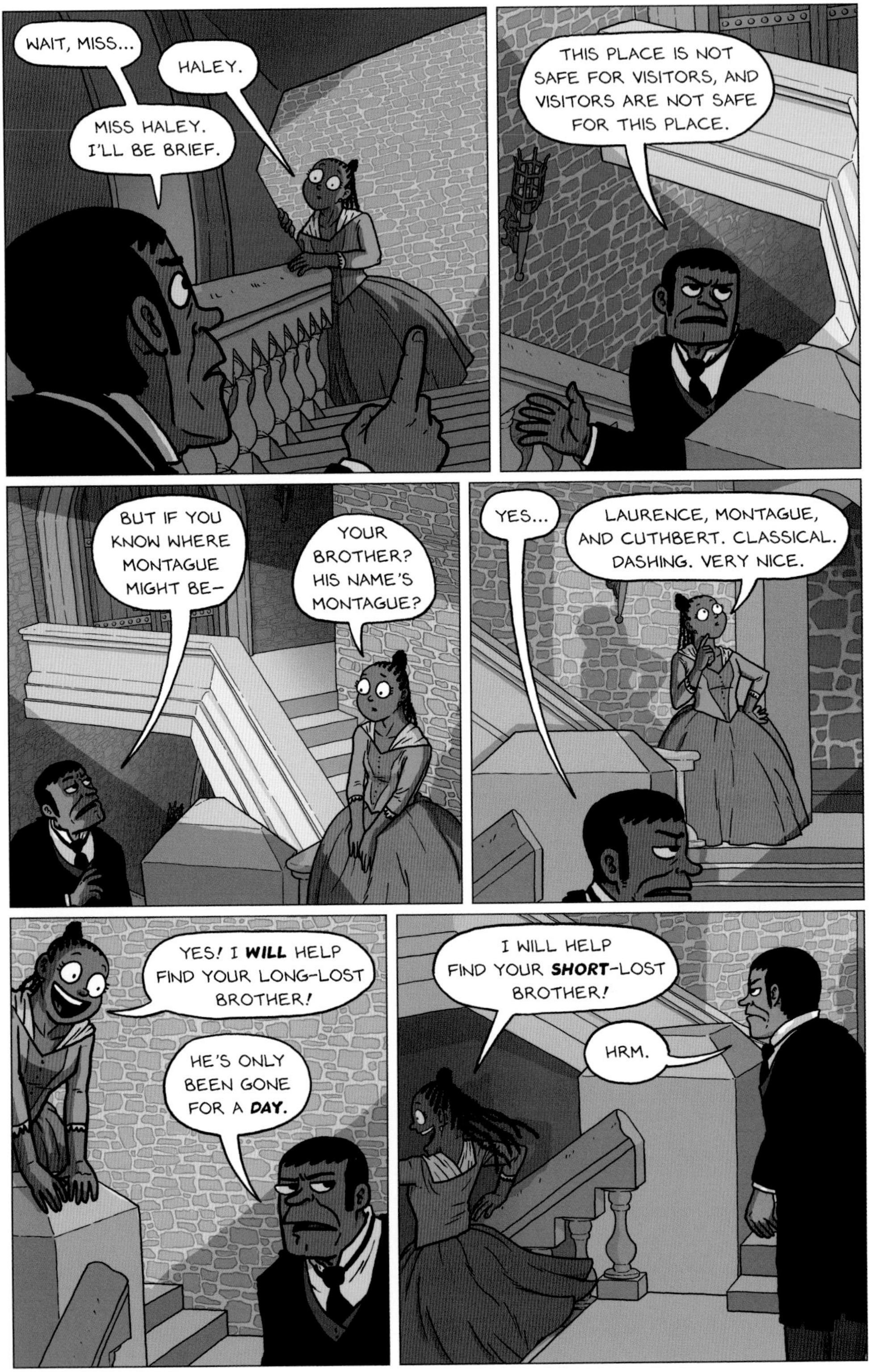

WAIT, MISS...
HALEY.
MISS HALEY. I'LL BE BRIEF.
THIS PLACE IS NOT SAFE FOR VISITORS, AND VISITORS ARE NOT SAFE FOR THIS PLACE.
BUT IF YOU KNOW WHERE MONTAGUE MIGHT BE—
YOUR BROTHER? HIS NAME'S MONTAGUE?
YES...
LAURENCE, MONTAGUE, AND CUTHBERT. CLASSICAL. DASHING. VERY NICE.
YES! I **WILL** HELP FIND YOUR LONG-LOST BROTHER!
HE'S ONLY BEEN GONE FOR A **DAY**.
I WILL HELP FIND YOUR **SHORT**-LOST BROTHER!
HRM.

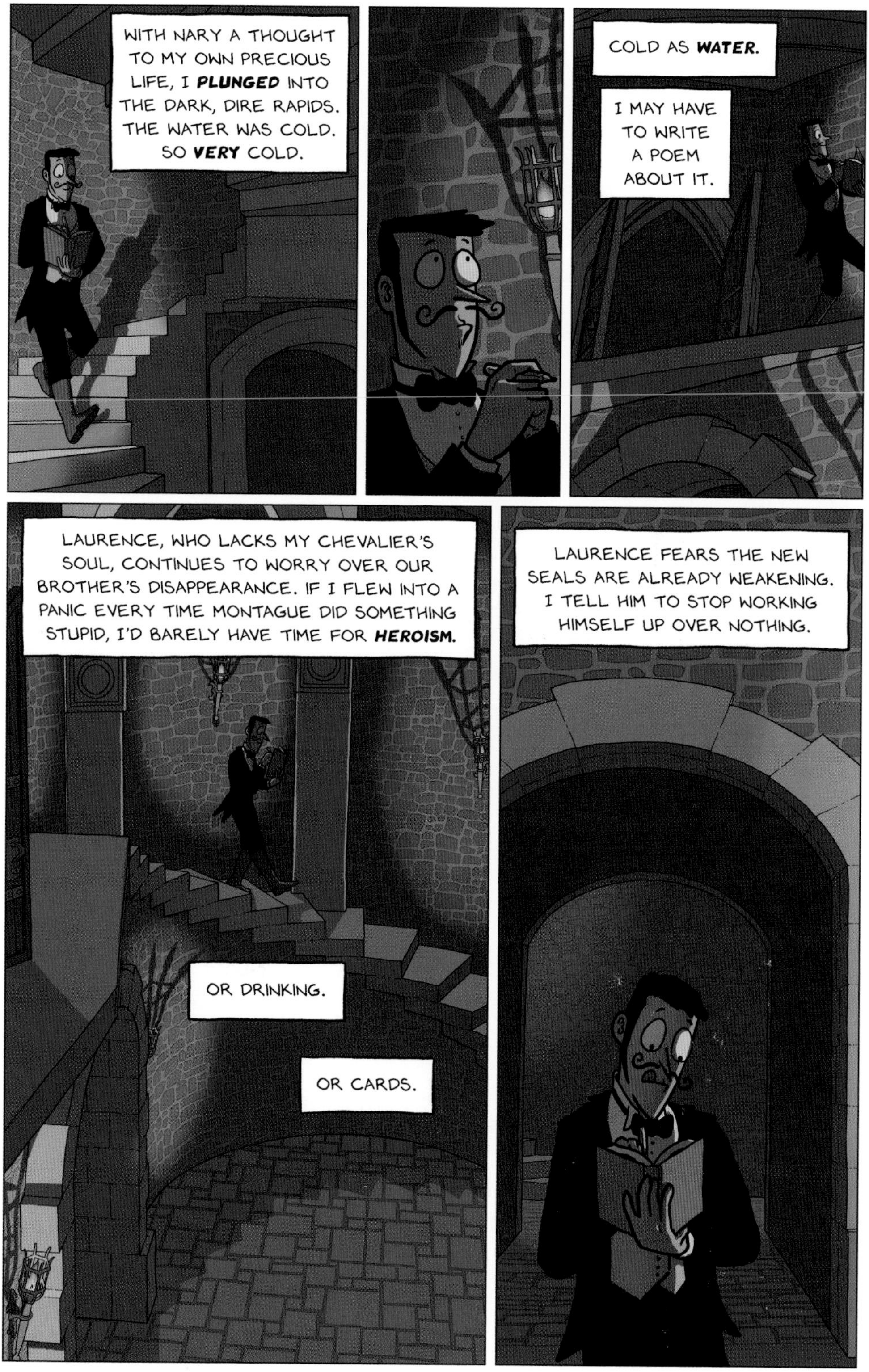
WITH NARY A THOUGHT TO MY OWN PRECIOUS LIFE, I **PLUNGED** INTO THE DARK, DIRE RAPIDS. THE WATER WAS COLD. SO **VERY** COLD.
COLD AS **WATER.**
I MAY HAVE TO WRITE A POEM ABOUT IT.
LAURENCE, WHO LACKS MY CHEVALIER'S SOUL, CONTINUES TO WORRY OVER OUR BROTHER'S DISAPPEARANCE. IF I FLEW INTO A PANIC EVERY TIME MONTAGUE DID SOMETHING STUPID, I'D BARELY HAVE TIME FOR **HEROISM.**
OR DRINKING.
OR CARDS.
LAURENCE FEARS THE NEW SEALS ARE ALREADY WEAKENING. I TELL HIM TO STOP WORKING HIMSELF UP OVER NOTHING.

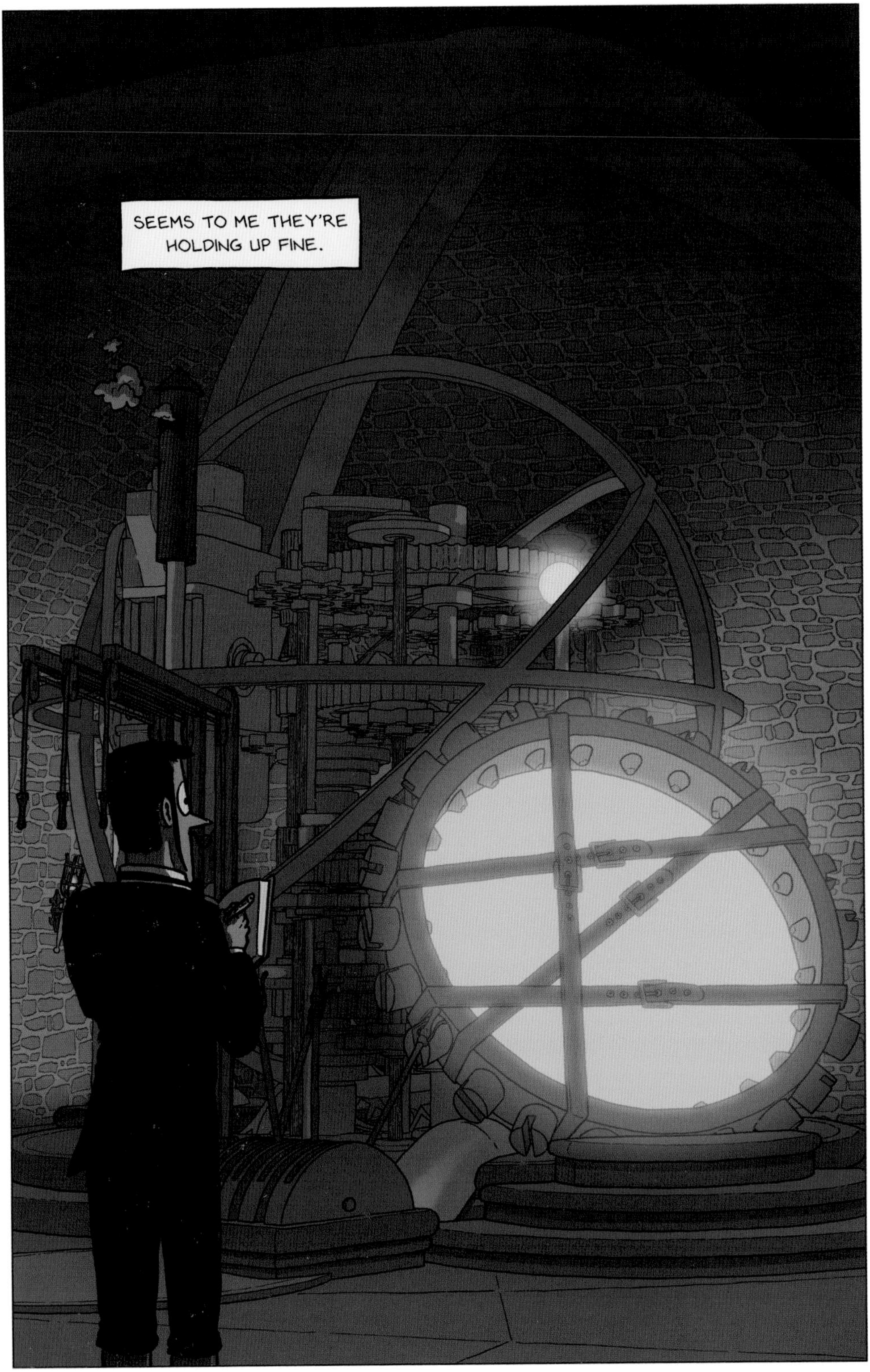
SEEMS TO ME THEY'RE HOLDING UP FINE.

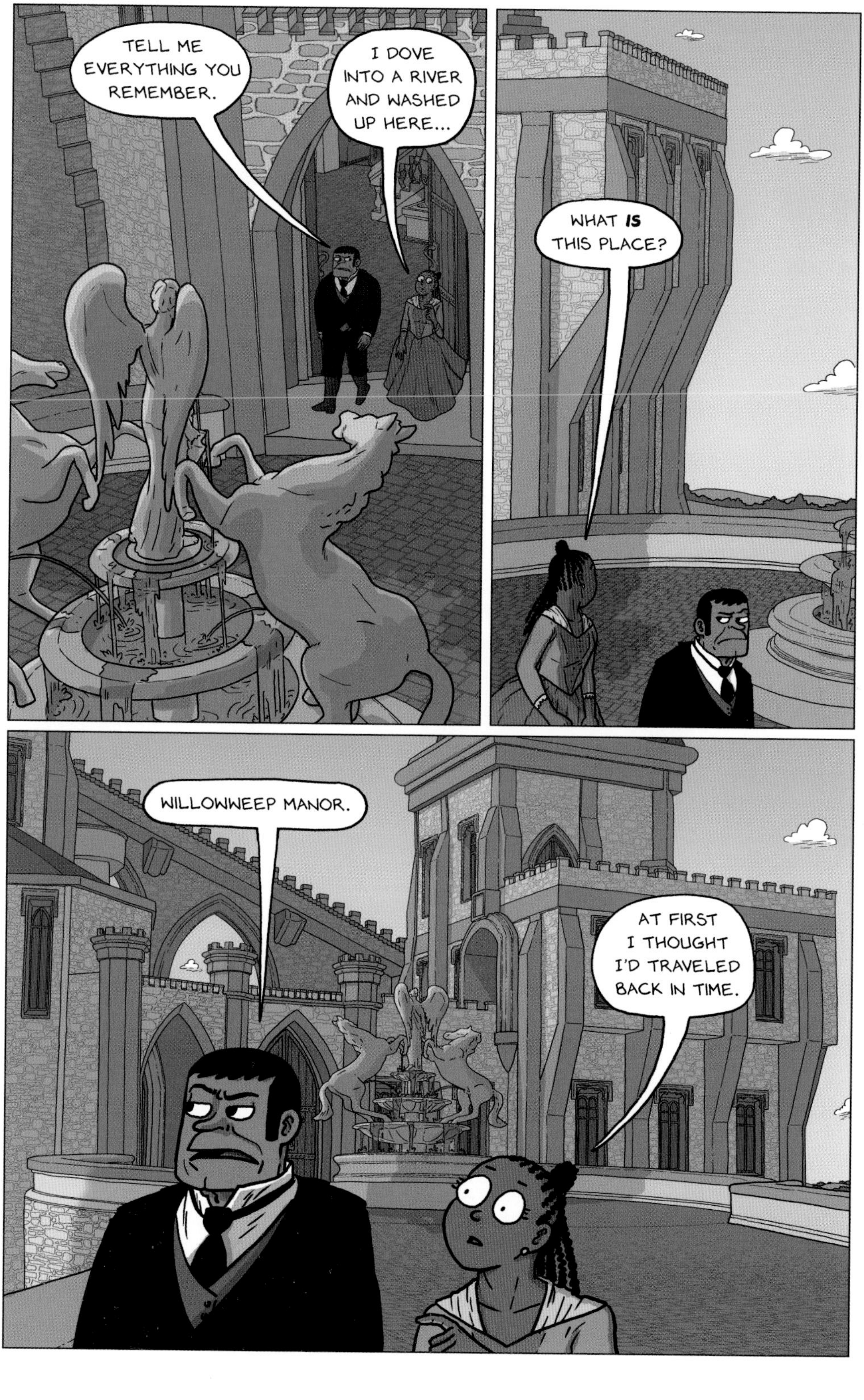
TELL ME EVERYTHING YOU REMEMBER.
I DOVE INTO A RIVER AND WASHED UP HERE...
WHAT **IS** THIS PLACE?
WILLOWWEEP MANOR.
AT FIRST I THOUGHT I'D TRAVELED BACK IN TIME.

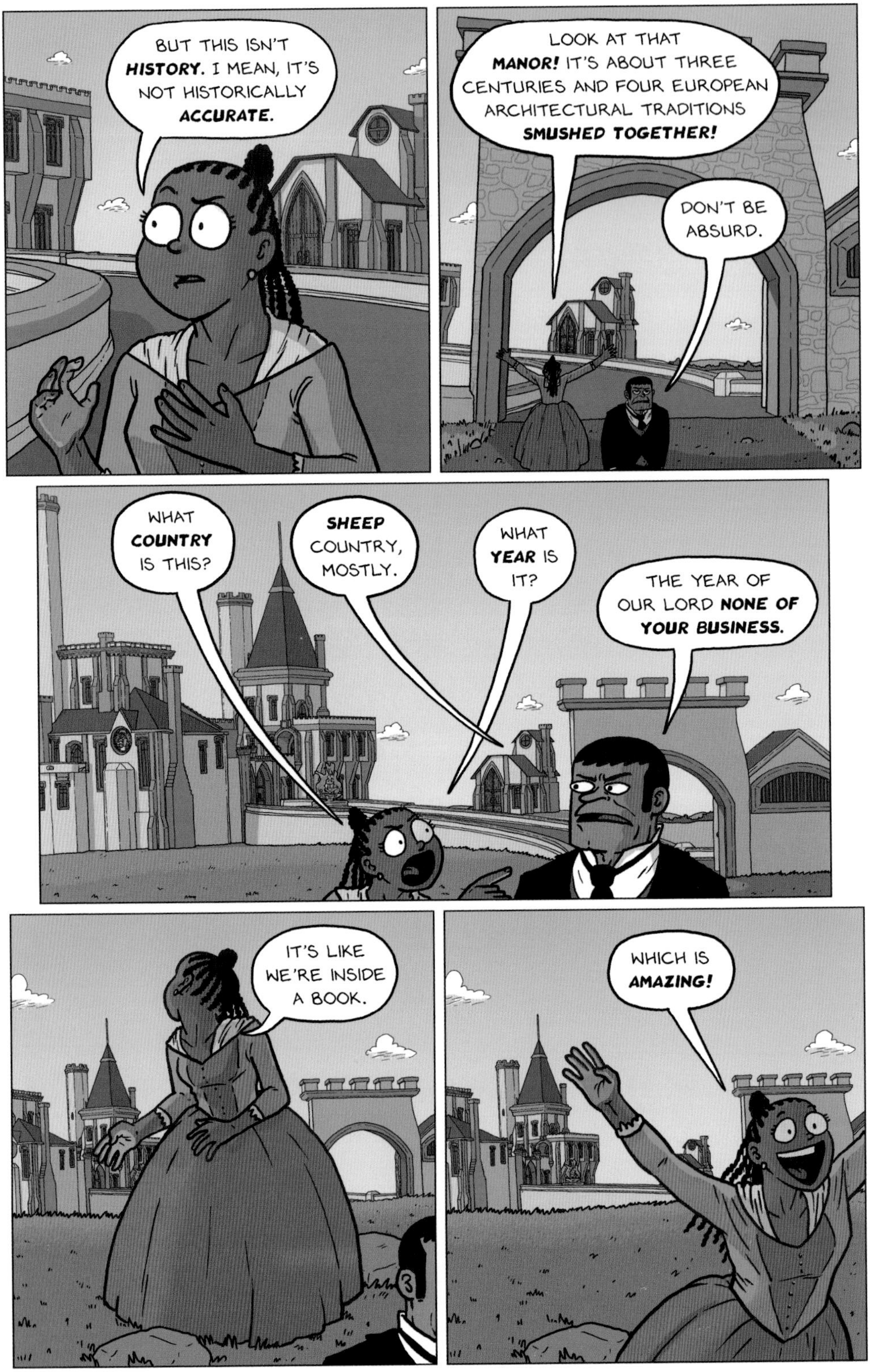
BUT THIS ISN'T **HISTORY**. I MEAN, IT'S NOT HISTORICALLY **ACCURATE**.
LOOK AT THAT **MANOR!** IT'S ABOUT THREE CENTURIES AND FOUR EUROPEAN ARCHITECTURAL TRADITIONS **SMUSHED TOGETHER!**
DON'T BE ABSURD.
WHAT **COUNTRY** IS THIS?
SHEEP COUNTRY, MOSTLY.
WHAT **YEAR** IS IT?
THE YEAR OF OUR LORD **NONE OF YOUR BUSINESS.**
IT'S LIKE WE'RE INSIDE A BOOK.
WHICH IS **AMAZING!**

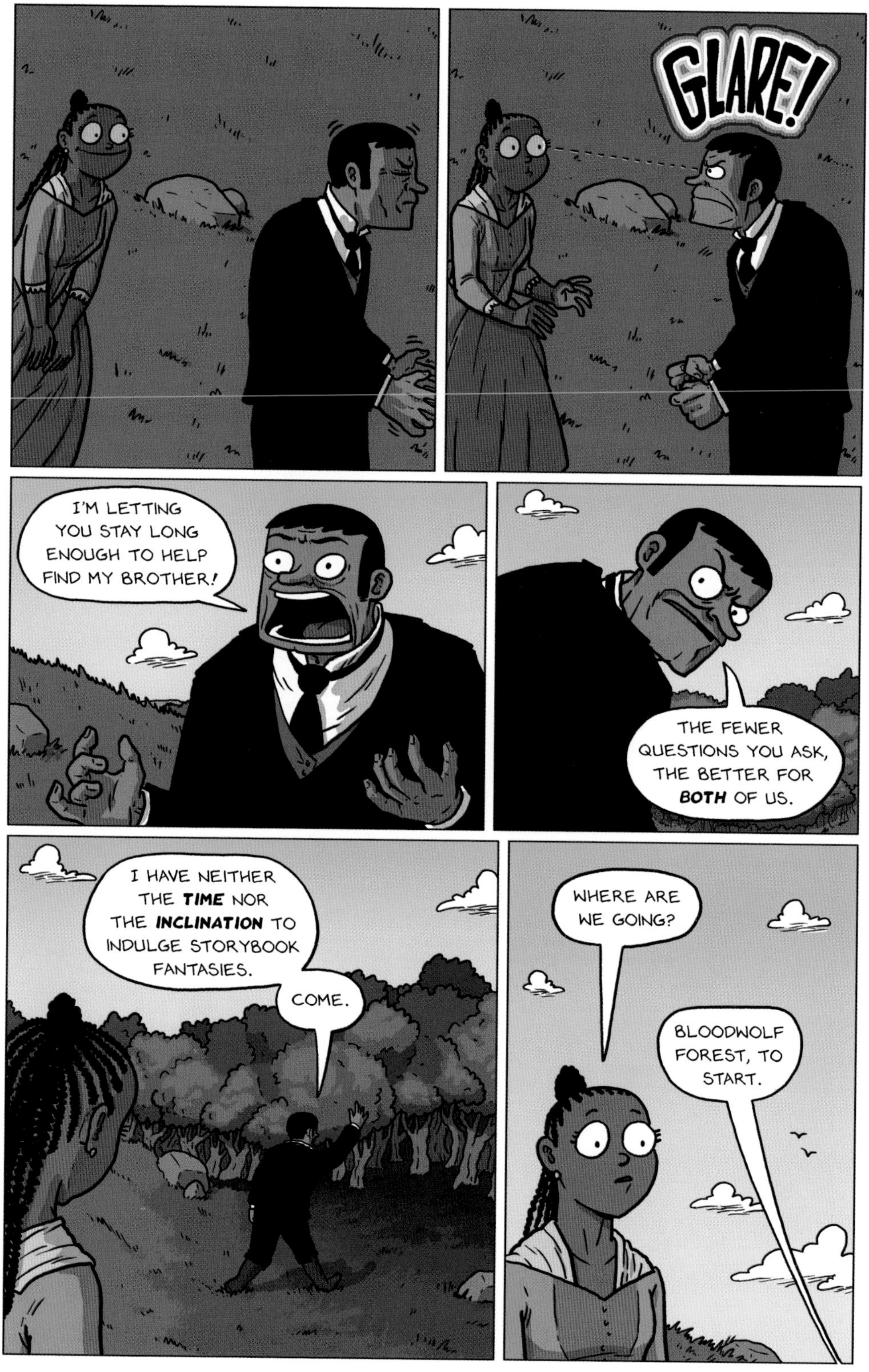
GLARE!
I'M LETTING YOU STAY LONG ENOUGH TO HELP FIND MY BROTHER!
THE FEWER QUESTIONS YOU ASK, THE BETTER FOR **BOTH** OF US.
I HAVE NEITHER THE **TIME** NOR THE **INCLINATION** TO INDULGE STORYBOOK FANTASIES.
COME.
WHERE ARE WE GOING?
BLOODWOLF FOREST, TO START.

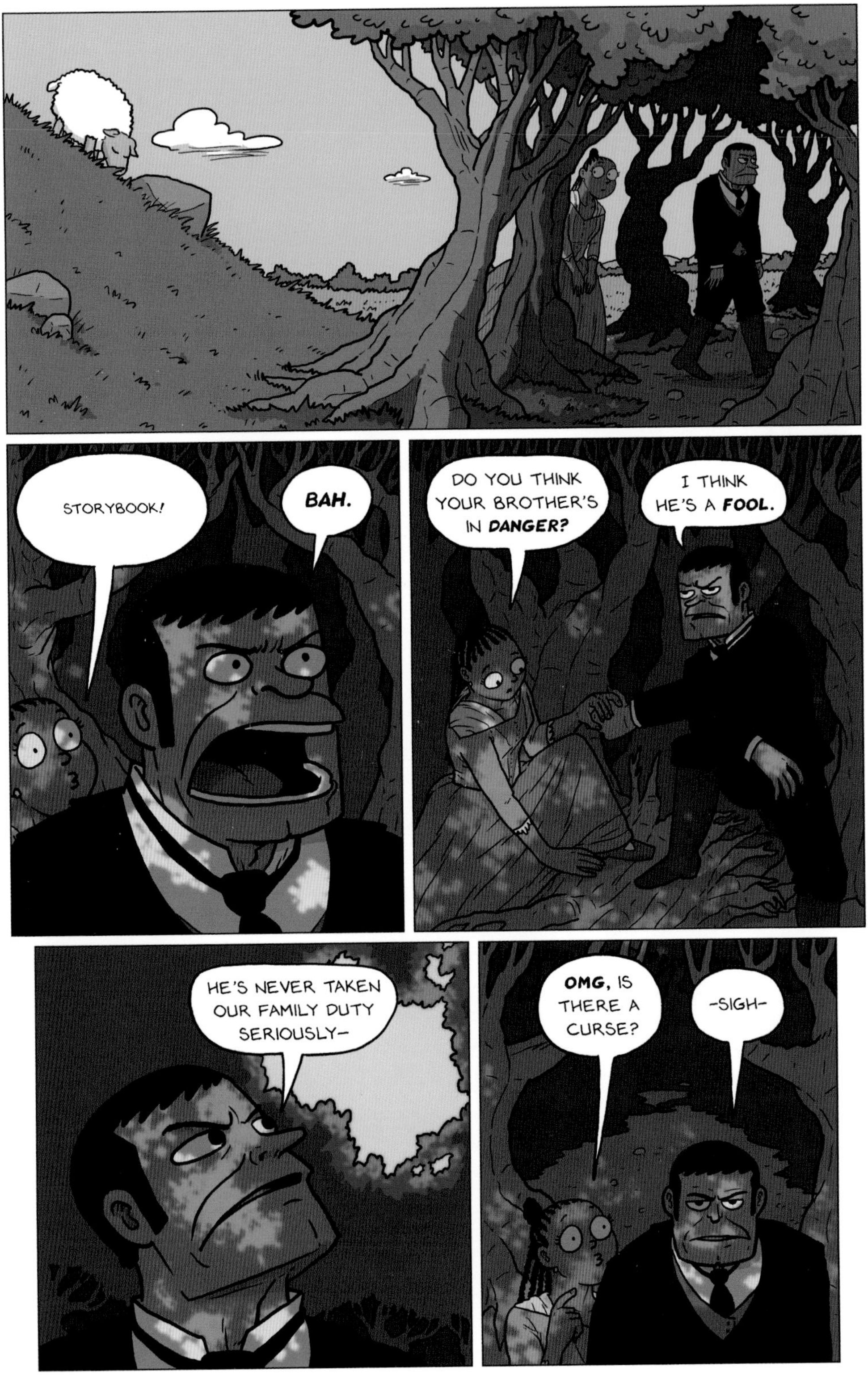
STORYBOOK!
BAH.
DO YOU THINK YOUR BROTHER'S IN **DANGER?**
I THINK HE'S A **FOOL.**
HE'S NEVER TAKEN OUR FAMILY DUTY SERIOUSLY–
OMG, IS THERE A CURSE?
-SIGH-

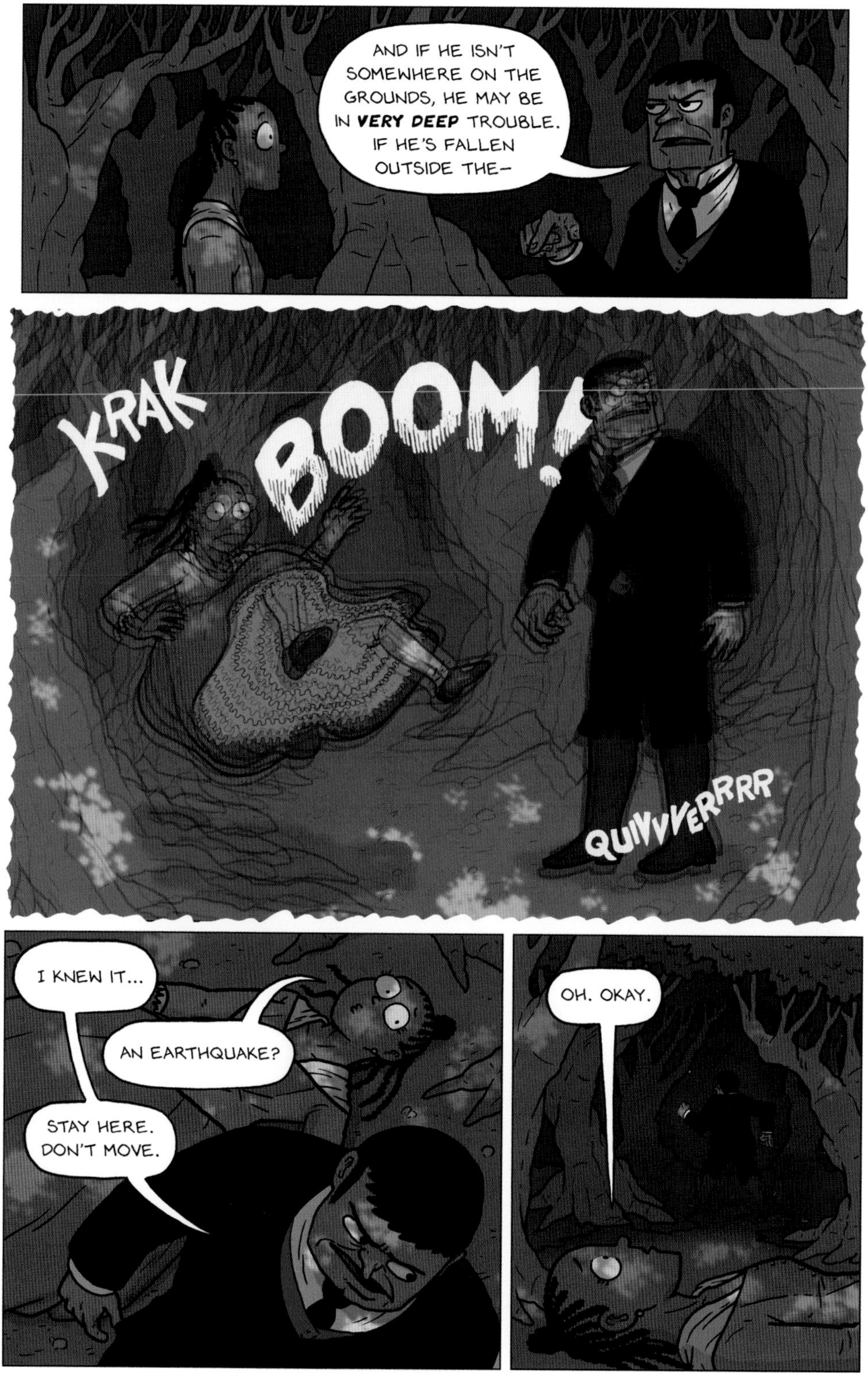
AND IF HE ISN'T SOMEWHERE ON THE GROUNDS, HE MAY BE IN **VERY DEEP** TROUBLE. IF HE'S FALLEN OUTSIDE THE–
KRAK
BOOM!
QUIVVVERRRR
I KNEW IT...
AN EARTHQUAKE?
STAY HERE. DON'T MOVE.
OH. OKAY.

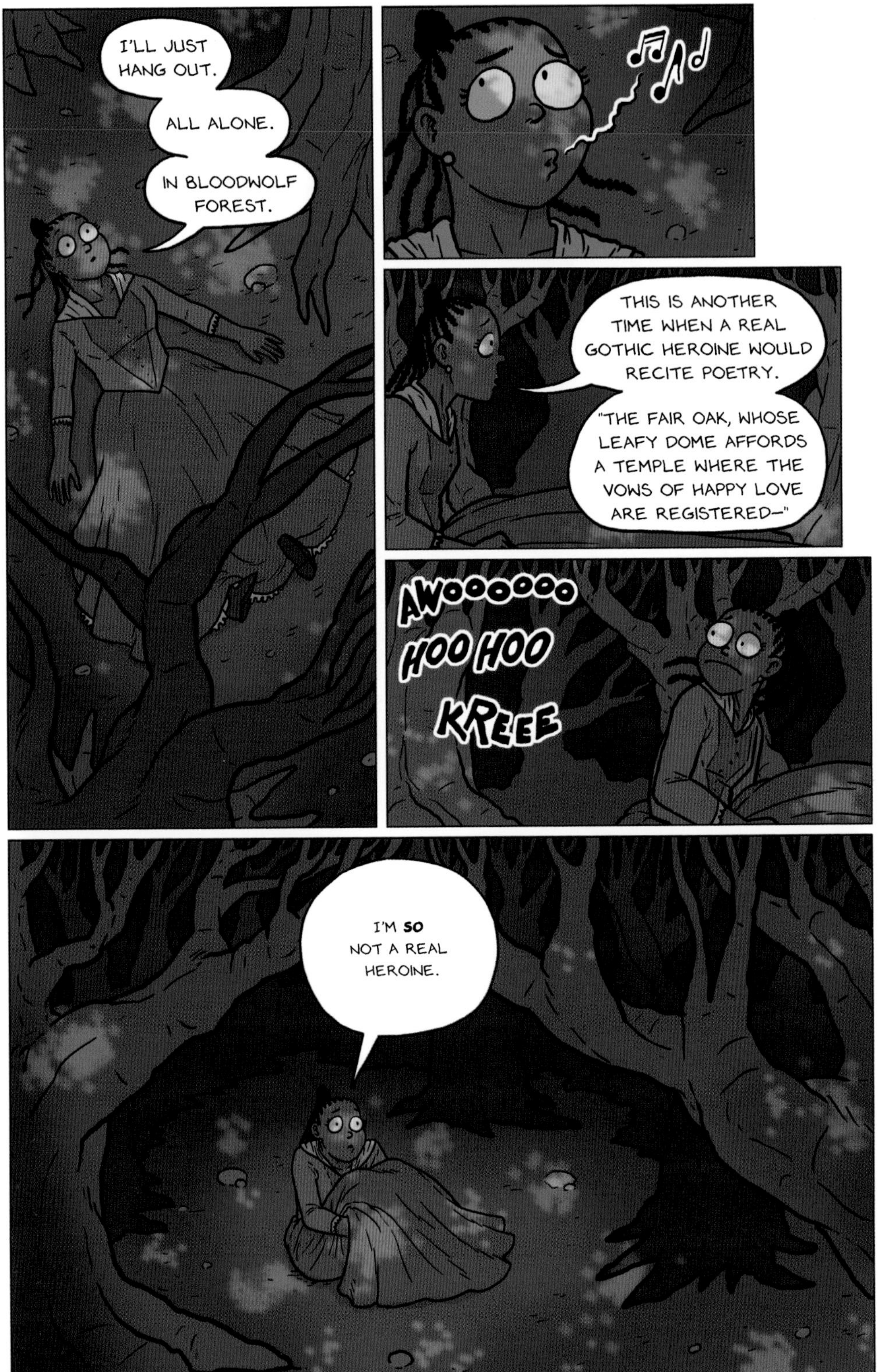
I'LL JUST HANG OUT.
ALL ALONE.
IN BLOODWOLF FOREST.
THIS IS ANOTHER TIME WHEN A REAL GOTHIC HEROINE WOULD RECITE POETRY.
"THE FAIR OAK, WHOSE LEAFY DOME AFFORDS A TEMPLE WHERE THE VOWS OF HAPPY LOVE ARE REGISTERED—"
AWOOOOOO
HOO HOO
KREEE
I'M **SO** NOT A REAL HEROINE.

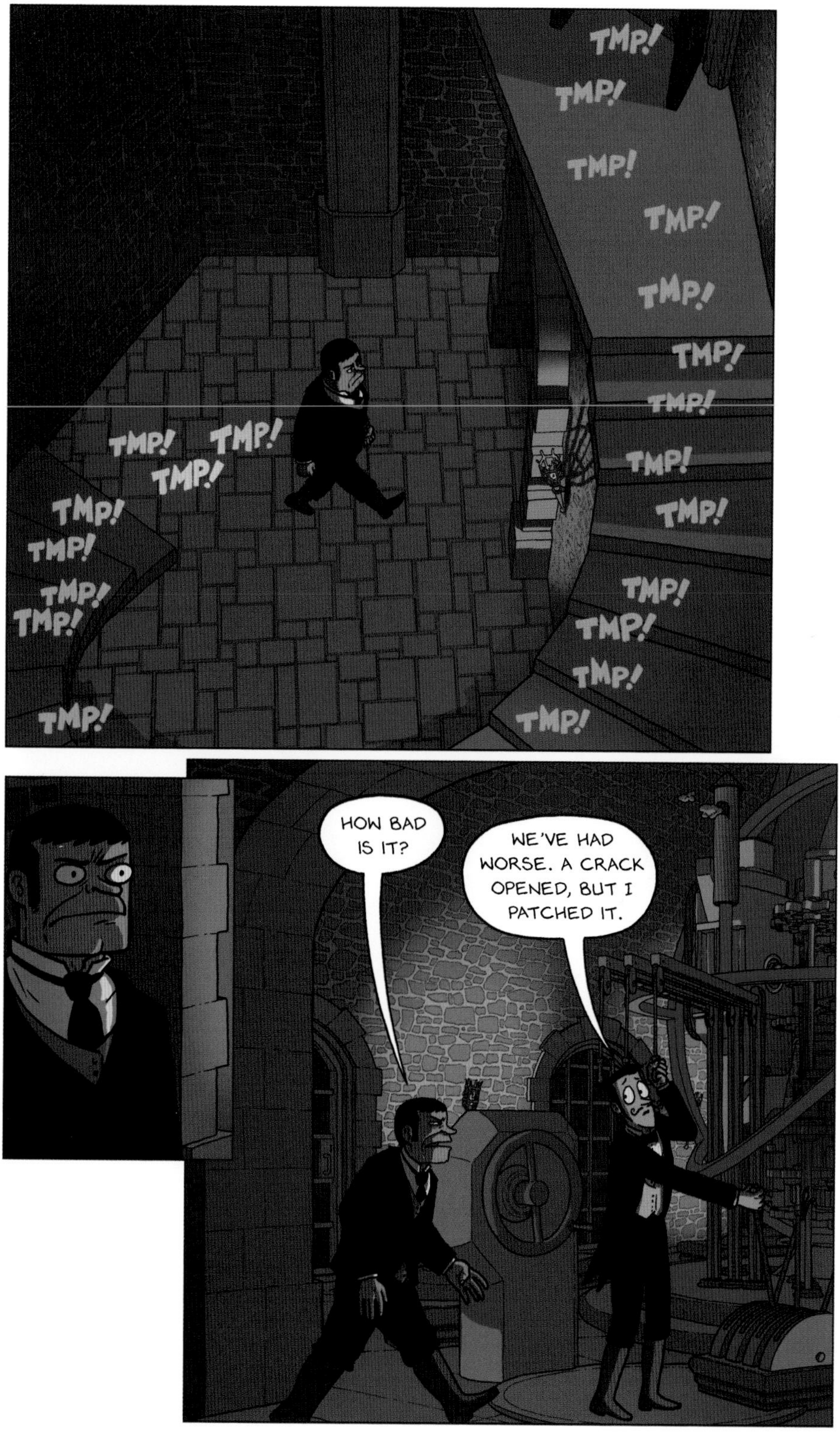
TMP!
TMP!
TMP!
TMP!
TMP!
TMP!
TMP!
TMP!
TMP!
TMP!
TMP!
TMP!
TMP!
TMP!
TMP!
TMP!
TMP!
TMP!
TMP!
TMP!
TMP!
HOW BAD IS IT?
WE'VE HAD WORSE. A CRACK OPENED, BUT I PATCHED IT.

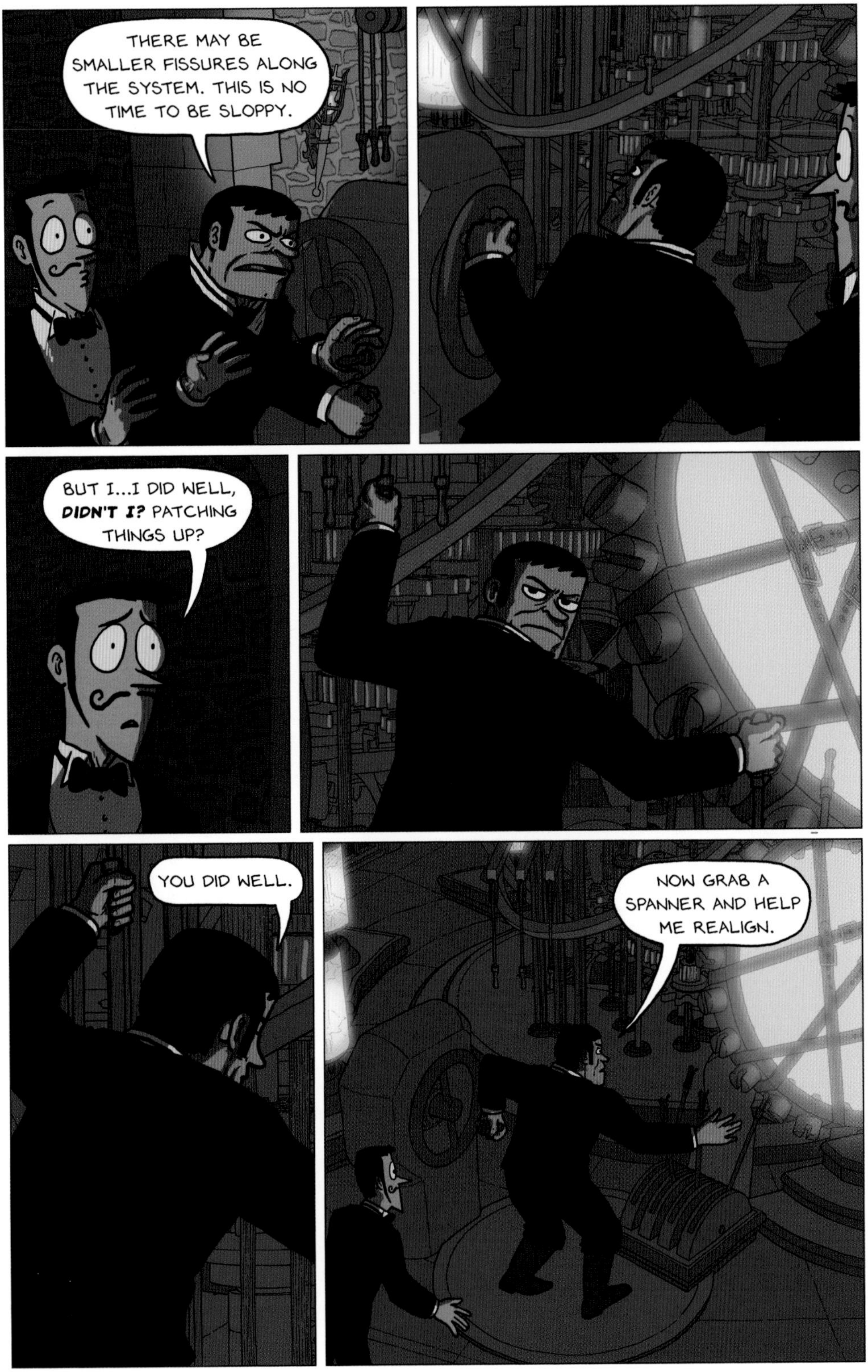
THERE MAY BE SMALLER FISSURES ALONG THE SYSTEM. THIS IS NO TIME TO BE SLOPPY.
BUT I...I DID WELL, **DIDN'T I?** PATCHING THINGS UP?
YOU DID WELL.
NOW GRAB A SPANNER AND HELP ME REALIGN.

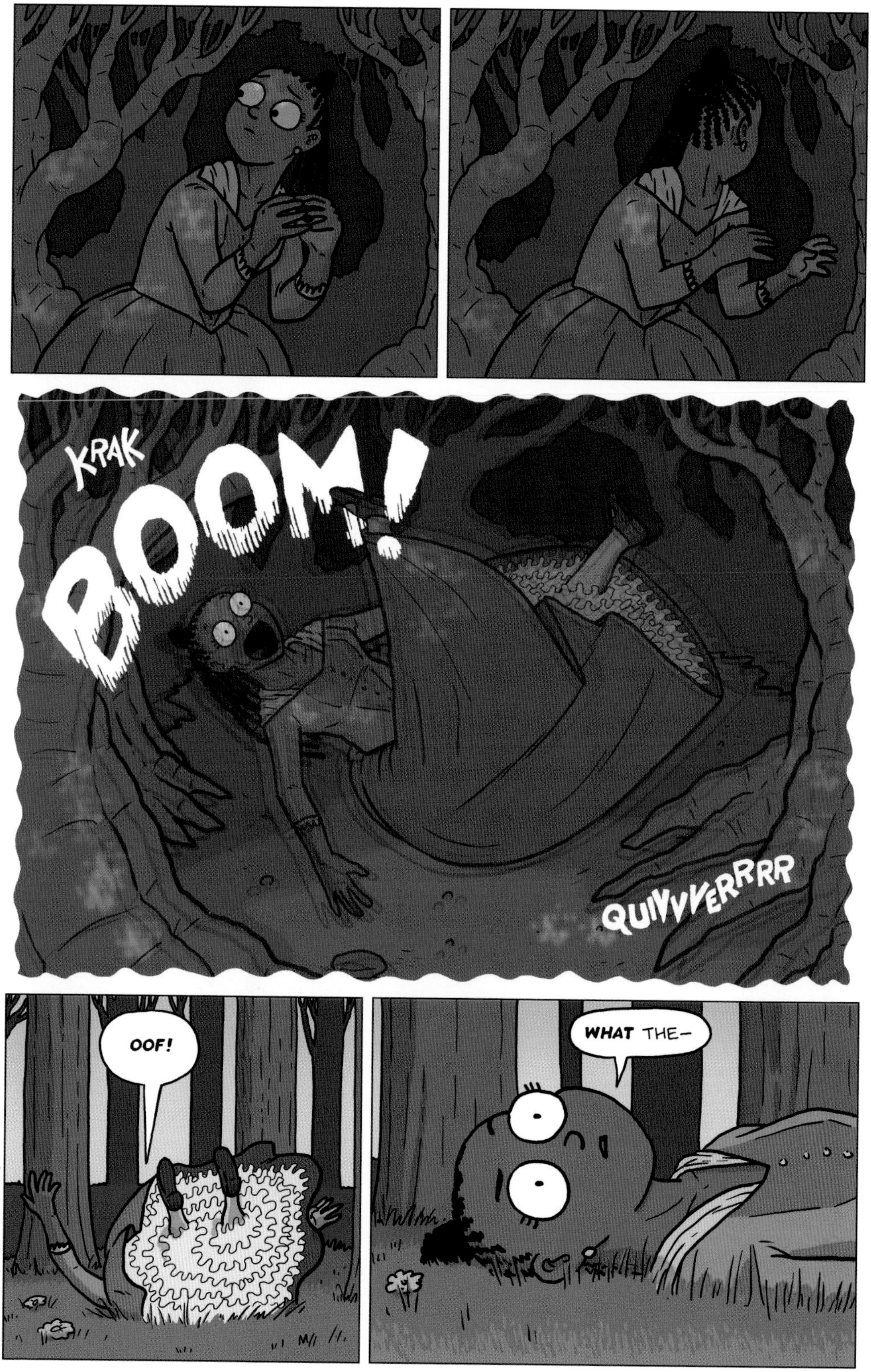
KRAK
BOOM!
QUIVVVERRRR
OOF!
WHAT THE–

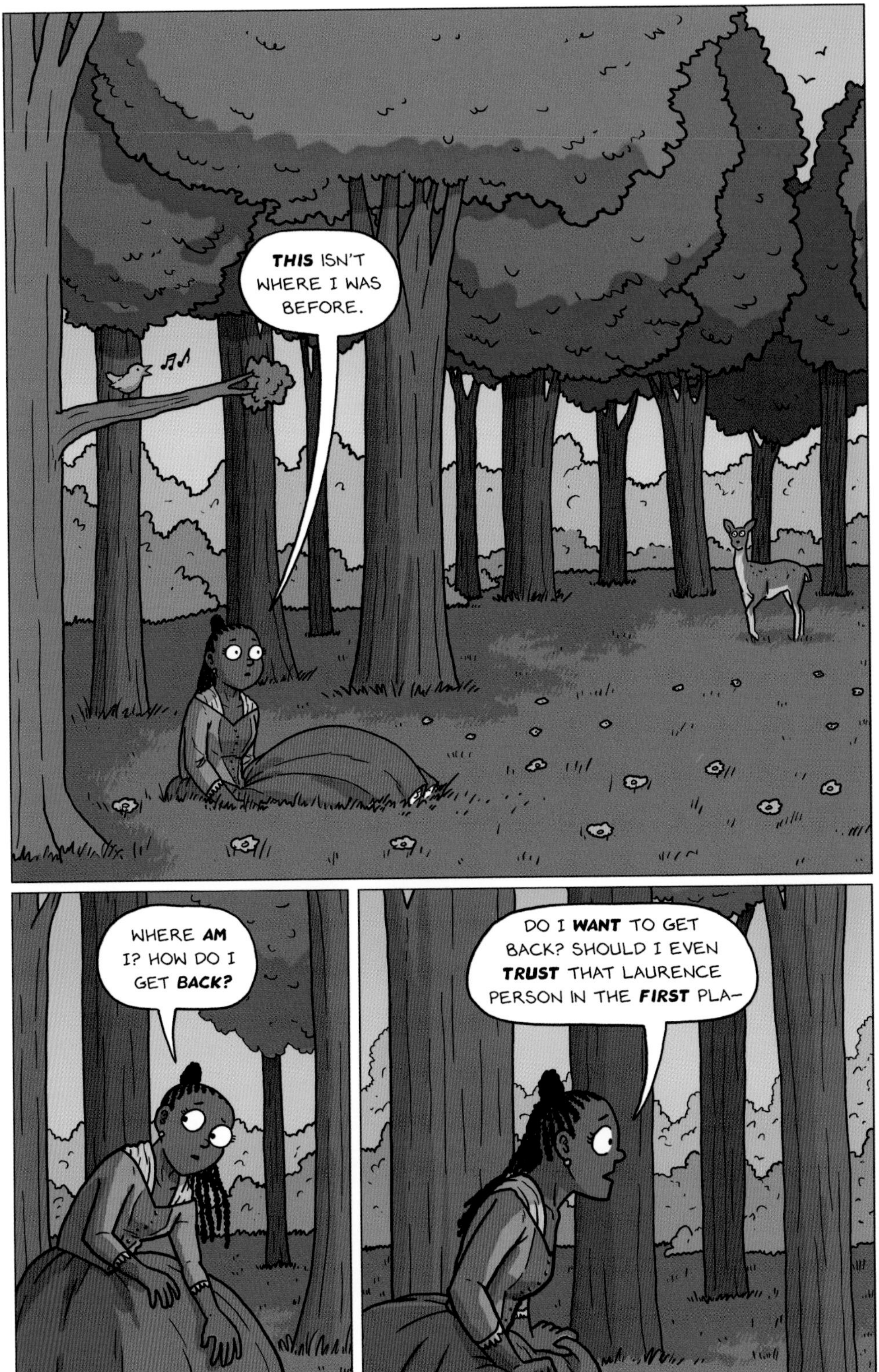
THIS ISN'T WHERE I WAS BEFORE.
WHERE **AM** I? HOW DO I GET **BACK?**
DO I **WANT** TO GET BACK? SHOULD I EVEN **TRUST** THAT LAURENCE PERSON IN THE **FIRST** PLA–

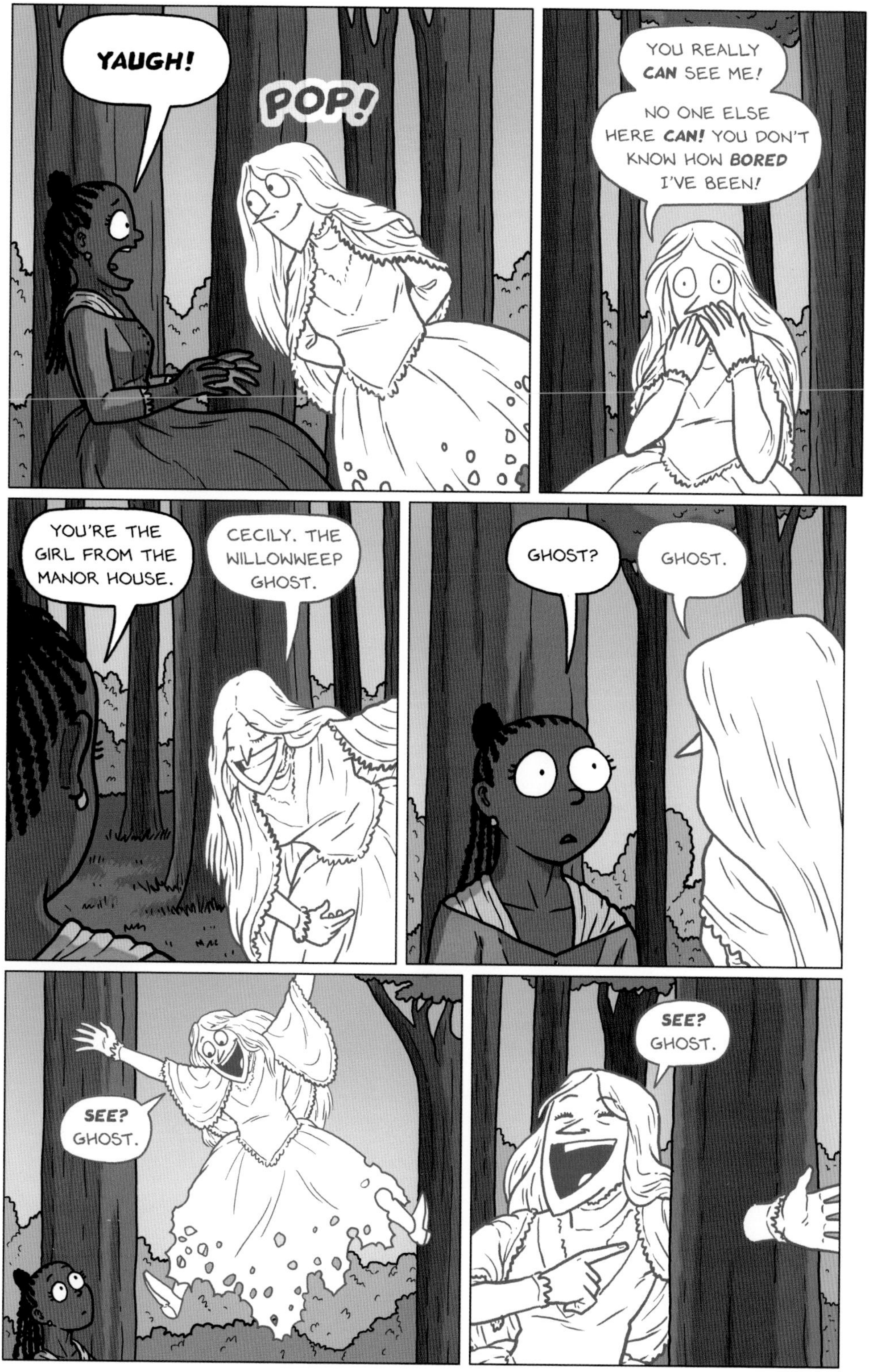
YAUGH!
POP!
YOU REALLY CAN SEE ME!
NO ONE ELSE HERE CAN! YOU DON'T KNOW HOW BORED I'VE BEEN!
YOU'RE THE GIRL FROM THE MANOR HOUSE.
CECILY. THE WILLOWWEEP GHOST.
GHOST?
GHOST.
SEE? GHOST.
SEE? GHOST.

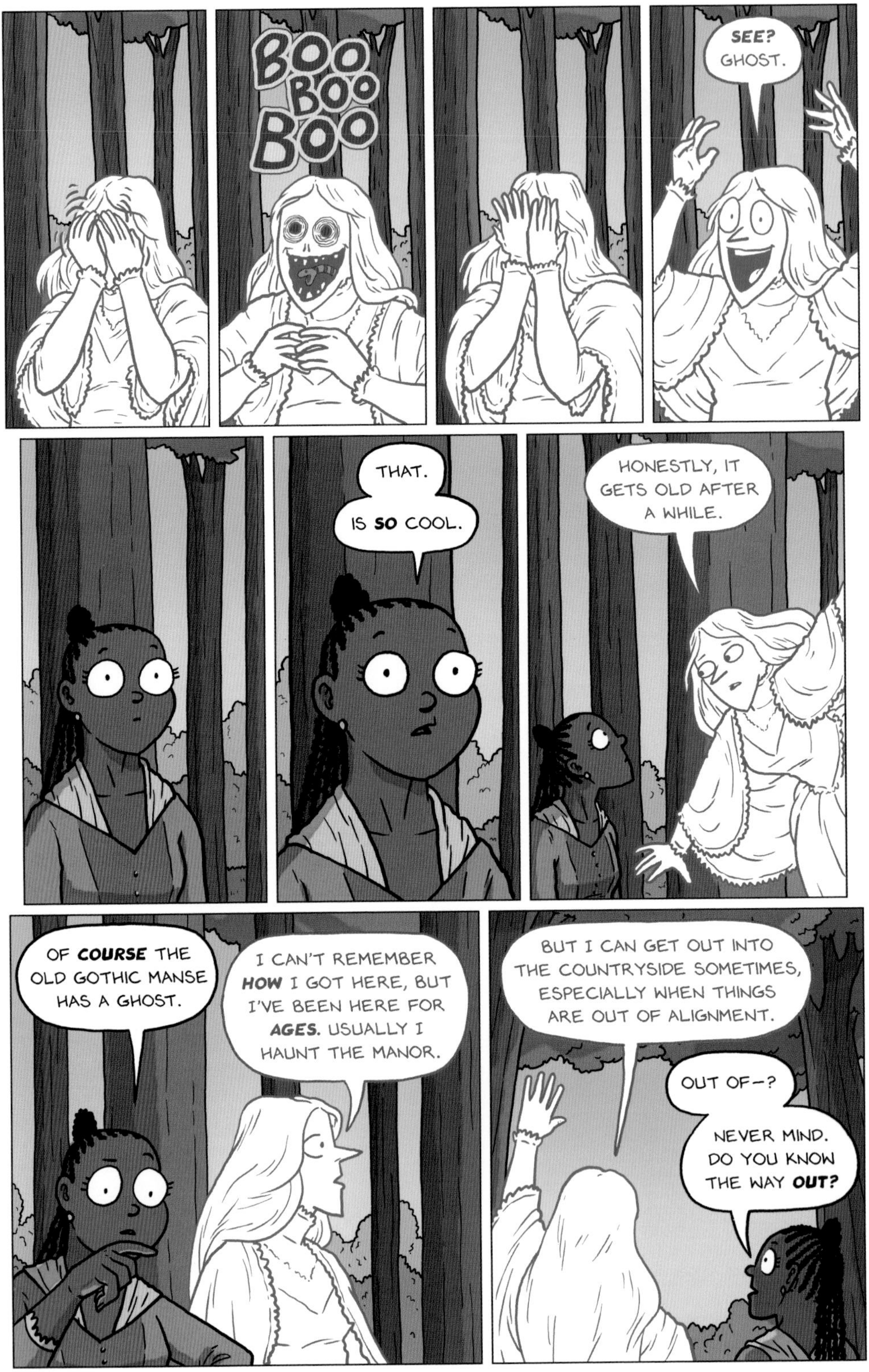
BOO BOO BOO
SEE? GHOST.
THAT.
IS **SO** COOL.
HONESTLY, IT GETS OLD AFTER A WHILE.
OF **COURSE** THE OLD GOTHIC MANSE HAS A GHOST.
I CAN'T REMEMBER **HOW** I GOT HERE, BUT I'VE BEEN HERE FOR **AGES.** USUALLY I HAUNT THE MANOR.
BUT I CAN GET OUT INTO THE COUNTRYSIDE SOMETIMES, ESPECIALLY WHEN THINGS ARE OUT OF ALIGNMENT.
OUT OF—?
NEVER MIND. DO YOU KNOW THE WAY **OUT?**

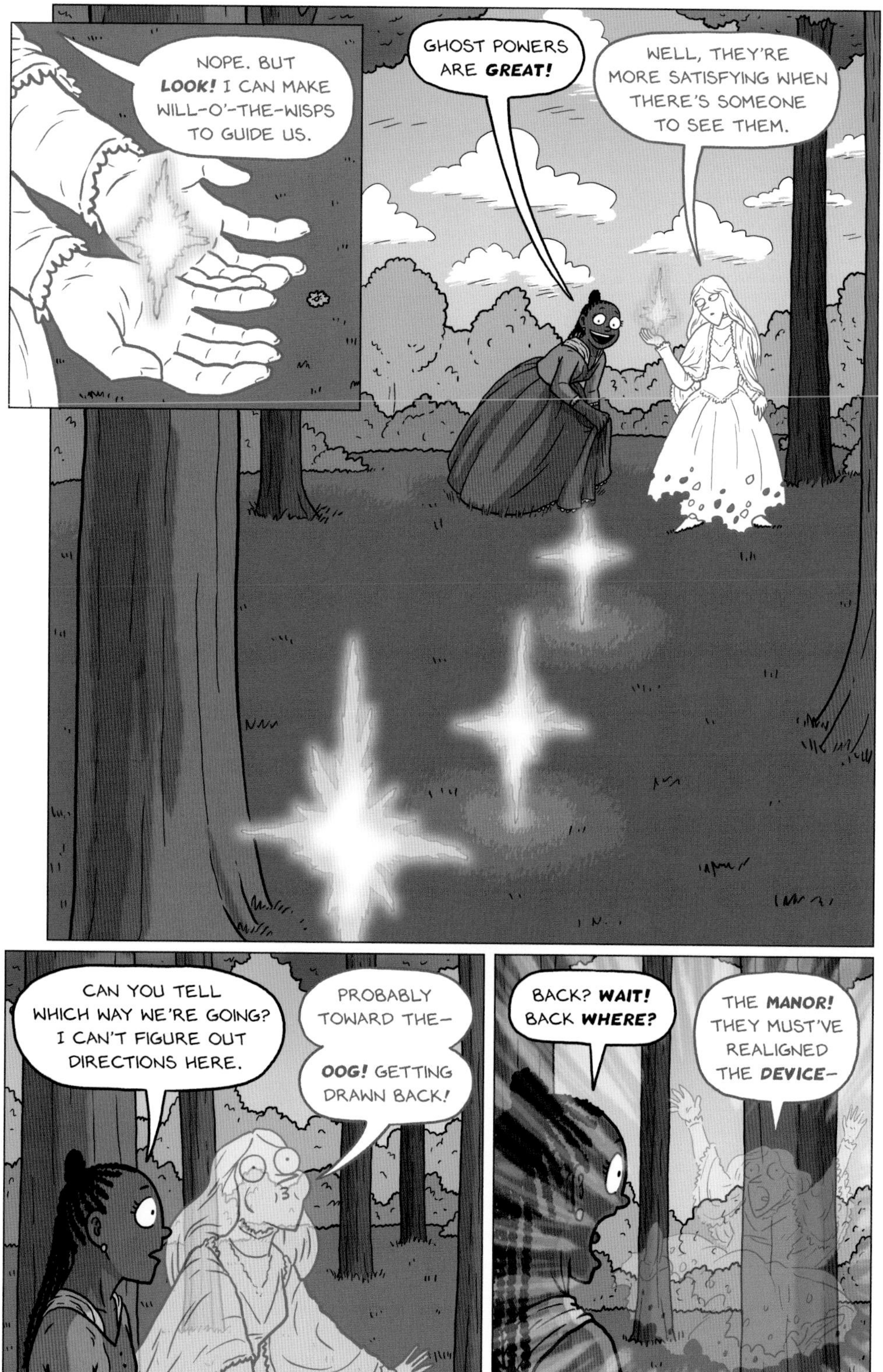
NOPE. BUT **LOOK!** I CAN MAKE WILL-O'-THE-WISPS TO GUIDE US.
GHOST POWERS ARE **GREAT!**
WELL, THEY'RE MORE SATISFYING WHEN THERE'S SOMEONE TO SEE THEM.
CAN YOU TELL WHICH WAY WE'RE GOING? I CAN'T FIGURE OUT DIRECTIONS HERE.
PROBABLY TOWARD THE–
OOG! GETTING DRAWN BACK!
BACK? **WAIT!** BACK **WHERE?**
THE **MANOR!** THEY MUST'VE REALIGNED THE **DEVICE**–

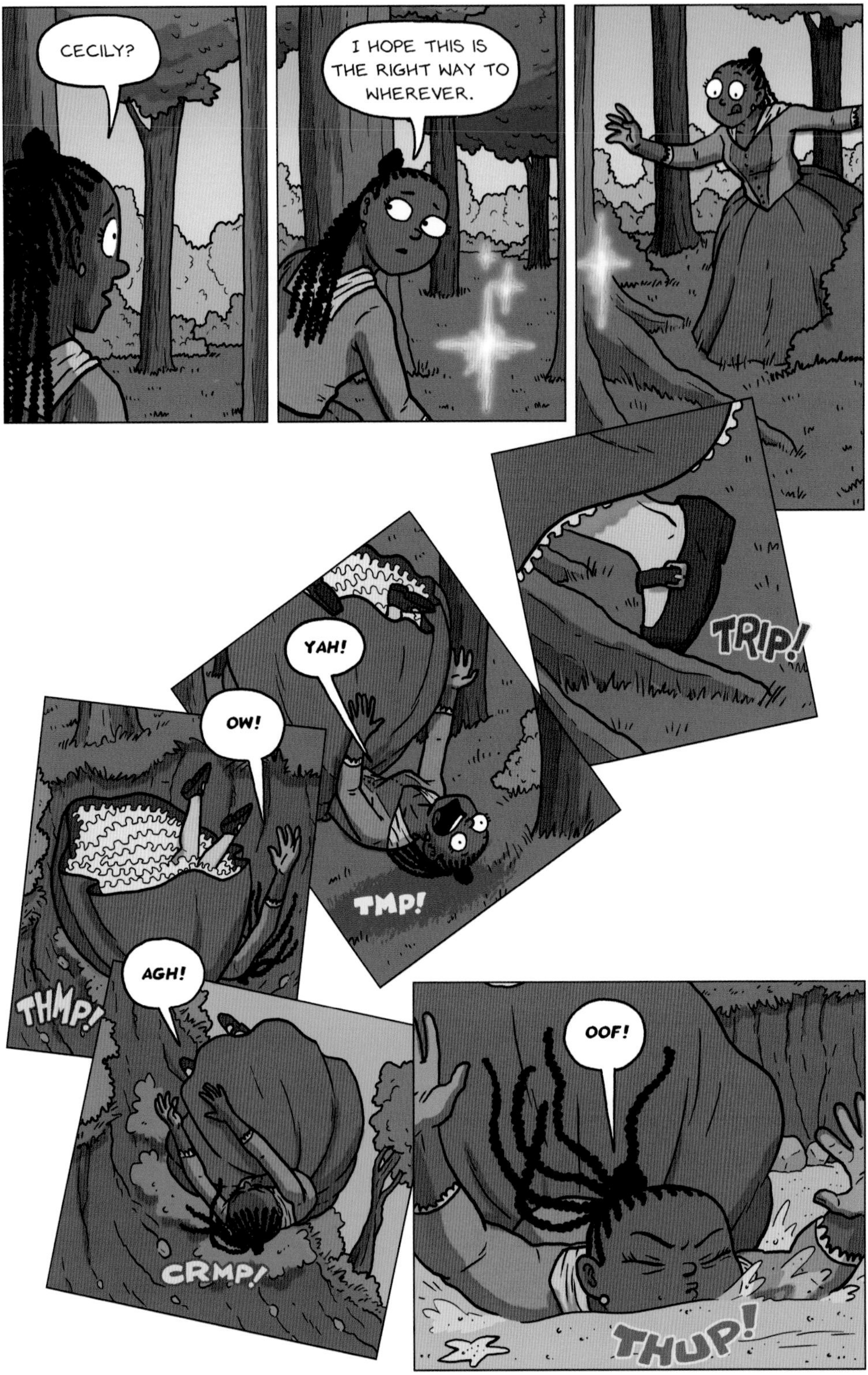
CECILY?
I HOPE THIS IS THE RIGHT WAY TO WHEREVER.
TRIP!
YAH!
TMP!
OW!
THMP!
AGH!
CRMP!
OOF!
THUP!

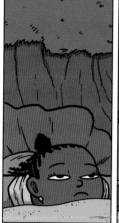

OH...

KREE KREE

FSSSH

FSSSSSH

MONTAGUE!

YOU ARE **SO** BROODING ON A STARK AND LONELY STRAND.

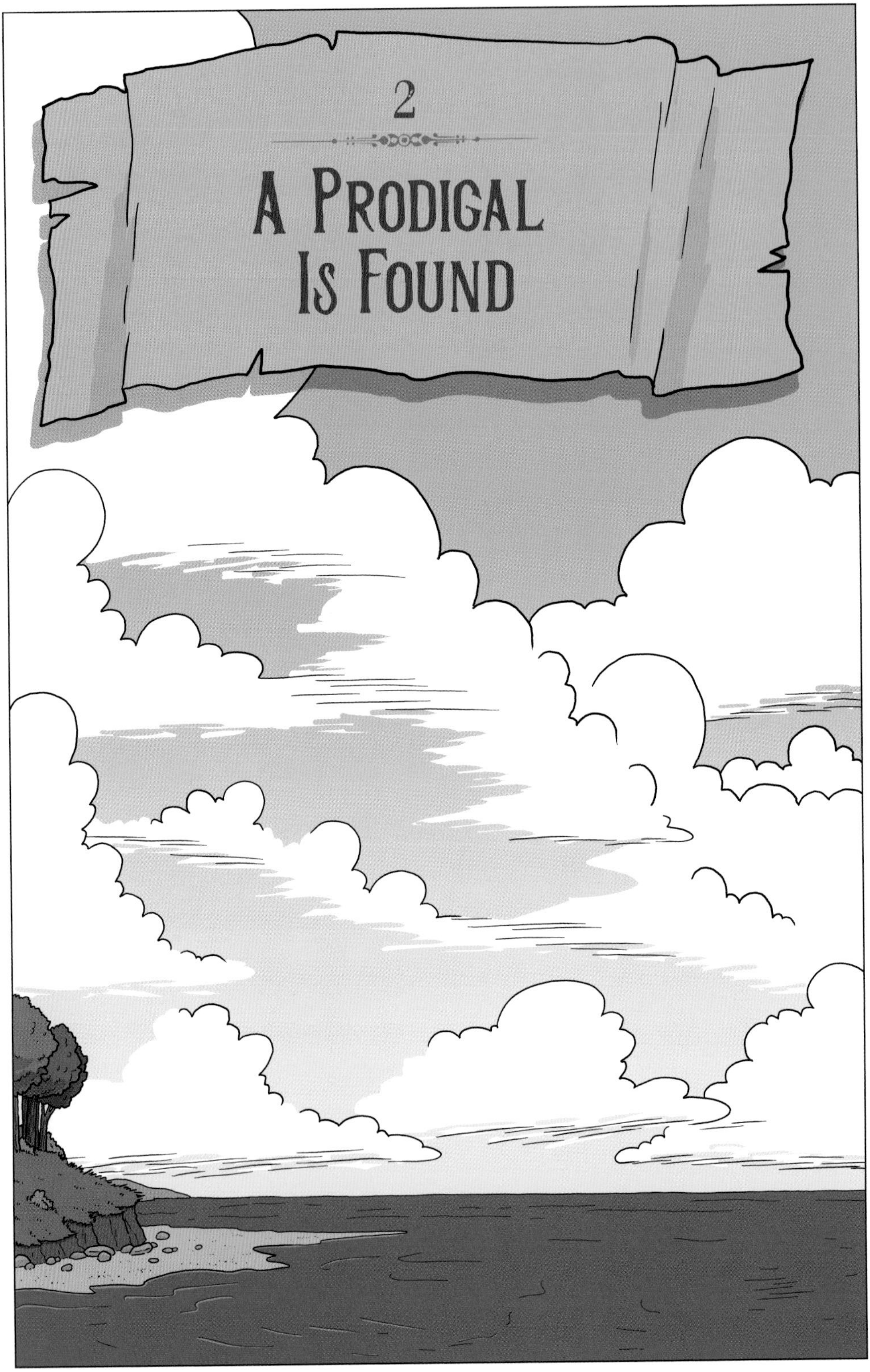
2
A Prodigal Is Found

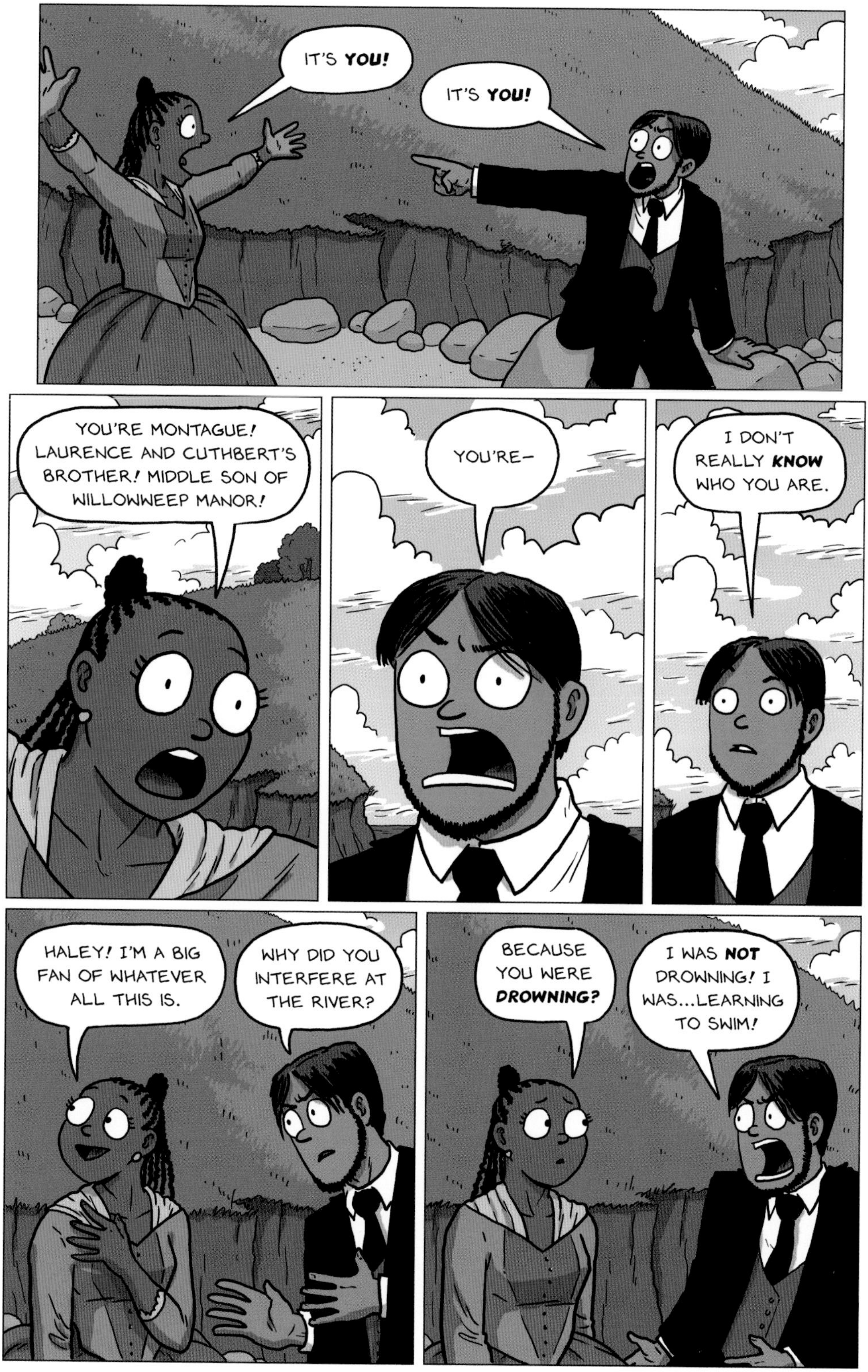
IT'S **YOU!**
IT'S **YOU!**
YOU'RE MONTAGUE! LAURENCE AND CUTHBERT'S BROTHER! MIDDLE SON OF WILLOWWEEP MANOR!
YOU'RE—
I DON'T REALLY **KNOW** WHO YOU ARE.
HALEY! I'M A BIG FAN OF WHATEVER ALL THIS IS.
WHY DID YOU INTERFERE AT THE RIVER?
BECAUSE YOU WERE **DROWNING?**
I WAS **NOT** DROWNING! I WAS...LEARNING TO SWIM!

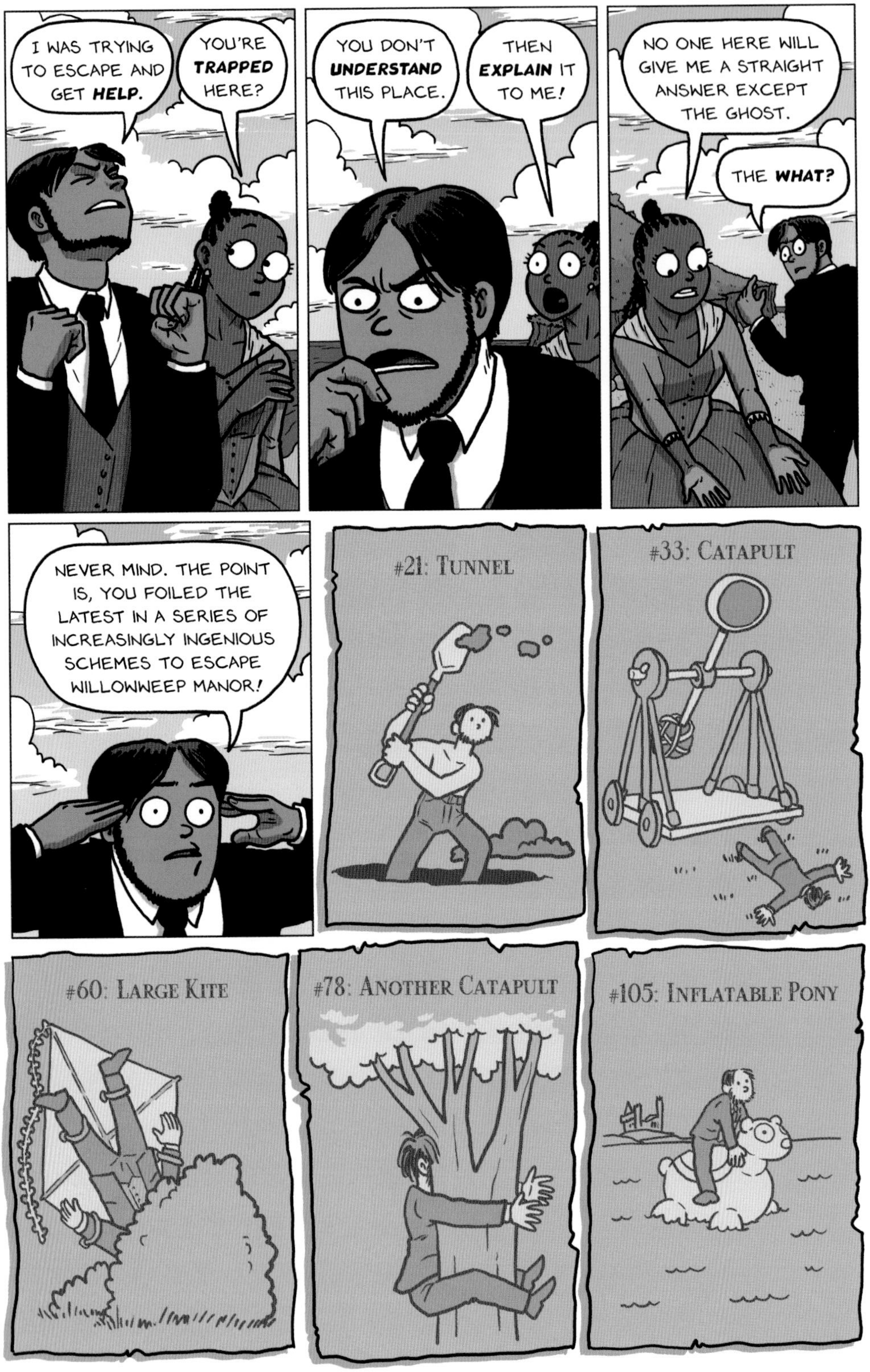
I WAS TRYING TO ESCAPE AND GET HELP.
YOU'RE TRAPPED HERE?
YOU DON'T UNDERSTAND THIS PLACE.
THEN EXPLAIN IT TO ME!
NO ONE HERE WILL GIVE ME A STRAIGHT ANSWER EXCEPT THE GHOST.
THE WHAT?
NEVER MIND. THE POINT IS, YOU FOILED THE LATEST IN A SERIES OF INCREASINGLY INGENIOUS SCHEMES TO ESCAPE WILLOWWEEP MANOR!
#21: TUNNEL
#33: CATAPULT
#60: LARGE KITE
#78: ANOTHER CATAPULT
#105: INFLATABLE PONY

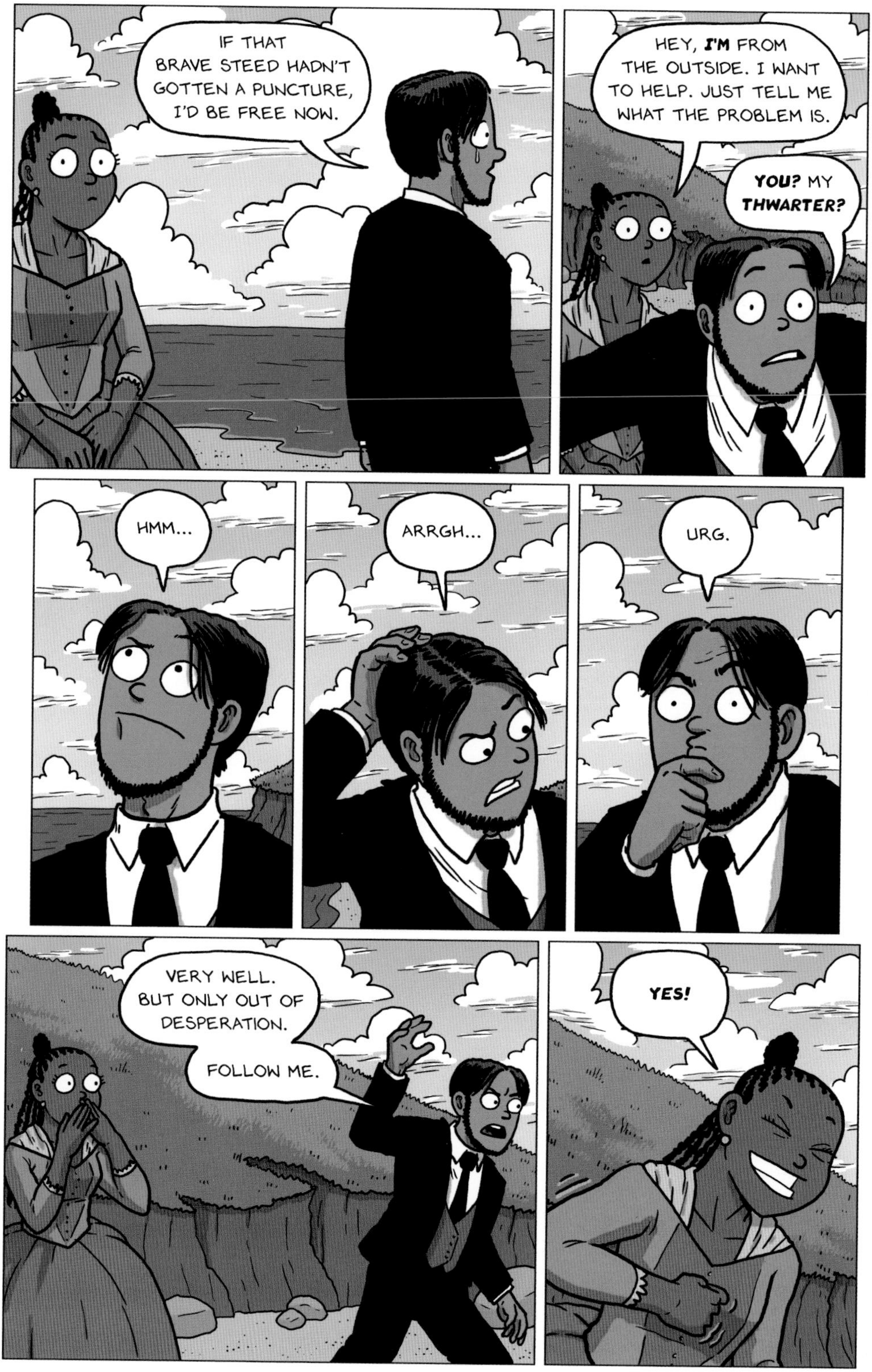
IF THAT BRAVE STEED HADN'T GOTTEN A PUNCTURE, I'D BE FREE NOW.
HEY, **I'M** FROM THE OUTSIDE. I WANT TO HELP. JUST TELL ME WHAT THE PROBLEM IS.
YOU? MY **THWARTER?**
HMM...
ARRGH...
URG.
VERY WELL. BUT ONLY OUT OF DESPERATION.
FOLLOW ME.
YES!

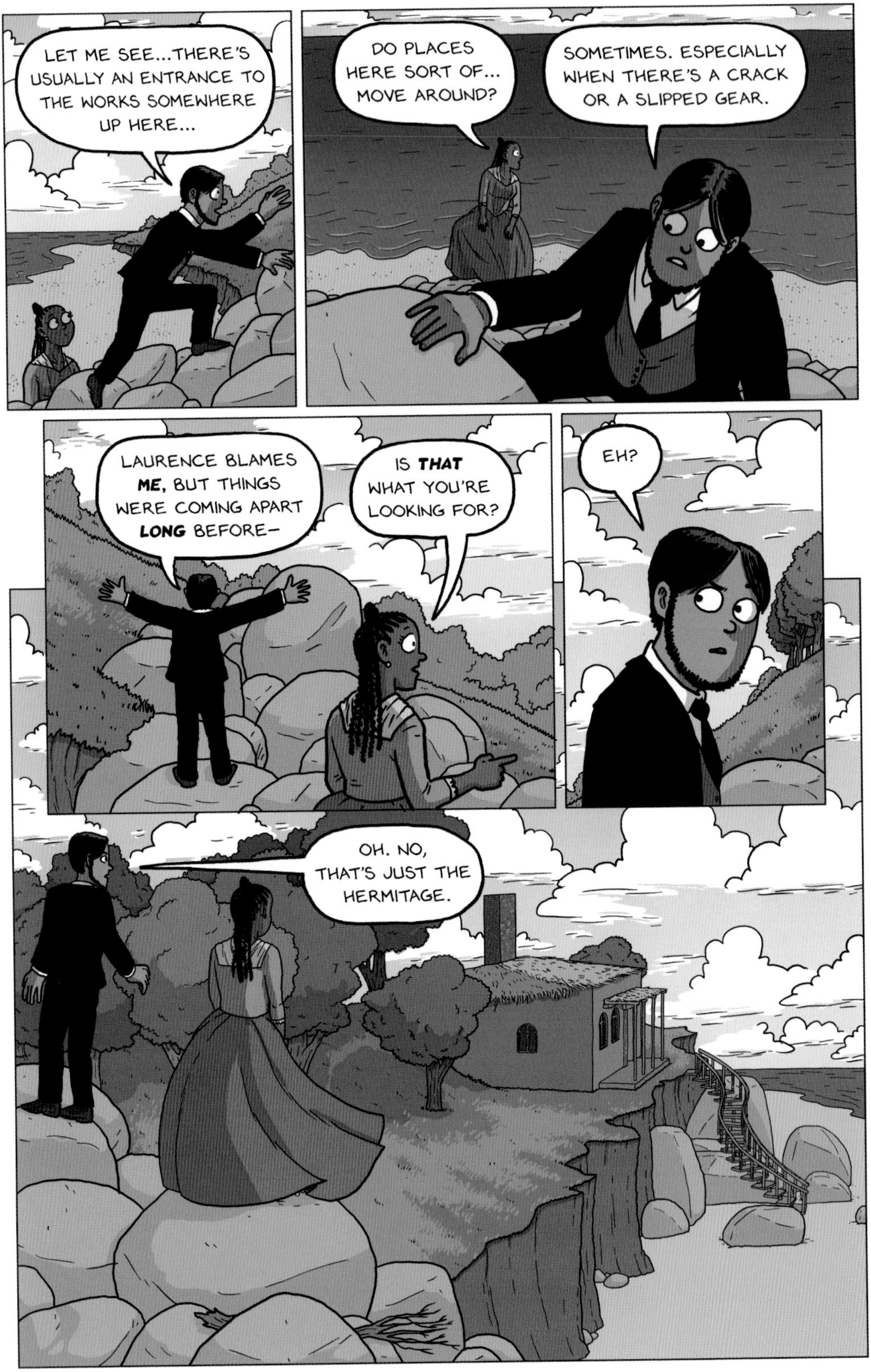
LET ME SEE...THERE'S USUALLY AN ENTRANCE TO THE WORKS SOMEWHERE UP HERE...
DO PLACES HERE SORT OF... MOVE AROUND?
SOMETIMES. ESPECIALLY WHEN THERE'S A CRACK OR A SLIPPED GEAR.
LAURENCE BLAMES **ME,** BUT THINGS WERE COMING APART **LONG** BEFORE—
IS **THAT** WHAT YOU'RE LOOKING FOR?
EH?
OH. NO, THAT'S JUST THE HERMITAGE.

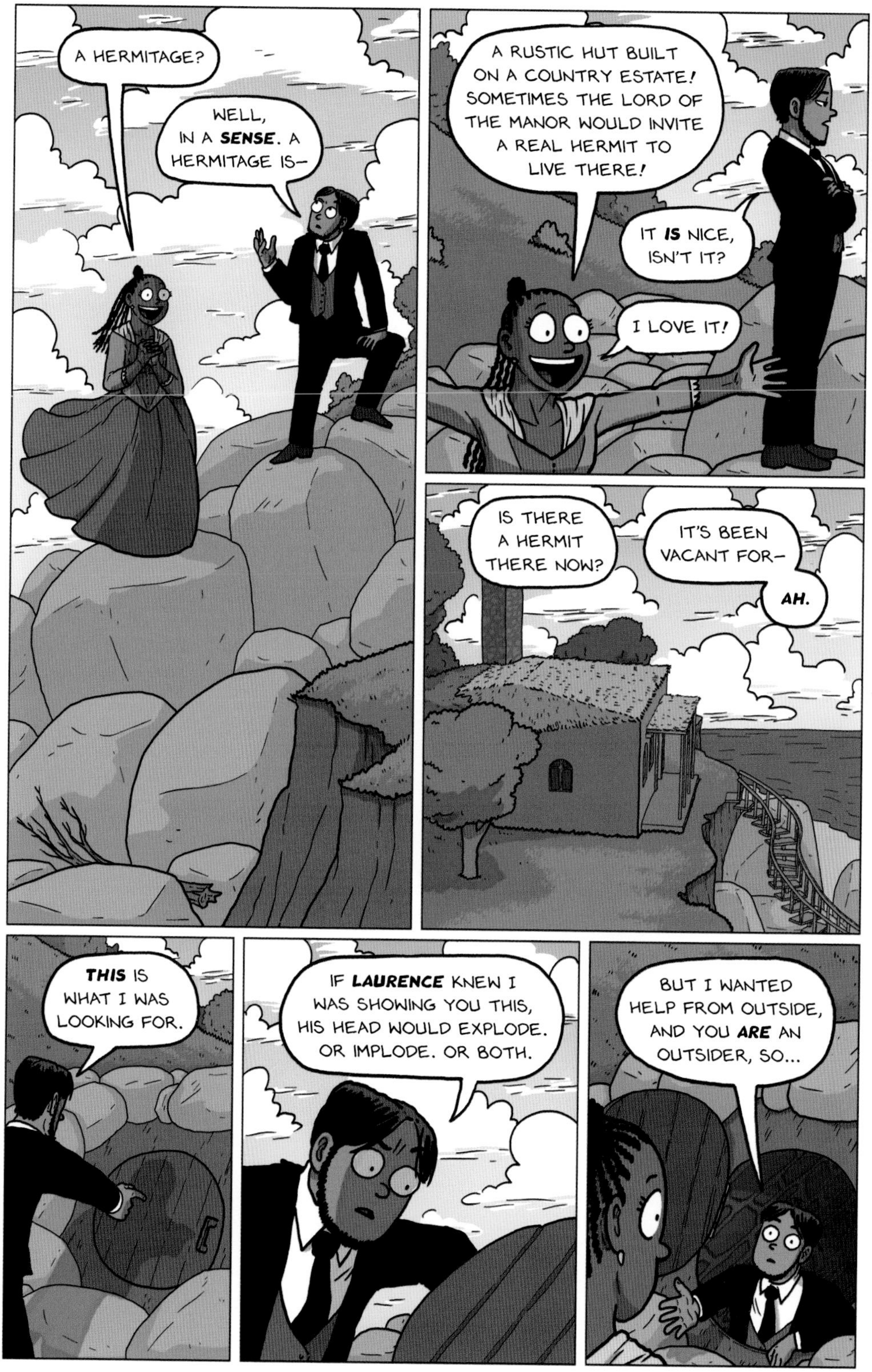
A HERMITAGE?
WELL, IN A **SENSE**. A HERMITAGE IS—
A RUSTIC HUT BUILT ON A COUNTRY ESTATE! SOMETIMES THE LORD OF THE MANOR WOULD INVITE A REAL HERMIT TO LIVE THERE!
IT **IS** NICE, ISN'T IT?
I LOVE IT!
IS THERE A HERMIT THERE NOW?
IT'S BEEN VACANT FOR—
AH.
THIS IS WHAT I WAS LOOKING FOR.
IF **LAURENCE** KNEW I WAS SHOWING YOU THIS, HIS HEAD WOULD EXPLODE. OR IMPLODE. OR BOTH.
BUT I WANTED HELP FROM OUTSIDE, AND YOU **ARE** AN OUTSIDER, SO...

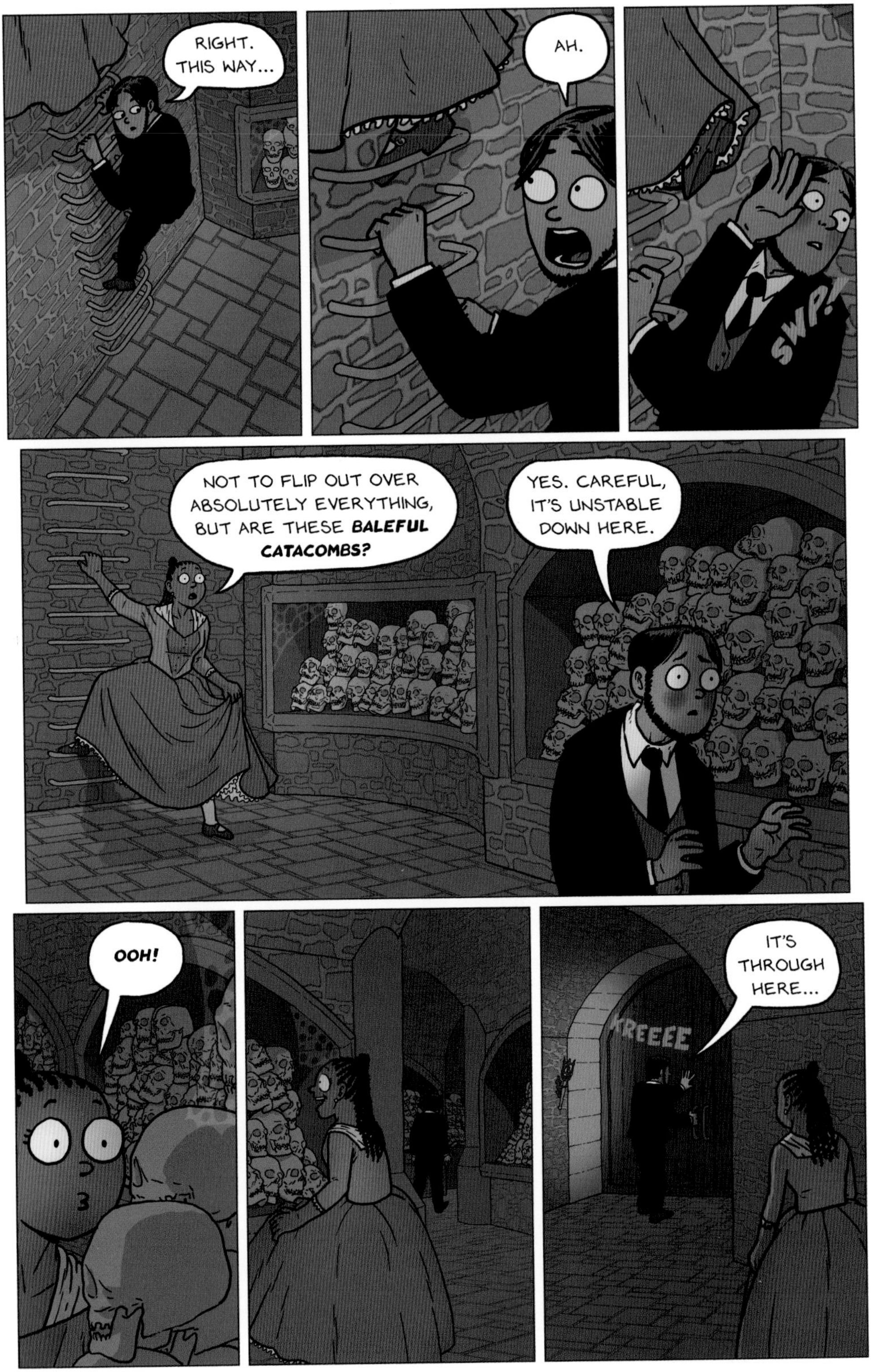
RIGHT. THIS WAY...
AH.
SWP!
NOT TO FLIP OUT OVER ABSOLUTELY EVERYTHING, BUT ARE THESE **BALEFUL CATACOMBS?**
YES. CAREFUL, IT'S UNSTABLE DOWN HERE.
OOH!
KREEEE
IT'S THROUGH HERE...

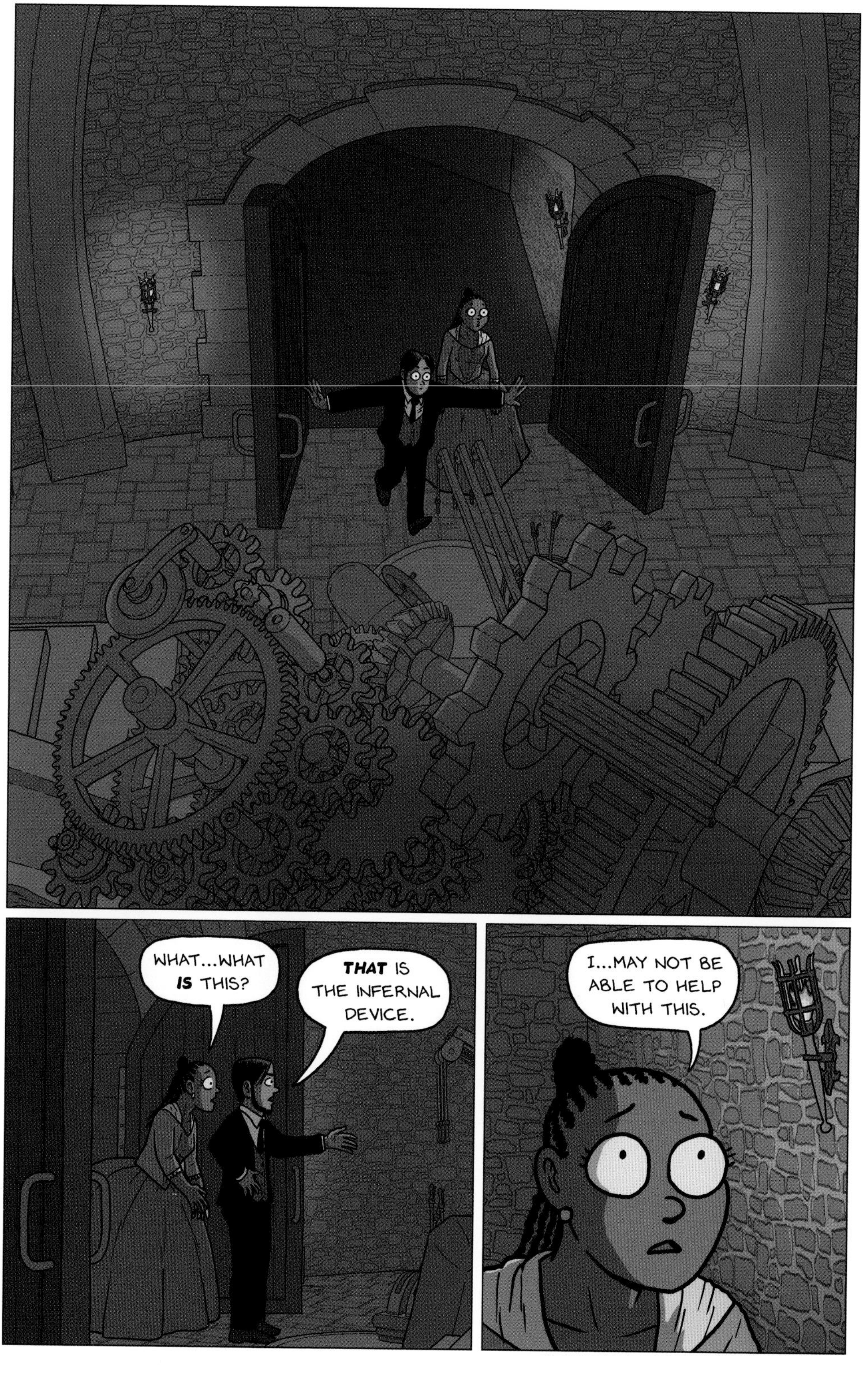
WHAT...WHAT **IS** THIS?
THAT IS THE INFERNAL DEVICE.
I...MAY NOT BE ABLE TO HELP WITH THIS.

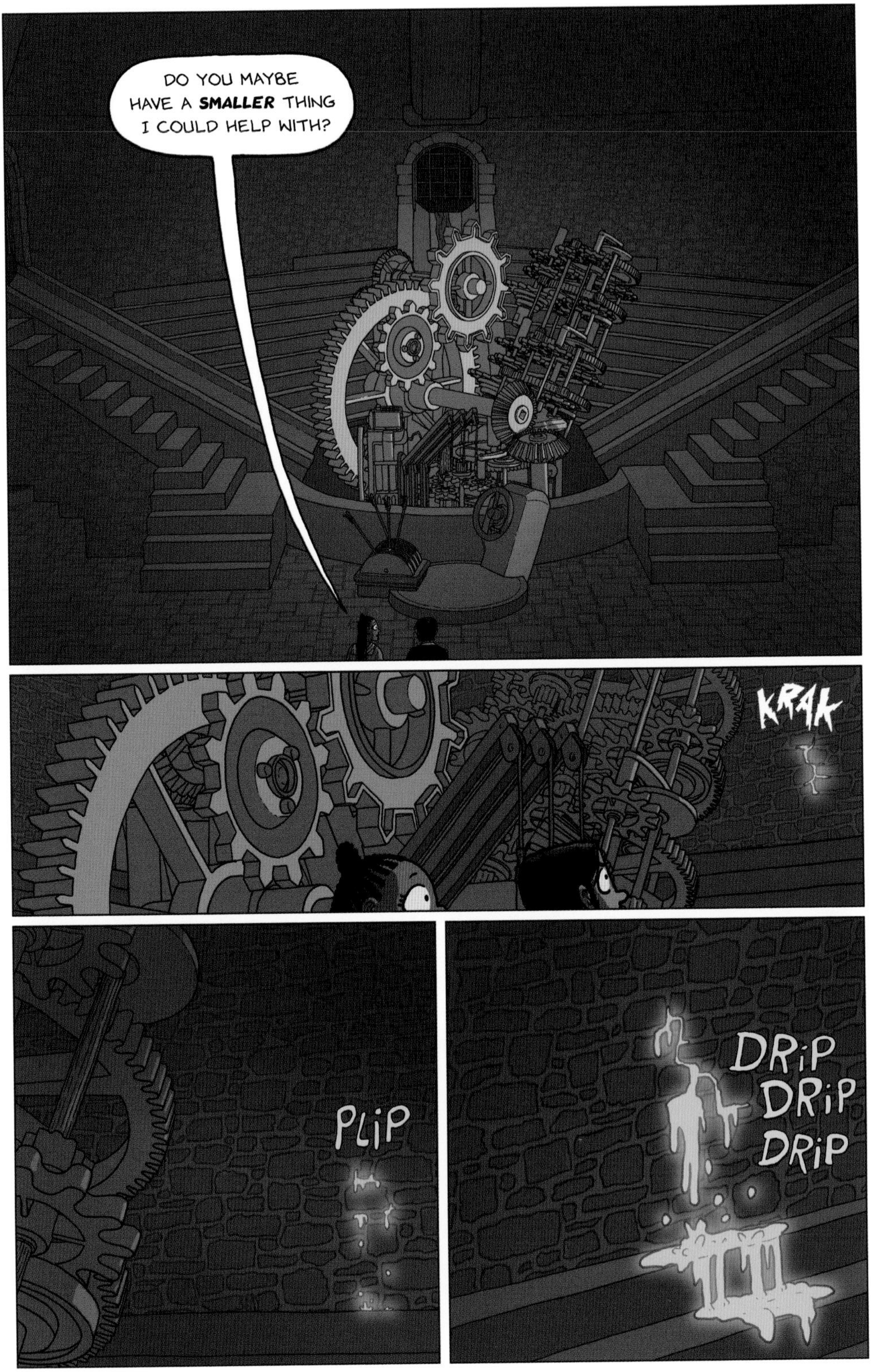
DO YOU MAYBE HAVE A **SMALLER** THING I COULD HELP WITH?
KRAK
PLIP
DRIP
DRIP
DRIP

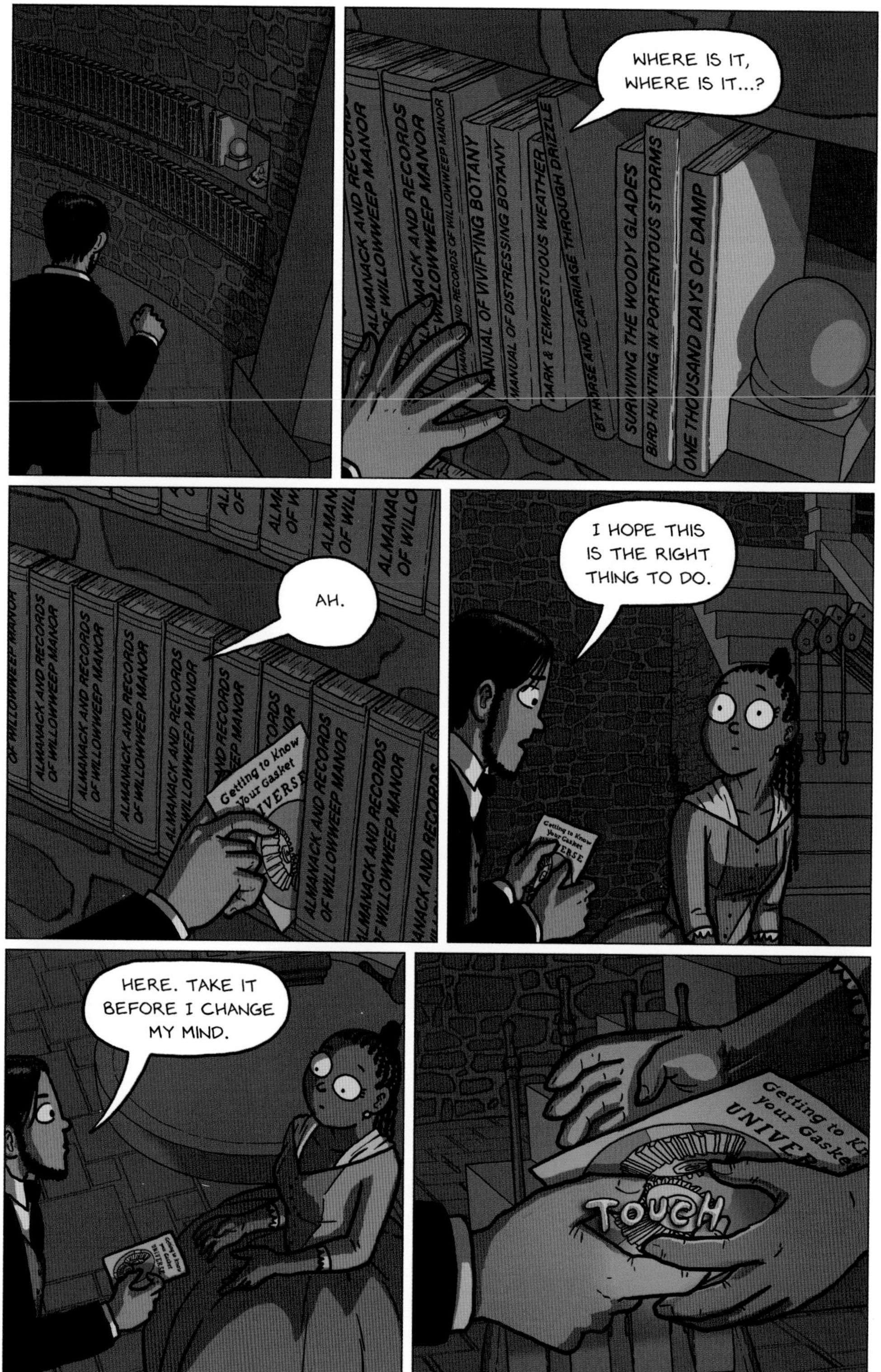
WHERE IS IT, WHERE IS IT...?
ALMANACK AND RECORDS OF WILLOWWEEP MANOR
MANUAL OF VIVIFYING BOTANY
MANUAL OF DISTRESSING BOTANY
DARK & TEMPESTUOUS WEATHER
BY HORSE AND CARRIAGE THROUGH DRIZZLE
SURVIVING THE WOODY GLADES
BIRD HUNTING IN PORTENTOUS STORMS
ONE THOUSAND DAYS OF DAMP
AH.
Getting to Know Your Gasket UNIVERSE
I HOPE THIS IS THE RIGHT THING TO DO.
HERE. TAKE IT BEFORE I CHANGE MY MIND.
TOUCH

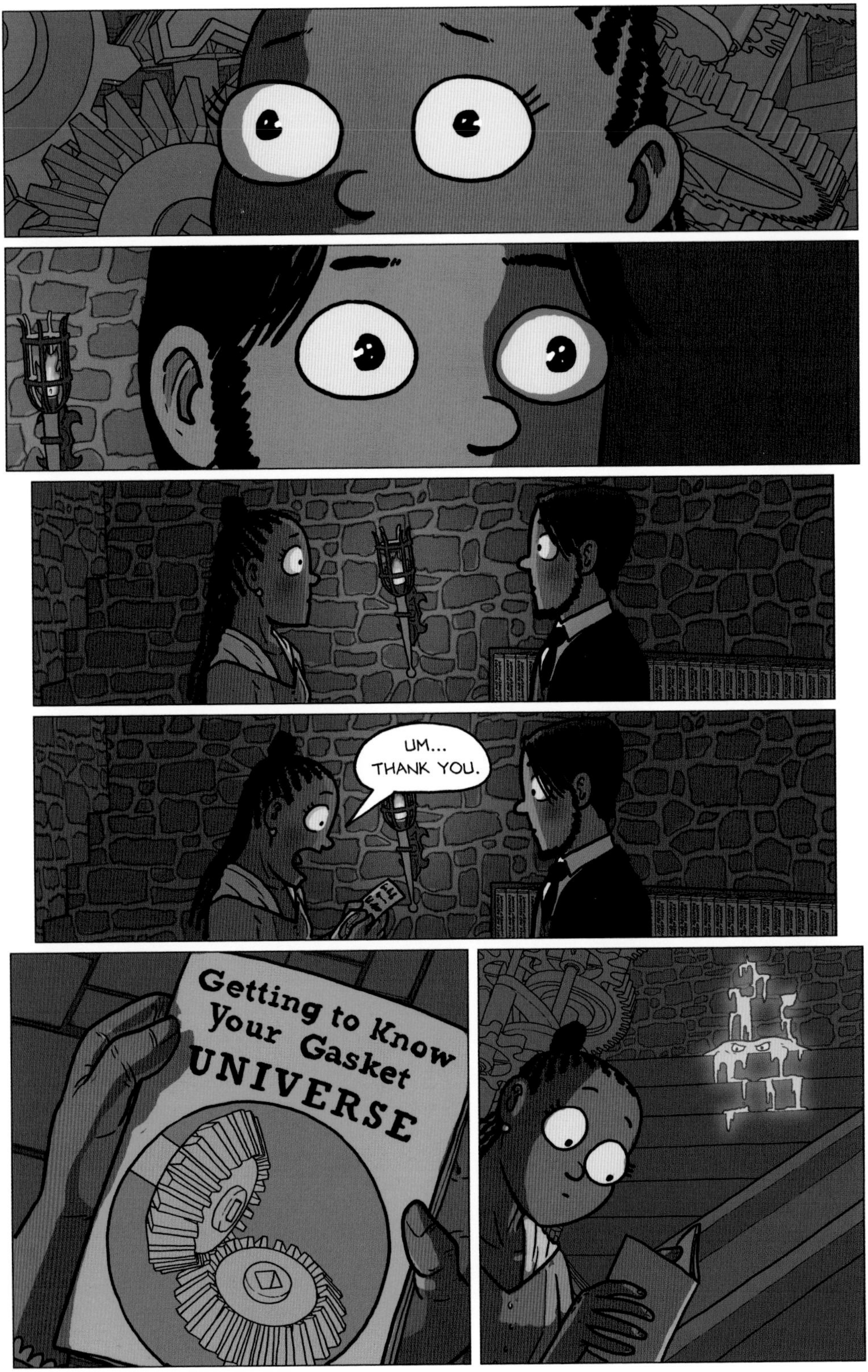
UM...
THANK YOU.
Getting to Know Your Gasket
UNIVERSE

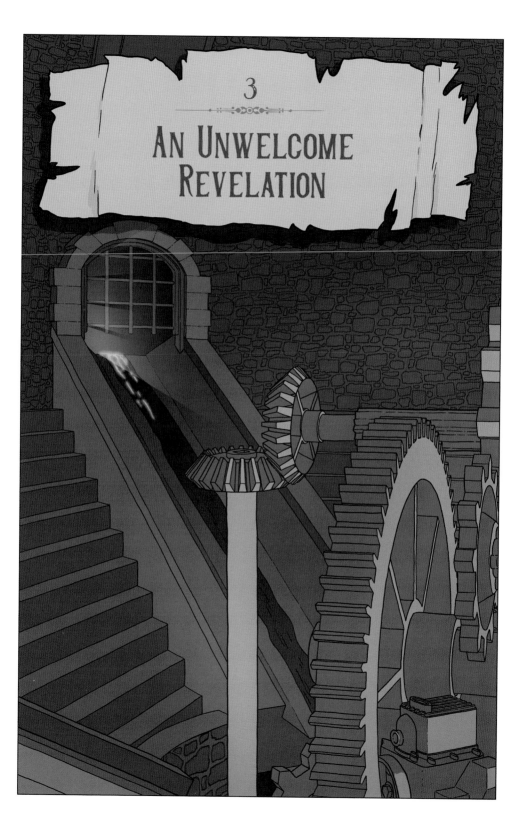

3

An Unwelcome Revelation

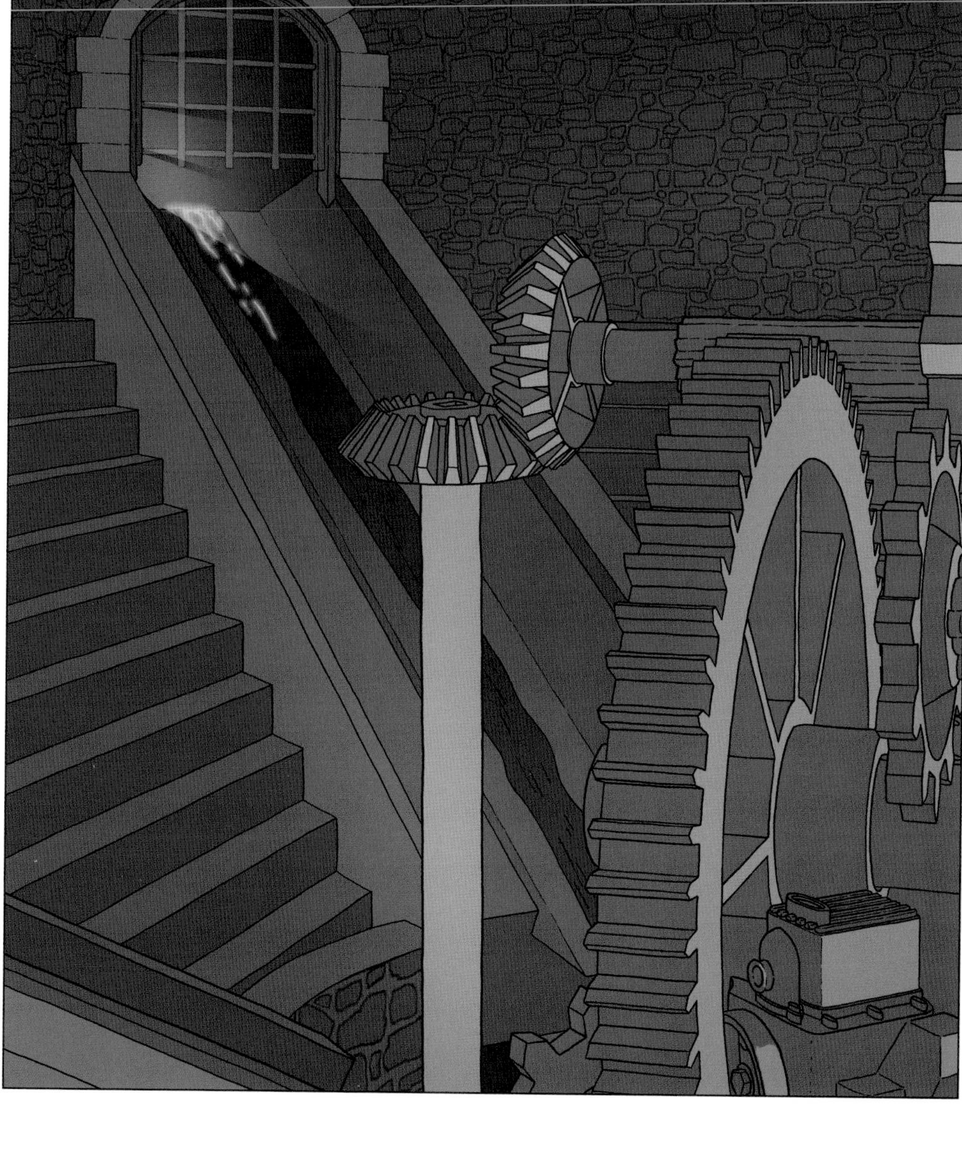

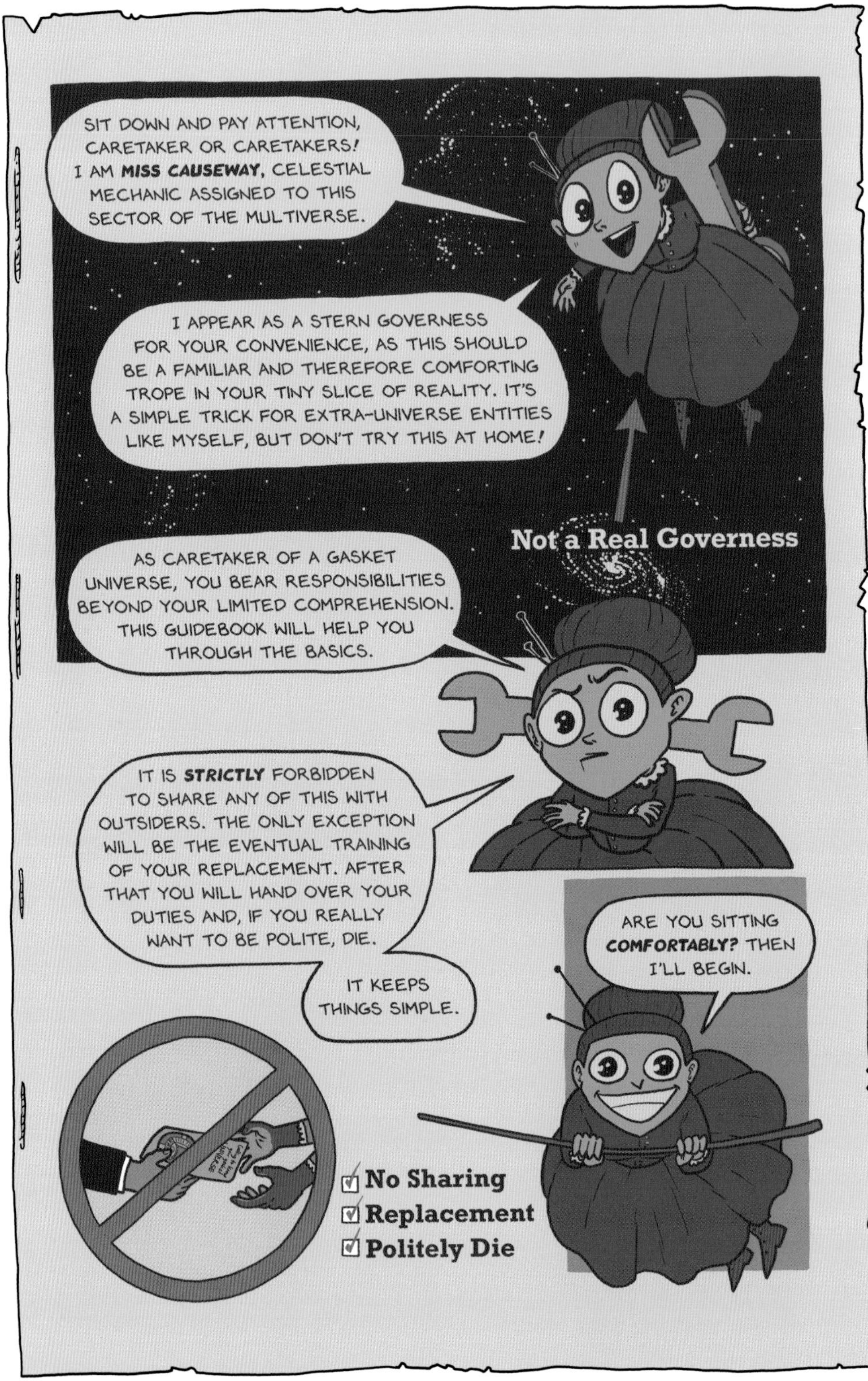
SIT DOWN AND PAY ATTENTION, CARETAKER OR CARETAKERS! I AM MISS CAUSEWAY, CELESTIAL MECHANIC ASSIGNED TO THIS SECTOR OF THE MULTIVERSE.
I APPEAR AS A STERN GOVERNESS FOR YOUR CONVENIENCE, AS THIS SHOULD BE A FAMILIAR AND THEREFORE COMFORTING TROPE IN YOUR TINY SLICE OF REALITY. IT'S A SIMPLE TRICK FOR EXTRA-UNIVERSE ENTITIES LIKE MYSELF, BUT DON'T TRY THIS AT HOME!
Not a Real Governess
AS CARETAKER OF A GASKET UNIVERSE, YOU BEAR RESPONSIBILITIES BEYOND YOUR LIMITED COMPREHENSION. THIS GUIDEBOOK WILL HELP YOU THROUGH THE BASICS.
IT IS STRICTLY FORBIDDEN TO SHARE ANY OF THIS WITH OUTSIDERS. THE ONLY EXCEPTION WILL BE THE EVENTUAL TRAINING OF YOUR REPLACEMENT. AFTER THAT YOU WILL HAND OVER YOUR DUTIES AND, IF YOU REALLY WANT TO BE POLITE, DIE.
IT KEEPS THINGS SIMPLE.
ARE YOU SITTING COMFORTABLY? THEN I'LL BEGIN.
No Sharing
Replacement
Politely Die

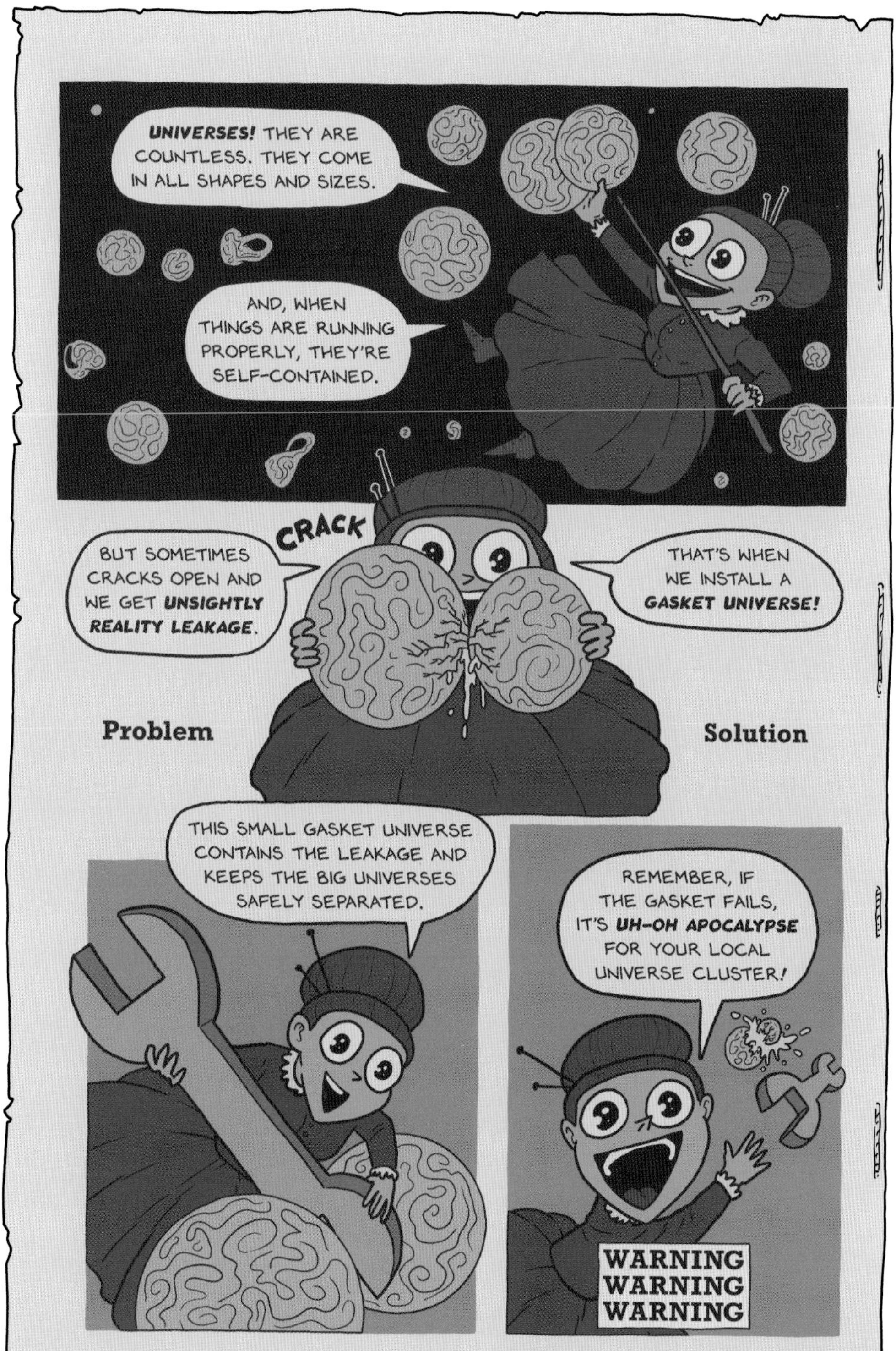
UNIVERSES! THEY ARE COUNTLESS. THEY COME IN ALL SHAPES AND SIZES.
AND, WHEN THINGS ARE RUNNING PROPERLY, THEY'RE SELF-CONTAINED.
CRACK
BUT SOMETIMES CRACKS OPEN AND WE GET UNSIGHTLY REALITY LEAKAGE.
THAT'S WHEN WE INSTALL A GASKET UNIVERSE!
Problem
Solution
THIS SMALL GASKET UNIVERSE CONTAINS THE LEAKAGE AND KEEPS THE BIG UNIVERSES SAFELY SEPARATED.
REMEMBER, IF THE GASKET FAILS, IT'S UH-OH APOCALYPSE FOR YOUR LOCAL UNIVERSE CLUSTER!
WARNING
WARNING
WARNING

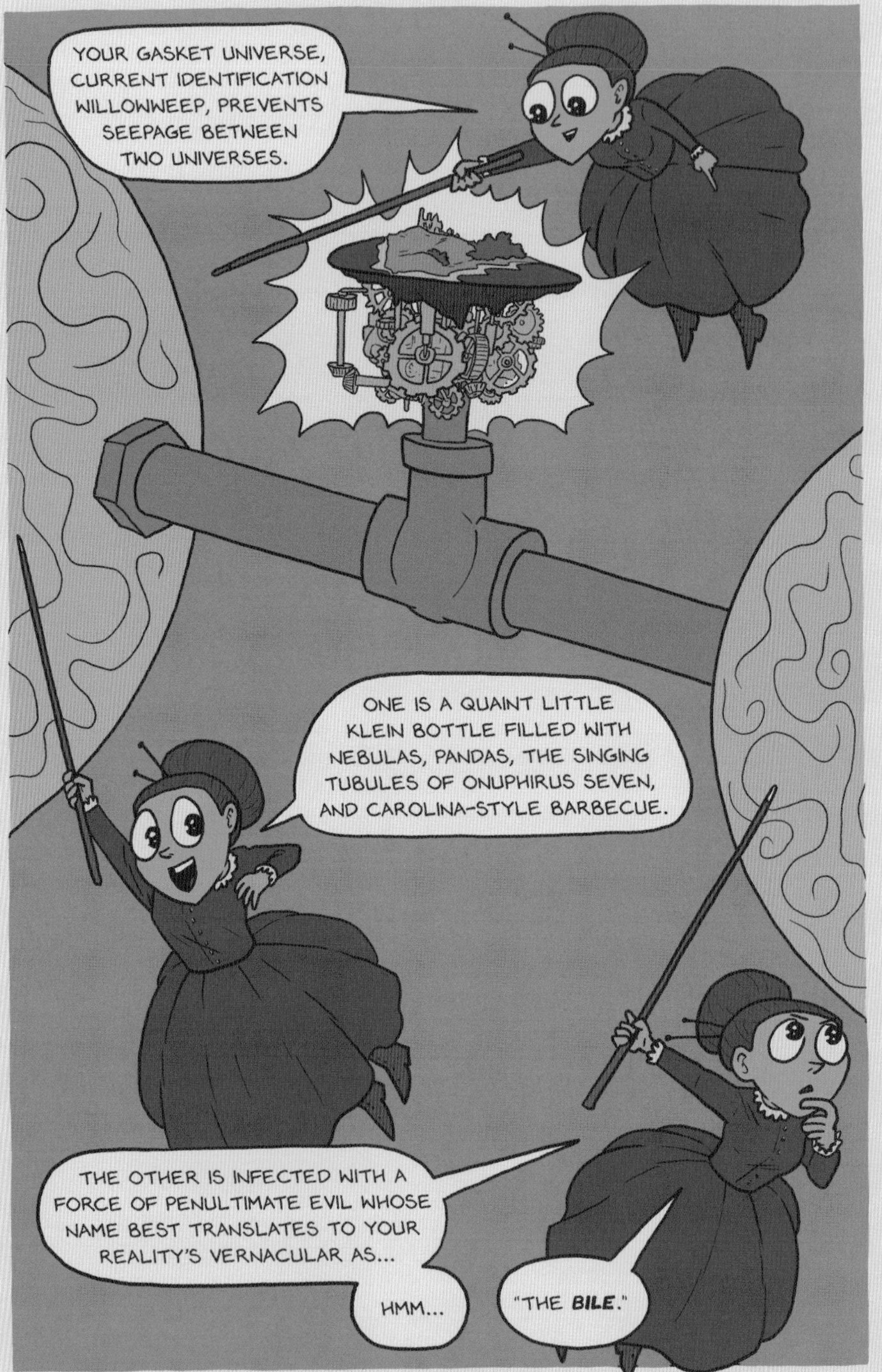
YOUR GASKET UNIVERSE, CURRENT IDENTIFICATION WILLOWWEEP, PREVENTS SEEPAGE BETWEEN TWO UNIVERSES.
ONE IS A QUAINT LITTLE KLEIN BOTTLE FILLED WITH NEBULAS, PANDAS, THE SINGING TUBULES OF ONUPHIRUS SEVEN, AND CAROLINA-STYLE BARBECUE.
THE OTHER IS INFECTED WITH A FORCE OF PENULTIMATE EVIL WHOSE NAME BEST TRANSLATES TO YOUR REALITY'S VERNACULAR AS...
HMM...
"THE **BILE**."

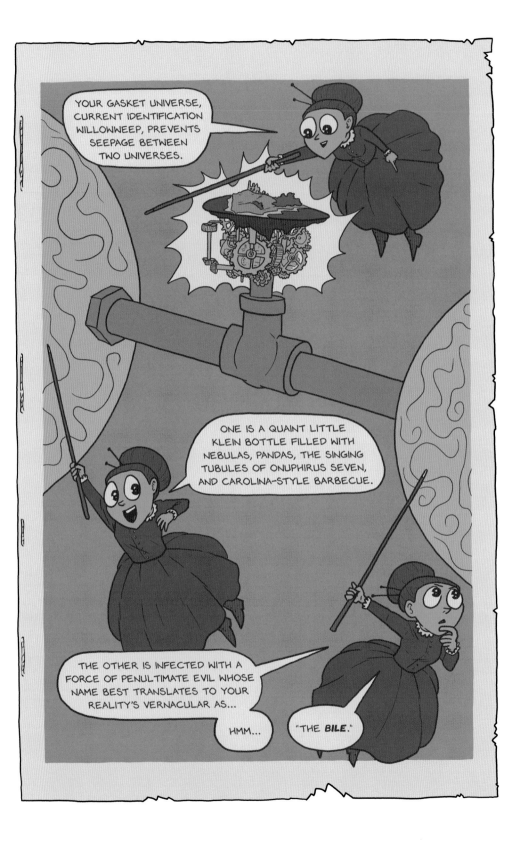

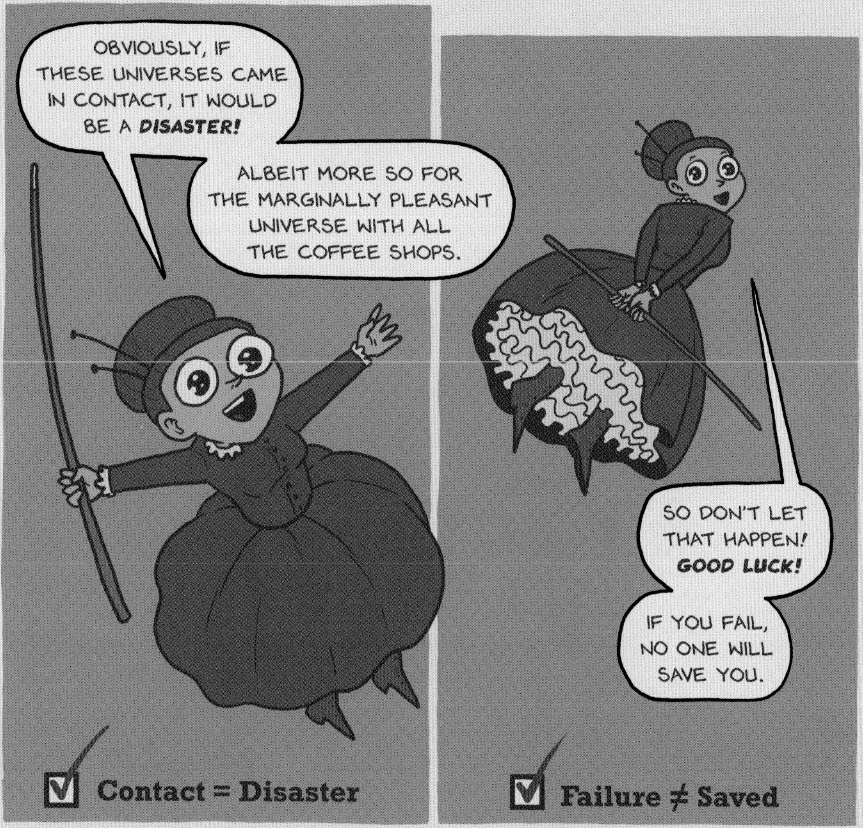
OBVIOUSLY, IF THESE UNIVERSES CAME IN CONTACT, IT WOULD BE A DISASTER!
ALBEIT MORE SO FOR THE MARGINALLY PLEASANT UNIVERSE WITH ALL THE COFFEE SHOPS.
Contact = Disaster
SO DON'T LET THAT HAPPEN! GOOD LUCK!
IF YOU FAIL, NO ONE WILL SAVE YOU.
Failure ≠ Saved

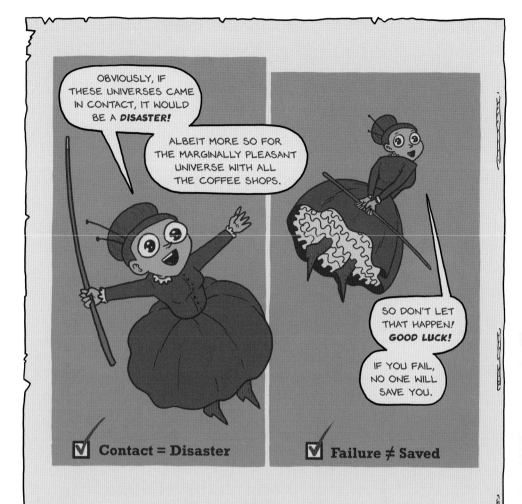

THIS HAS BEEN A MESSAGE FROM

ALL CREATION ITSELF

WE RUN THINGS.
YOU'RE WELCOME.

COMPLAINTS? Call your mom. Maybe she'll make you some nice soup.

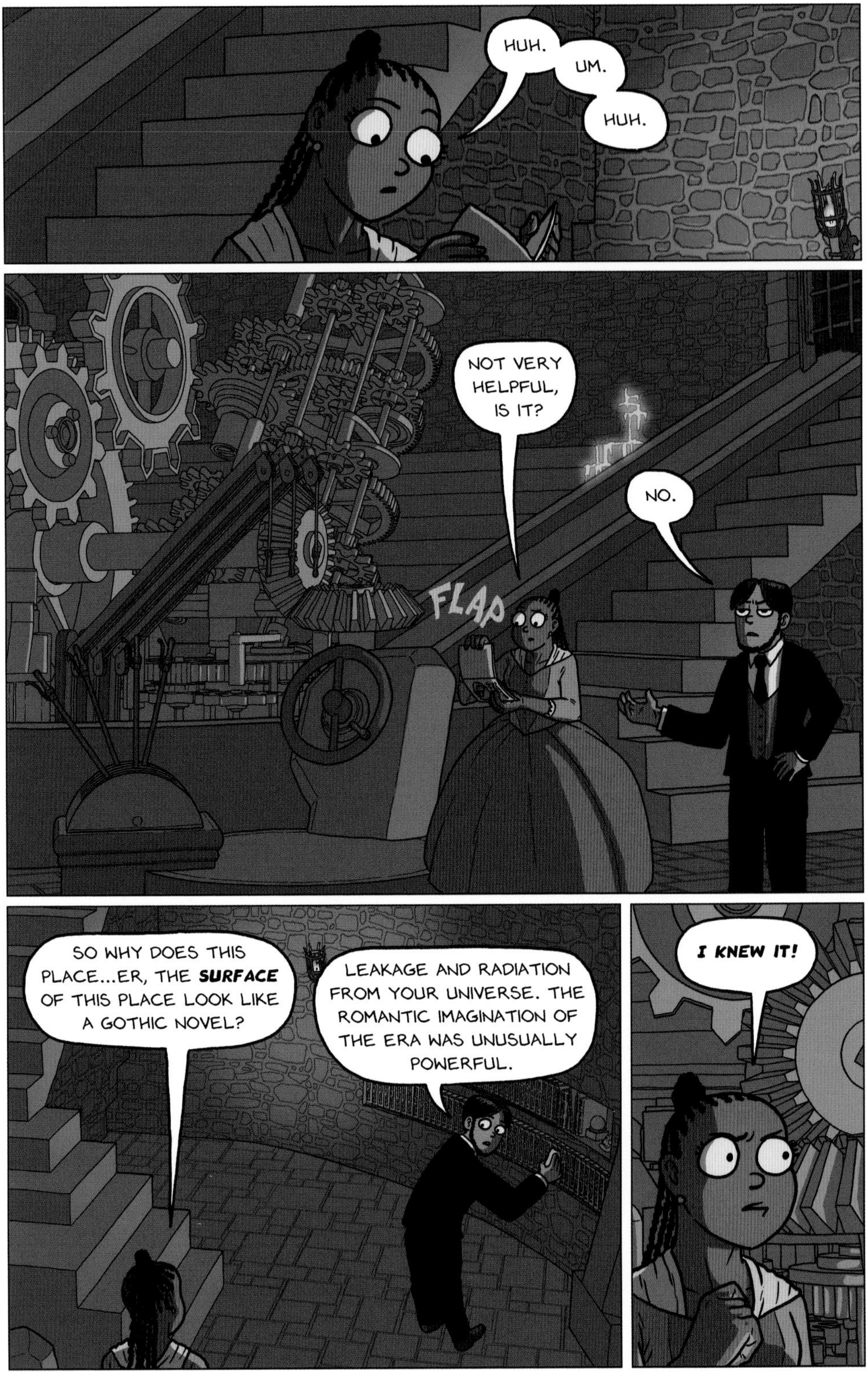
HUH.
UM.
HUH.
NOT VERY HELPFUL, IS IT?
NO.
FLAP
SO WHY DOES THIS PLACE...ER, THE **SURFACE** OF THIS PLACE LOOK LIKE A GOTHIC NOVEL?
LEAKAGE AND RADIATION FROM YOUR UNIVERSE. THE ROMANTIC IMAGINATION OF THE ERA WAS UNUSUALLY POWERFUL.
I KNEW IT!

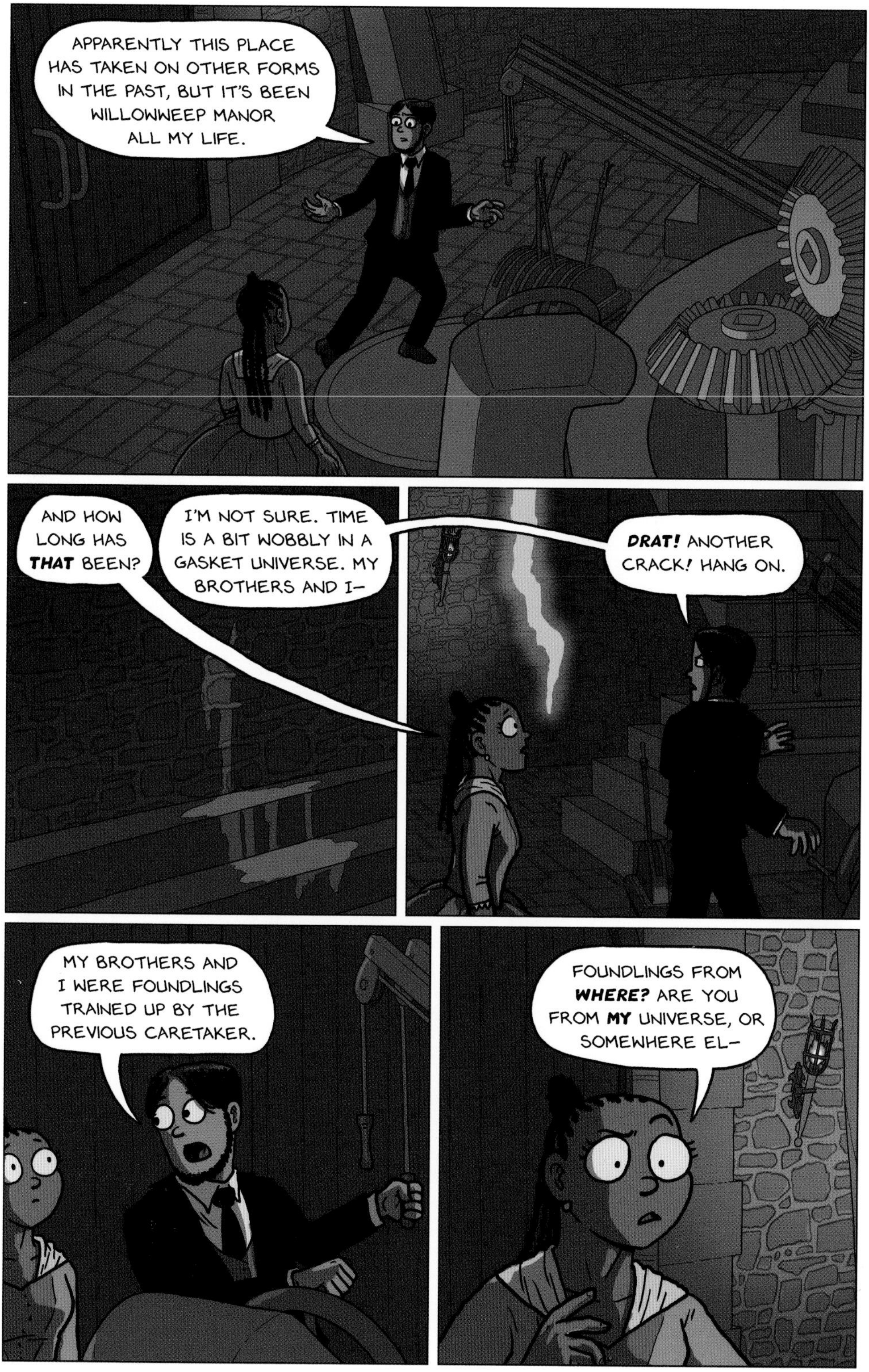
APPARENTLY THIS PLACE HAS TAKEN ON OTHER FORMS IN THE PAST, BUT IT'S BEEN WILLOWWEEP MANOR ALL MY LIFE.
AND HOW LONG HAS **THAT** BEEN?
I'M NOT SURE. TIME IS A BIT WOBBLY IN A GASKET UNIVERSE. MY BROTHERS AND I—
DRAT! ANOTHER CRACK! HANG ON.
MY BROTHERS AND I WERE FOUNDLINGS TRAINED UP BY THE PREVIOUS CARETAKER.
FOUNDLINGS FROM **WHERE?** ARE YOU FROM **MY** UNIVERSE, OR SOMEWHERE EL—

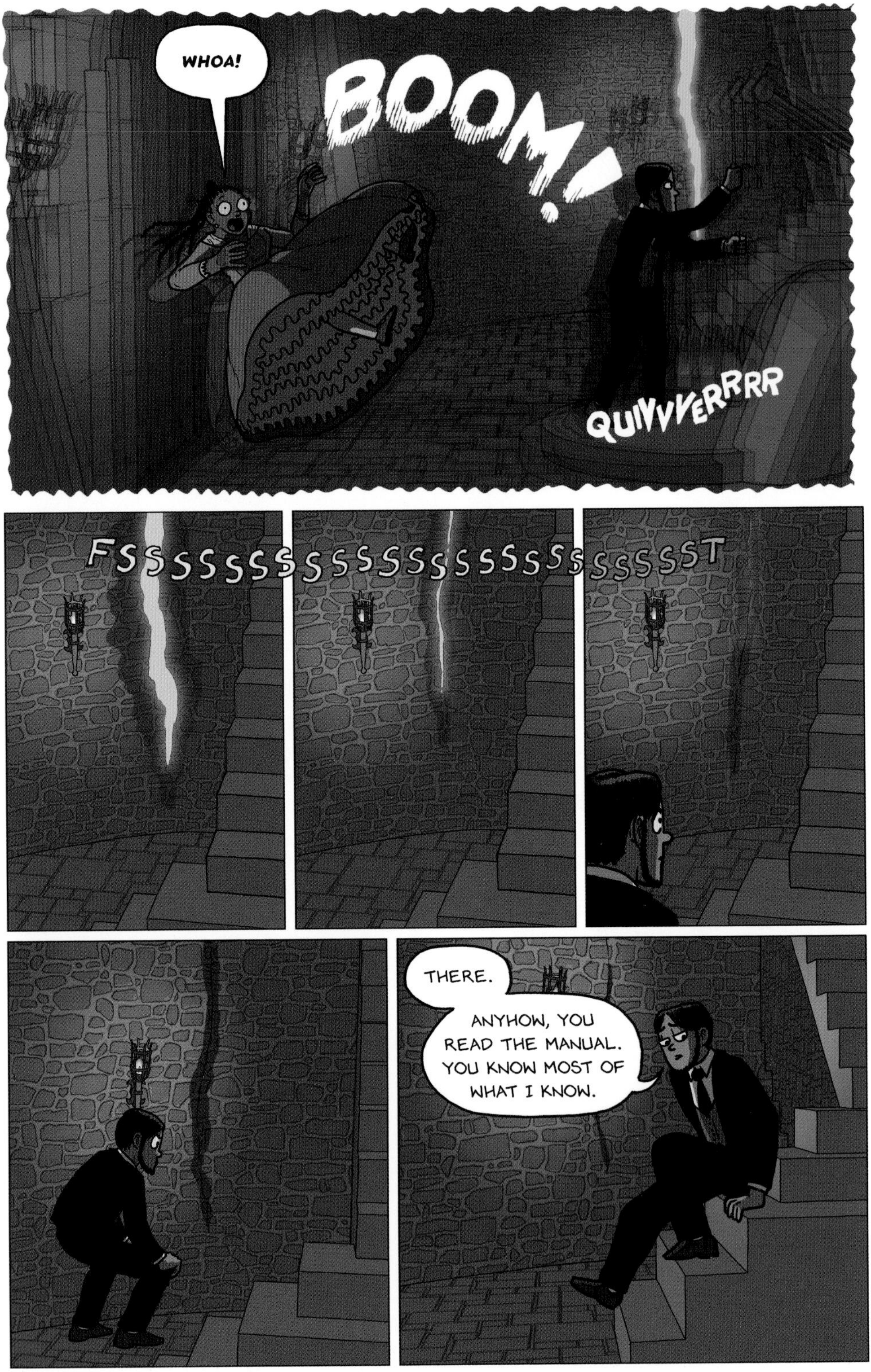
WHOA!
BOOM!
QUIVVVERRRR
FSSSSSSSSSSSSSSSSSSSSSSSSST
THERE.
ANYHOW, YOU READ THE MANUAL. YOU KNOW MOST OF WHAT I KNOW.

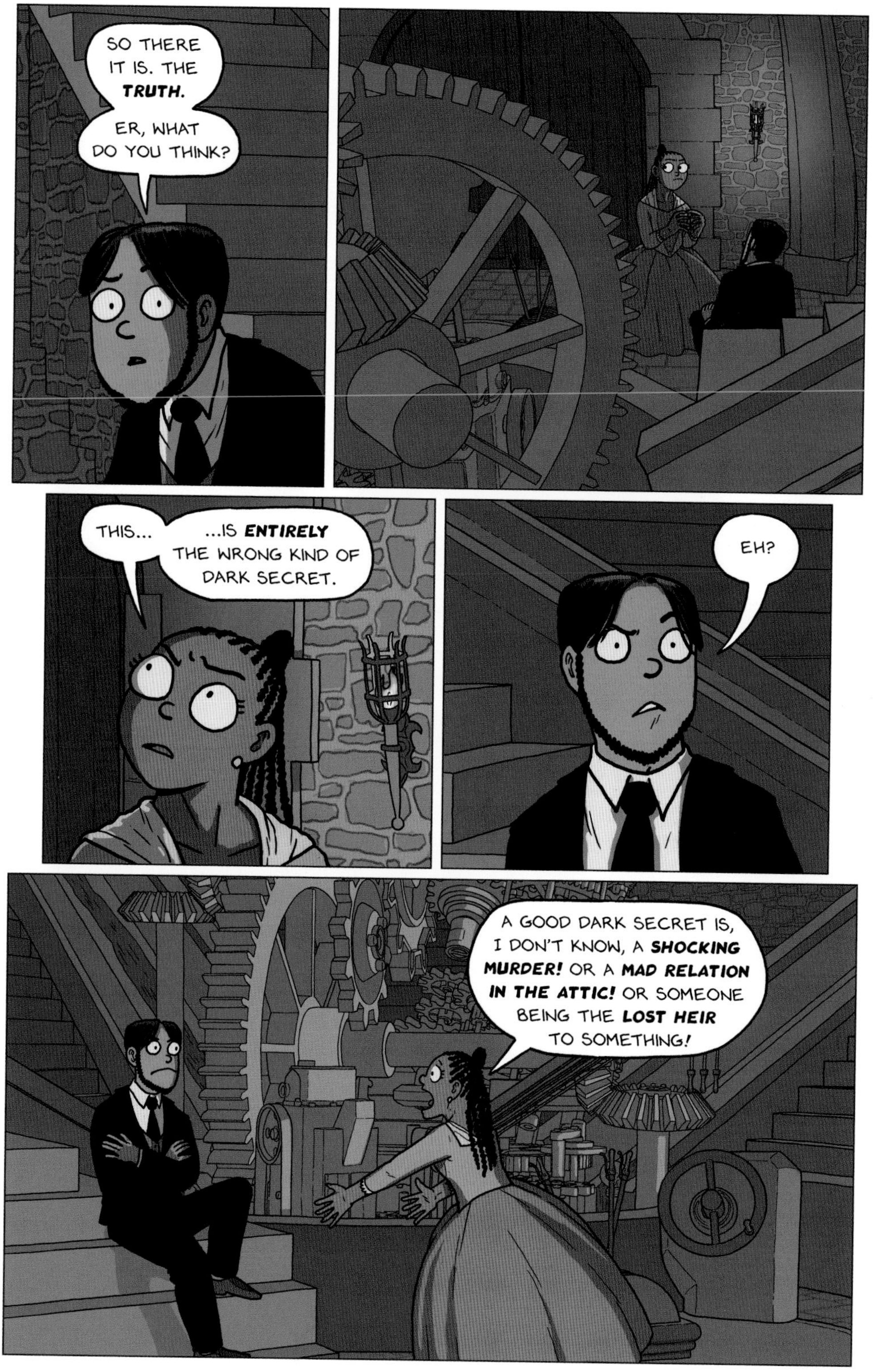
SO THERE IT IS. THE **TRUTH.**
ER, WHAT DO YOU THINK?
THIS...
...IS **ENTIRELY** THE WRONG KIND OF DARK SECRET.
EH?
A GOOD DARK SECRET IS, I DON'T KNOW, A **SHOCKING MURDER!** OR A **MAD RELATION IN THE ATTIC!** OR SOMEONE BEING THE **LOST HEIR** TO SOMETHING!

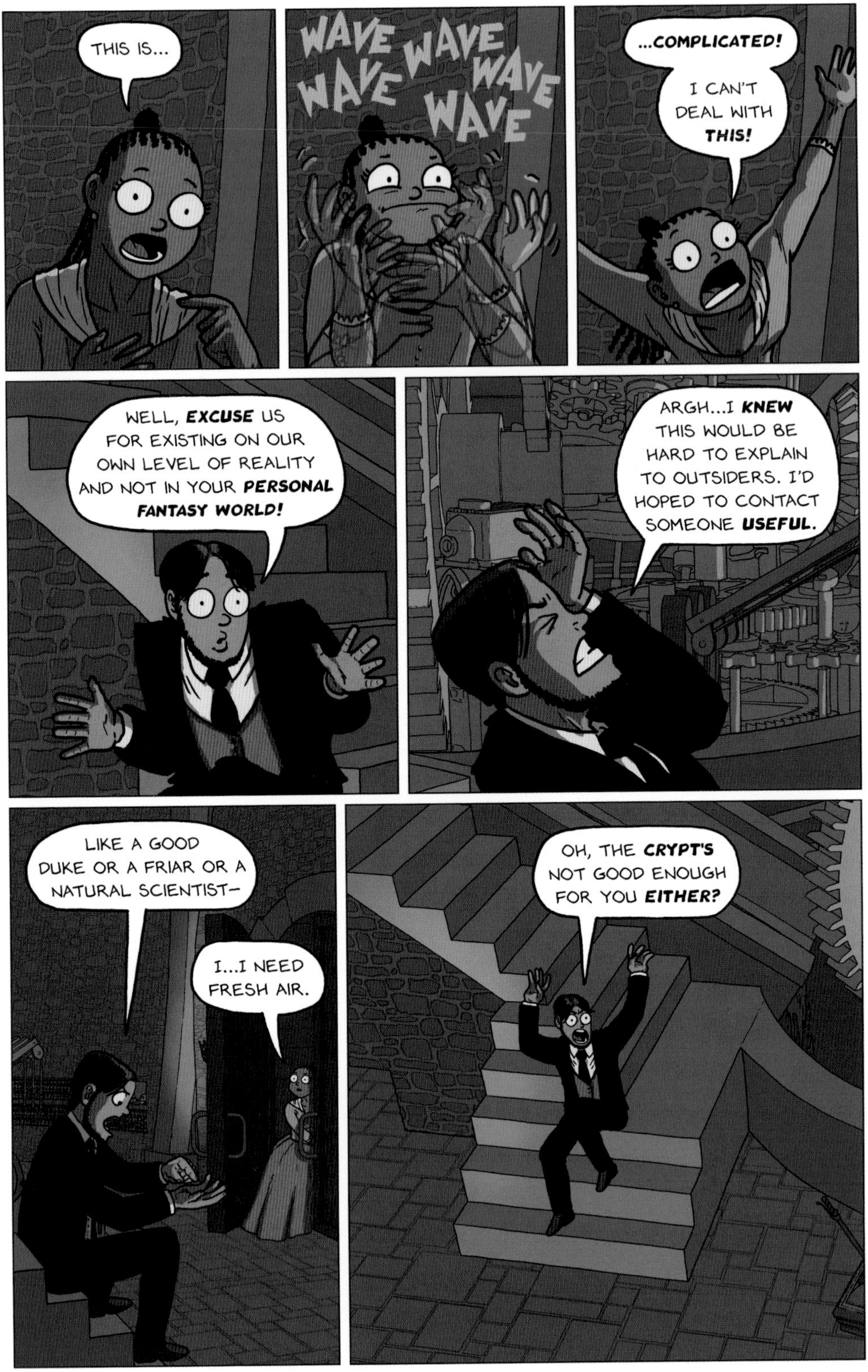
THIS IS...
WAVE WAVE WAVE WAVE WAVE
...COMPLICATED!
I CAN'T DEAL WITH THIS!
WELL, EXCUSE US FOR EXISTING ON OUR OWN LEVEL OF REALITY AND NOT IN YOUR PERSONAL FANTASY WORLD!
ARGH...I KNEW THIS WOULD BE HARD TO EXPLAIN TO OUTSIDERS. I'D HOPED TO CONTACT SOMEONE USEFUL.
LIKE A GOOD DUKE OR A FRIAR OR A NATURAL SCIENTIST—
I...I NEED FRESH AIR.
OH, THE CRYPT'S NOT GOOD ENOUGH FOR YOU EITHER?

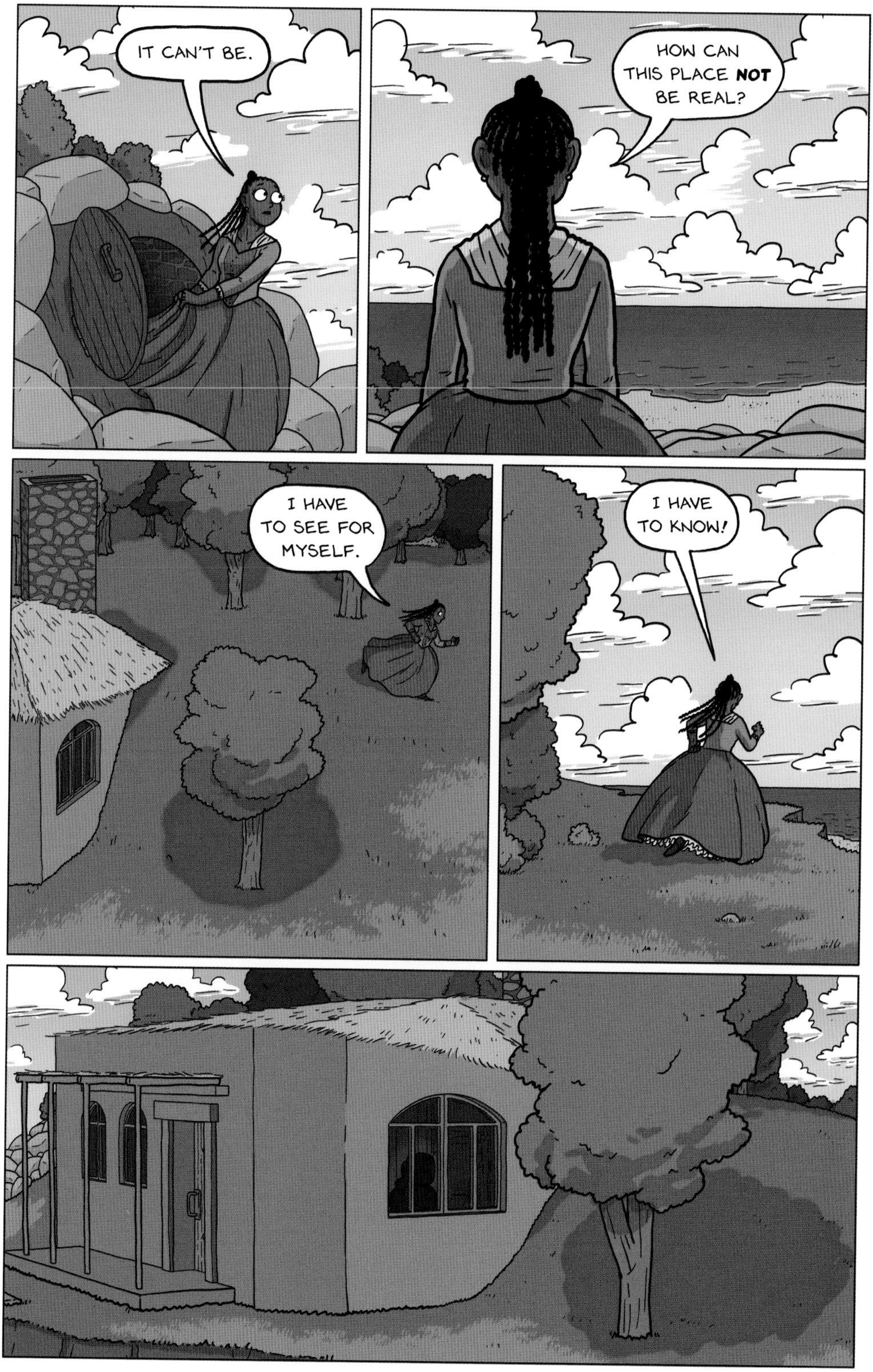
IT CAN'T BE.
HOW CAN THIS PLACE **NOT** BE REAL?
I HAVE TO SEE FOR MYSELF.
I HAVE TO KNOW!

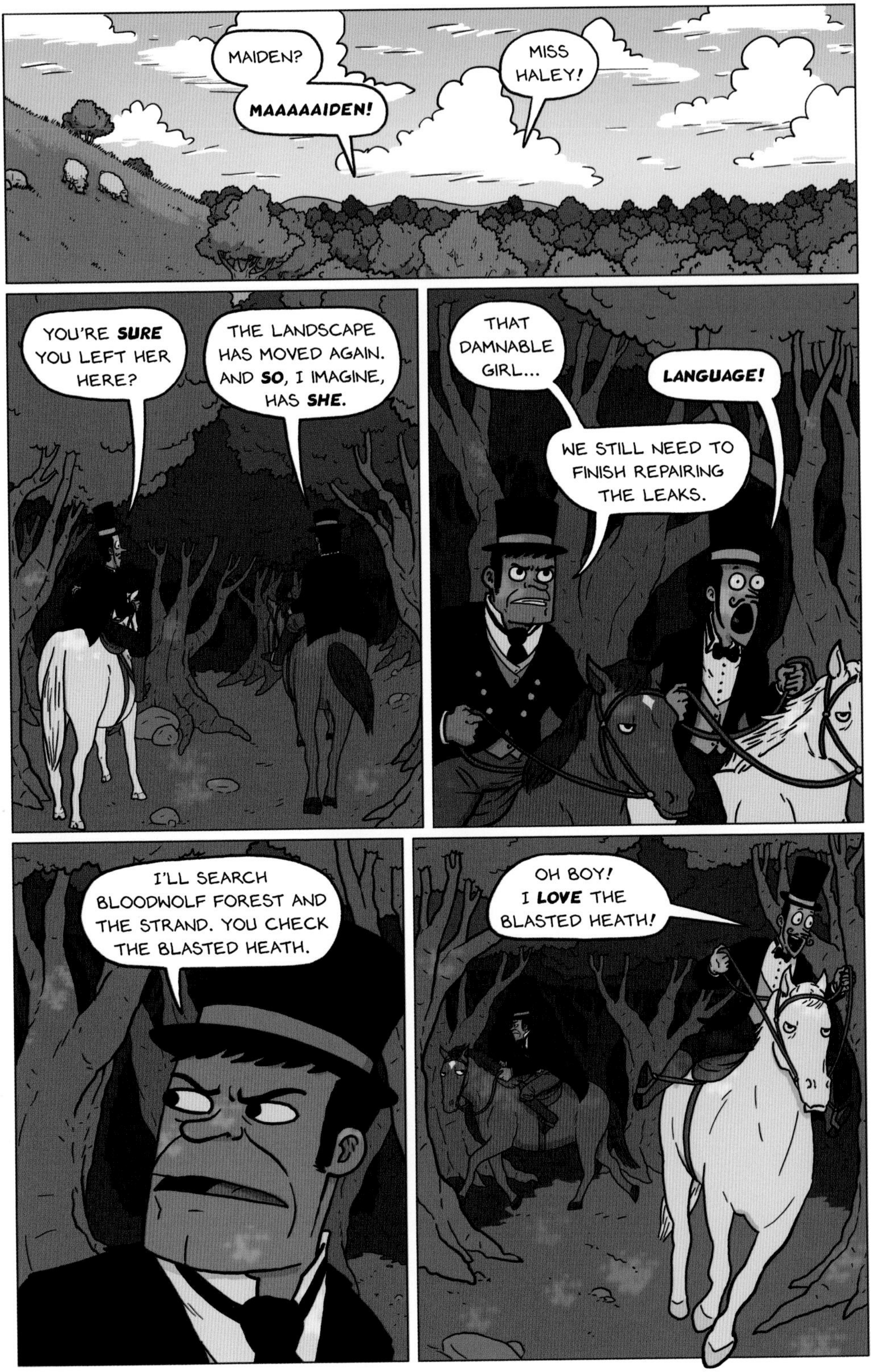
MAIDEN?
MAAAAAIDEN!
MISS HALEY!
YOU'RE **SURE** YOU LEFT HER HERE?
THE LANDSCAPE HAS MOVED AGAIN. AND **SO**, I IMAGINE, HAS **SHE**.
THAT DAMNABLE GIRL...
WE STILL NEED TO FINISH REPAIRING THE LEAKS.
LANGUAGE!
I'LL SEARCH BLOODWOLF FOREST AND THE STRAND. YOU CHECK THE BLASTED HEATH.
OH BOY! I **LOVE** THE BLASTED HEATH!

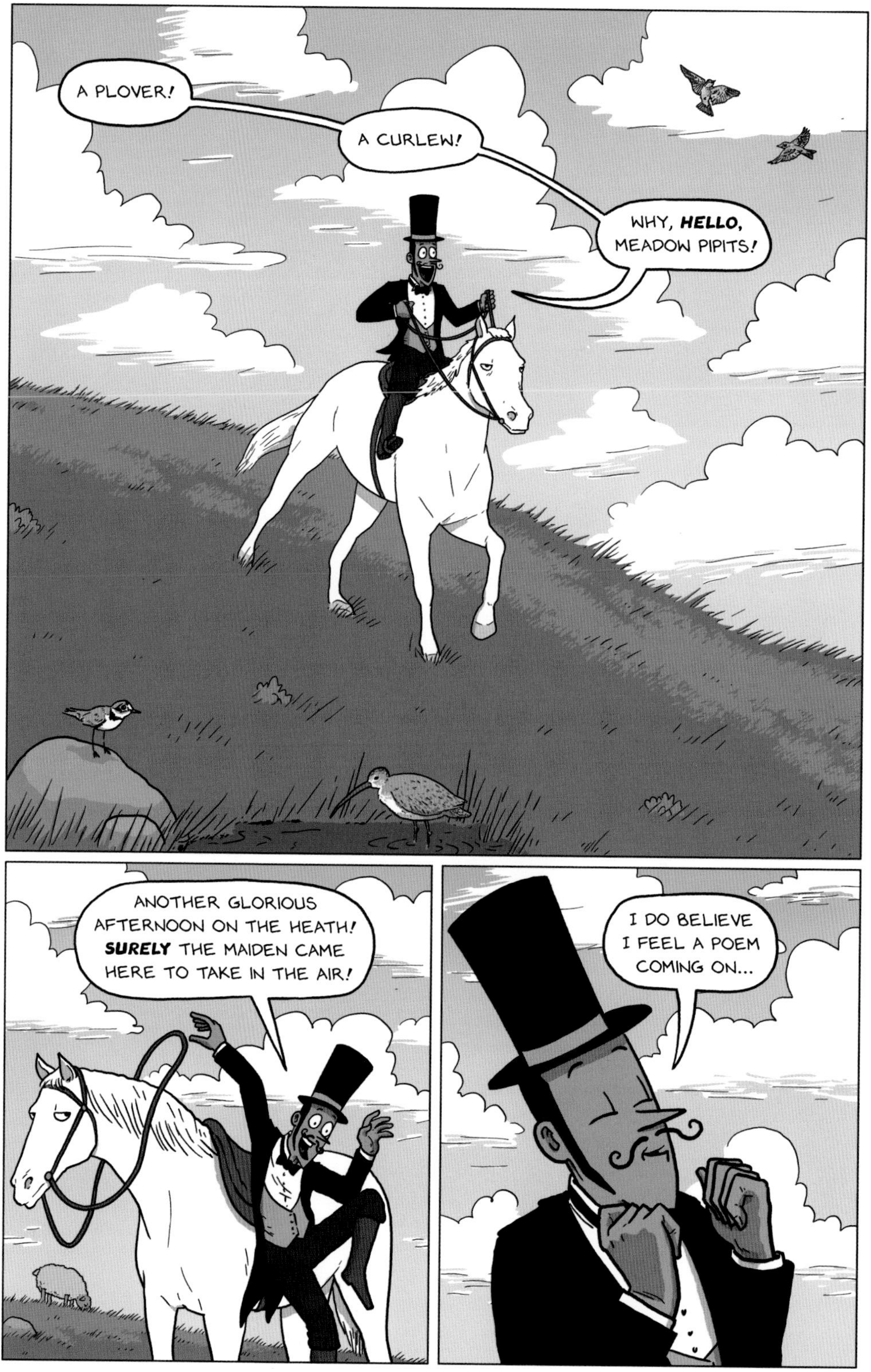
A PLOVER!
A CURLEW!
WHY, **HELLO,** MEADOW PIPITS!
ANOTHER GLORIOUS AFTERNOON ON THE HEATH! **SURELY** THE MAIDEN CAME HERE TO TAKE IN THE AIR!
I DO BELIEVE I FEEL A POEM COMING ON...

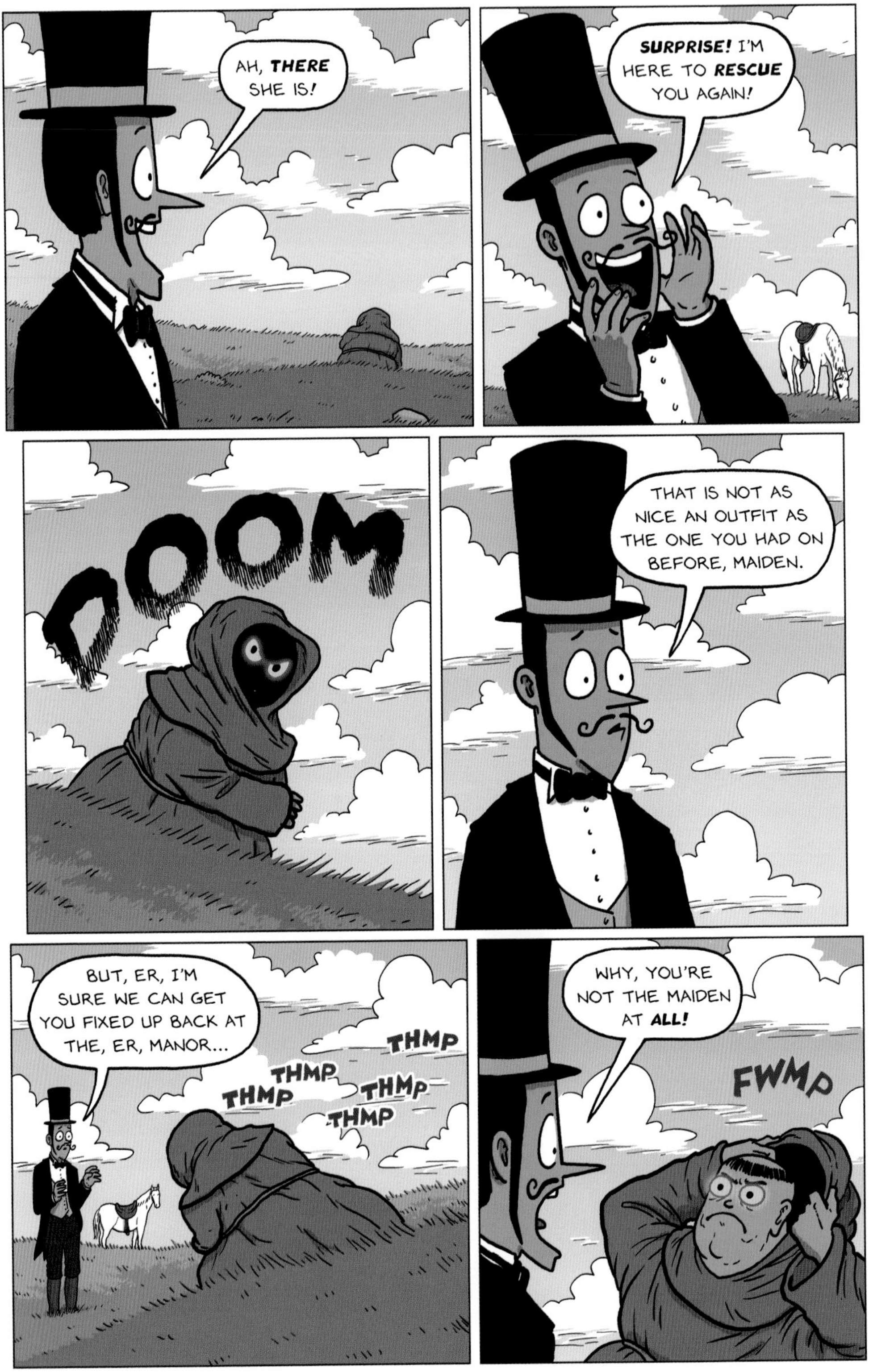
AH, **THERE** SHE IS!
SURPRISE! I'M HERE TO **RESCUE** YOU AGAIN!
DOOM
THAT IS NOT AS NICE AN OUTFIT AS THE ONE YOU HAD ON BEFORE, MAIDEN.
BUT, ER, I'M SURE WE CAN GET YOU FIXED UP BACK AT THE, ER, MANOR...
THMP
THMP
THMP
THMP
THMP
WHY, YOU'RE NOT THE MAIDEN AT **ALL!**
FWMP

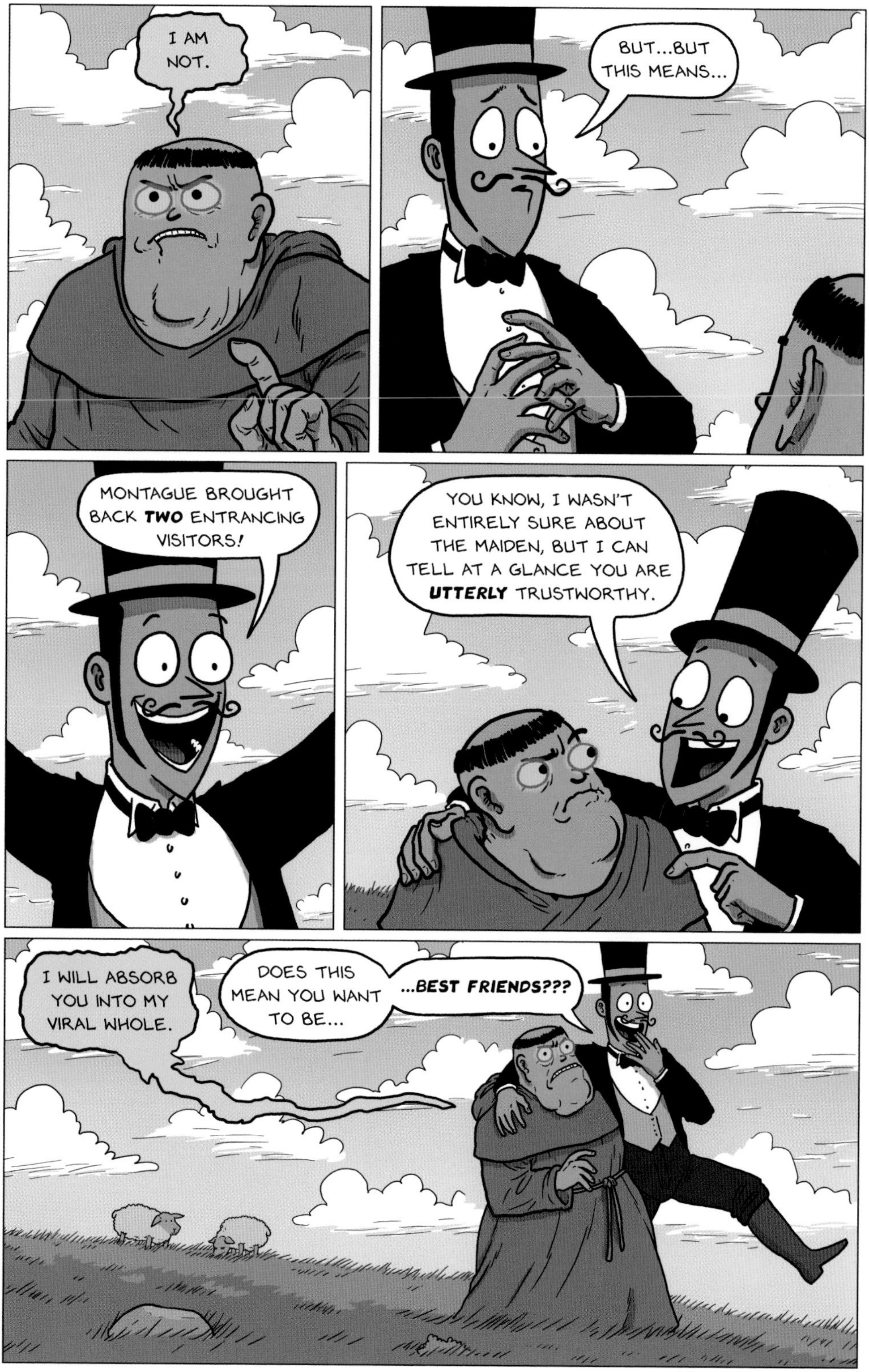
I AM NOT.
BUT...BUT THIS MEANS...
MONTAGUE BROUGHT BACK **TWO** ENTRANCING VISITORS!
YOU KNOW, I WASN'T ENTIRELY SURE ABOUT THE MAIDEN, BUT I CAN TELL AT A GLANCE YOU ARE **UTTERLY** TRUSTWORTHY.
I WILL ABSORB YOU INTO MY VIRAL WHOLE.
DOES THIS MEAN YOU WANT TO BE...
...BEST FRIENDS???

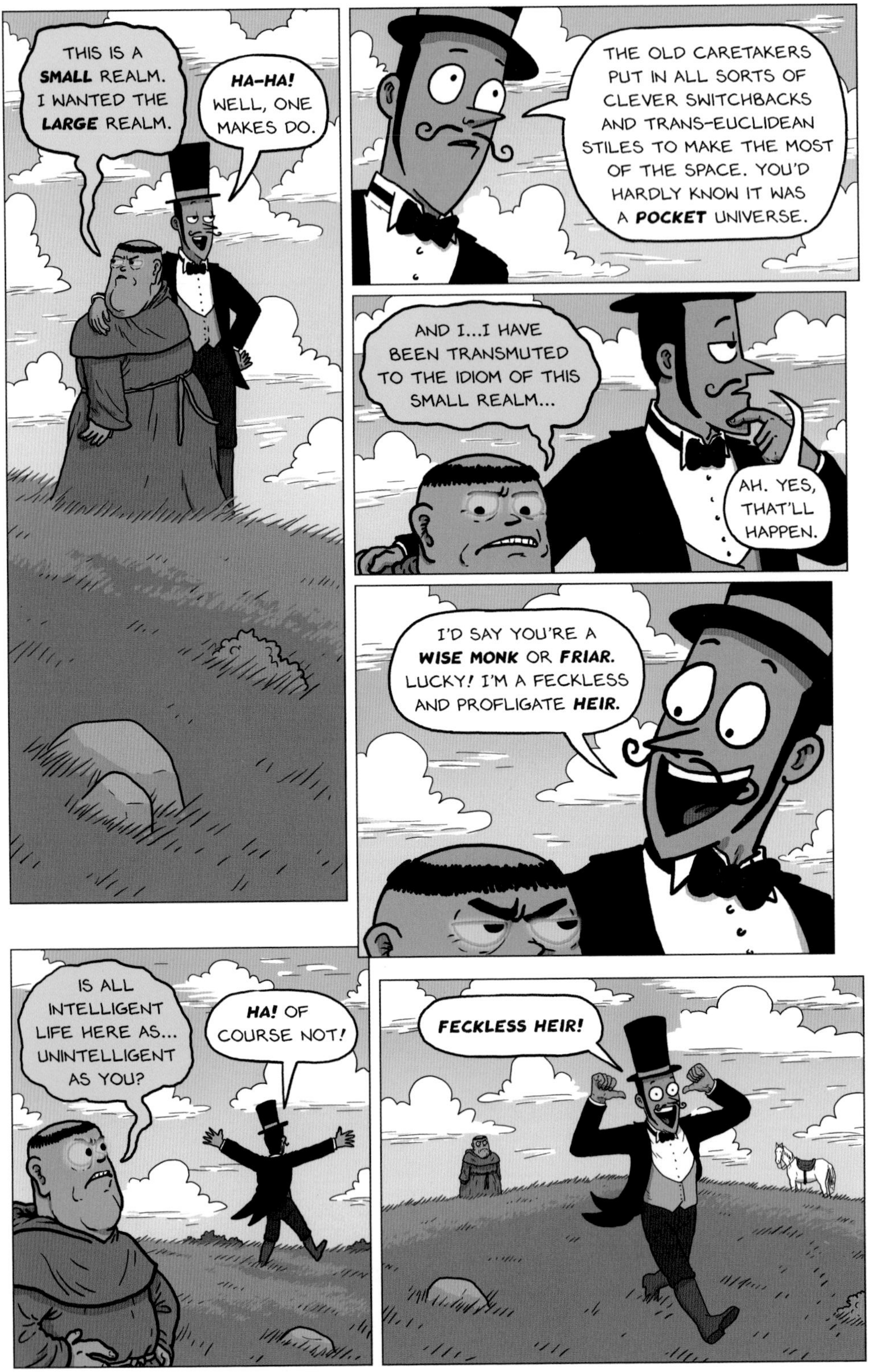

THIS IS A **SMALL** REALM. I WANTED THE **LARGE** REALM.
HA-HA! WELL, ONE MAKES DO.
THE OLD CARETAKERS PUT IN ALL SORTS OF CLEVER SWITCHBACKS AND TRANS-EUCLIDEAN STILES TO MAKE THE MOST OF THE SPACE. YOU'D HARDLY KNOW IT WAS A **POCKET** UNIVERSE.
AND I...I HAVE BEEN TRANSMUTED TO THE IDIOM OF THIS SMALL REALM...
AH. YES, THAT'LL HAPPEN.
I'D SAY YOU'RE A **WISE MONK** OR **FRIAR**. LUCKY! I'M A FECKLESS AND PROFLIGATE **HEIR**.
IS ALL INTELLIGENT LIFE HERE AS... UNINTELLIGENT AS YOU?
HA! OF COURSE NOT!
FECKLESS HEIR!

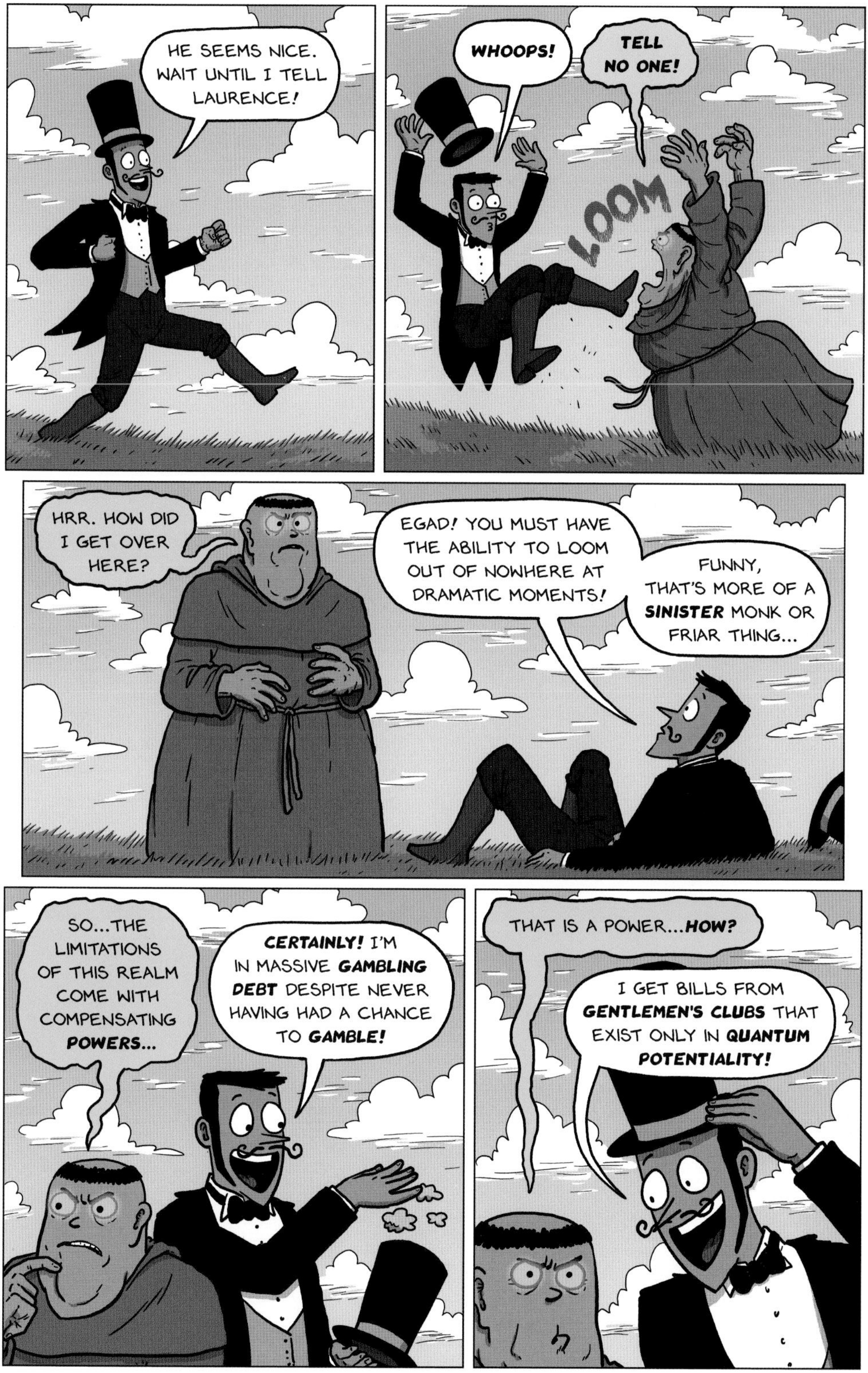
HE SEEMS NICE. WAIT UNTIL I TELL LAURENCE!
WHOOPS!
TELL NO ONE!
LOOM
HRR. HOW DID I GET OVER HERE?
EGAD! YOU MUST HAVE THE ABILITY TO LOOM OUT OF NOWHERE AT DRAMATIC MOMENTS!
FUNNY, THAT'S MORE OF A **SINISTER** MONK OR FRIAR THING...
SO...THE LIMITATIONS OF THIS REALM COME WITH COMPENSATING **POWERS...**
CERTAINLY! I'M IN MASSIVE **GAMBLING DEBT** DESPITE NEVER HAVING HAD A CHANCE TO **GAMBLE!**
THAT IS A POWER...**HOW?**
I GET BILLS FROM **GENTLEMEN'S CLUBS** THAT EXIST ONLY IN **QUANTUM POTENTIALITY!**

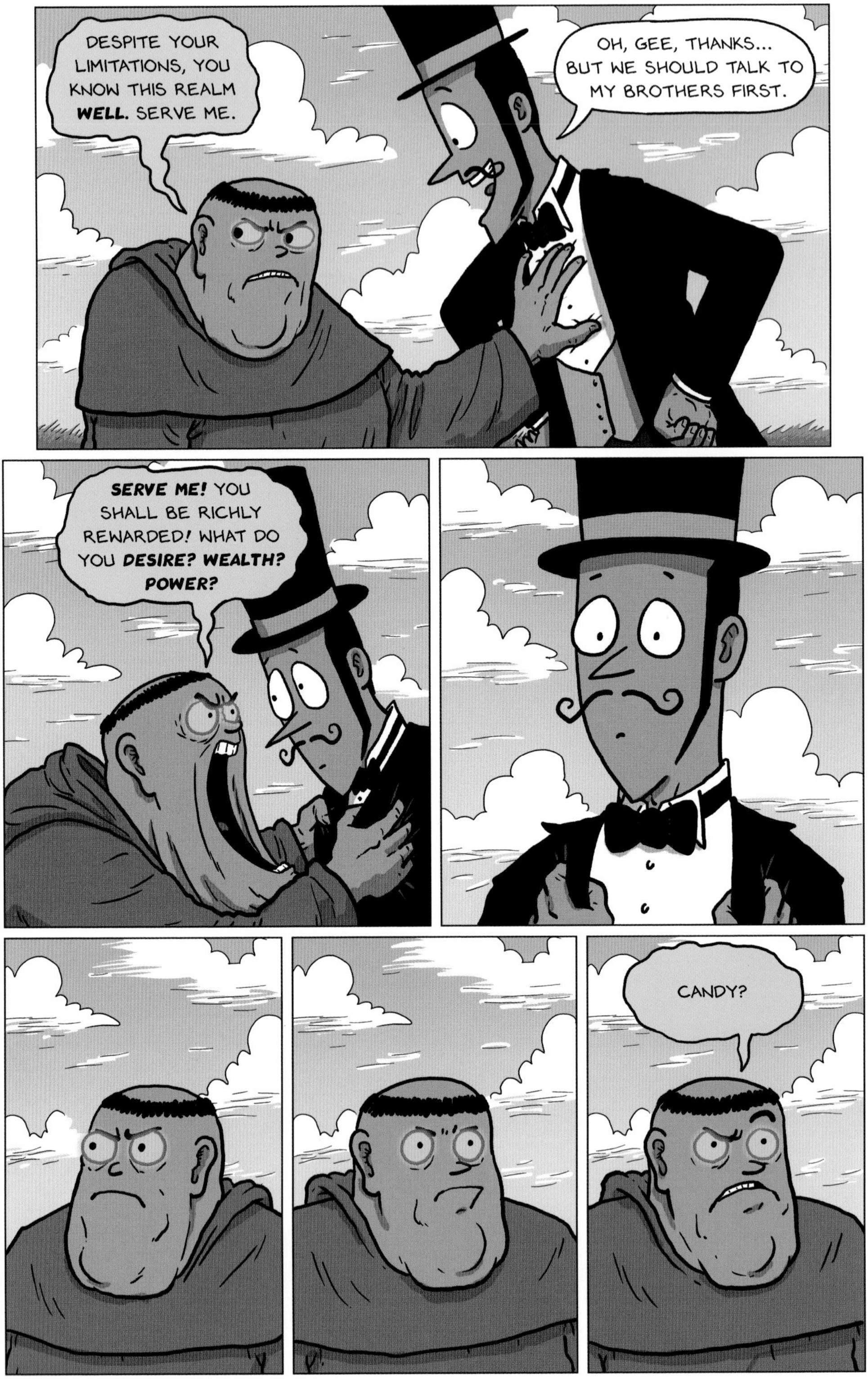
DESPITE YOUR LIMITATIONS, YOU KNOW THIS REALM **WELL.** SERVE ME.
OH, GEE, THANKS... BUT WE SHOULD TALK TO MY BROTHERS FIRST.
SERVE ME! YOU SHALL BE RICHLY REWARDED! WHAT DO YOU **DESIRE? WEALTH? POWER?**
CANDY?

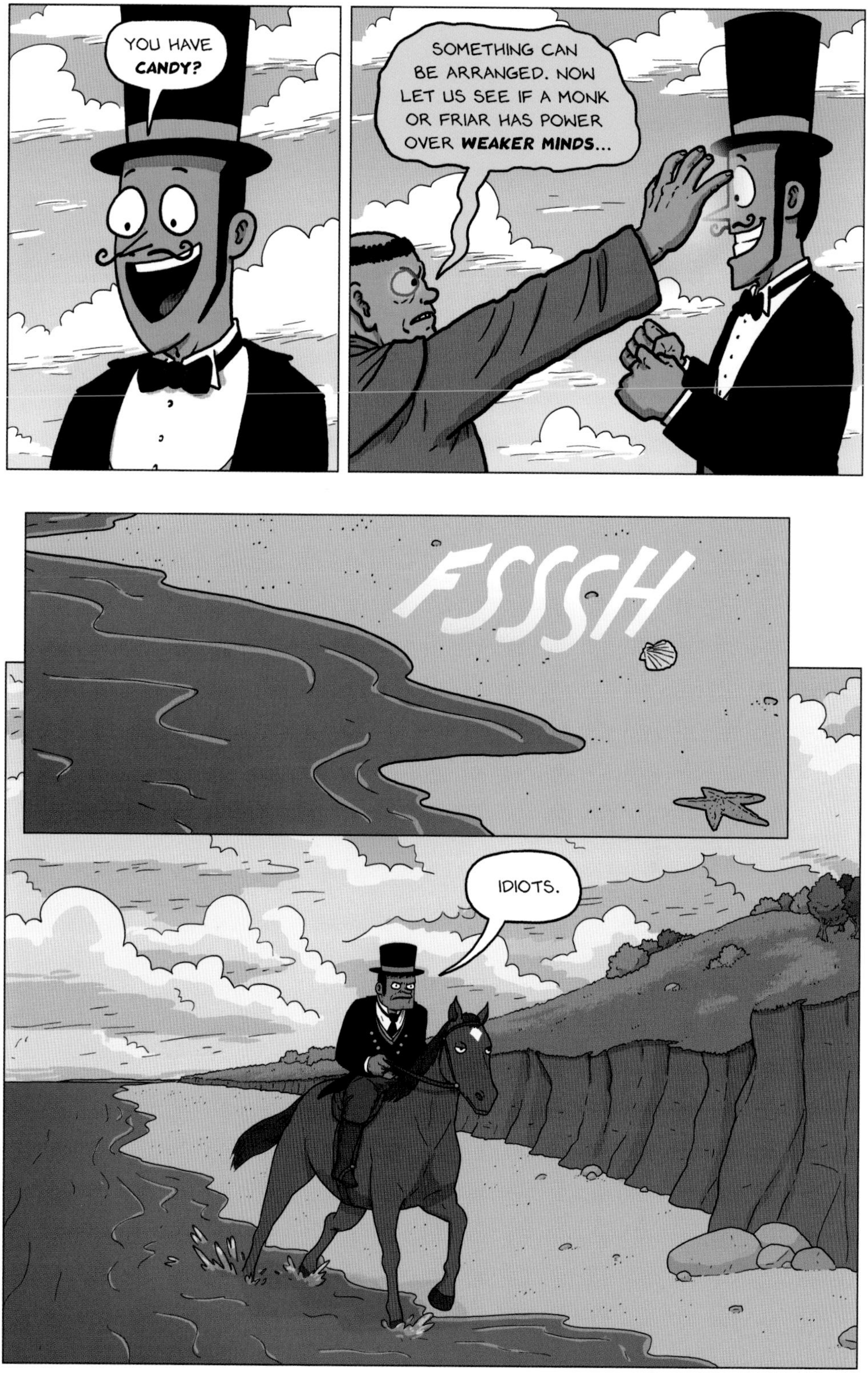
YOU HAVE **CANDY?**
SOMETHING CAN BE ARRANGED. NOW LET US SEE IF A MONK OR FRIAR HAS POWER OVER **WEAKER MINDS...**
FSSSH
IDIOTS.

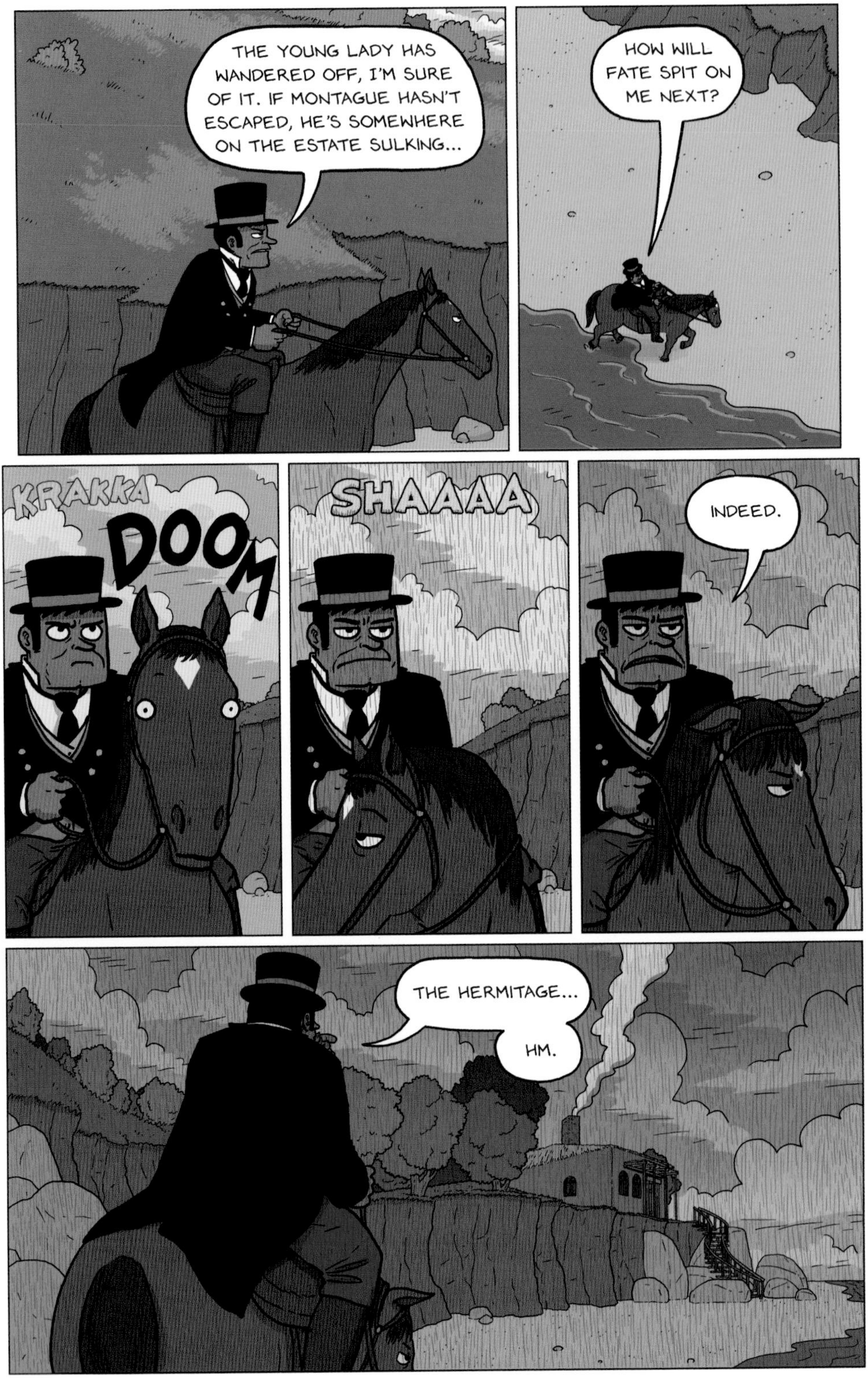
THE YOUNG LADY HAS WANDERED OFF, I'M SURE OF IT. IF MONTAGUE HASN'T ESCAPED, HE'S SOMEWHERE ON THE ESTATE SULKING...
HOW WILL FATE SPIT ON ME NEXT?
KRAKKA
DOOM
SHAAAA
INDEED.
THE HERMITAGE...
HM.

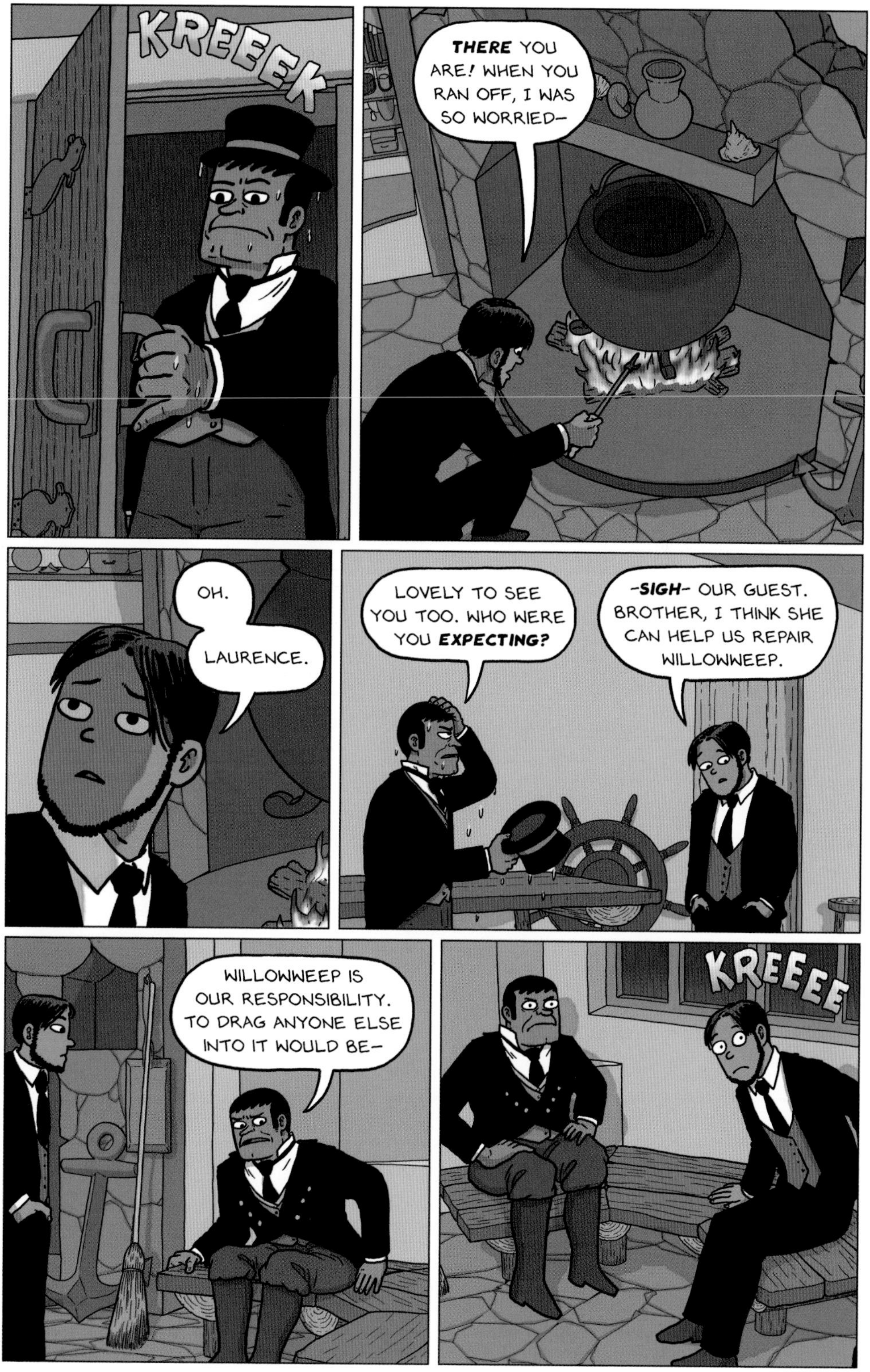
KREEEK
THERE YOU ARE! WHEN YOU RAN OFF, I WAS SO WORRIED—
OH.
LAURENCE.
LOVELY TO SEE YOU TOO. WHO WERE YOU EXPECTING?
-SIGH- OUR GUEST. BROTHER, I THINK SHE CAN HELP US REPAIR WILLOWWEEP.
WILLOWWEEP IS OUR RESPONSIBILITY. TO DRAG ANYONE ELSE INTO IT WOULD BE—
KREEEE

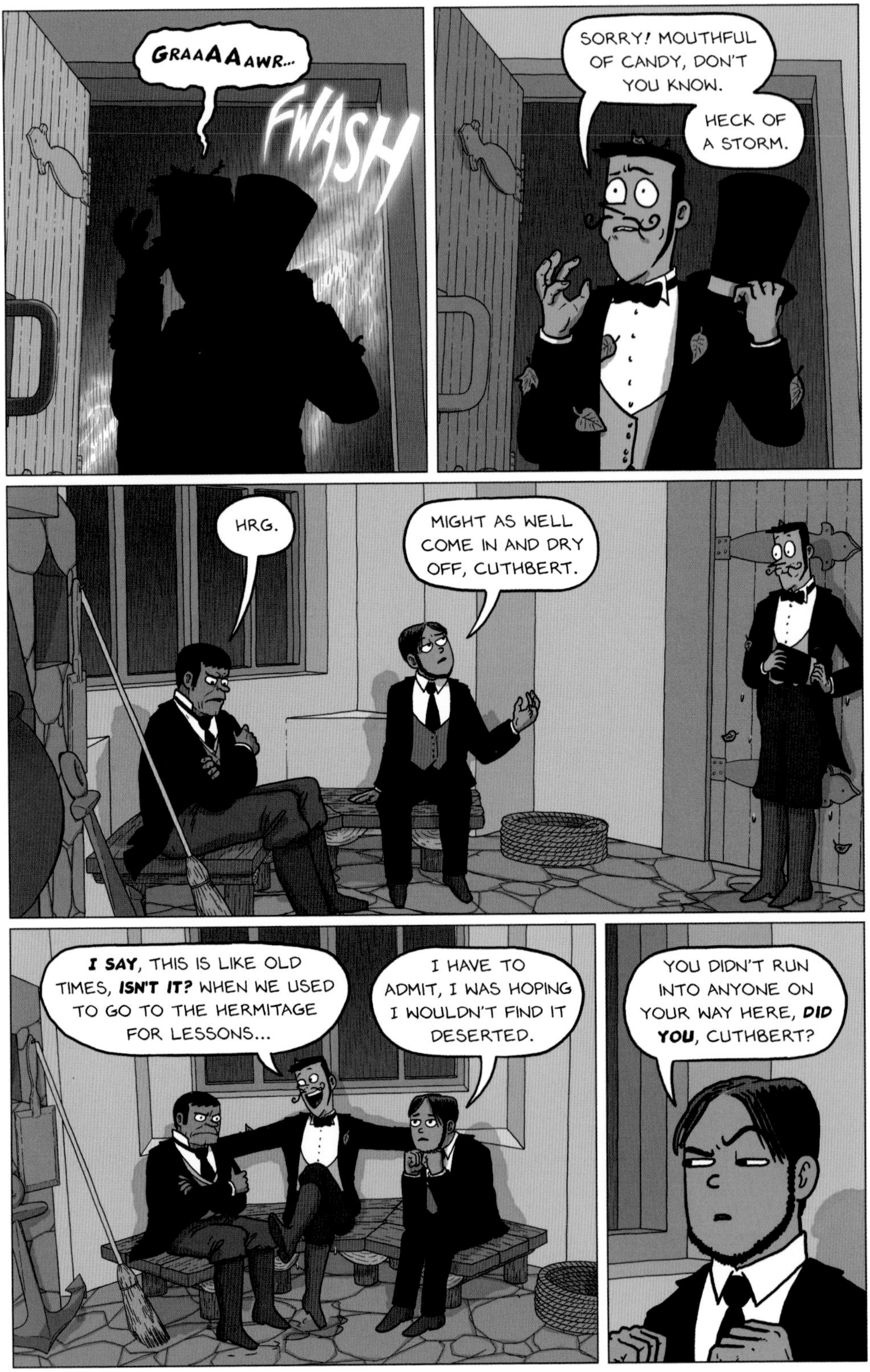
GRAAAAAWR...
FWASH
SORRY! MOUTHFUL OF CANDY, DON'T YOU KNOW.
HECK OF A STORM.
HRG.
MIGHT AS WELL COME IN AND DRY OFF, CUTHBERT.
I SAY, THIS IS LIKE OLD TIMES, ISN'T IT? WHEN WE USED TO GO TO THE HERMITAGE FOR LESSONS...
I HAVE TO ADMIT, I WAS HOPING I WOULDN'T FIND IT DESERTED.
YOU DIDN'T RUN INTO ANYONE ON YOUR WAY HERE, DID YOU, CUTHBERT?

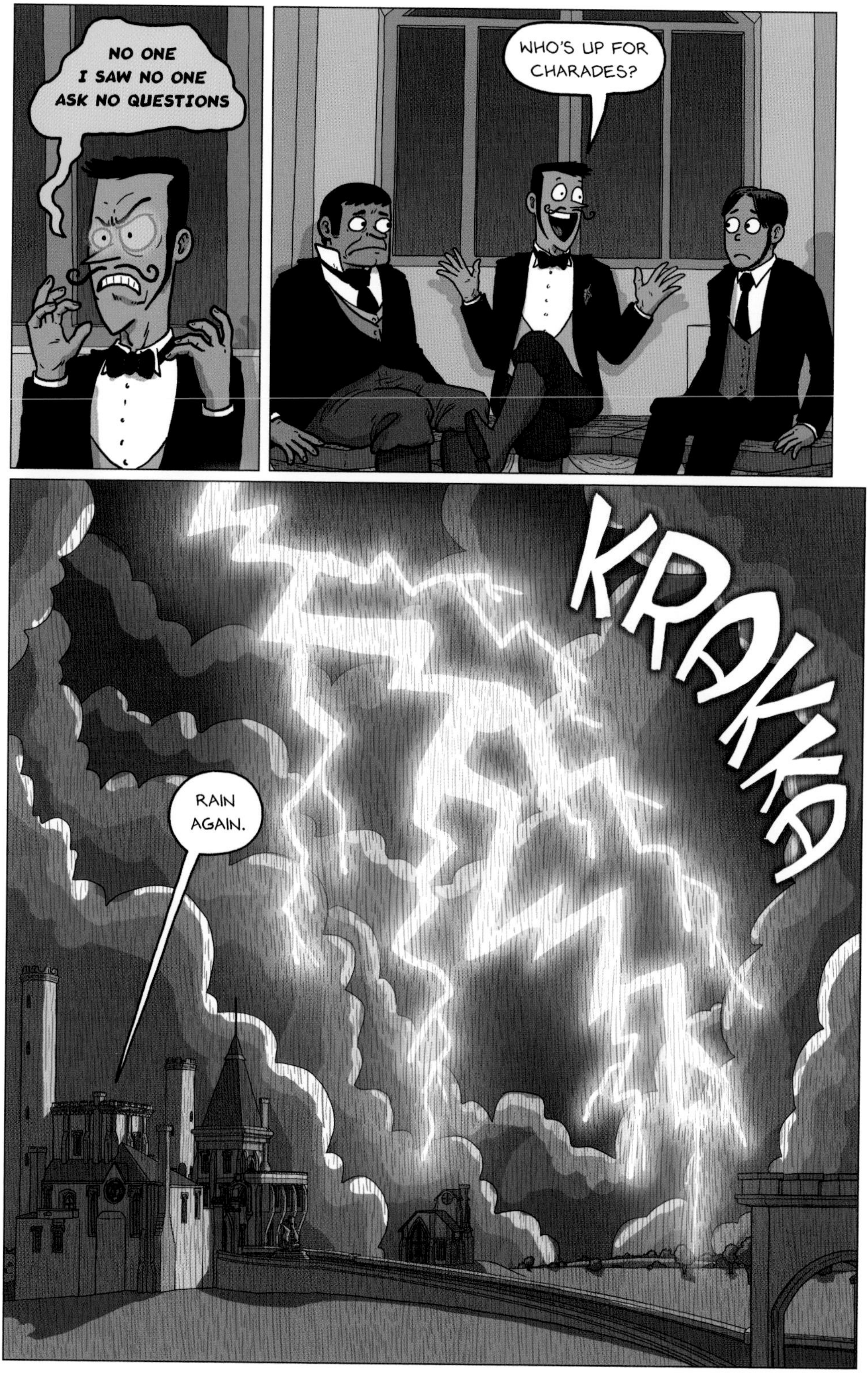
NO ONE
I SAW NO ONE
ASK NO QUESTIONS
WHO'S UP FOR CHARADES?
KRAKKA
RAIN AGAIN.

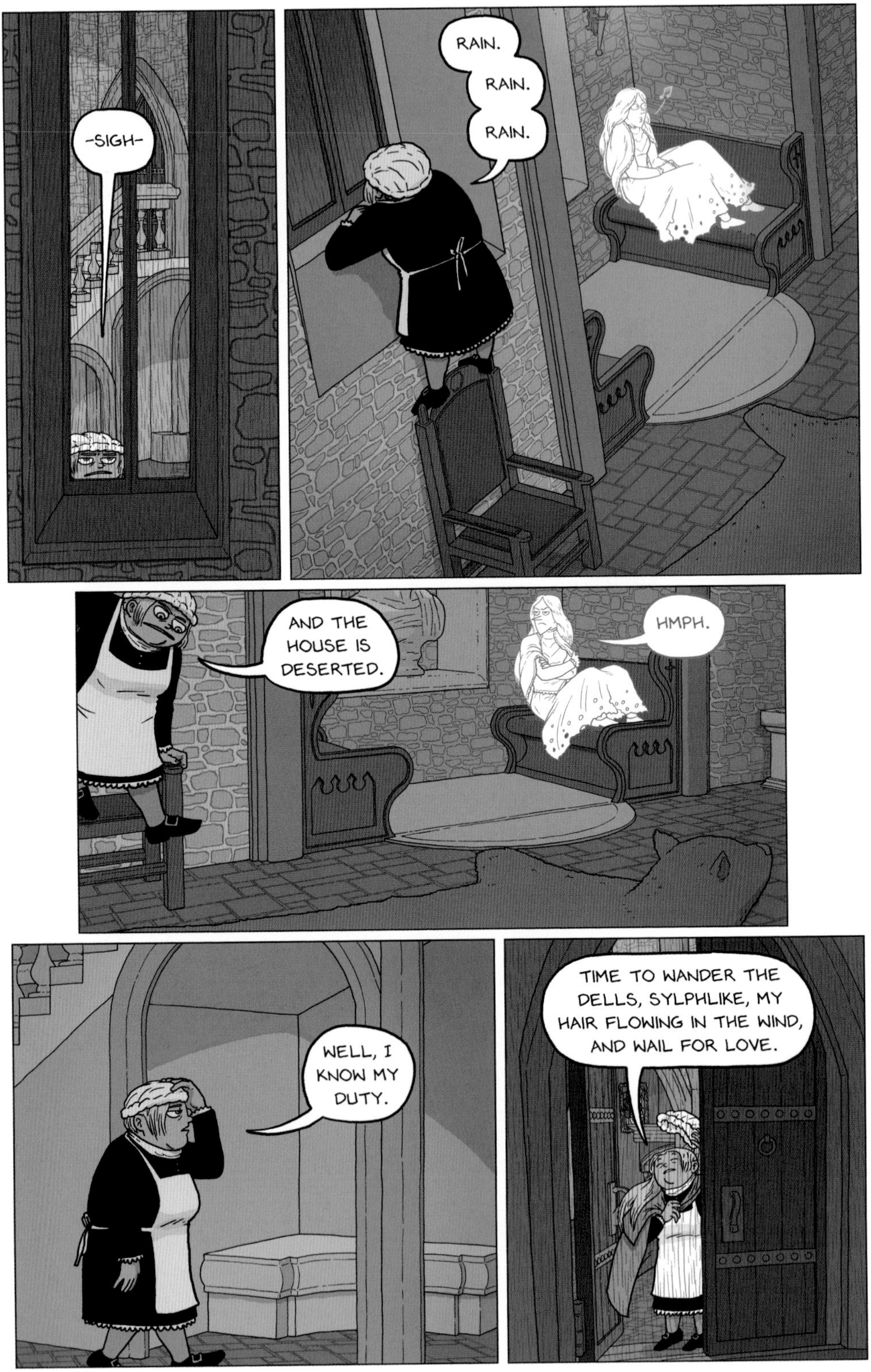
-SIGH-
RAIN.
RAIN.
RAIN.
AND THE HOUSE IS DESERTED.
HMPH.
WELL, I KNOW MY DUTY.
TIME TO WANDER THE DELLS, SYLPHLIKE, MY HAIR FLOWING IN THE WIND, AND WAIL FOR LOVE.

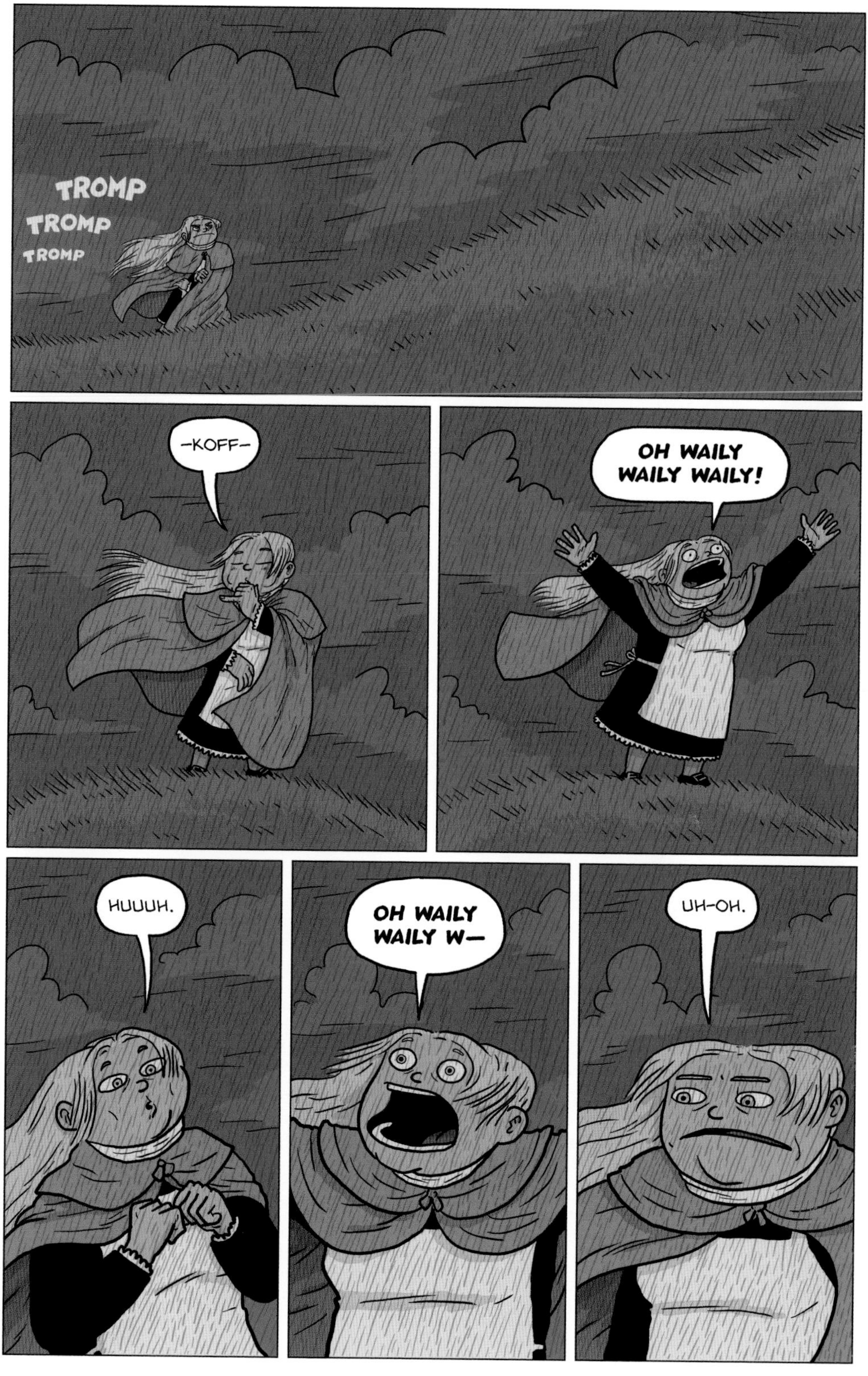
TROMP
TROMP
TROMP
-KOFF-
OH WAILY WAILY WAILY!
HUUUH.
OH WAILY WAILY W—
UH-OH.

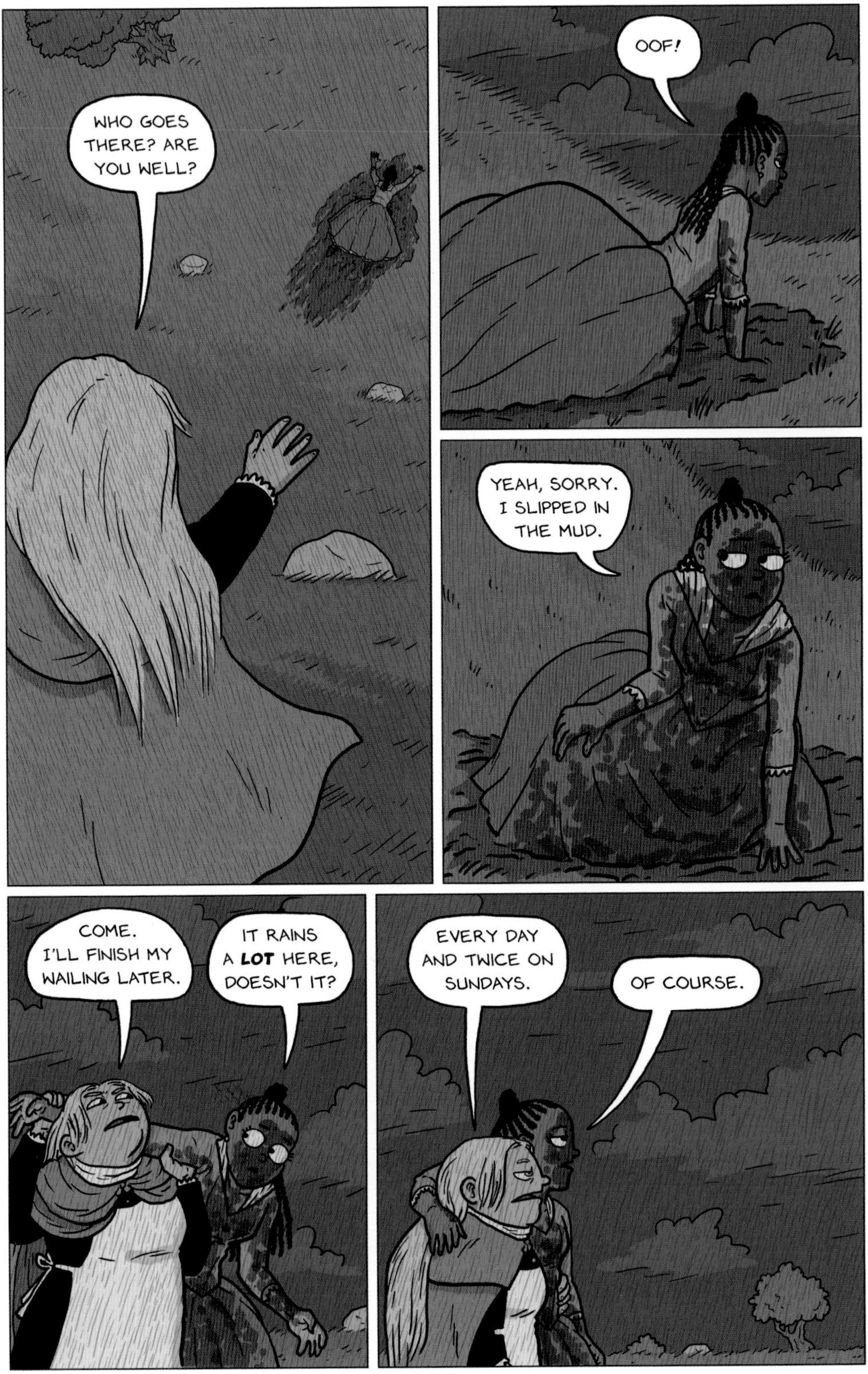
WHO GOES THERE? ARE YOU WELL?
OOF!
YEAH, SORRY. I SLIPPED IN THE MUD.
COME. I'LL FINISH MY WAILING LATER.
IT RAINS A **LOT** HERE, DOESN'T IT?
EVERY DAY AND TWICE ON SUNDAYS.
OF COURSE.

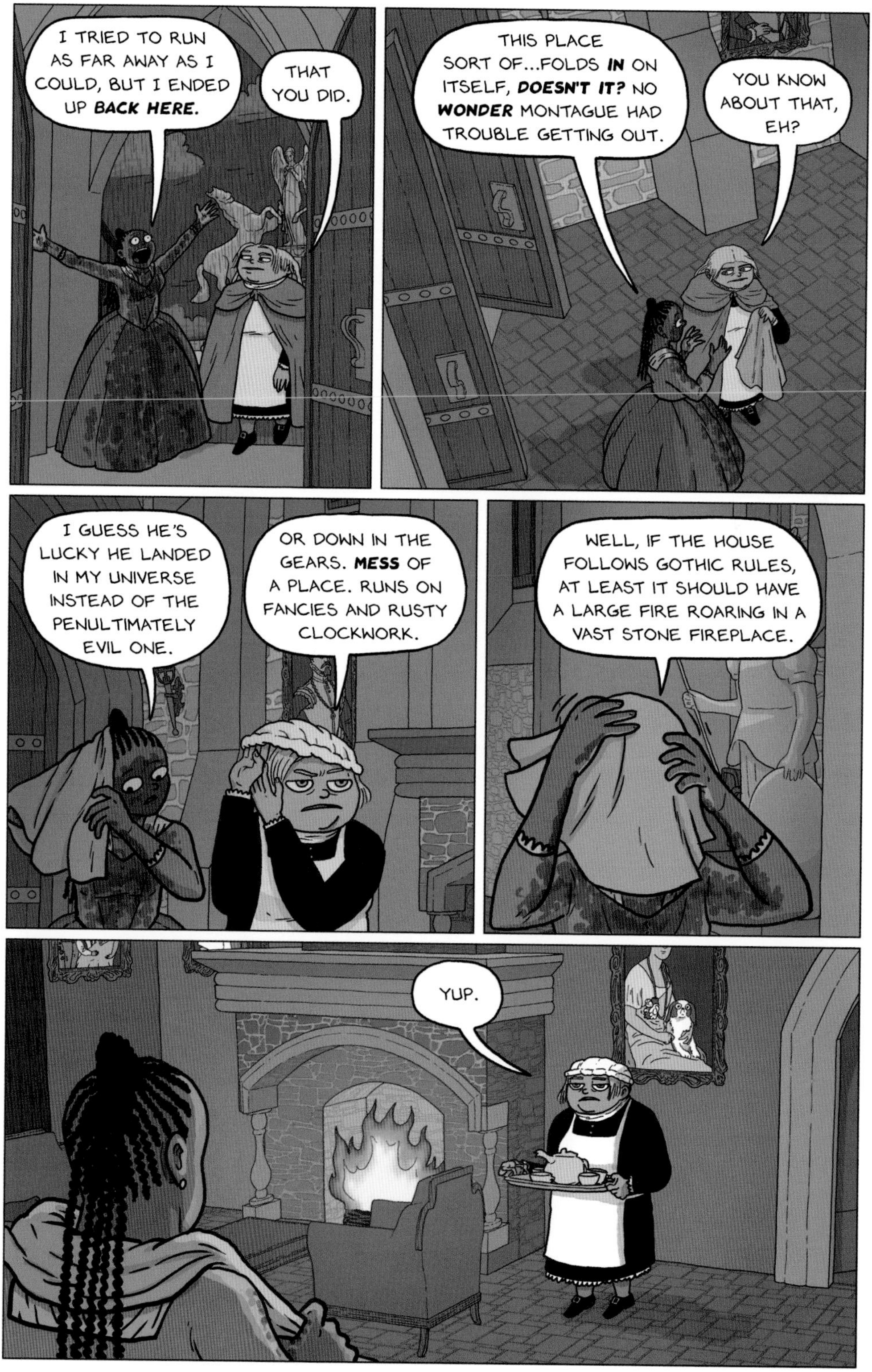
I TRIED TO RUN AS FAR AWAY AS I COULD, BUT I ENDED UP **BACK HERE.**
THAT YOU DID.
THIS PLACE SORT OF...FOLDS **IN** ON ITSELF, ***DOESN'T IT?*** NO **WONDER** MONTAGUE HAD TROUBLE GETTING OUT.
YOU KNOW ABOUT THAT, EH?
I GUESS HE'S LUCKY HE LANDED IN MY UNIVERSE INSTEAD OF THE PENULTIMATELY EVIL ONE.
OR DOWN IN THE GEARS. **MESS** OF A PLACE. RUNS ON FANCIES AND RUSTY CLOCKWORK.
WELL, IF THE HOUSE FOLLOWS GOTHIC RULES, AT LEAST IT SHOULD HAVE A LARGE FIRE ROARING IN A VAST STONE FIREPLACE.
YUP.

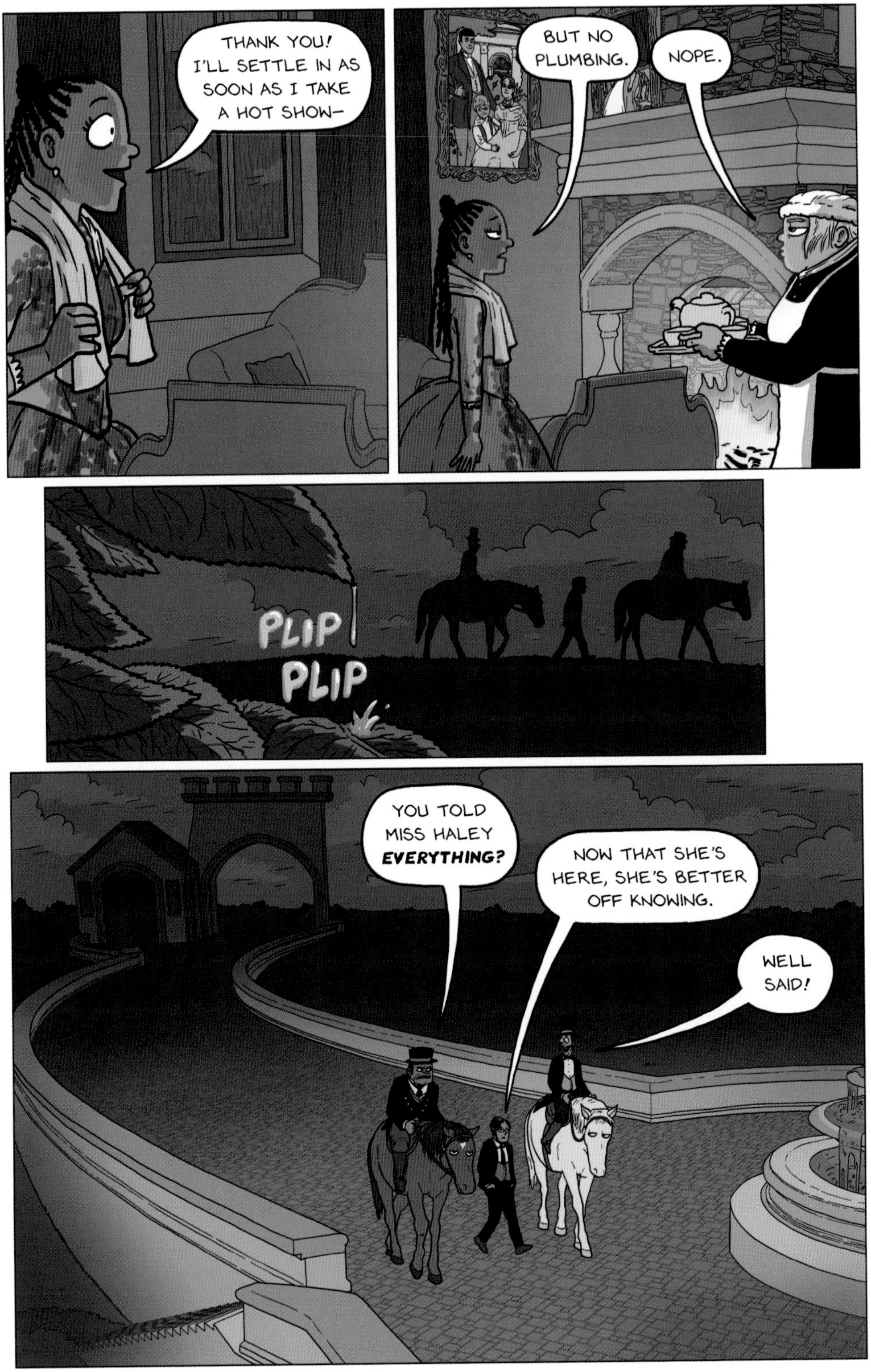
THANK YOU! I'LL SETTLE IN AS SOON AS I TAKE A HOT SHOW–
BUT NO PLUMBING.
NOPE.
PLIP
PLIP
YOU TOLD MISS HALEY EVERYTHING?
NOW THAT SHE'S HERE, SHE'S BETTER OFF KNOWING.
WELL SAID!

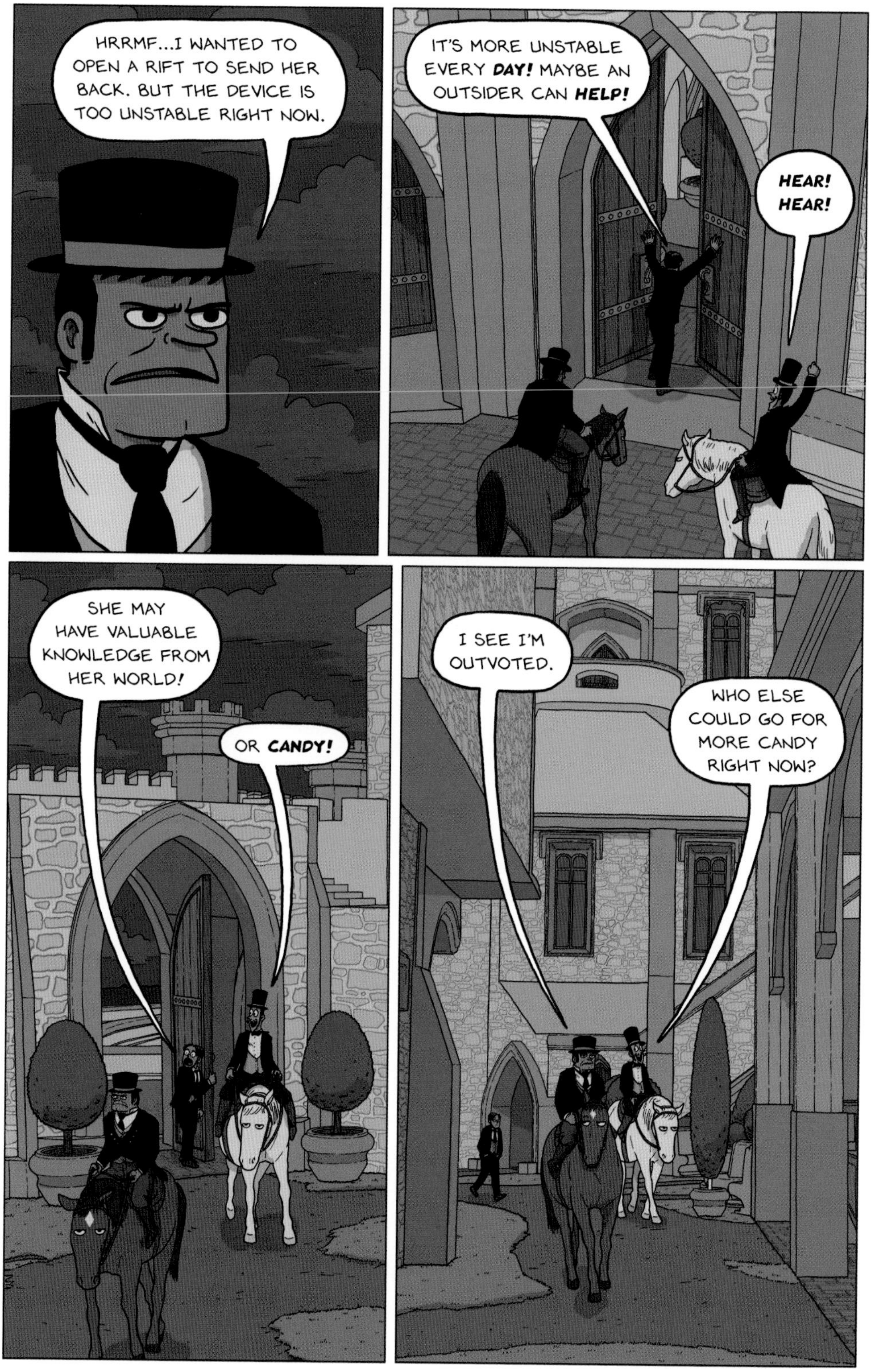
HRRMF...I WANTED TO OPEN A RIFT TO SEND HER BACK. BUT THE DEVICE IS TOO UNSTABLE RIGHT NOW.
IT'S MORE UNSTABLE EVERY **DAY!** MAYBE AN OUTSIDER CAN **HELP!**
HEAR! HEAR!
SHE MAY HAVE VALUABLE KNOWLEDGE FROM HER WORLD!
OR **CANDY!**
I SEE I'M OUTVOTED.
WHO ELSE COULD GO FOR MORE CANDY RIGHT NOW?

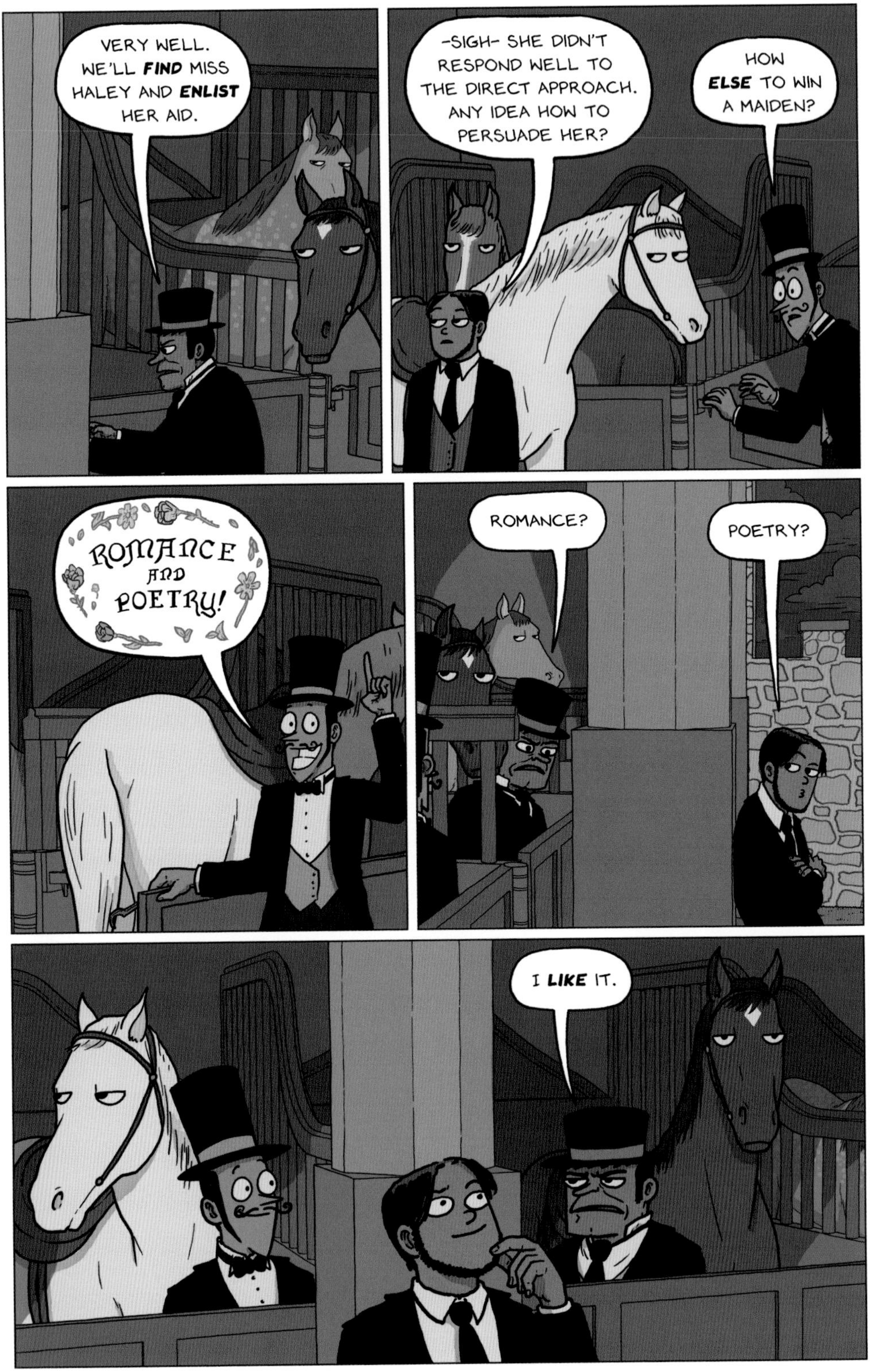
VERY WELL. WE'LL **FIND** MISS HALEY AND **ENLIST** HER AID.
-SIGH- SHE DIDN'T RESPOND WELL TO THE DIRECT APPROACH. ANY IDEA HOW TO PERSUADE HER?
HOW **ELSE** TO WIN A MAIDEN?
ROMANCE AND POETRY!
ROMANCE?
POETRY?
I **LIKE** IT.

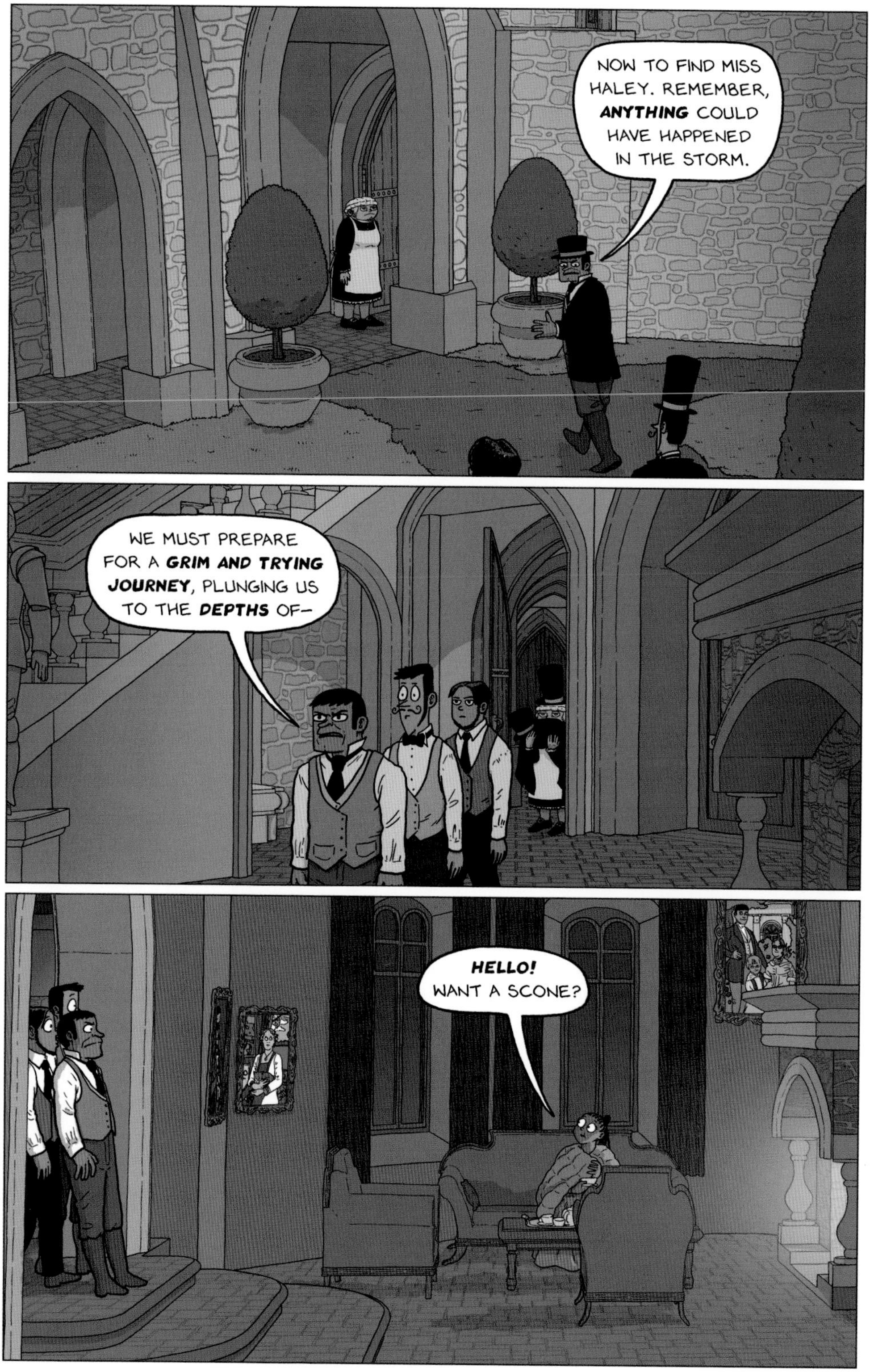
NOW TO FIND MISS HALEY. REMEMBER, **ANYTHING** COULD HAVE HAPPENED IN THE STORM.
WE MUST PREPARE FOR A **GRIM AND TRYING JOURNEY**, PLUNGING US TO THE **DEPTHS** OF—
HELLO! WANT A SCONE?

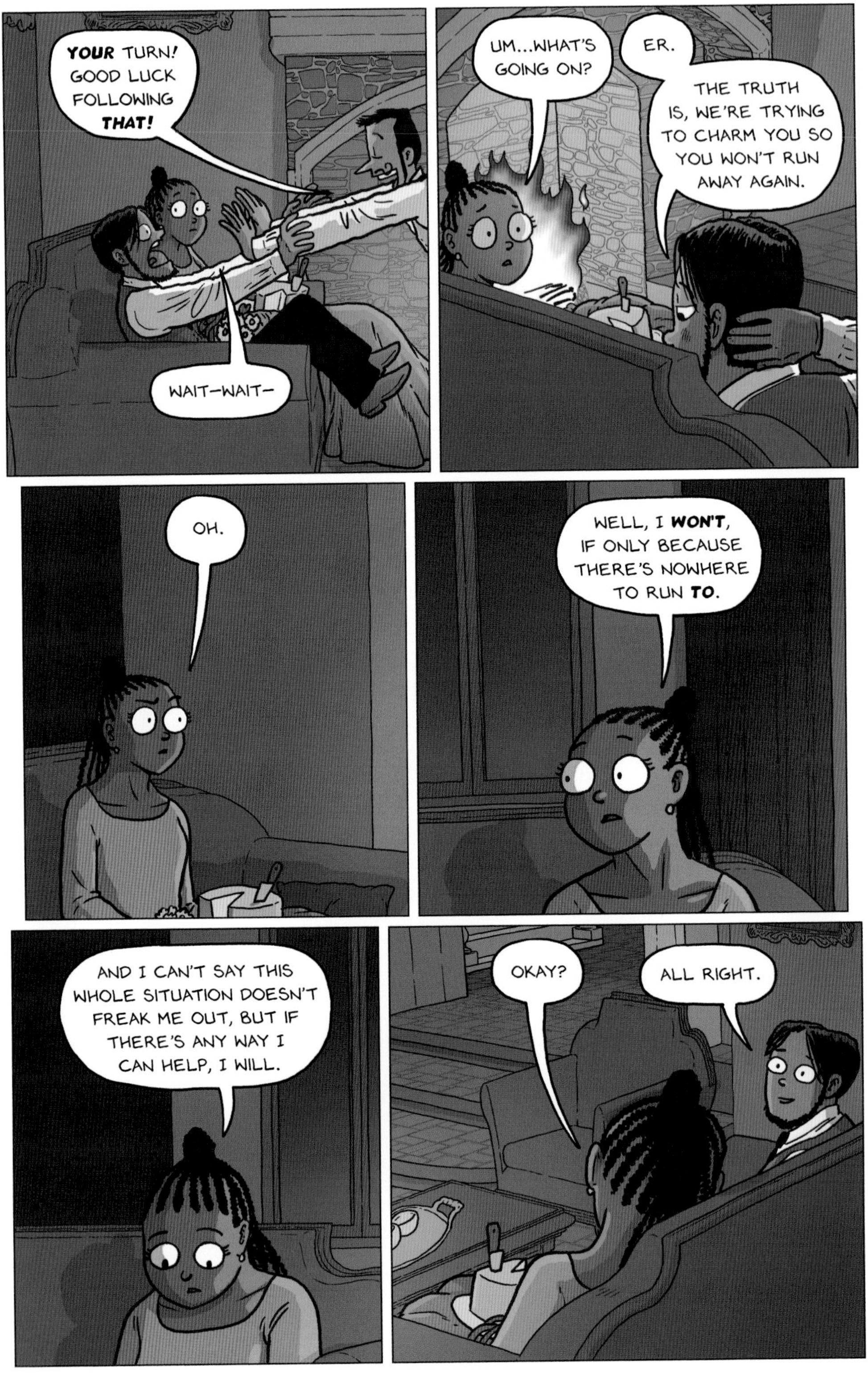
YOUR TURN! GOOD LUCK FOLLOWING **THAT!**
WAIT—WAIT—
UM...WHAT'S GOING ON?
ER.
THE TRUTH IS, WE'RE TRYING TO CHARM YOU SO YOU WON'T RUN AWAY AGAIN.
OH.
WELL, I **WON'T**, IF ONLY BECAUSE THERE'S NOWHERE TO RUN **TO**.
AND I CAN'T SAY THIS WHOLE SITUATION DOESN'T FREAK ME OUT, BUT IF THERE'S ANY WAY I CAN HELP, I WILL.
OKAY?
ALL RIGHT.

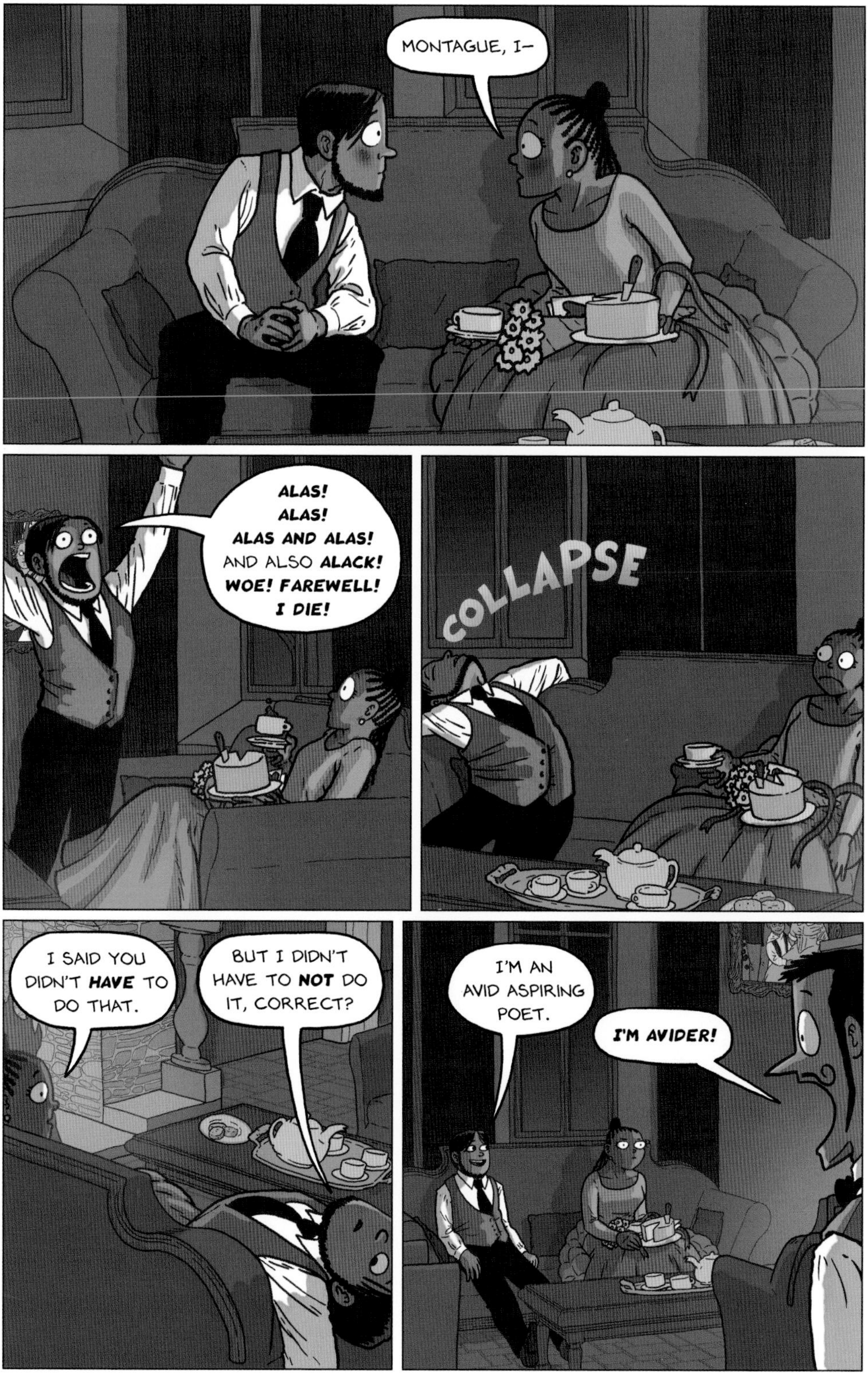
MONTAGUE, I–
ALAS! ALAS! ALAS AND ALAS! AND ALSO ALACK! WOE! FAREWELL! I DIE!
COLLAPSE
I SAID YOU DIDN'T HAVE TO DO THAT.
BUT I DIDN'T HAVE TO NOT DO IT, CORRECT?
I'M AN AVID ASPIRING POET.
I'M AVIDER!

4
The Bile Spreads

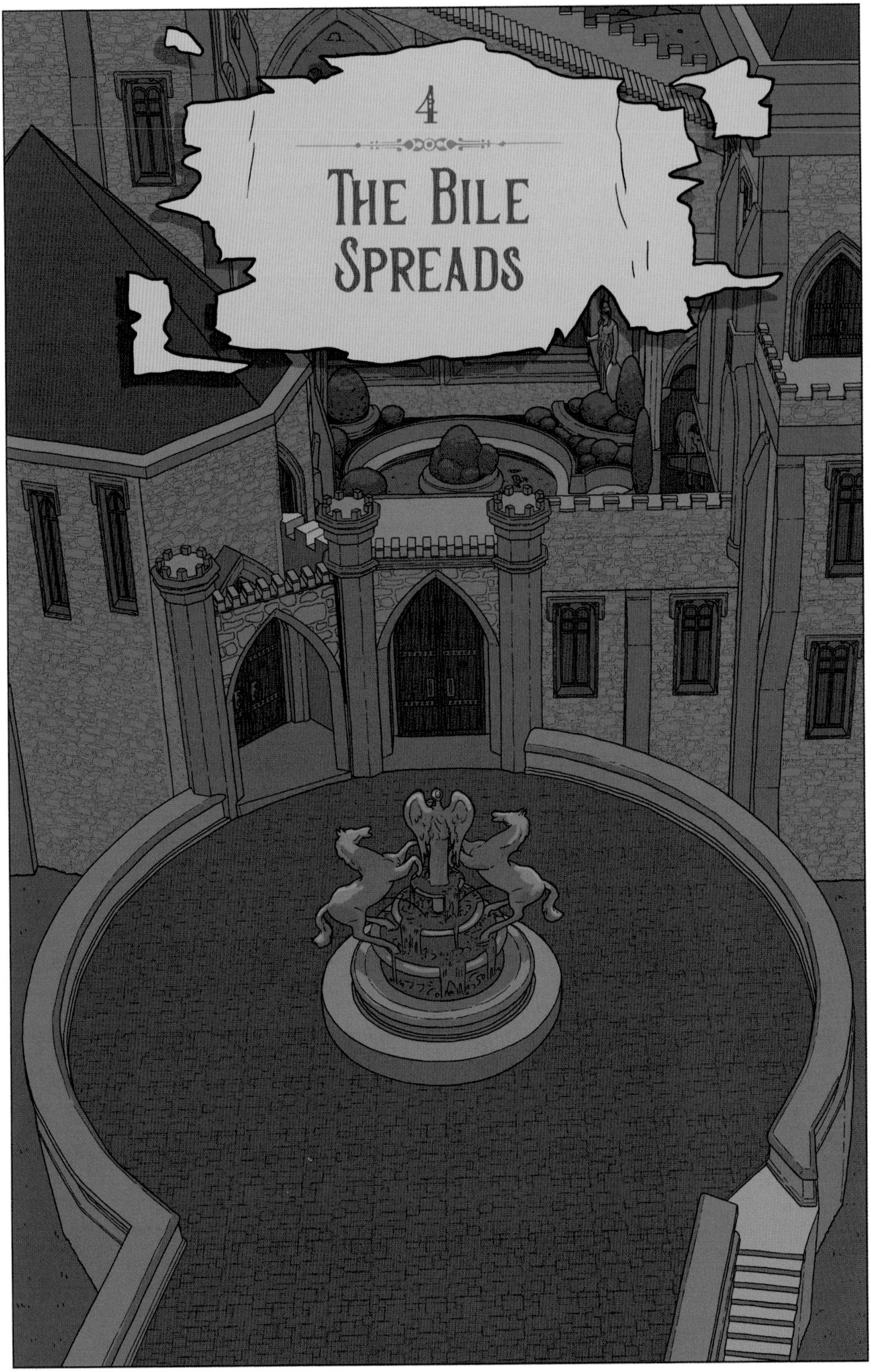

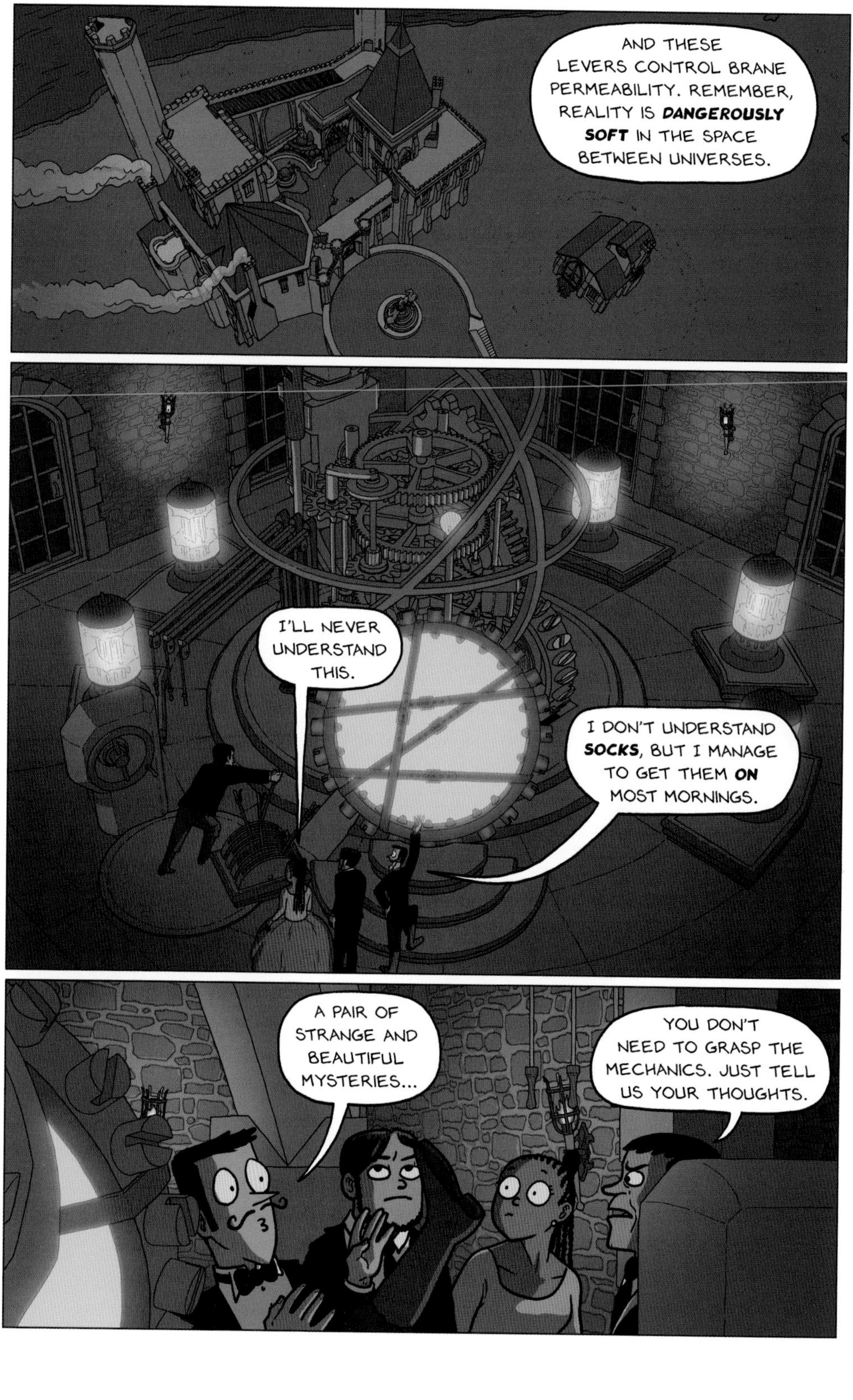
AND THESE LEVERS CONTROL BRANE PERMEABILITY. REMEMBER, REALITY IS **DANGEROUSLY SOFT** IN THE SPACE BETWEEN UNIVERSES.
I'LL NEVER UNDERSTAND THIS.
I DON'T UNDERSTAND **SOCKS**, BUT I MANAGE TO GET THEM **ON** MOST MORNINGS.
A PAIR OF STRANGE AND BEAUTIFUL MYSTERIES...
YOU DON'T NEED TO GRASP THE MECHANICS. JUST TELL US YOUR THOUGHTS.

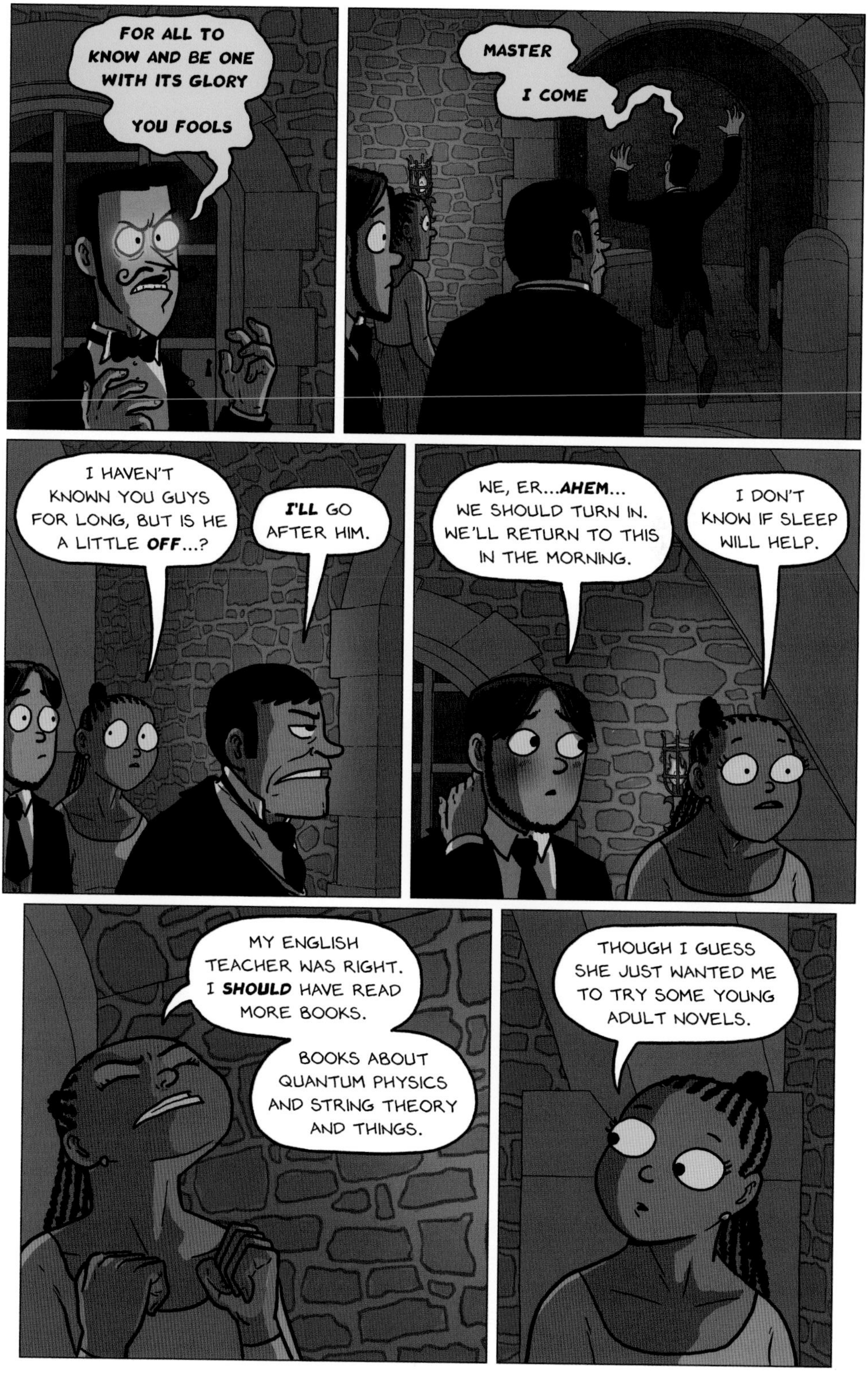
FOR ALL TO KNOW AND BE ONE WITH ITS GLORY
YOU FOOLS
MASTER
I COME
I HAVEN'T KNOWN YOU GUYS FOR LONG, BUT IS HE A LITTLE **OFF**...?
I'LL GO AFTER HIM.
WE, ER...**AHEM**... WE SHOULD TURN IN. WE'LL RETURN TO THIS IN THE MORNING.
I DON'T KNOW IF SLEEP WILL HELP.
MY ENGLISH TEACHER WAS RIGHT. I **SHOULD** HAVE READ MORE BOOKS.
BOOKS ABOUT QUANTUM PHYSICS AND STRING THEORY AND THINGS.
THOUGH I GUESS SHE JUST WANTED ME TO TRY SOME YOUNG ADULT NOVELS.

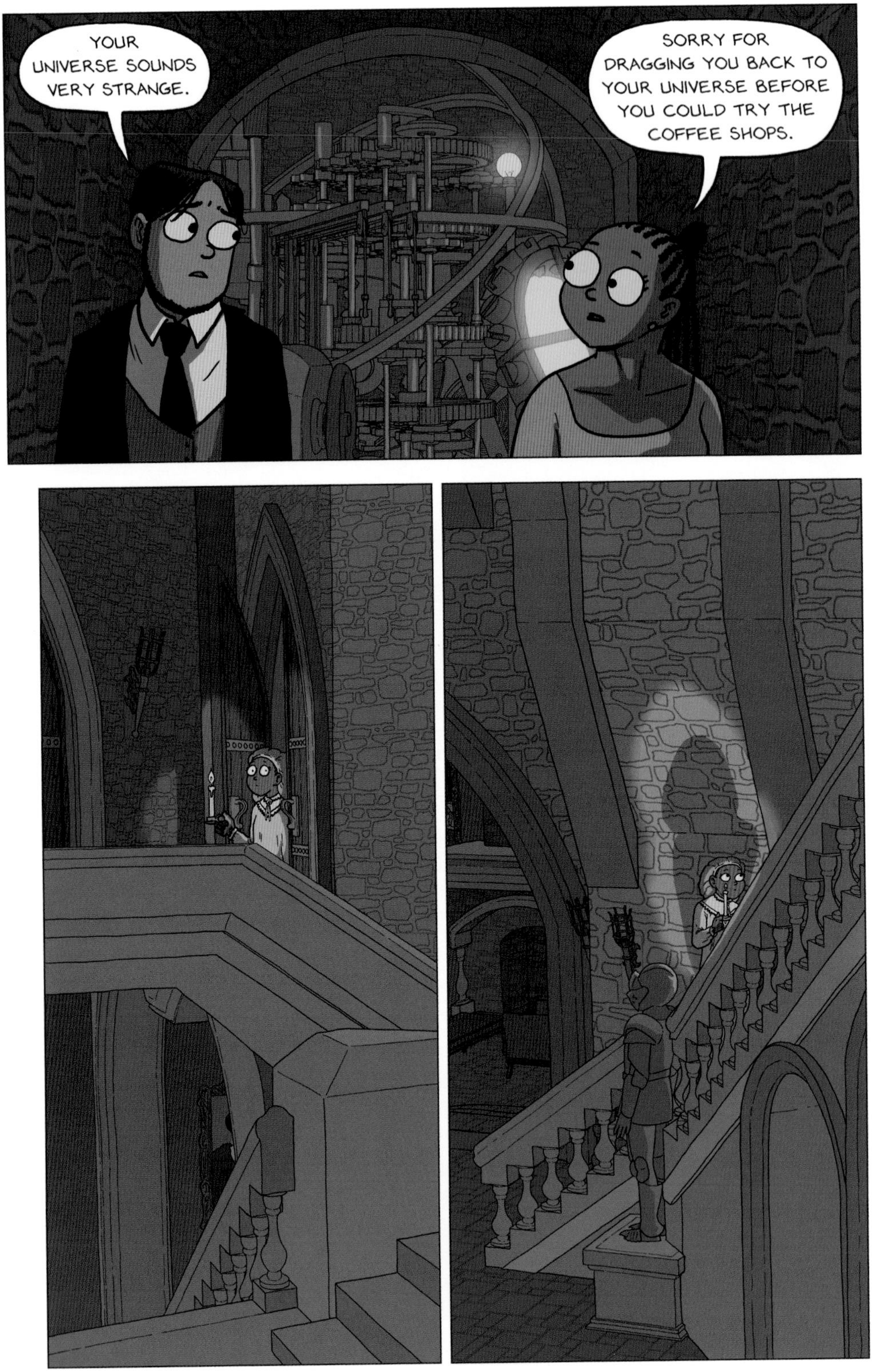
YOUR UNIVERSE SOUNDS VERY STRANGE.
SORRY FOR DRAGGING YOU BACK TO YOUR UNIVERSE BEFORE YOU COULD TRY THE COFFEE SHOPS.

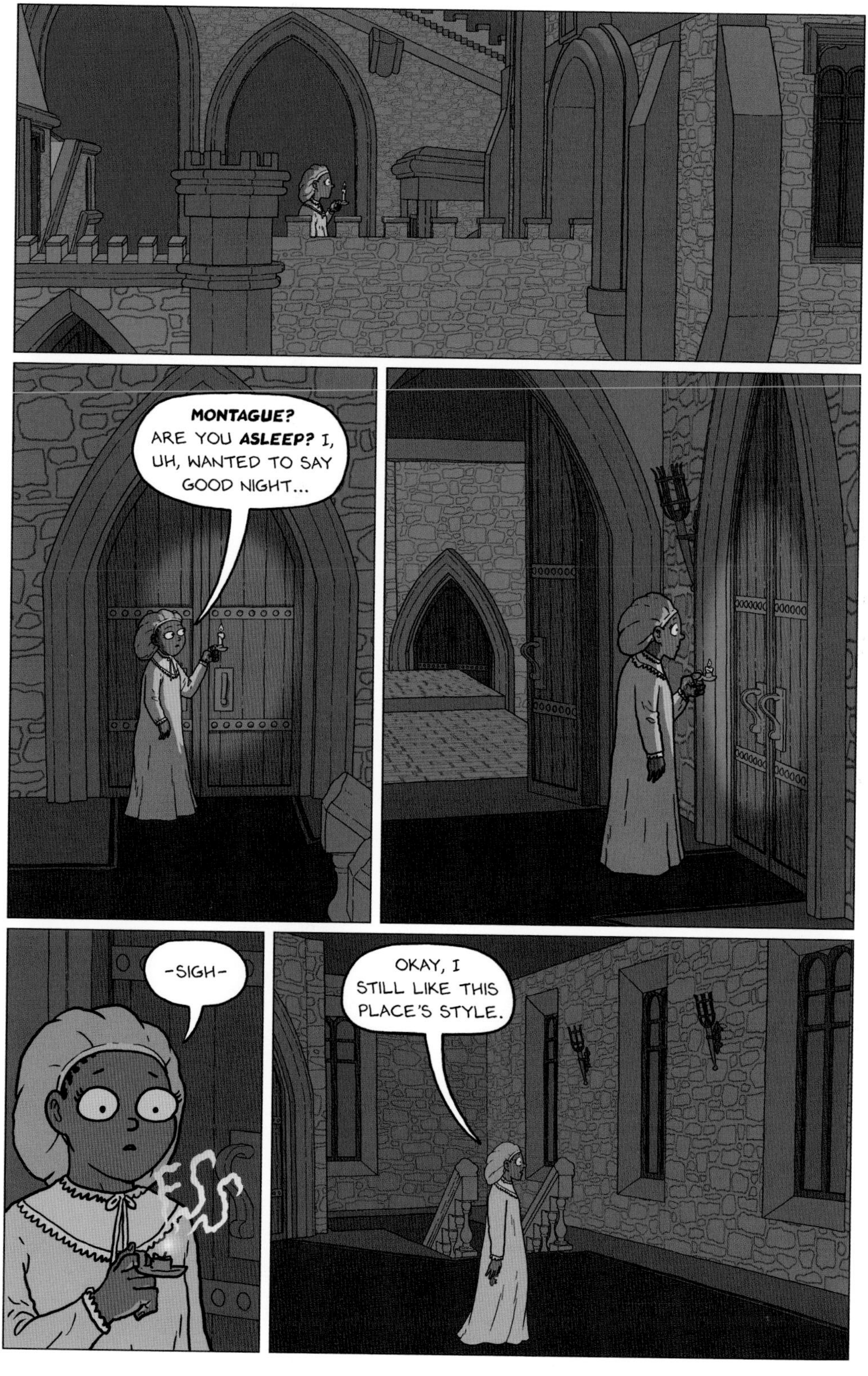
MONTAGUE? ARE YOU ASLEEP? I, UH, WANTED TO SAY GOOD NIGHT...
-SIGH-
OKAY, I STILL LIKE THIS PLACE'S STYLE.

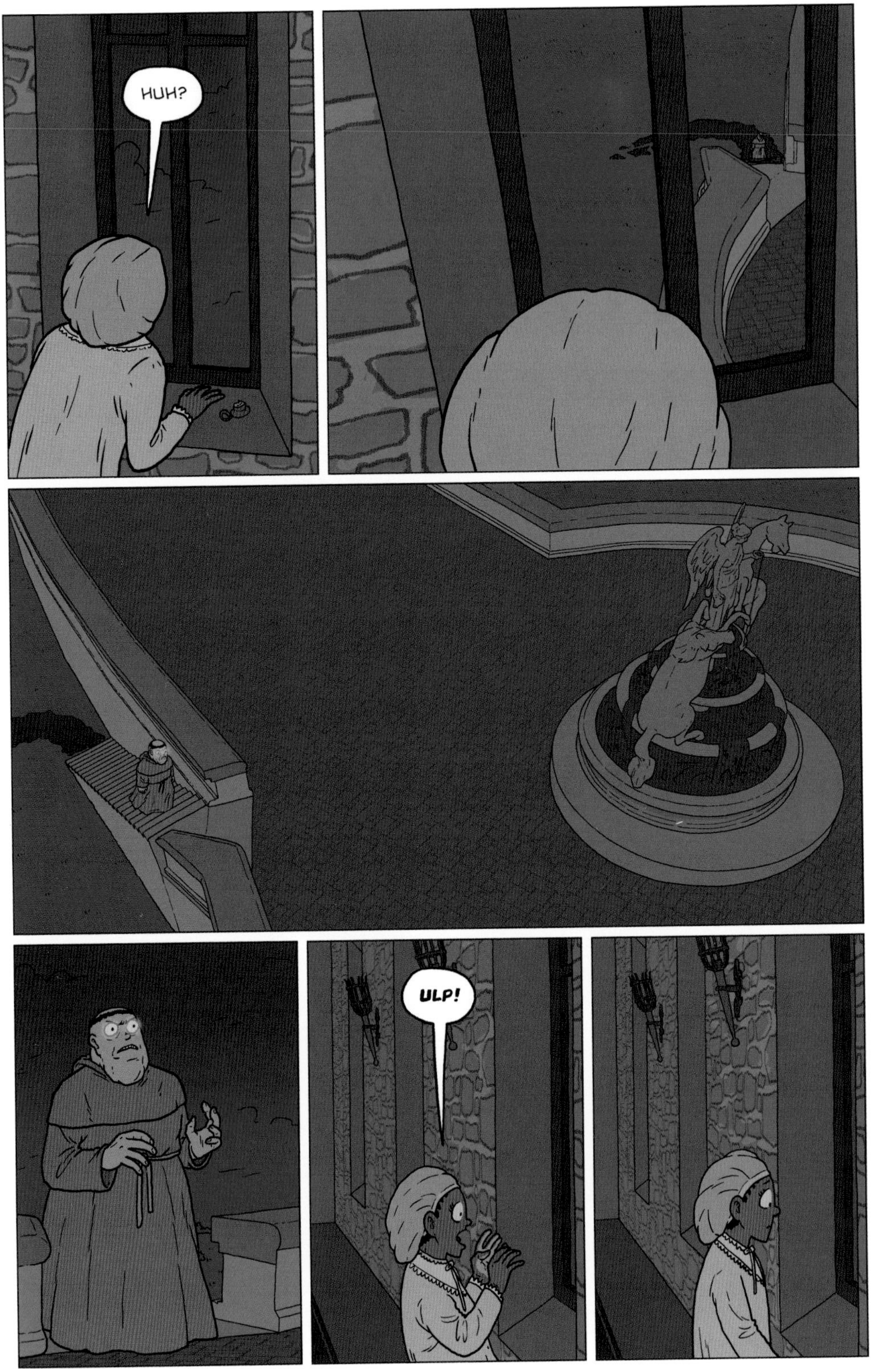
HUH?
ULP!

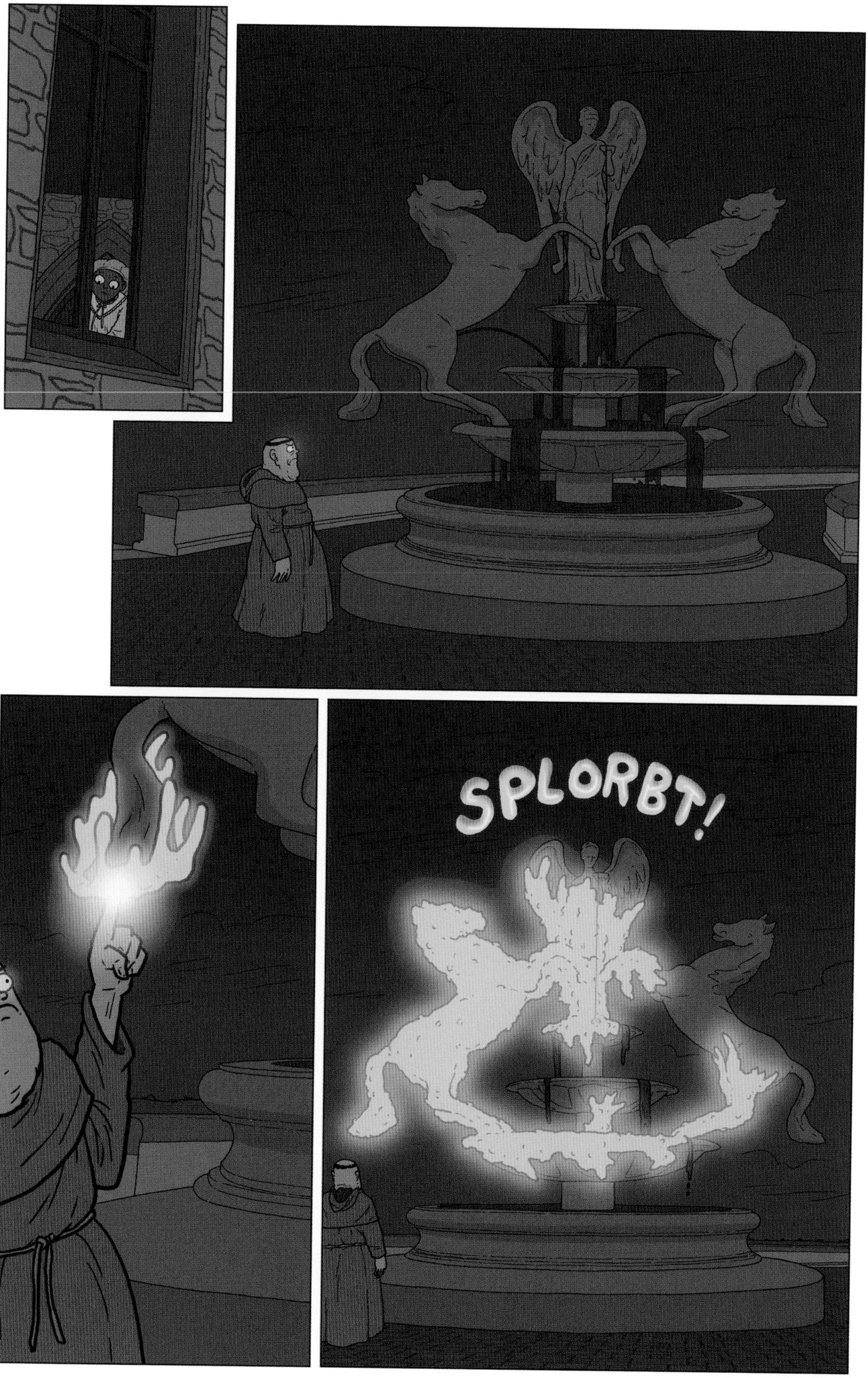
SPLORBT!

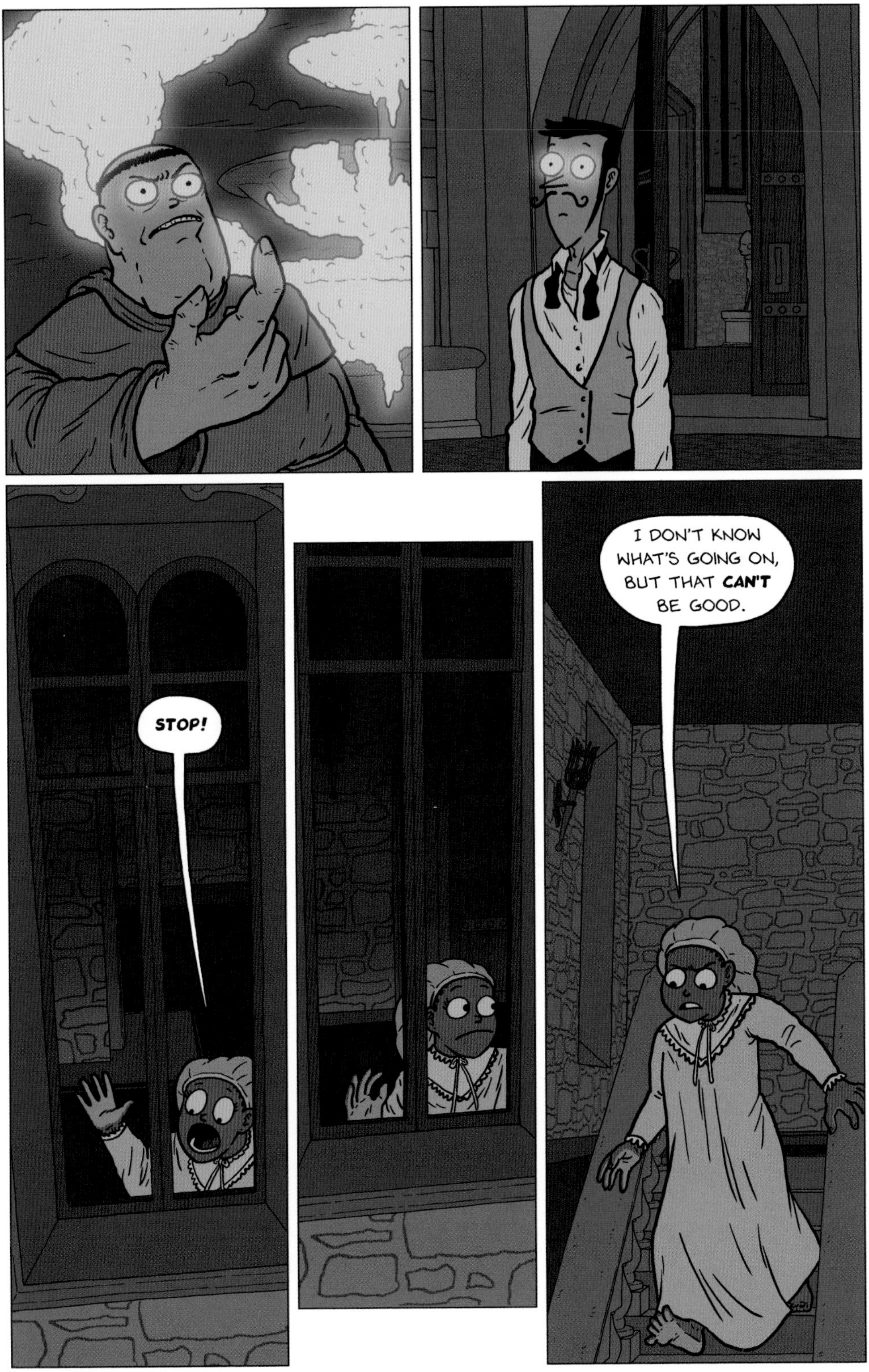
STOP!
I DON'T KNOW WHAT'S GOING ON, BUT THAT CAN'T BE GOOD.

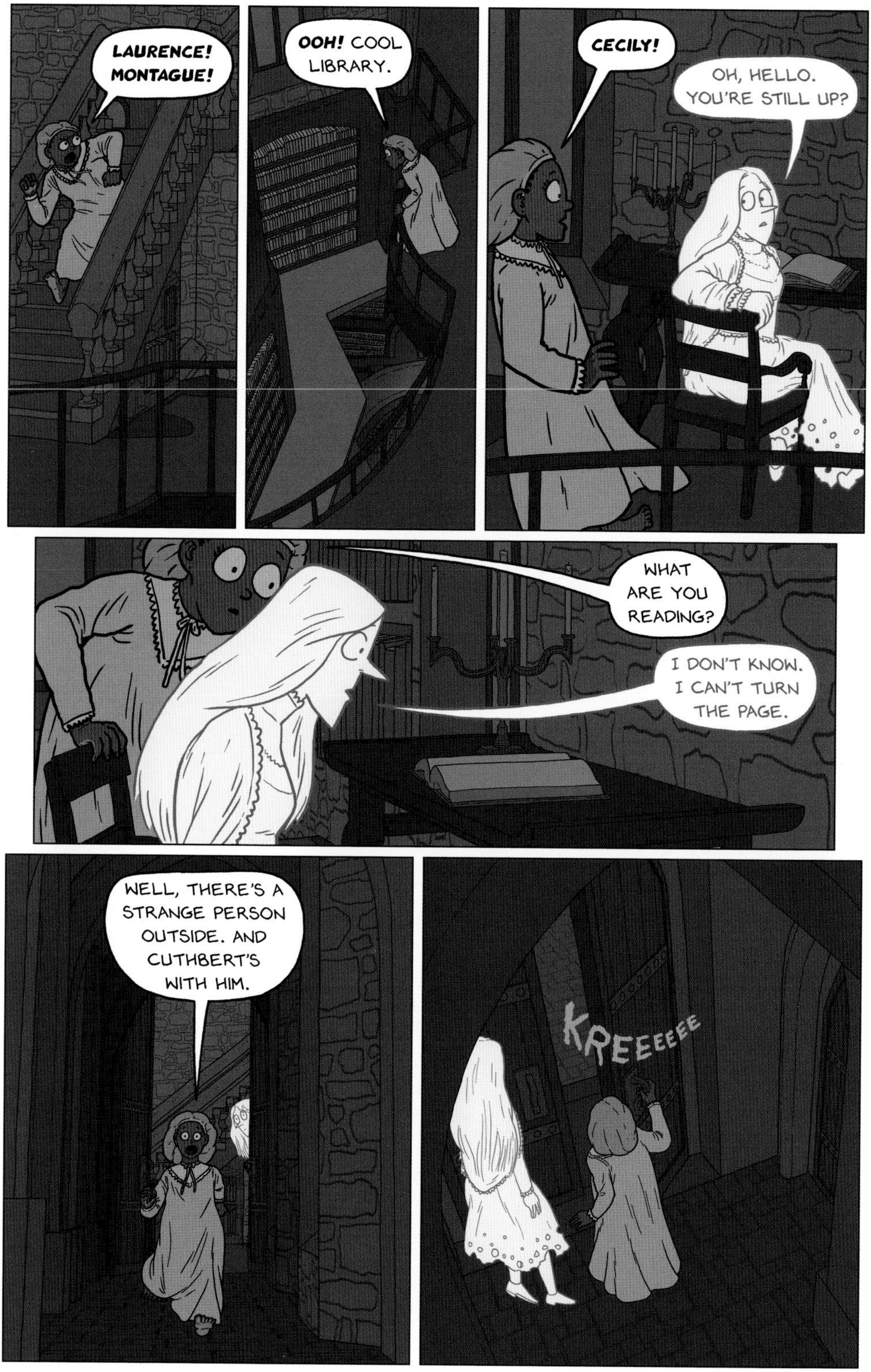
LAURENCE! MONTAGUE!
OOH! COOL LIBRARY.
CECILY!
OH, HELLO. YOU'RE STILL UP?
WHAT ARE YOU READING?
I DON'T KNOW. I CAN'T TURN THE PAGE.
WELL, THERE'S A STRANGE PERSON OUTSIDE. AND CUTHBERT'S WITH HIM.
KREEEEEE

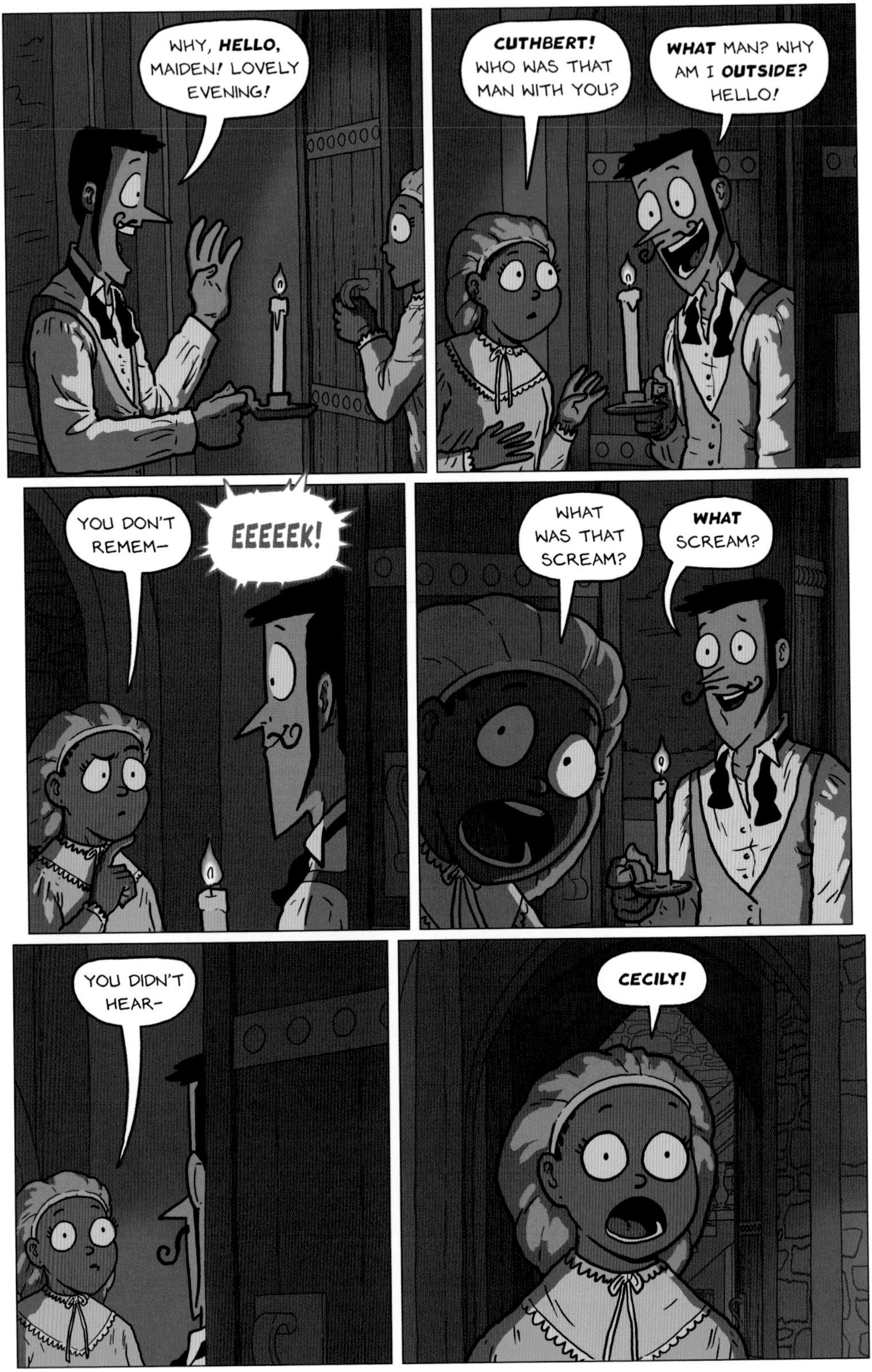
WHY, HELLO, MAIDEN! LOVELY EVENING!
CUTHBERT! WHO WAS THAT MAN WITH YOU?
WHAT MAN? WHY AM I OUTSIDE? HELLO!
YOU DON'T REMEM—
EEEEEK!
WHAT WAS THAT SCREAM?
WHAT SCREAM?
YOU DIDN'T HEAR-
CECILY!

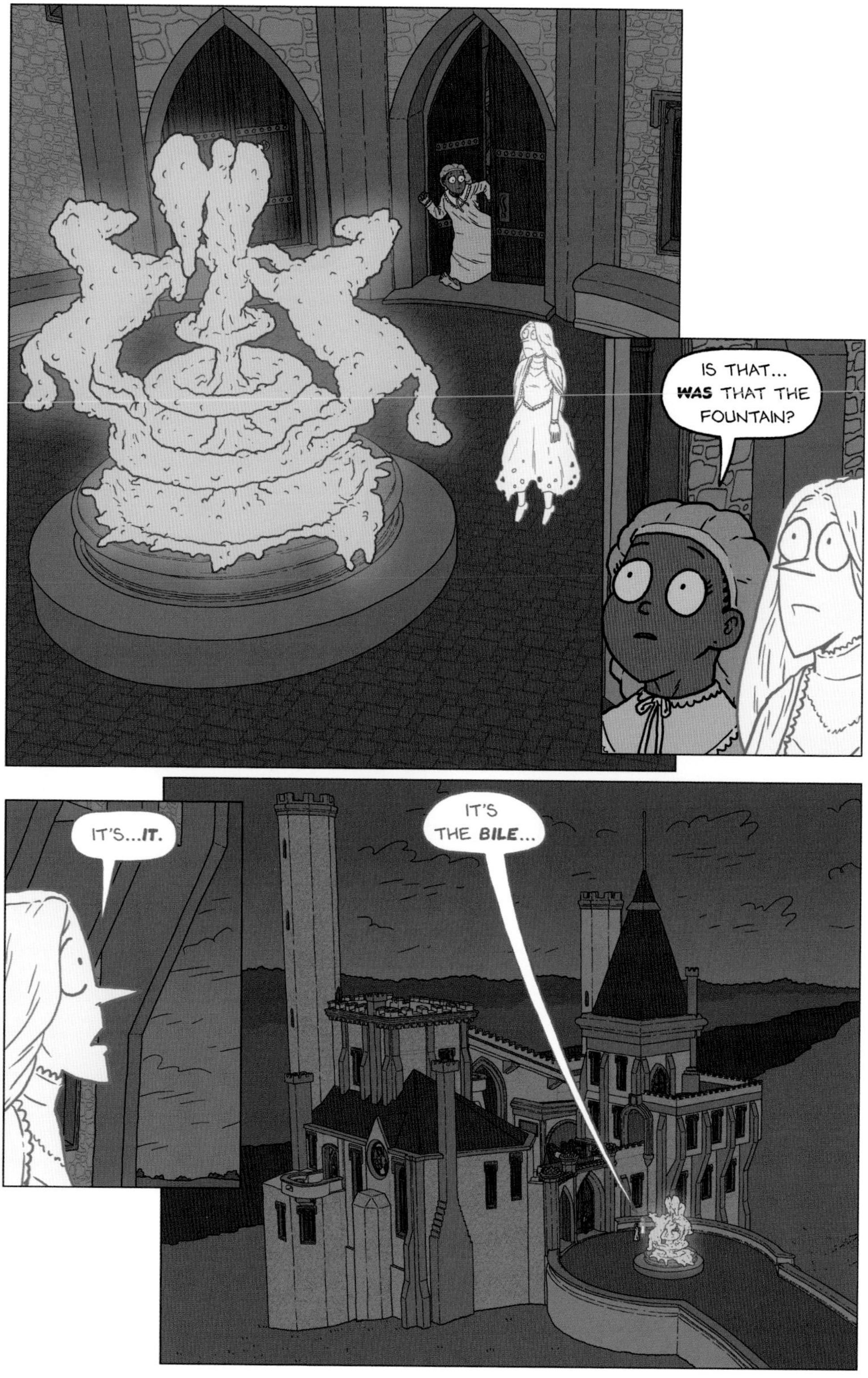
IS THAT... WAS THAT THE FOUNTAIN?
IT'S...IT.
IT'S THE BILE...

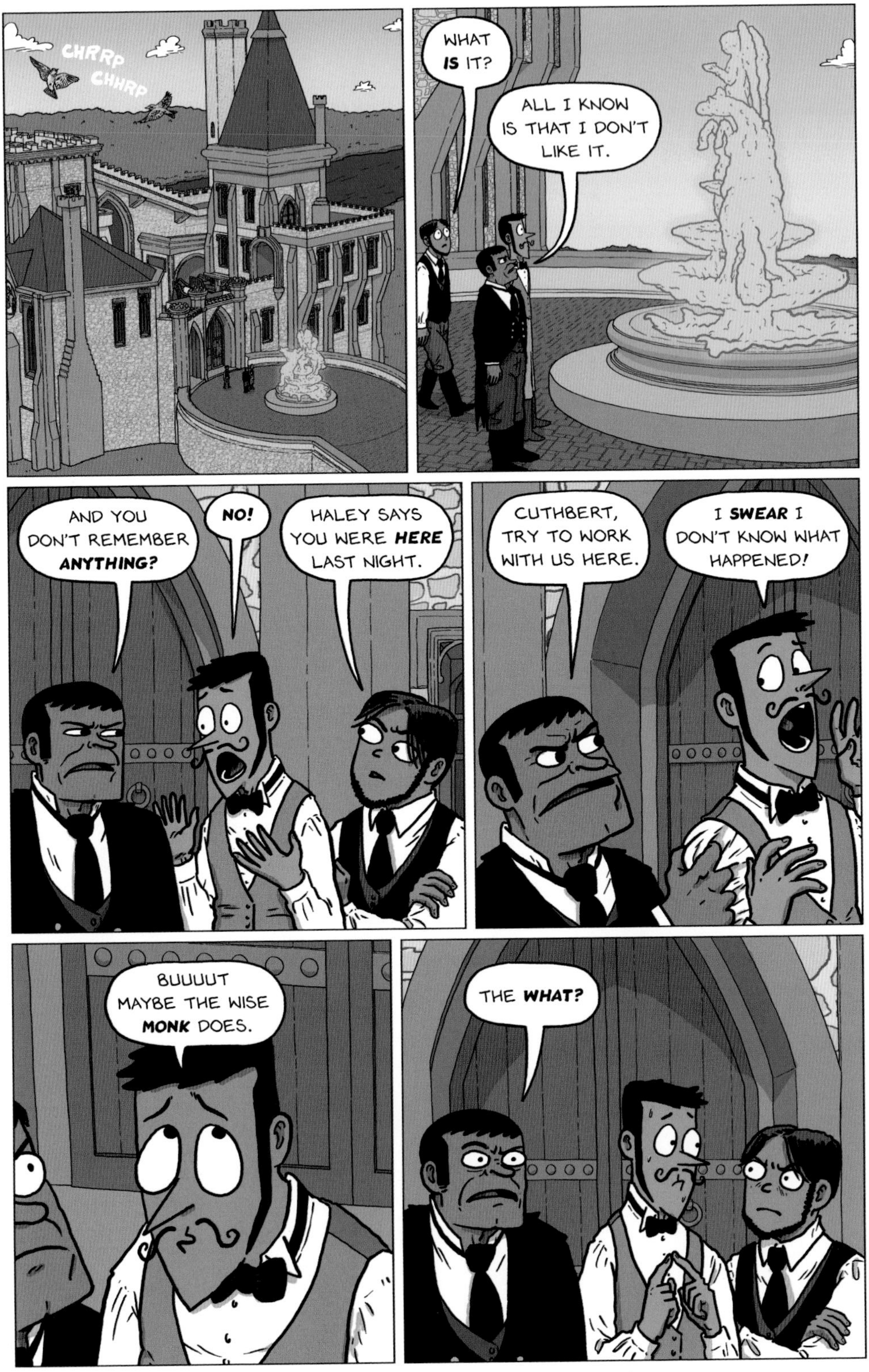
CHRRP
CHHRP
WHAT IS IT?
ALL I KNOW IS THAT I DON'T LIKE IT.
AND YOU DON'T REMEMBER ANYTHING?
NO!
HALEY SAYS YOU WERE HERE LAST NIGHT.
CUTHBERT, TRY TO WORK WITH US HERE.
I SWEAR I DON'T KNOW WHAT HAPPENED!
BUUUUT MAYBE THE WISE MONK DOES.
THE WHAT?

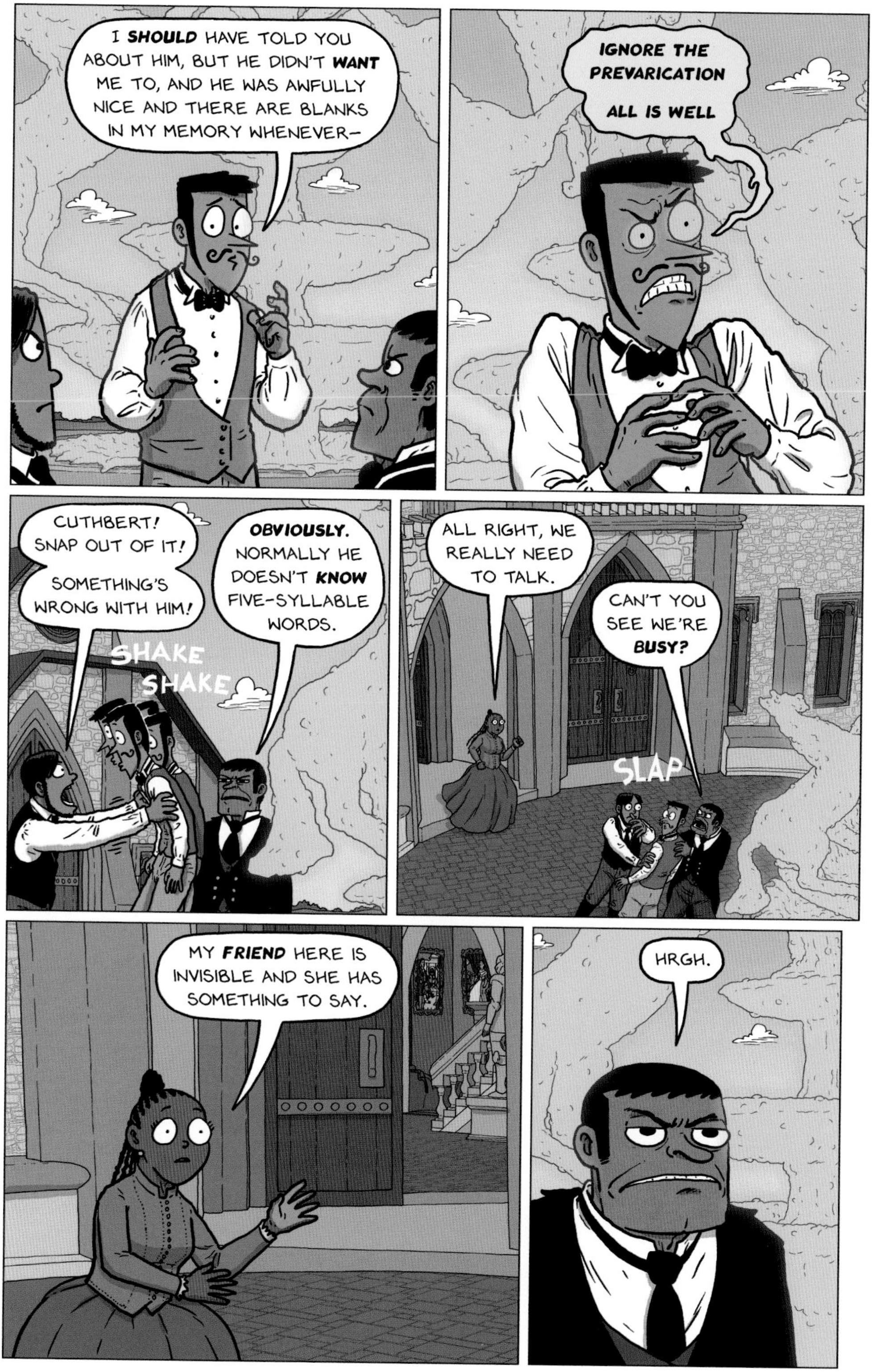
I **SHOULD** HAVE TOLD YOU ABOUT HIM, BUT HE DIDN'T **WANT** ME TO, AND HE WAS AWFULLY NICE AND THERE ARE BLANKS IN MY MEMORY WHENEVER–
IGNORE THE PREVARICATION
ALL IS WELL
CUTHBERT! SNAP OUT OF IT!
SOMETHING'S WRONG WITH HIM!
SHAKE SHAKE
OBVIOUSLY. NORMALLY HE DOESN'T **KNOW** FIVE-SYLLABLE WORDS.
ALL RIGHT, WE REALLY NEED TO TALK.
CAN'T YOU SEE WE'RE **BUSY?**
SLAP
MY **FRIEND** HERE IS INVISIBLE AND SHE HAS SOMETHING TO SAY.
HRGH.

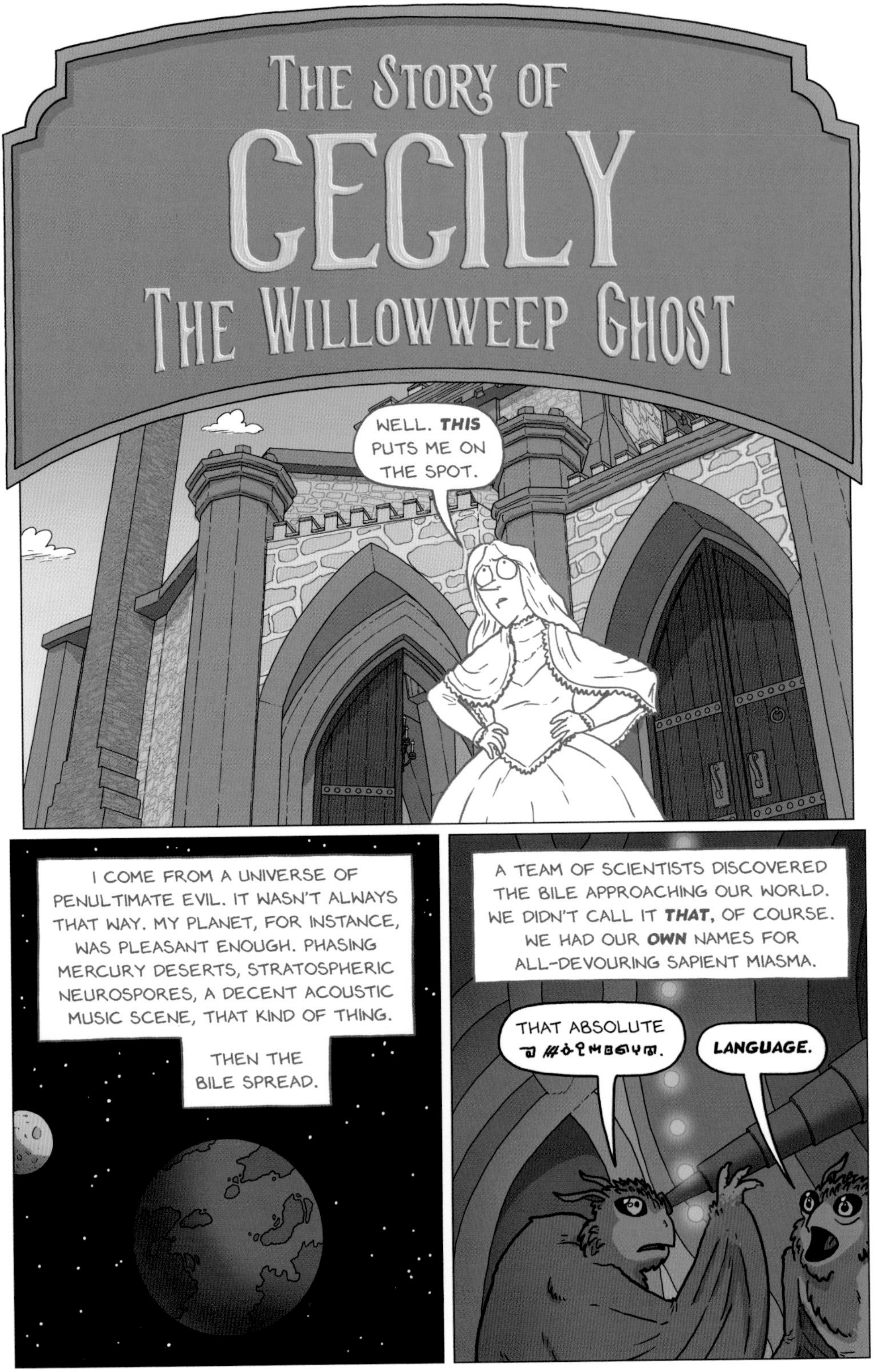
THE STORY OF
CECILY
THE WILLOWWEEP GHOST
WELL. THIS PUTS ME ON THE SPOT.
I COME FROM A UNIVERSE OF PENULTIMATE EVIL. IT WASN'T ALWAYS THAT WAY. MY PLANET, FOR INSTANCE, WAS PLEASANT ENOUGH. PHASING MERCURY DESERTS, STRATOSPHERIC NEUROSPORES, A DECENT ACOUSTIC MUSIC SCENE, THAT KIND OF THING.
THEN THE BILE SPREAD.
A TEAM OF SCIENTISTS DISCOVERED THE BILE APPROACHING OUR WORLD. WE DIDN'T CALL IT THAT, OF COURSE. WE HAD OUR OWN NAMES FOR ALL-DEVOURING SAPIENT MIASMA.
THAT ABSOLUTE
LANGUAGE.

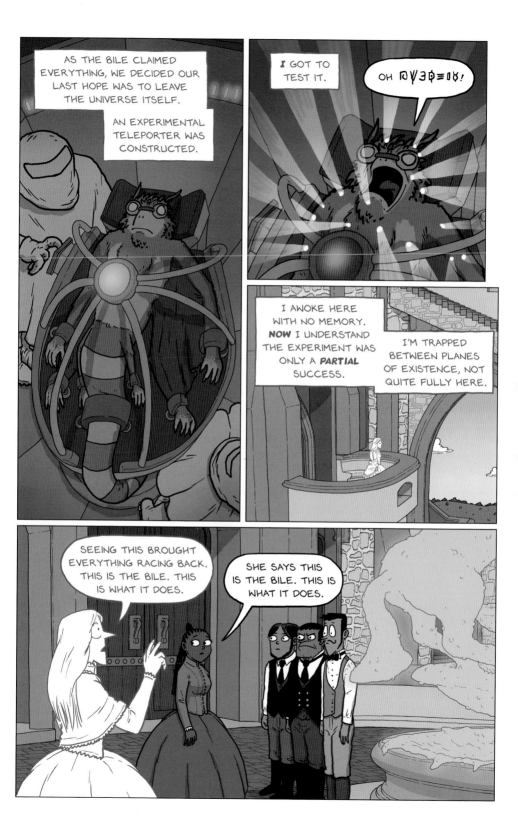

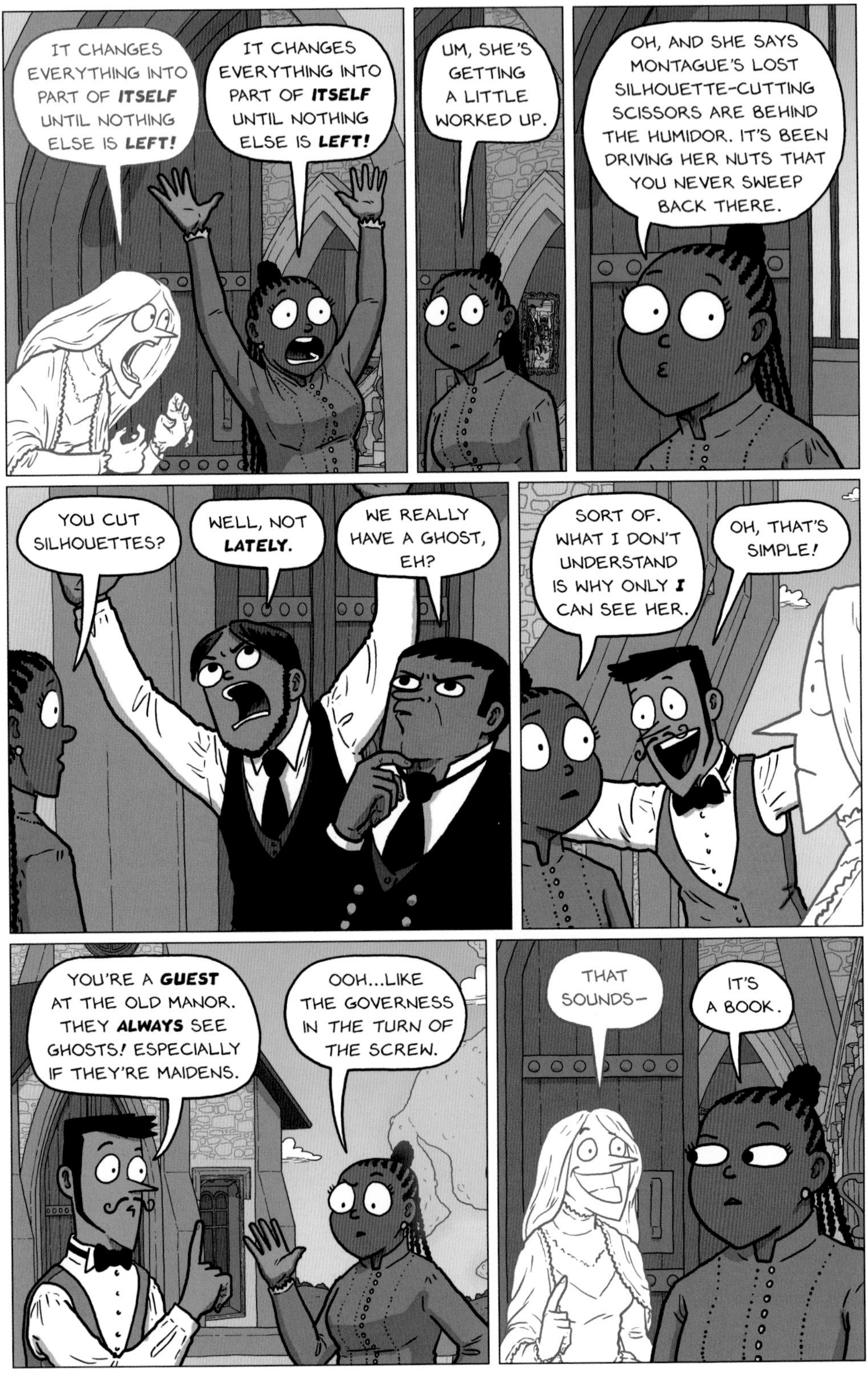
IT CHANGES EVERYTHING INTO PART OF **ITSELF** UNTIL NOTHING ELSE IS **LEFT!**
IT CHANGES EVERYTHING INTO PART OF **ITSELF** UNTIL NOTHING ELSE IS **LEFT!**
UM, SHE'S GETTING A LITTLE WORKED UP.
OH, AND SHE SAYS MONTAGUE'S LOST SILHOUETTE-CUTTING SCISSORS ARE BEHIND THE HUMIDOR. IT'S BEEN DRIVING HER NUTS THAT YOU NEVER SWEEP BACK THERE.
YOU CUT SILHOUETTES?
WELL, NOT **LATELY.**
WE REALLY HAVE A GHOST, EH?
SORT OF. WHAT I DON'T UNDERSTAND IS WHY ONLY **I** CAN SEE HER.
OH, THAT'S SIMPLE!
YOU'RE A **GUEST** AT THE OLD MANOR. THEY **ALWAYS** SEE GHOSTS! ESPECIALLY IF THEY'RE MAIDENS.
OOH...LIKE THE GOVERNESS IN THE TURN OF THE SCREW.
THAT SOUNDS—
IT'S A BOOK.

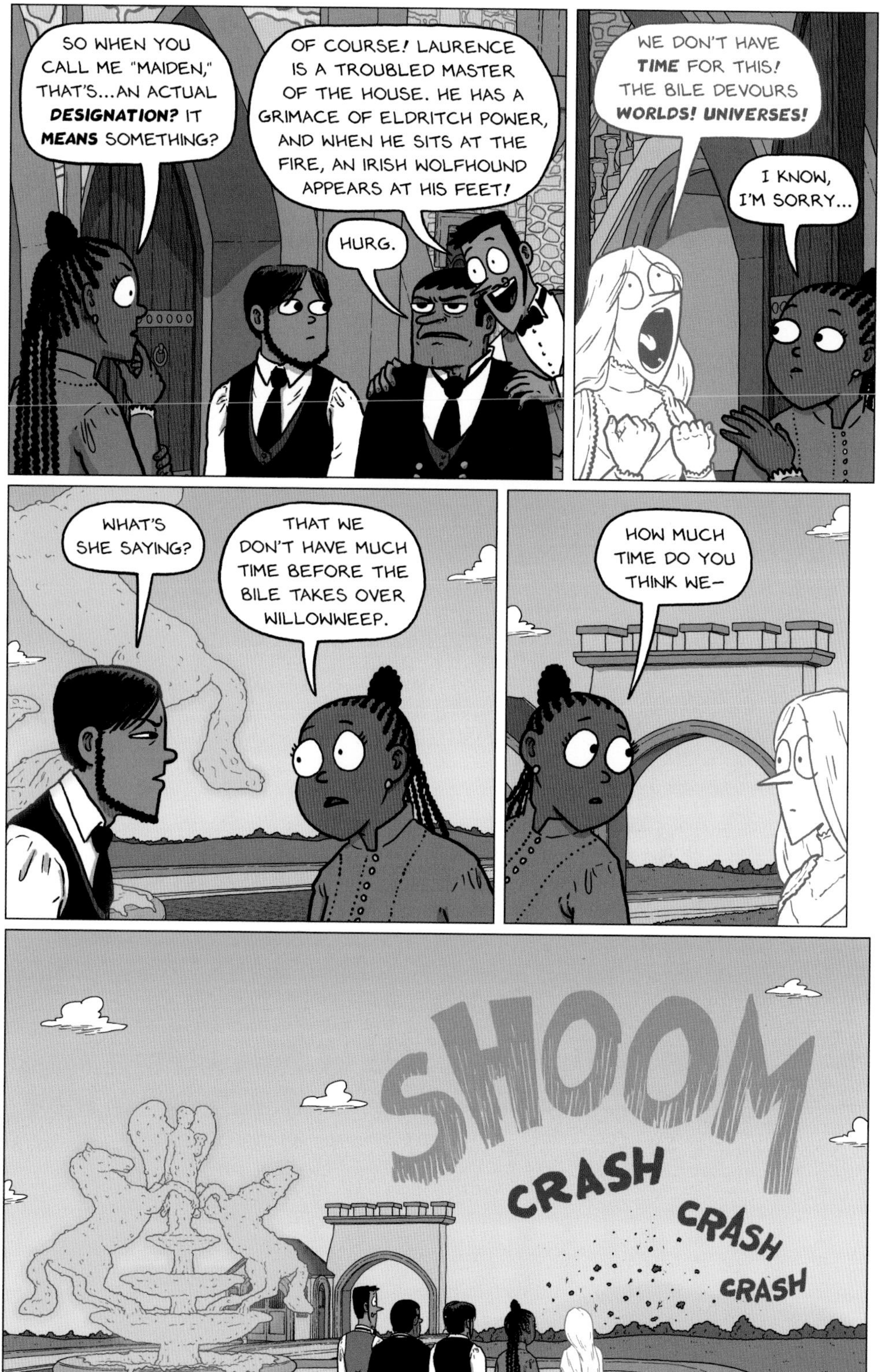

SO WHEN YOU CALL ME "MAIDEN," THAT'S...AN ACTUAL **DESIGNATION?** IT **MEANS** SOMETHING?
OF COURSE! LAURENCE IS A TROUBLED MASTER OF THE HOUSE. HE HAS A GRIMACE OF ELDRITCH POWER, AND WHEN HE SITS AT THE FIRE, AN IRISH WOLFHOUND APPEARS AT HIS FEET!
HURG.
WE DON'T HAVE **TIME** FOR THIS! THE BILE DEVOURS **WORLDS! UNIVERSES!**
I KNOW, I'M SORRY...
WHAT'S SHE SAYING?
THAT WE DON'T HAVE MUCH TIME BEFORE THE BILE TAKES OVER WILLOWWEEP.
HOW MUCH TIME DO YOU THINK WE—
SHOOM
CRASH
CRASH
CRASH

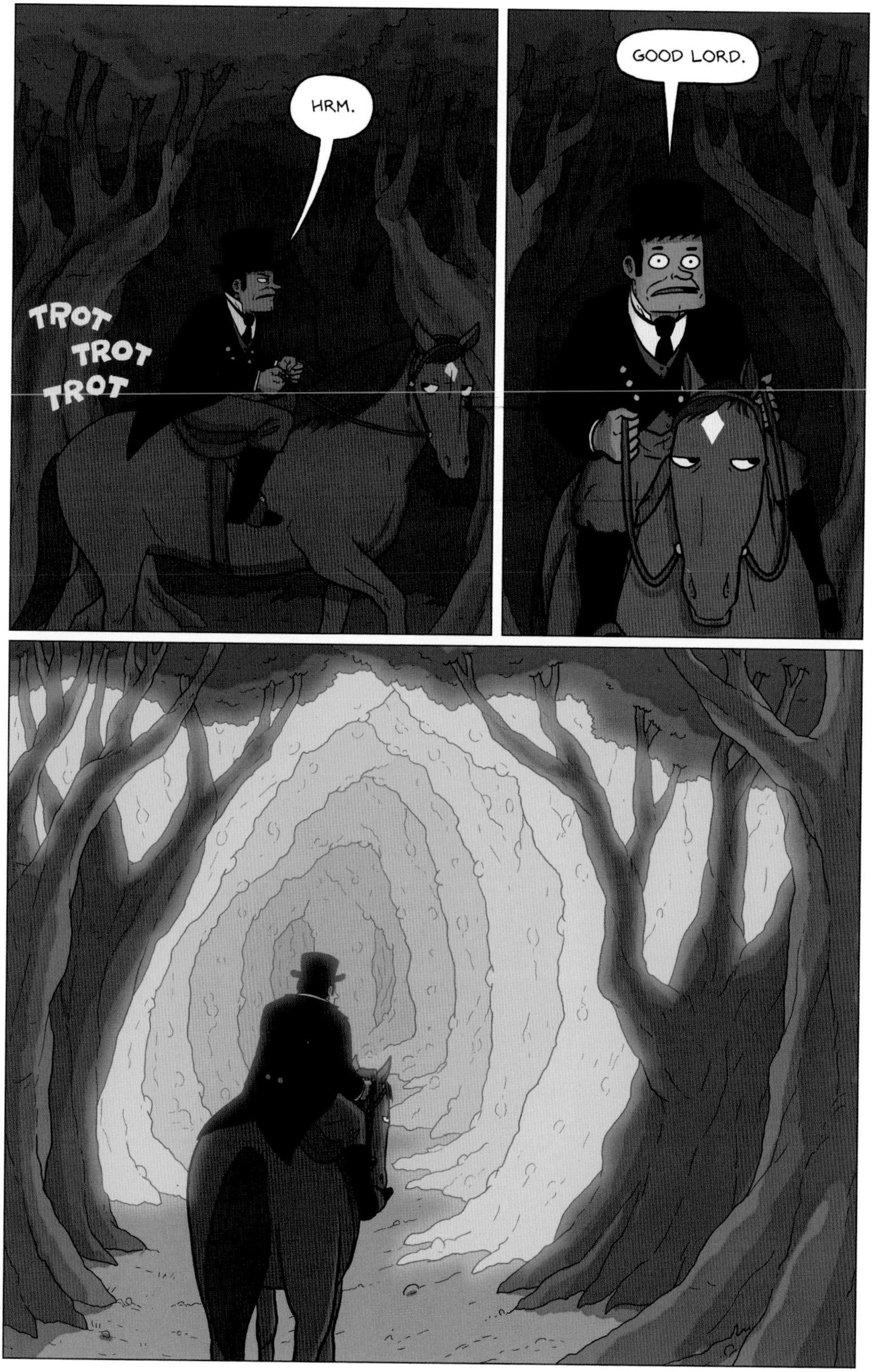
HRM.
TROT
TROT
TROT
GOOD LORD.

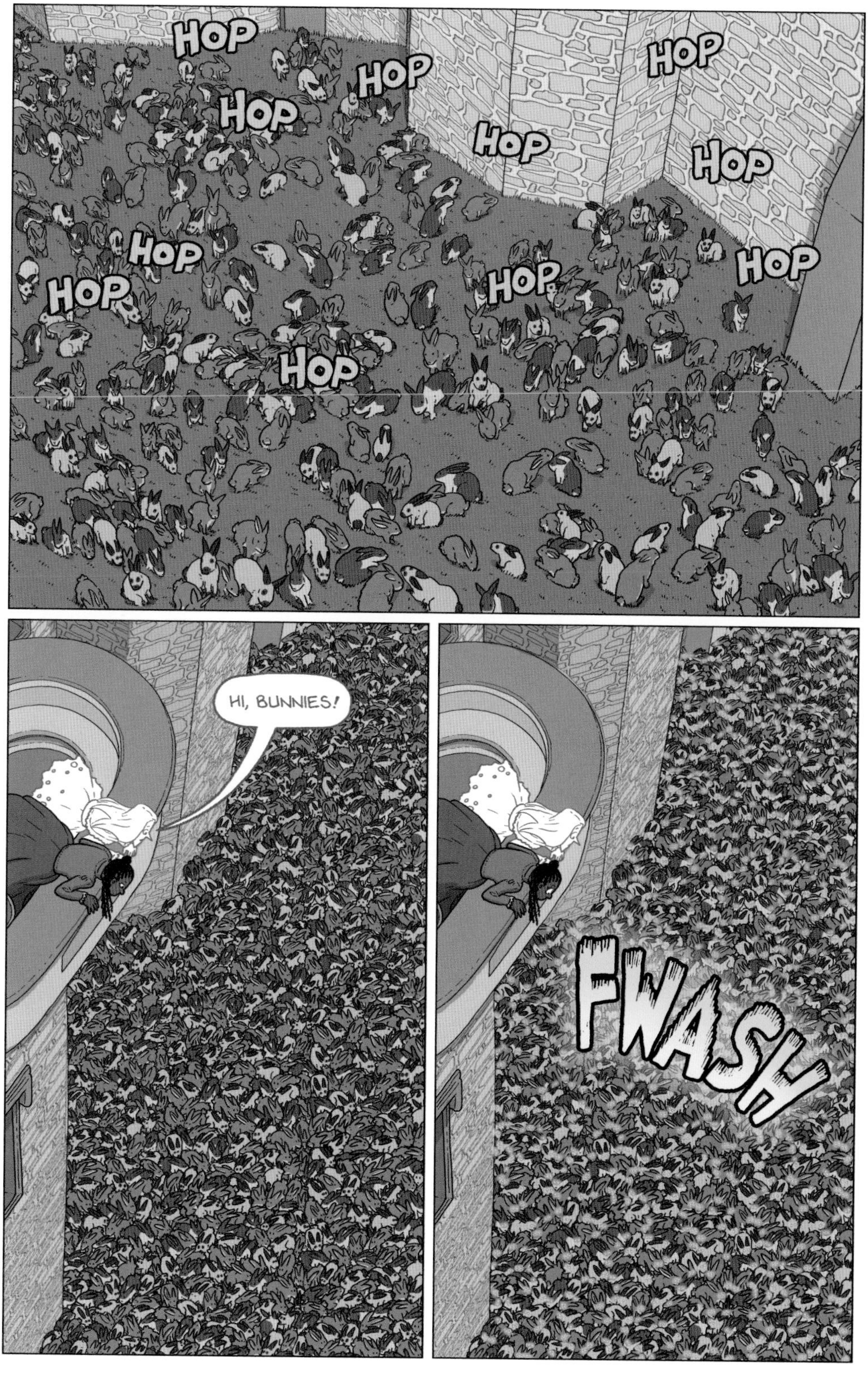
HOP
HOP
HOP
HOP
HOP
HOP
HOP
HOP
HOP
HOP
HOP
HI, BUNNIES!
FWASH

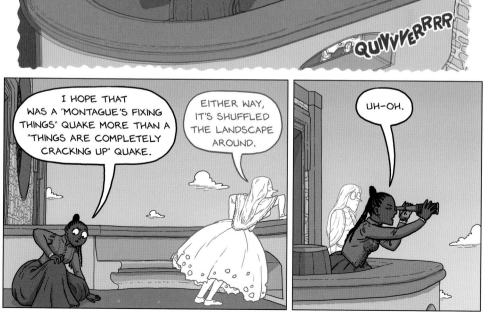

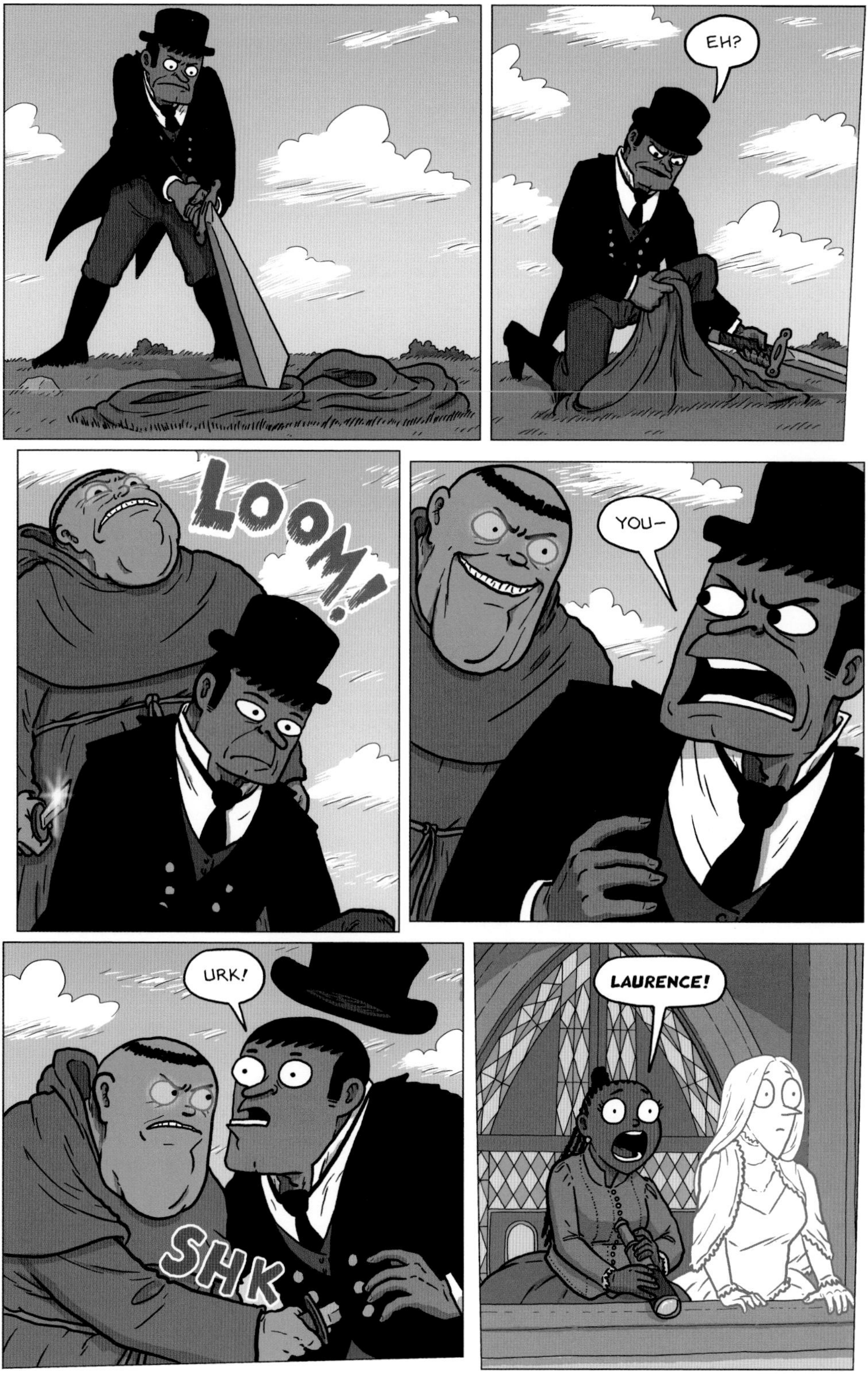
EH?
LOOM!
YOU—
URK!
SHK
LAURENCE!

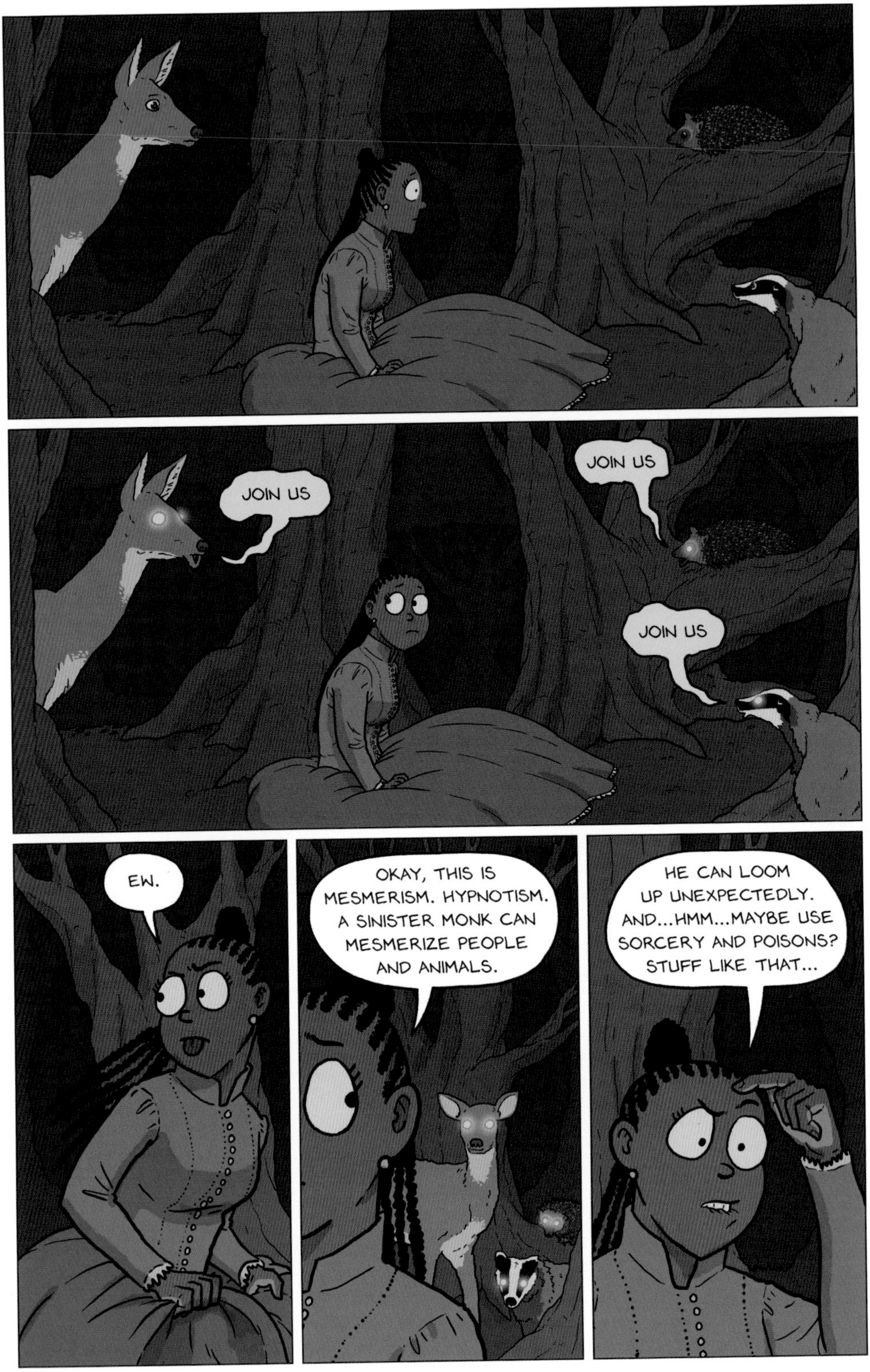
JOIN US
JOIN US
JOIN US
EW.
OKAY, THIS IS MESMERISM. HYPNOTISM. A SINISTER MONK CAN MESMERIZE PEOPLE AND ANIMALS.
HE CAN LOOM UP UNEXPECTEDLY. AND...HMM...MAYBE USE SORCERY AND POISONS? STUFF LIKE THAT...

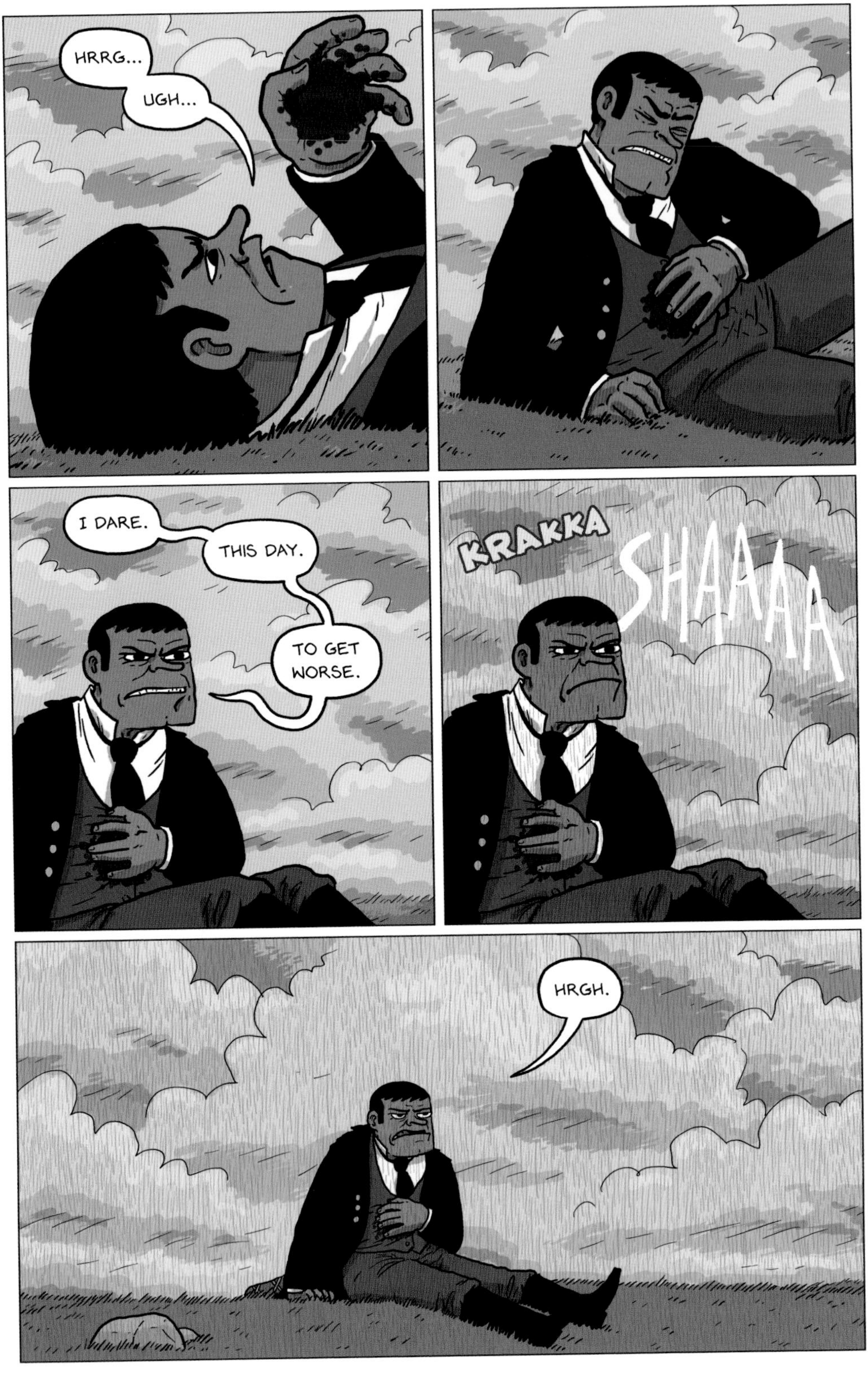
HRRG...
UGH...
I DARE.
THIS DAY.
TO GET WORSE.
KRAKKA
SHAAAAA
HRGH.

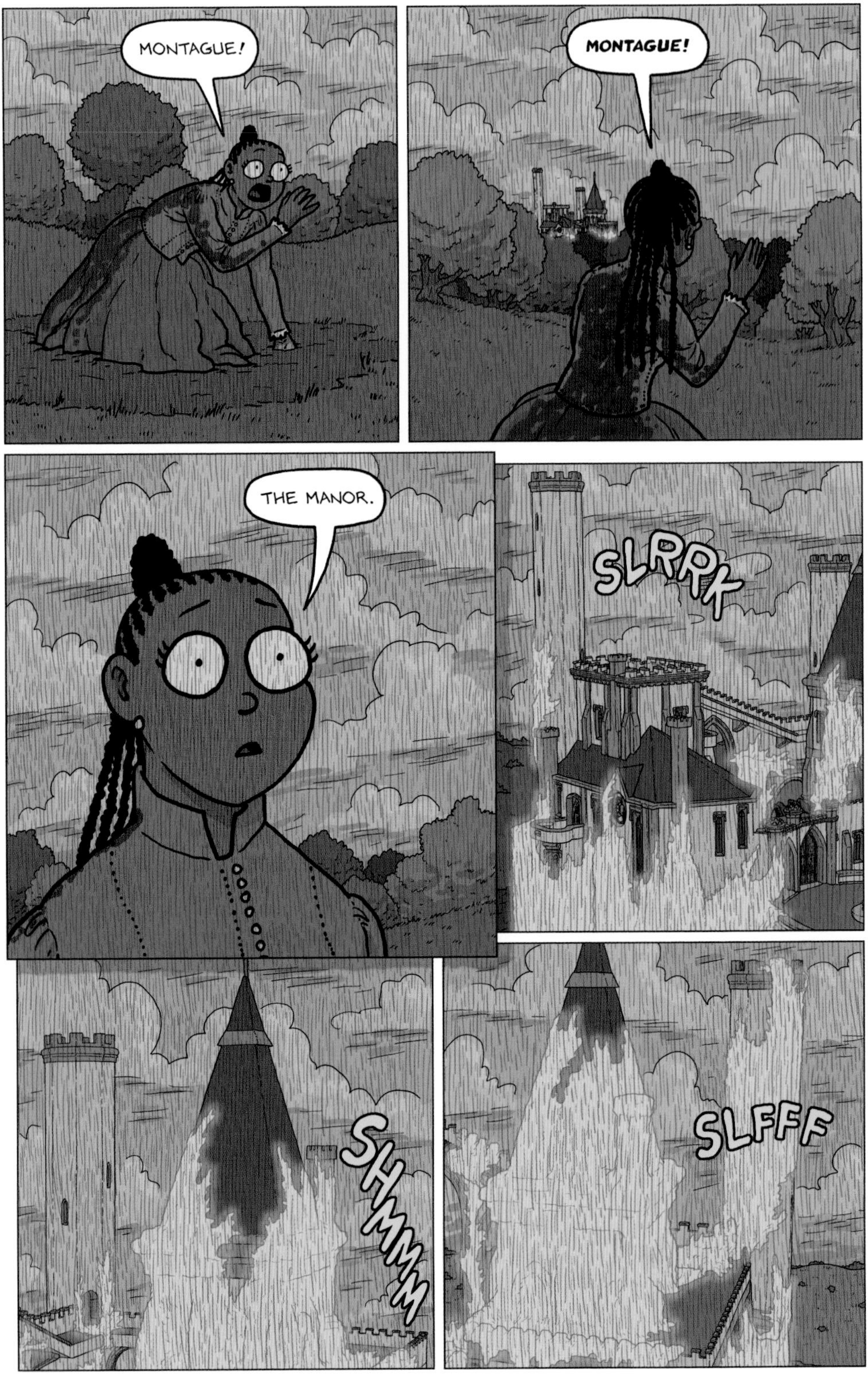
MONTAGUE!
MONTAGUE!
THE MANOR.
SLRRK
SHMMM
SLFFF

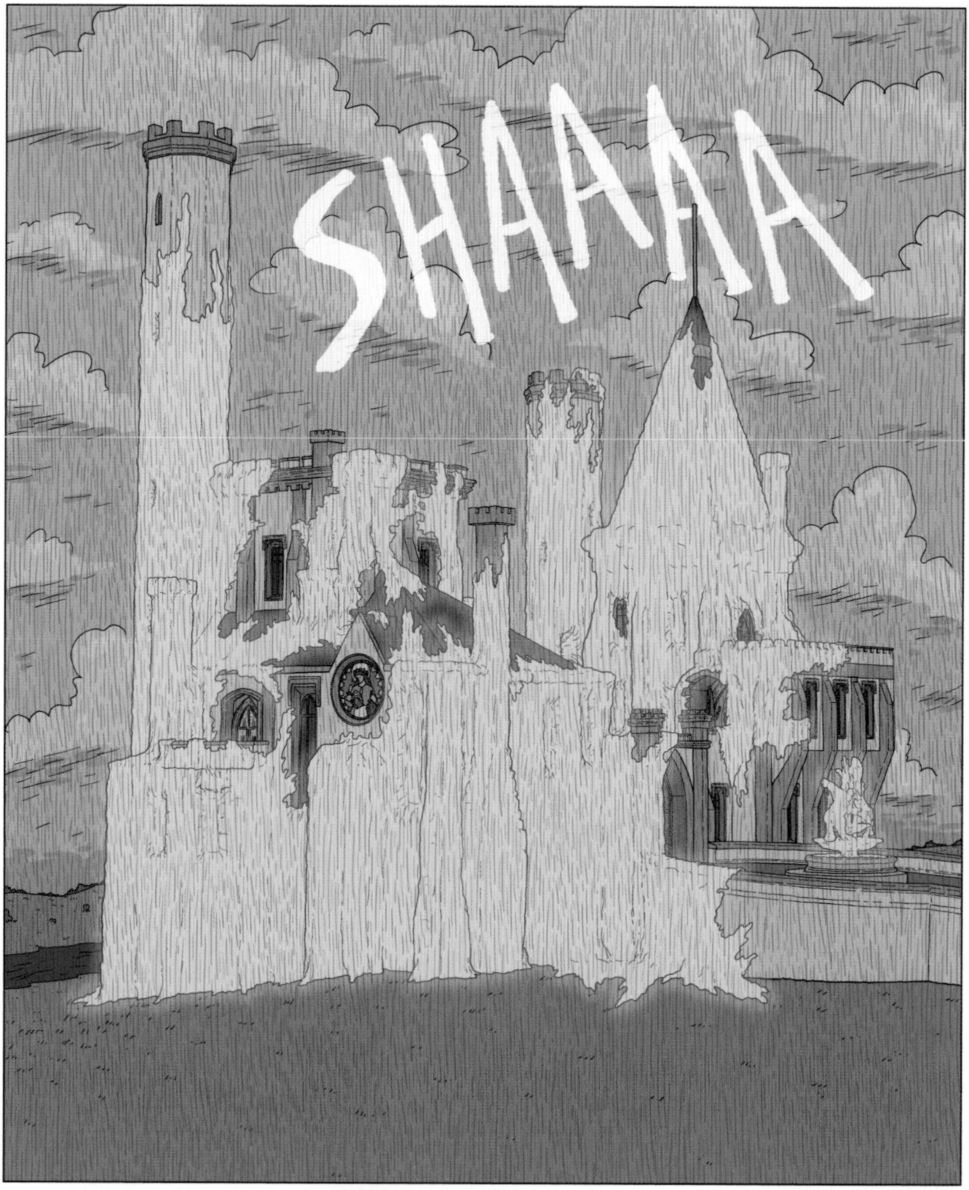
SHAAAA

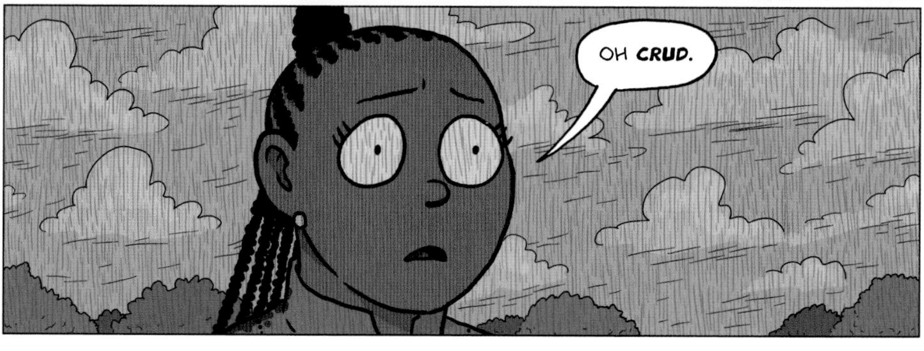
OH **CRUD.**

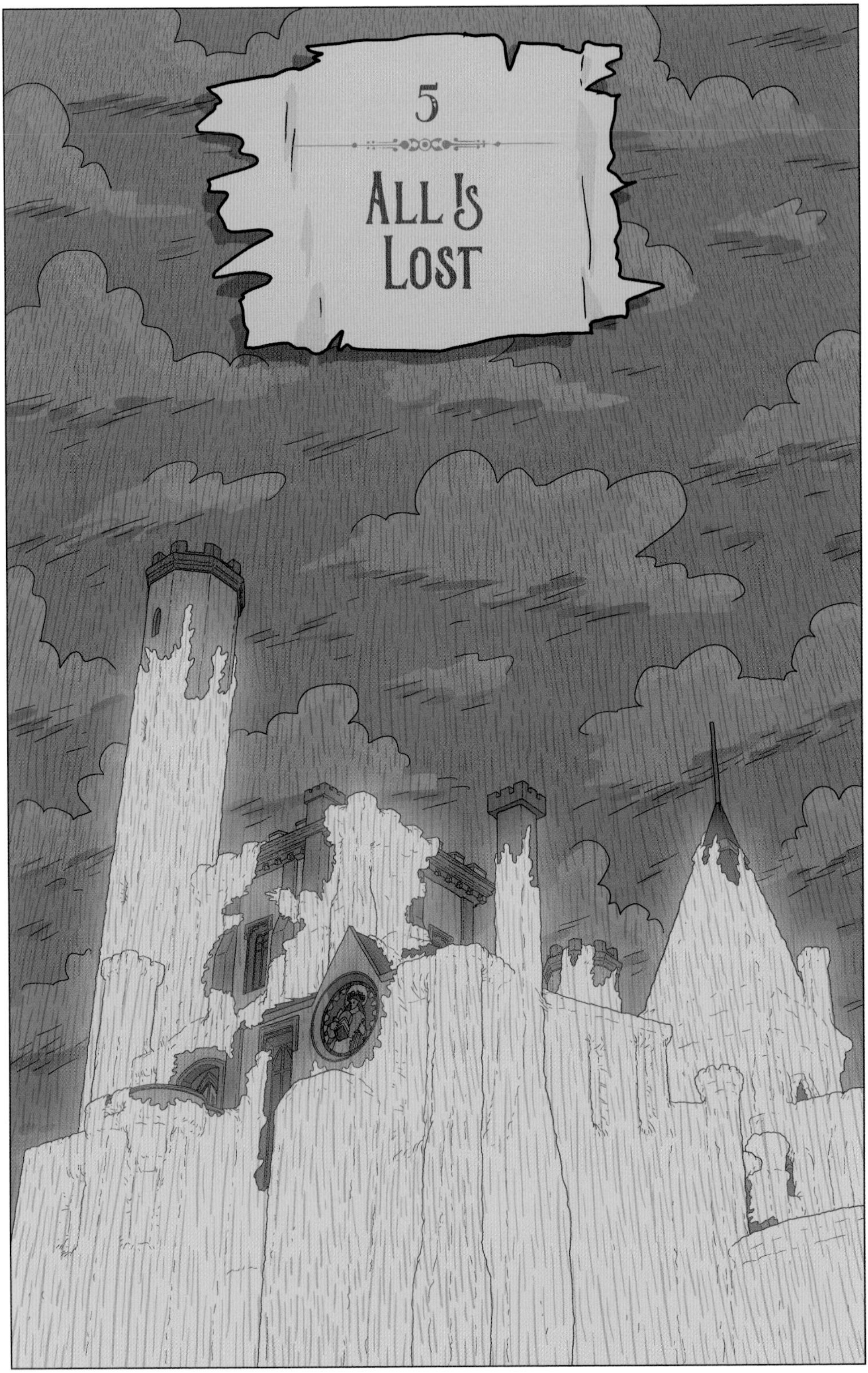
5
All Is Lost

6
A Desperate Stand

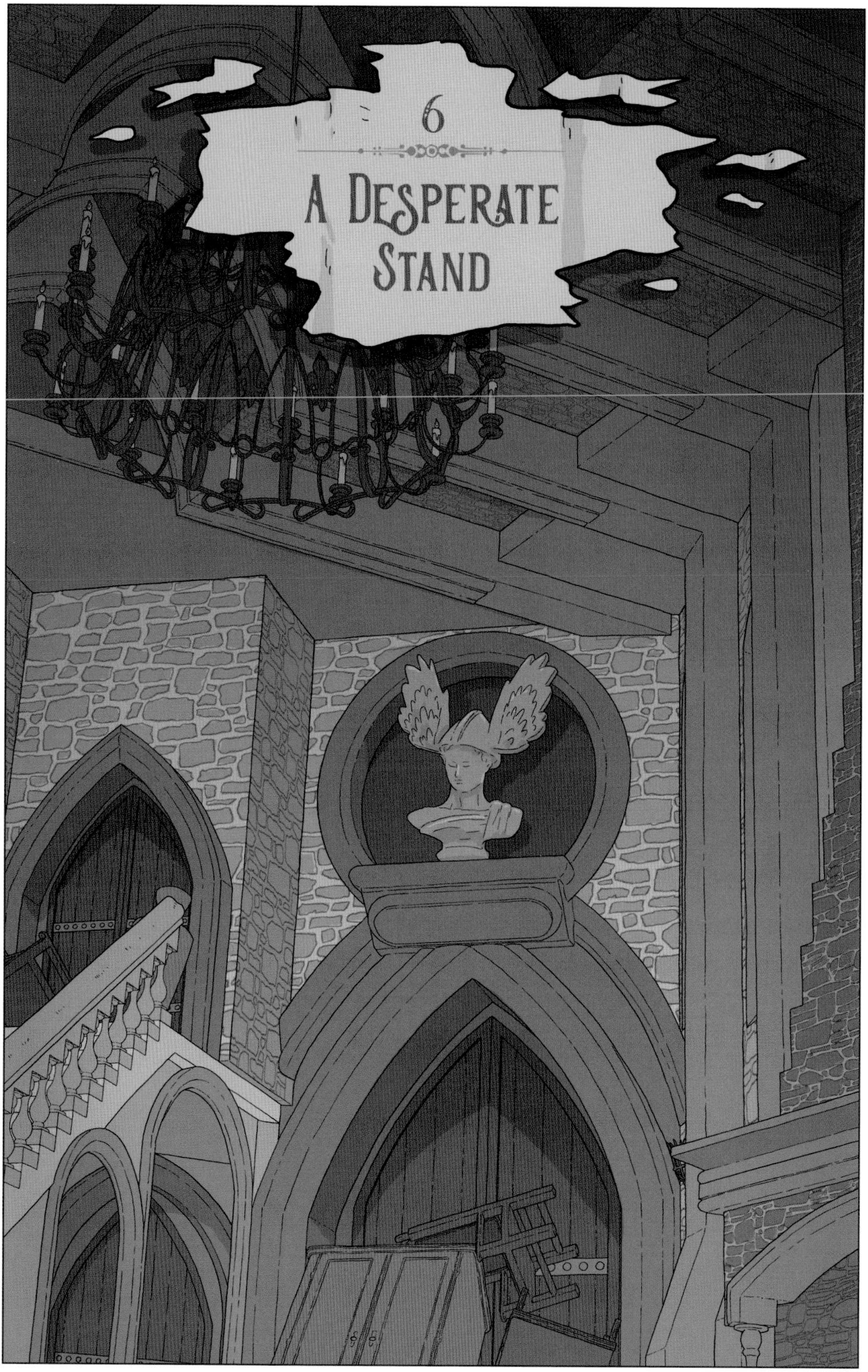

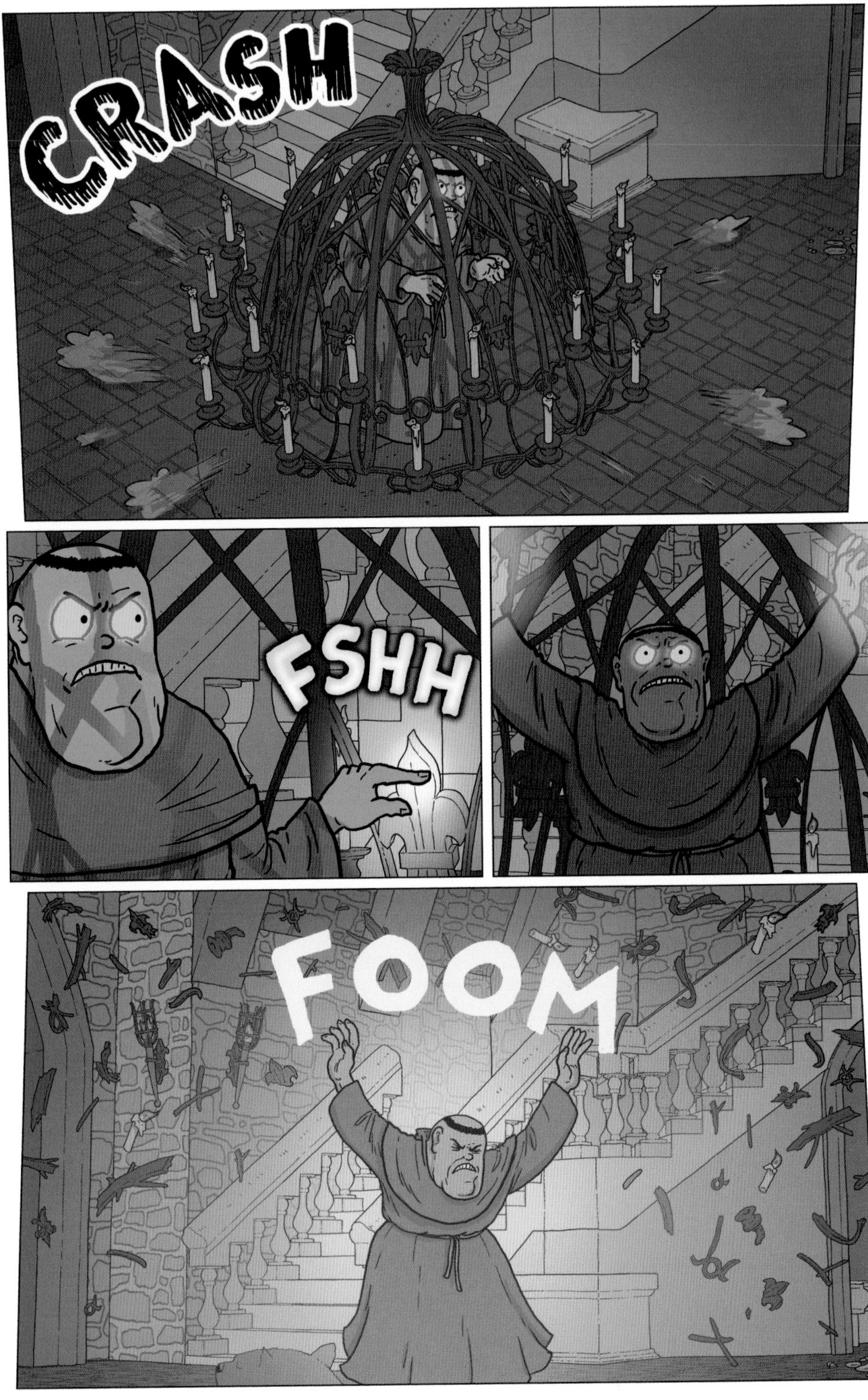
CRASH
FSHH
FOOM

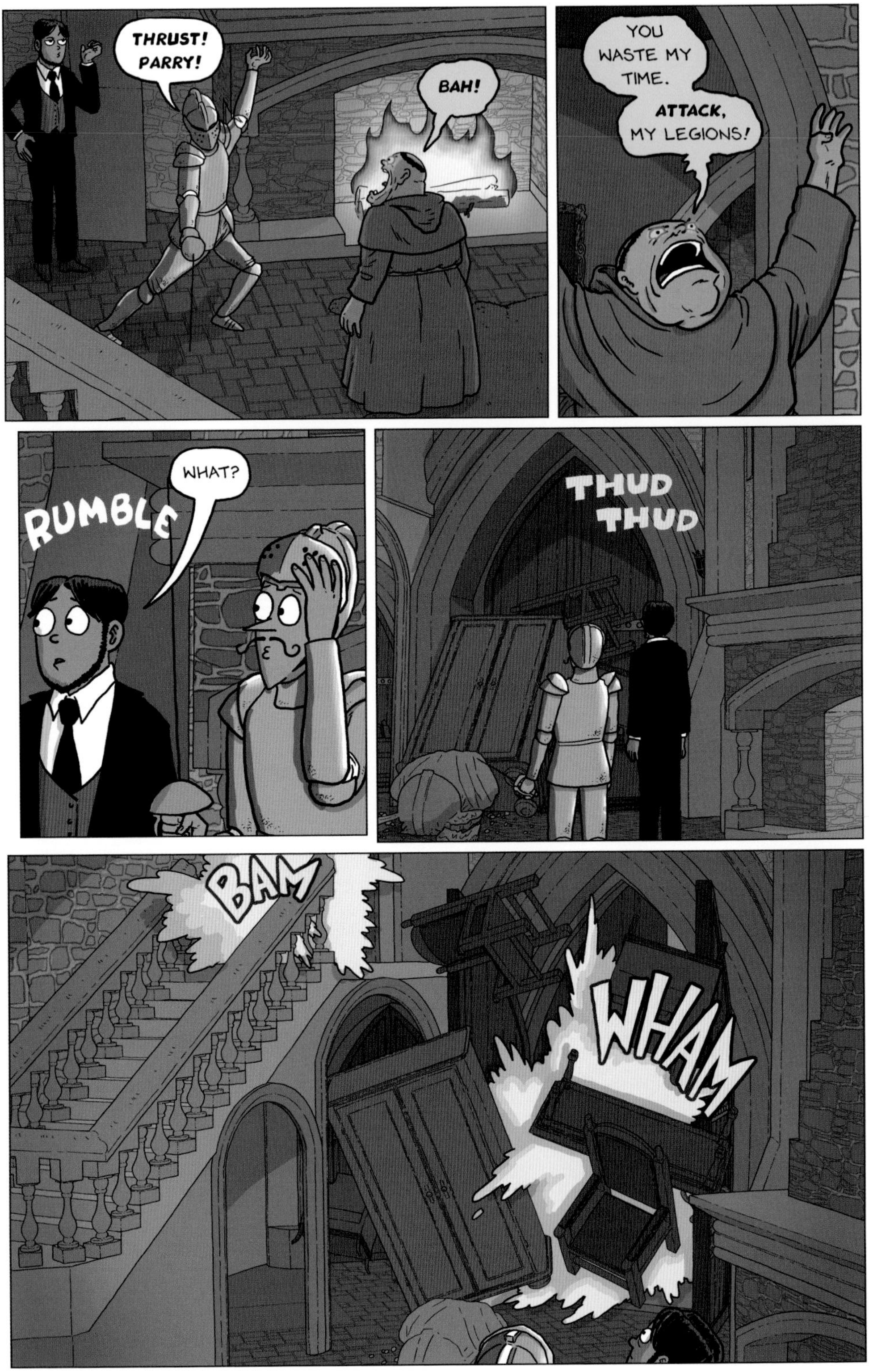
THRUST! PARRY!
BAH!
YOU WASTE MY TIME.
ATTACK, MY LEGIONS!
RUMBLE
WHAT?
THUD THUD
BAM
WHAM

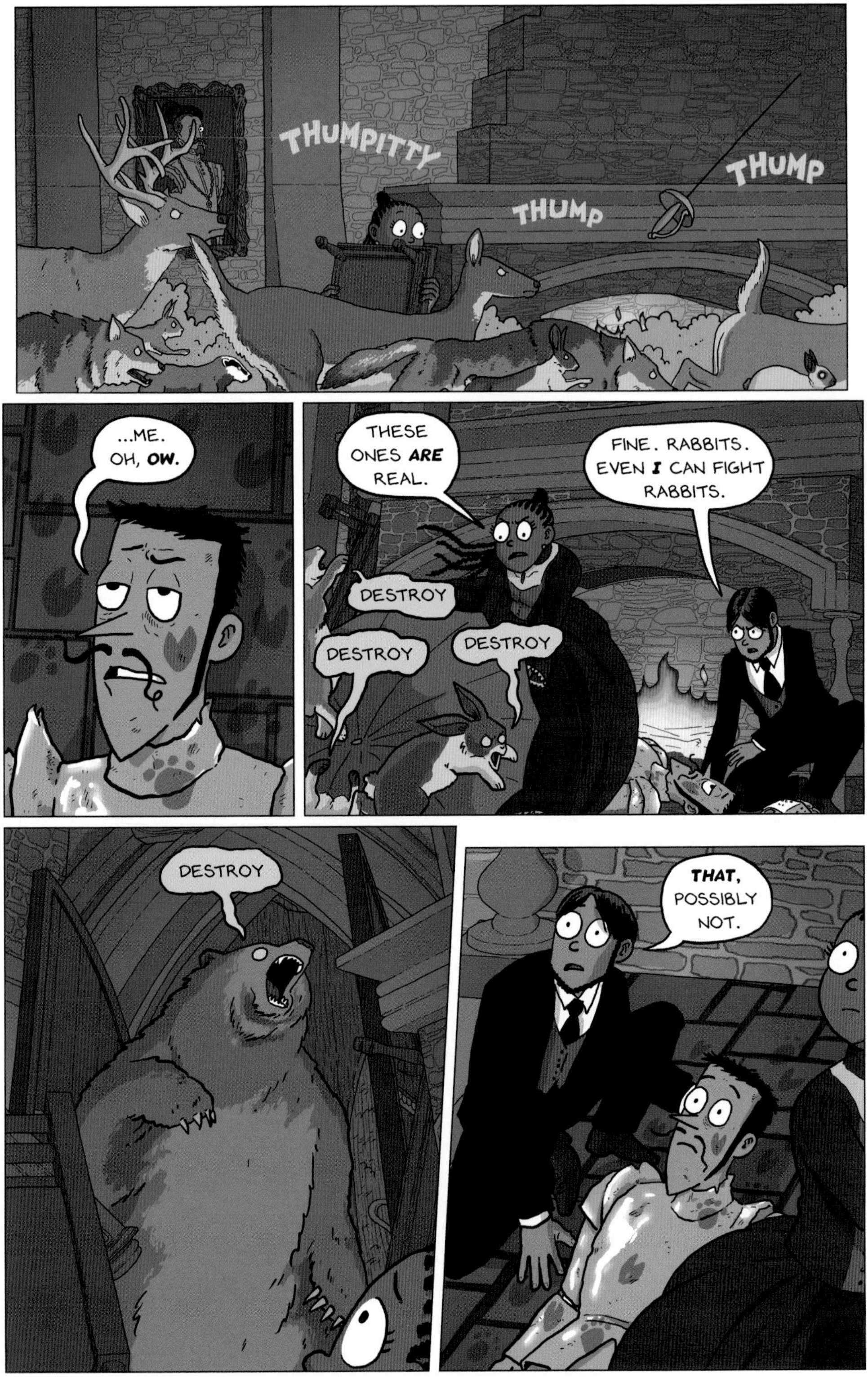
THUMPITTY
THUMP
THUMP
...ME. OH, **OW.**
THESE ONES **ARE** REAL.
DESTROY
DESTROY
DESTROY
FINE. RABBITS. EVEN **I** CAN FIGHT RABBITS.
DESTROY
THAT, POSSIBLY NOT.

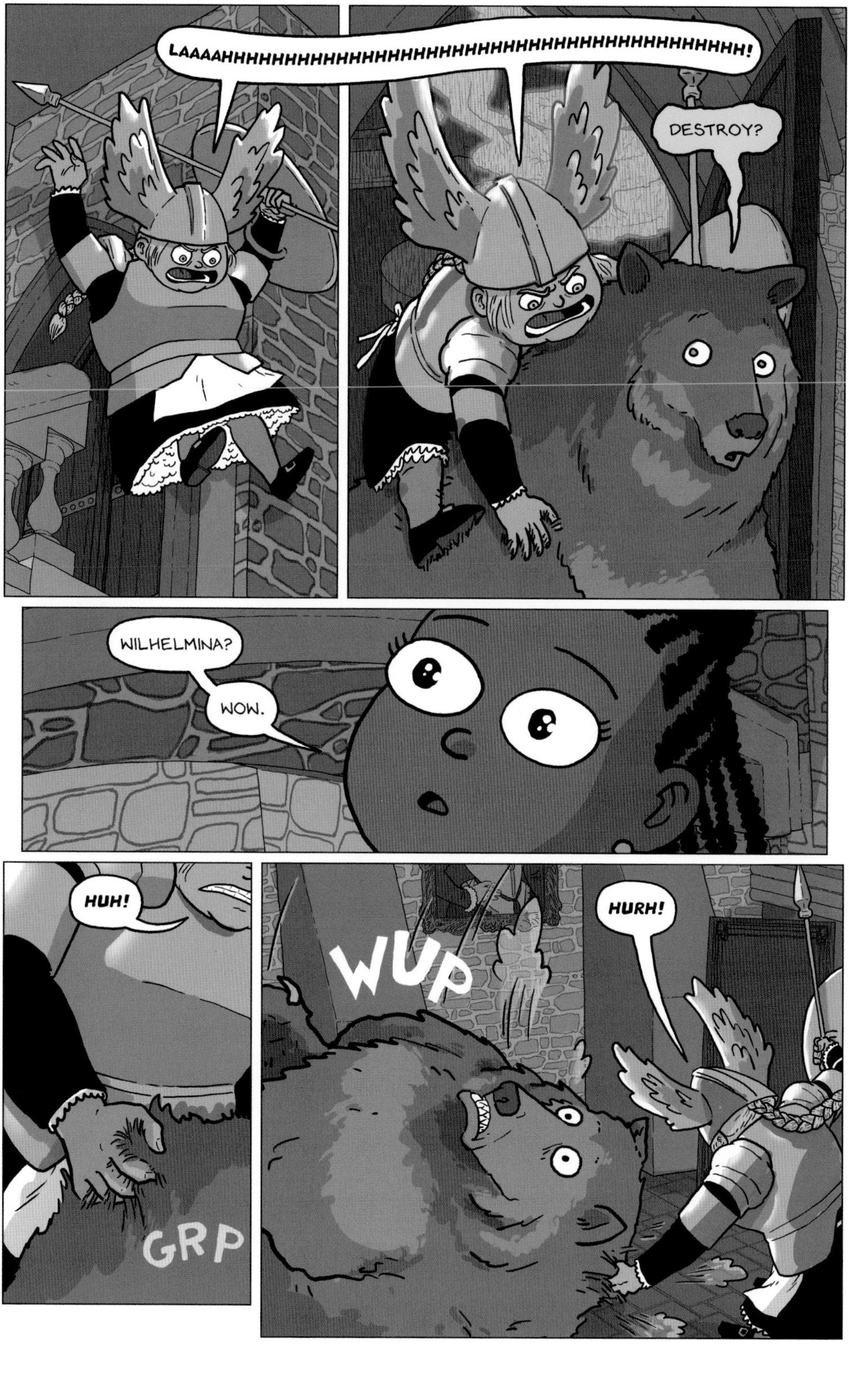
LAAAAHHHHHHHHHHHHHHHHHHHHHHHHHHHHHHHHHHHHHHHH!
DESTROY?
WILHELMINA?
WOW.
HUH!
GRP
HURH!
WUP

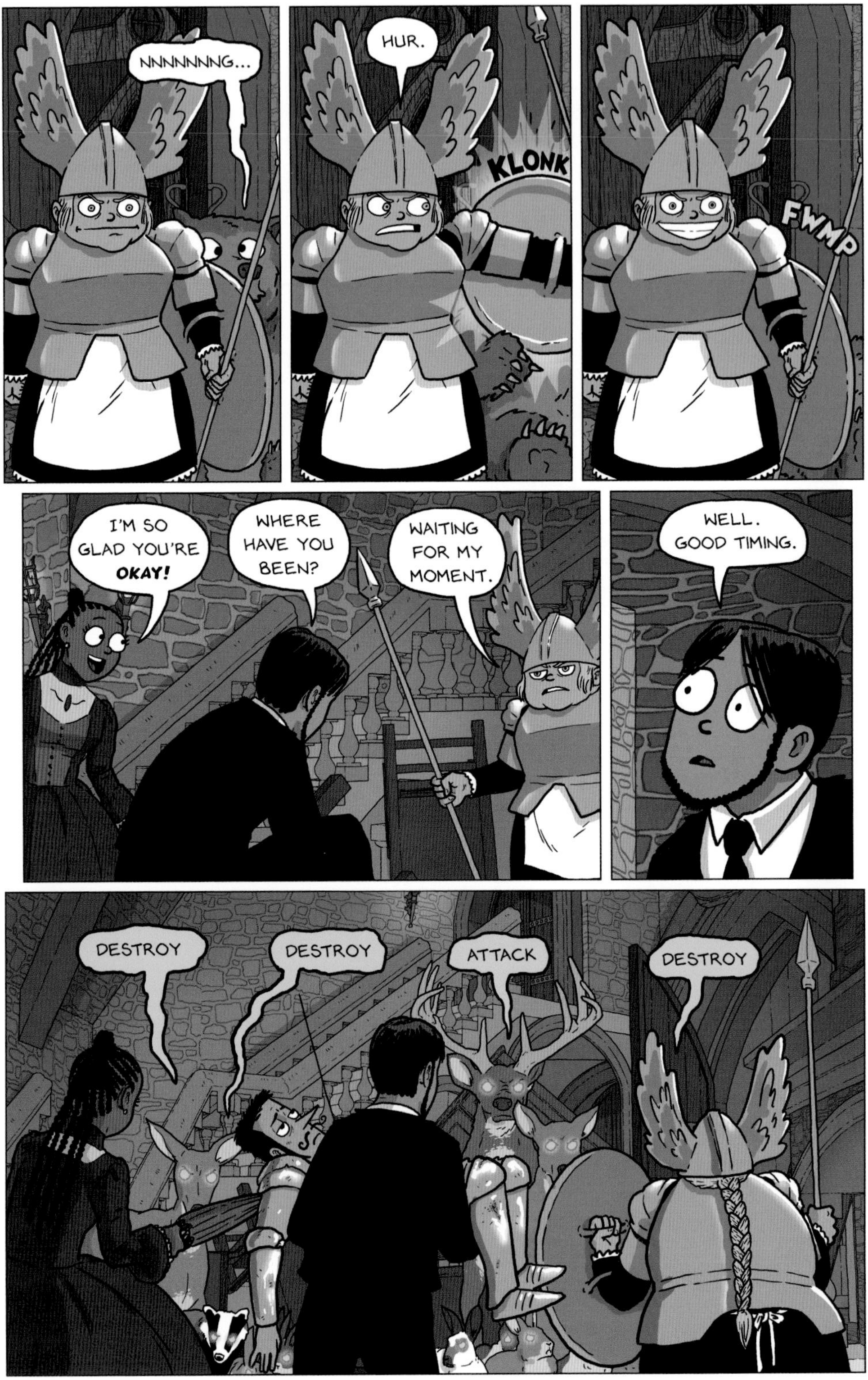
NNNNNNNG...
HUR.
KLONK
FWMP
I'M SO GLAD YOU'RE OKAY!
WHERE HAVE YOU BEEN?
WAITING FOR MY MOMENT.
WELL. GOOD TIMING.
DESTROY
DESTROY
ATTACK
DESTROY

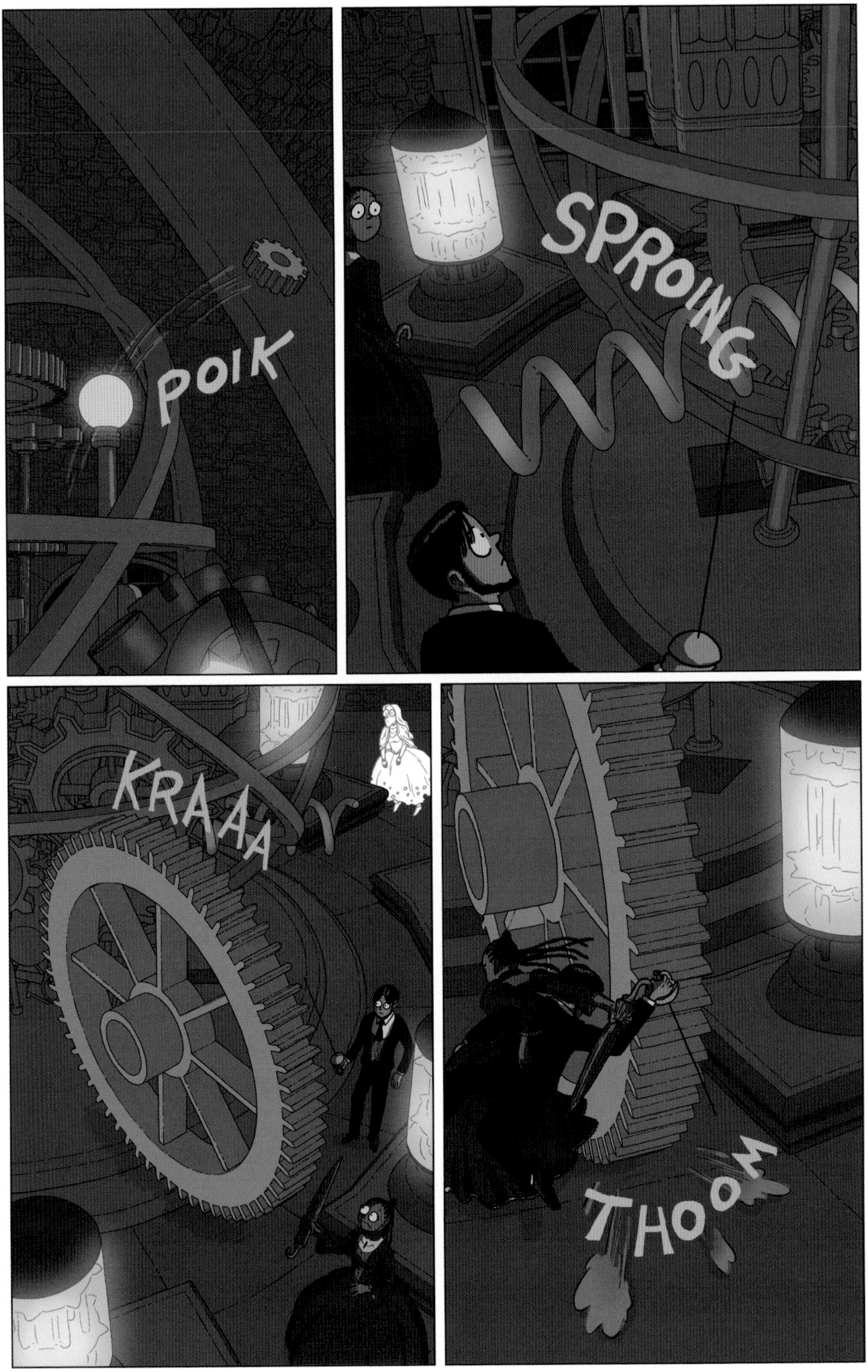
POIK
SPROING
KRAAA
THOOM

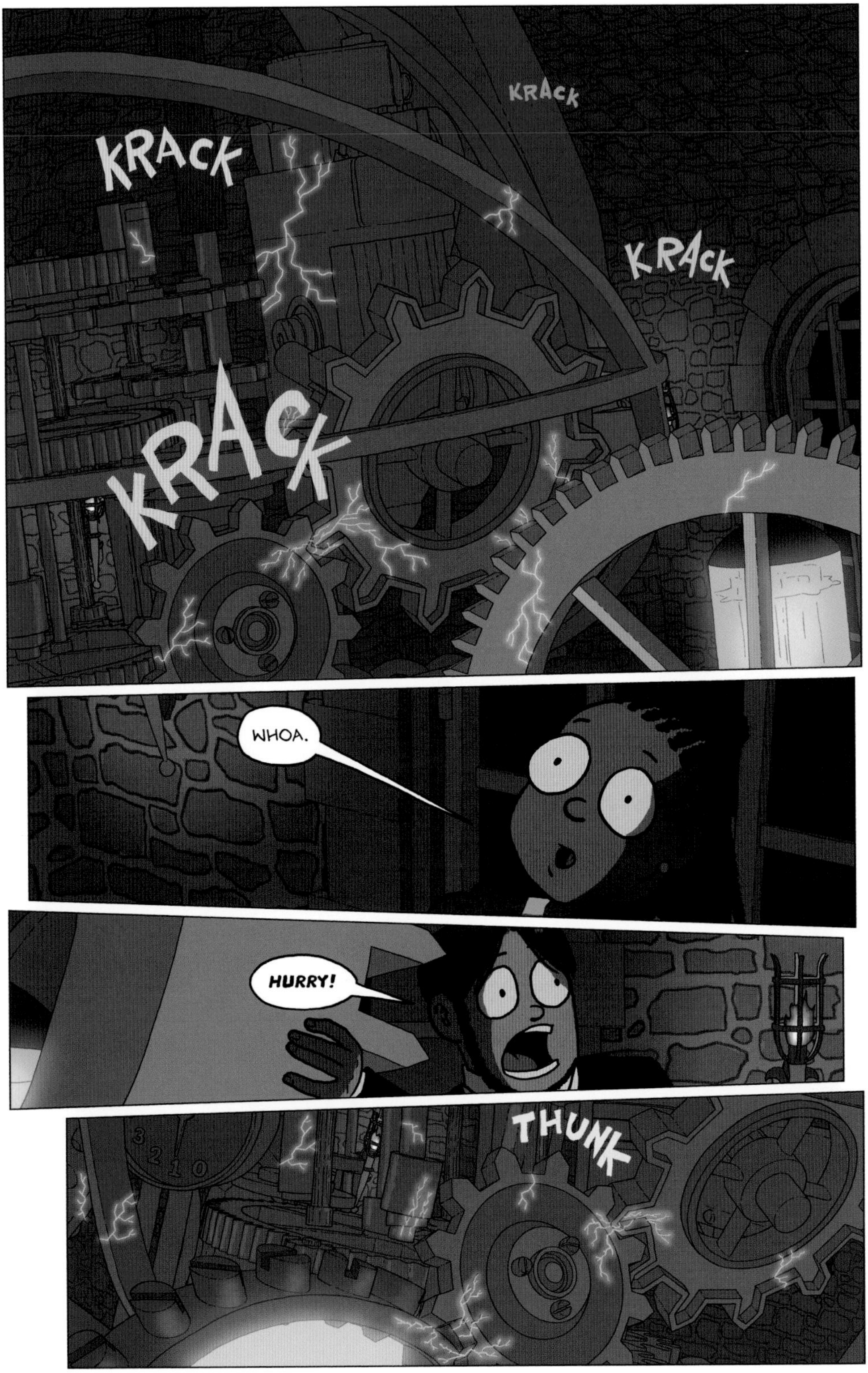
KRACK
KRACK
KRACK
KRACK
WHOA.
HURRY!
THUNK

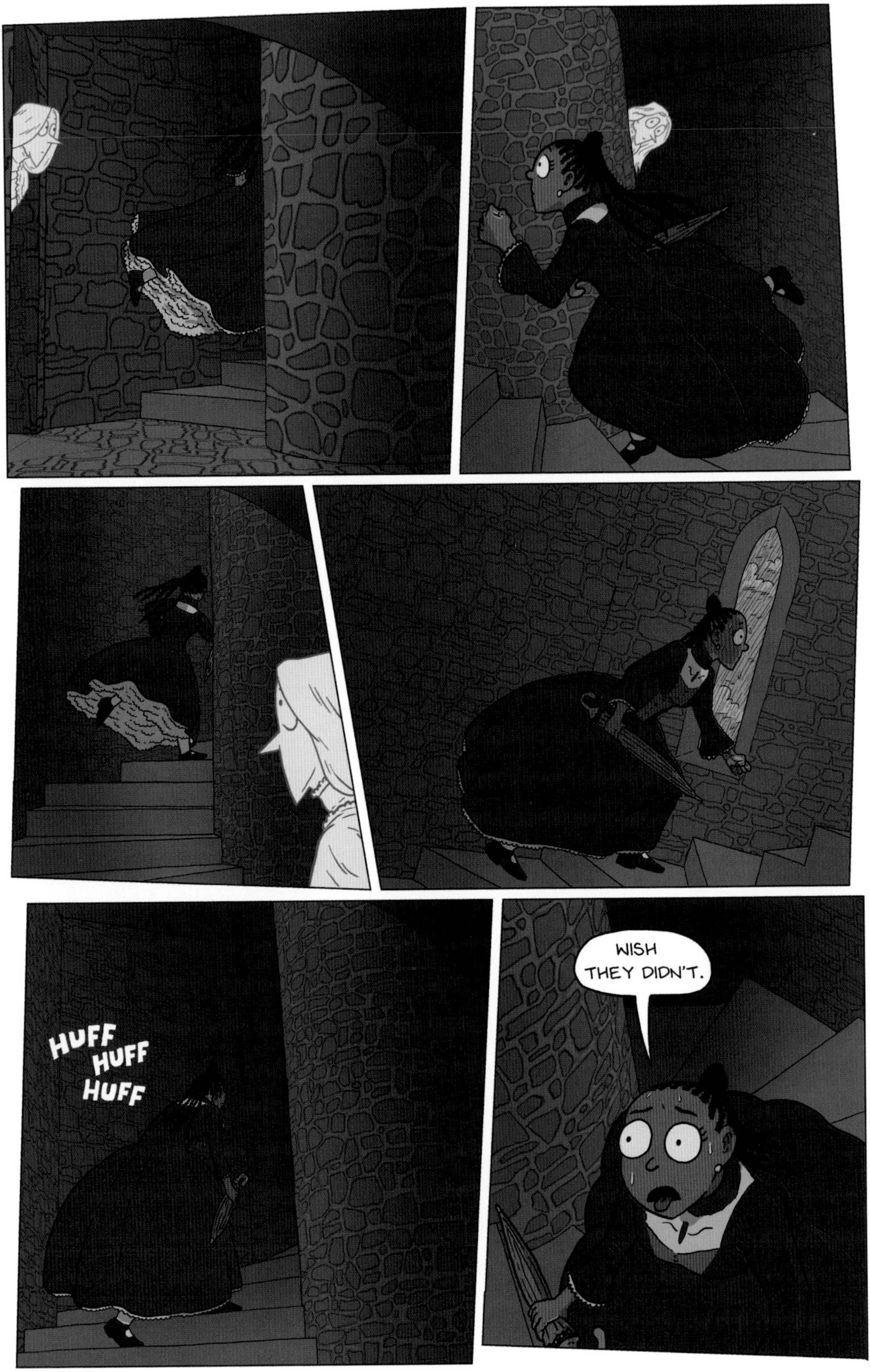
HUFF
HUFF
HUFF
WISH
THEY DIDN'T.

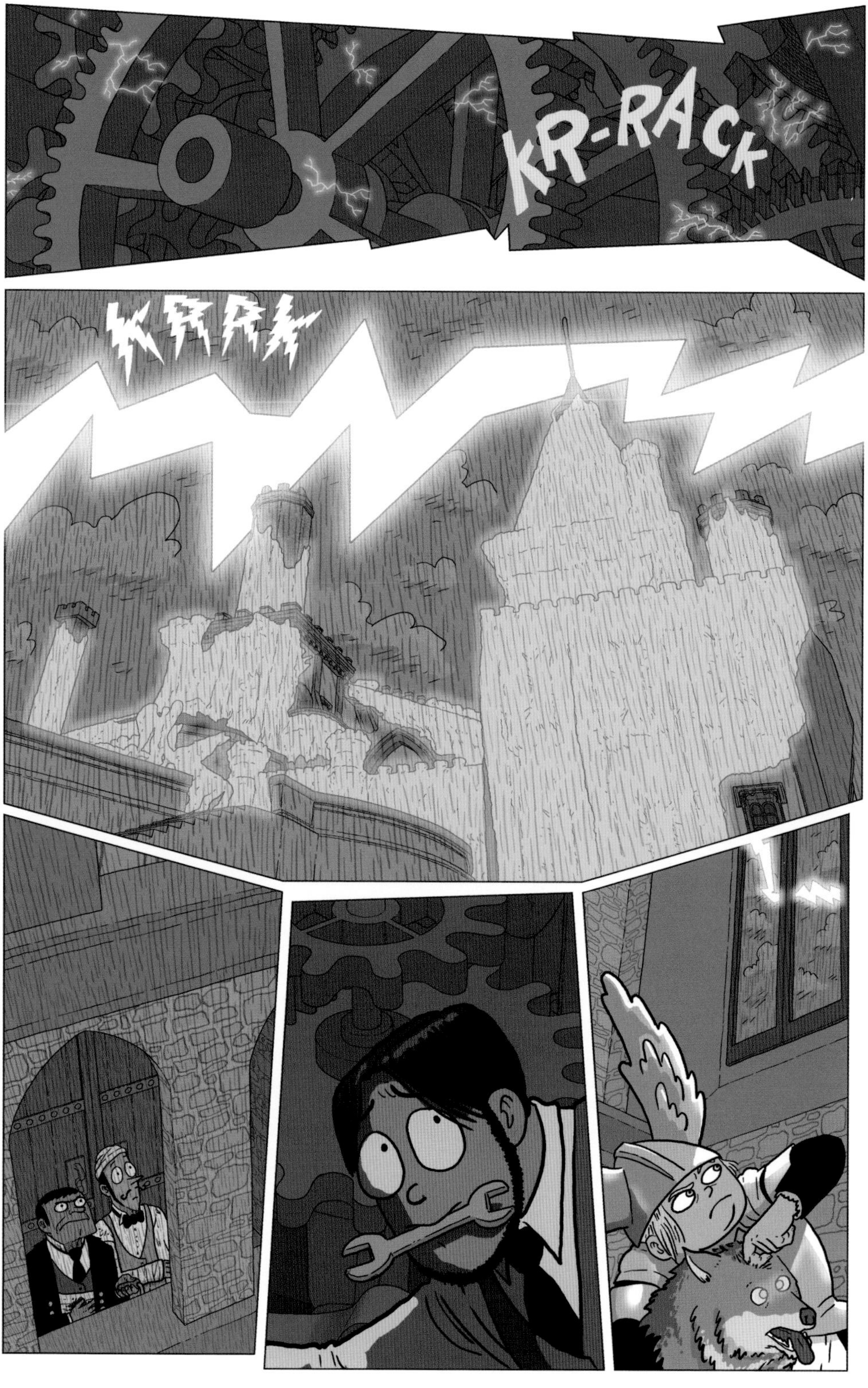
KR-RACK
KRRK

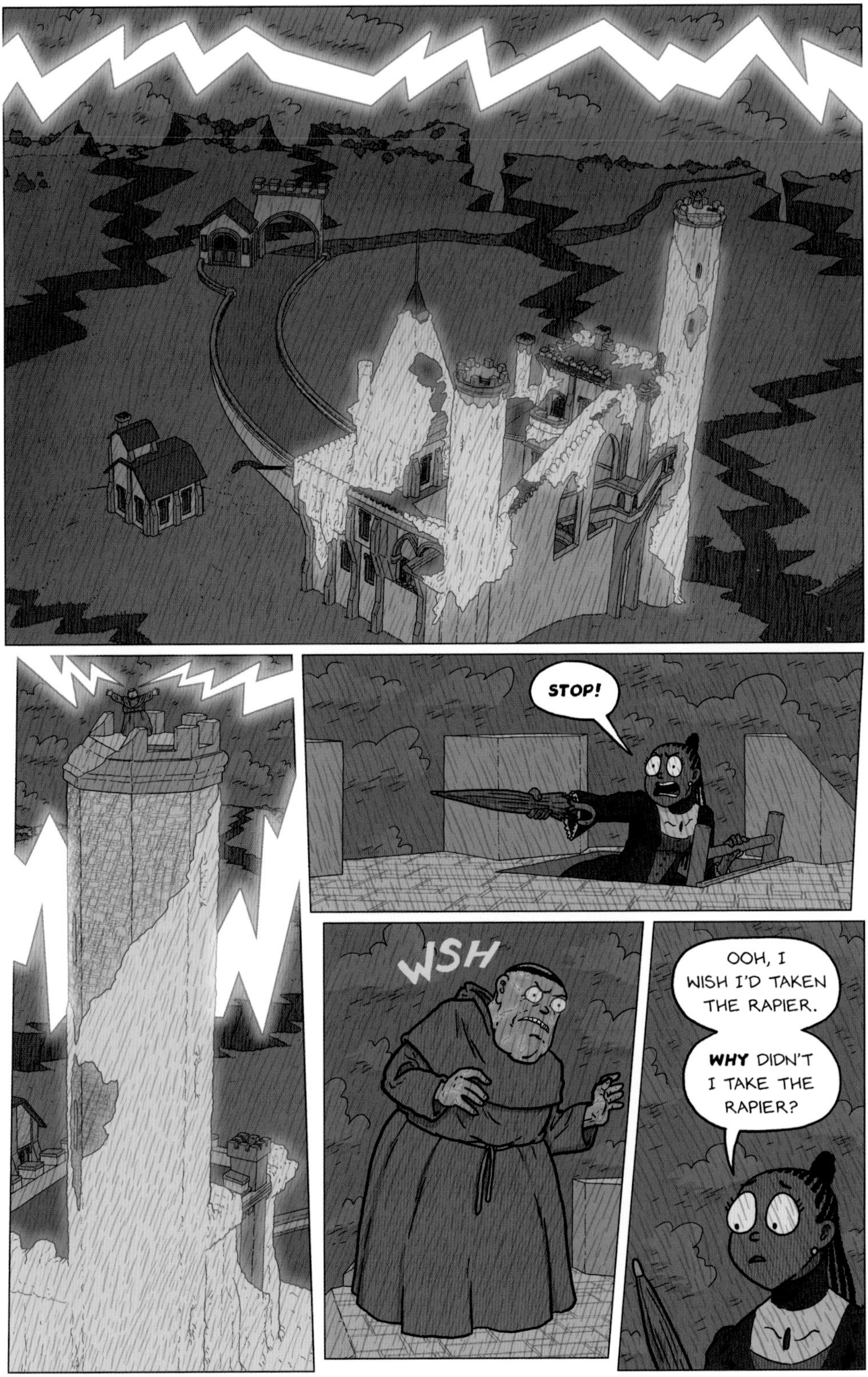
STOP!
WSH
OOH, I WISH I'D TAKEN THE RAPIER.
WHY DIDN'T I TAKE THE RAPIER?

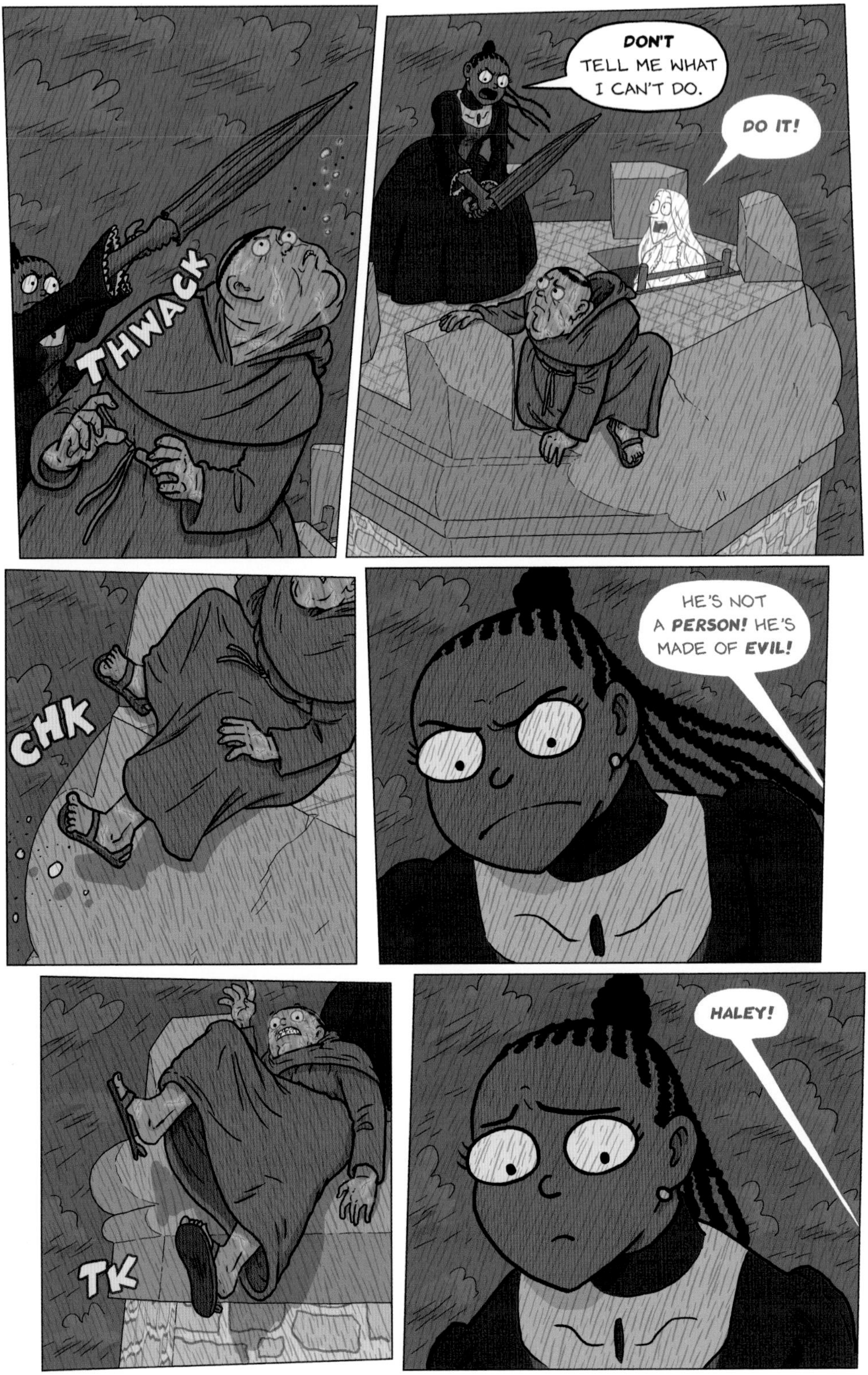
THWACK
DON'T TELL ME WHAT I CAN'T DO.
DO IT!
CHK
HE'S NOT A PERSON! HE'S MADE OF EVIL!
TK
HALEY!

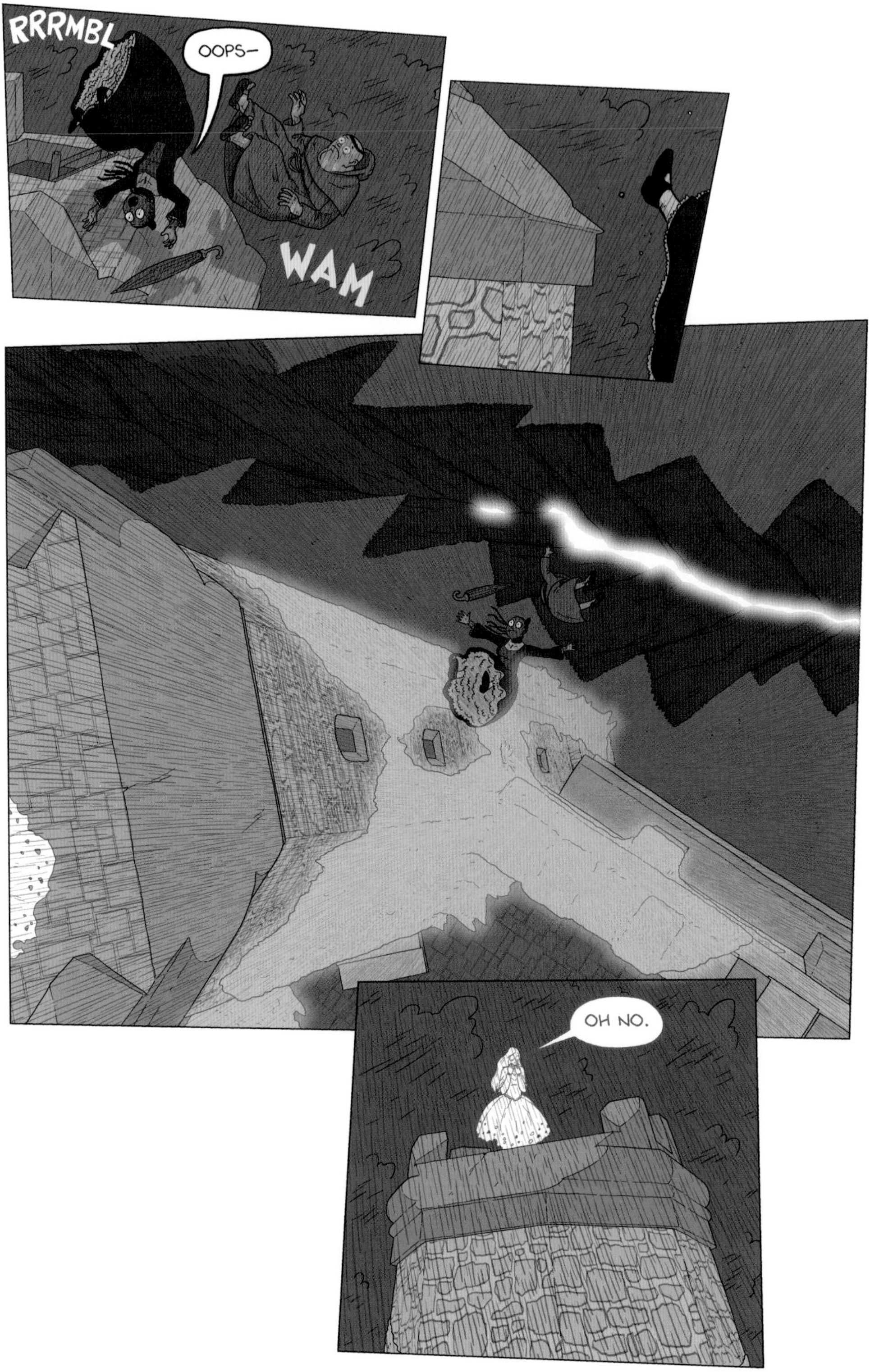
RRRMBL
OOPS—
WAM
OH NO.

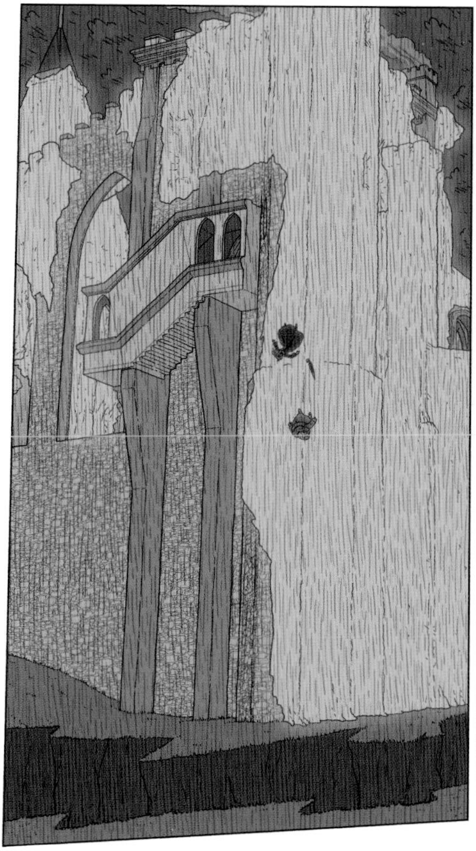

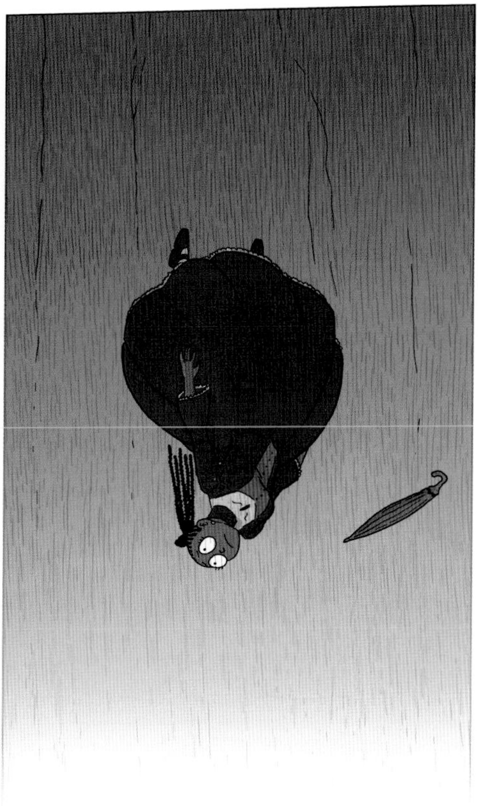

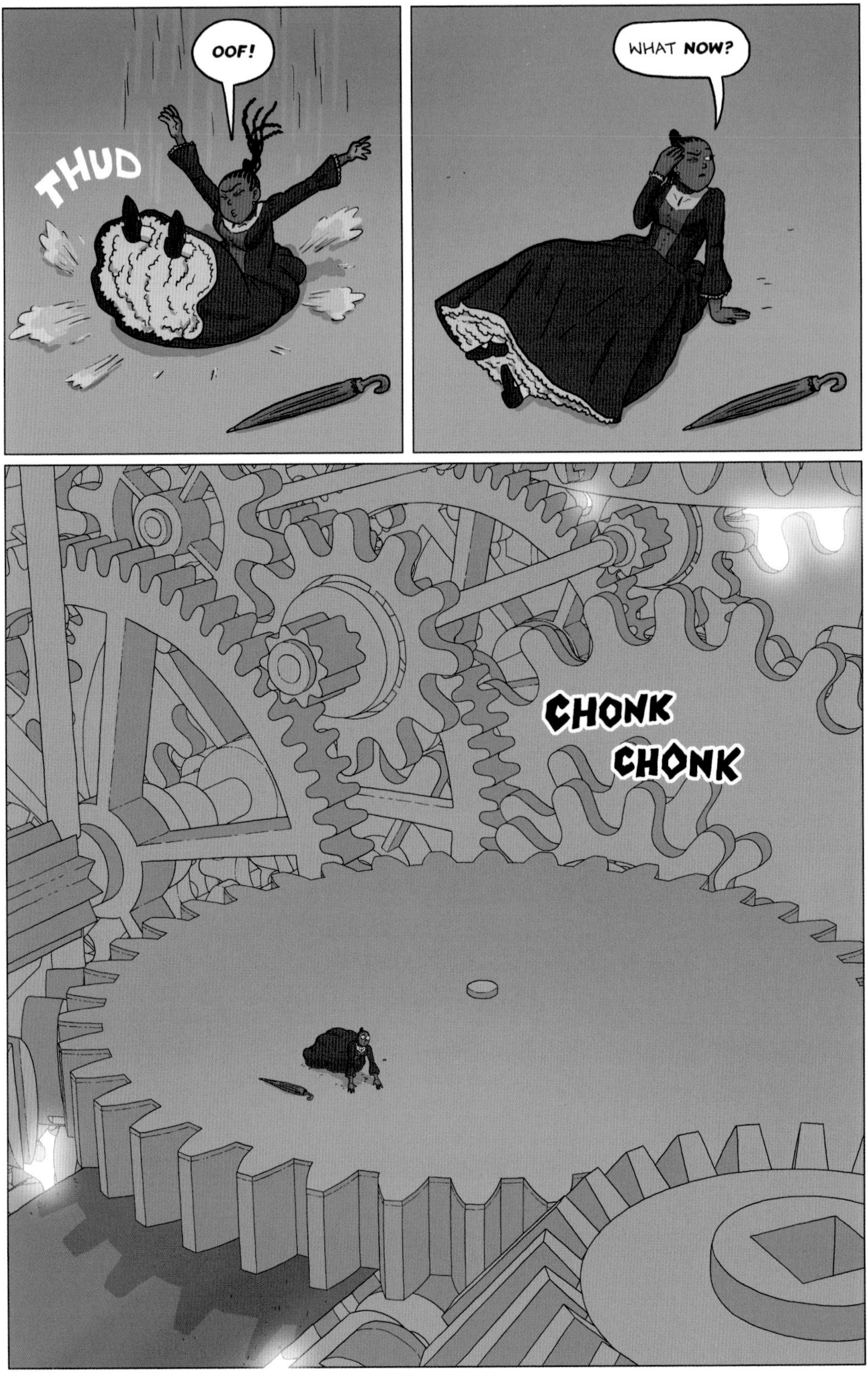
OOF!
THUD
WHAT NOW?
CHONK
CHONK

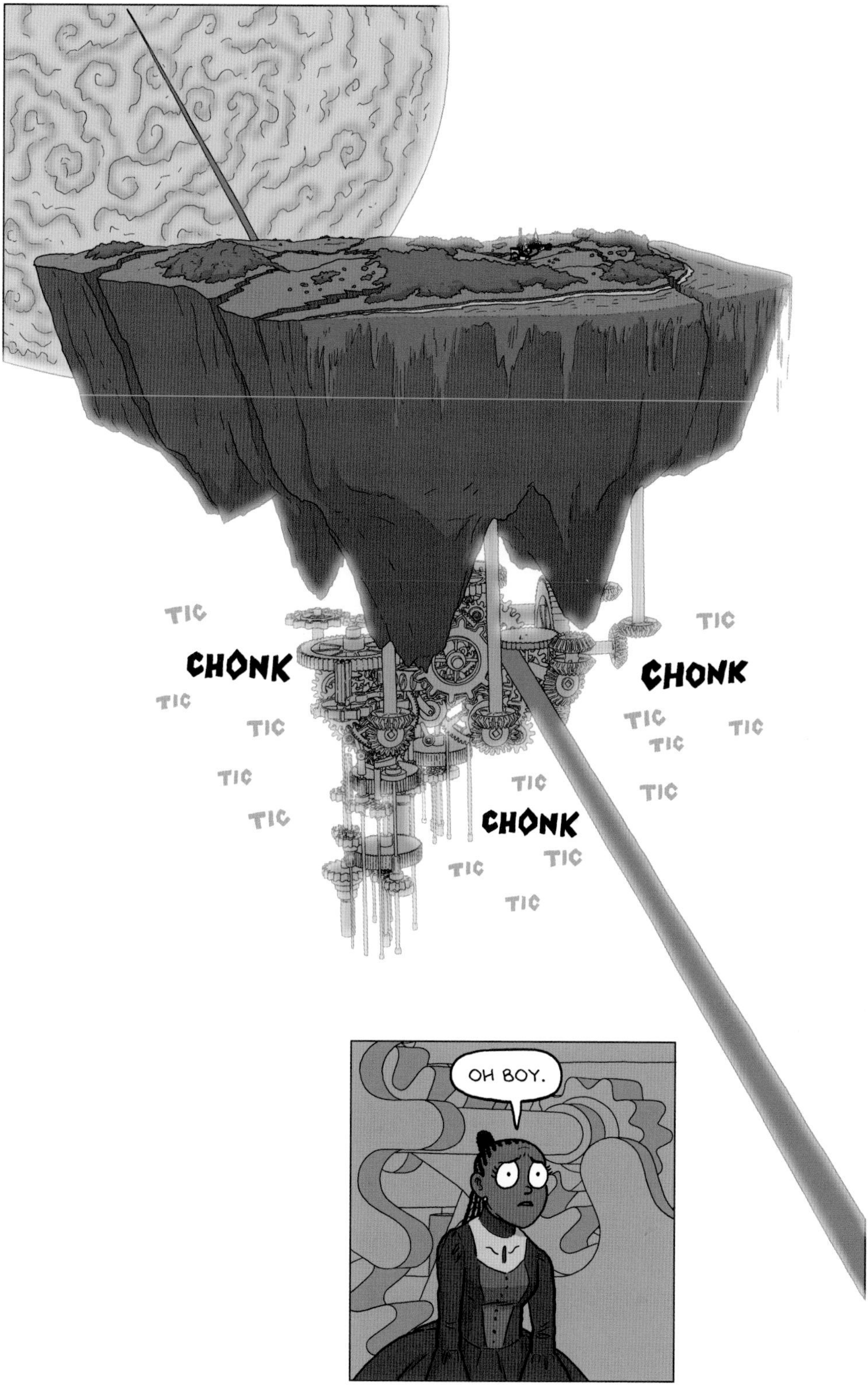
TIC
TIC
CHONK
CHONK
TIC
TIC
TIC
TIC
TIC
TIC
TIC
TIC
TIC
CHONK
TIC
TIC
TIC
OH BOY.

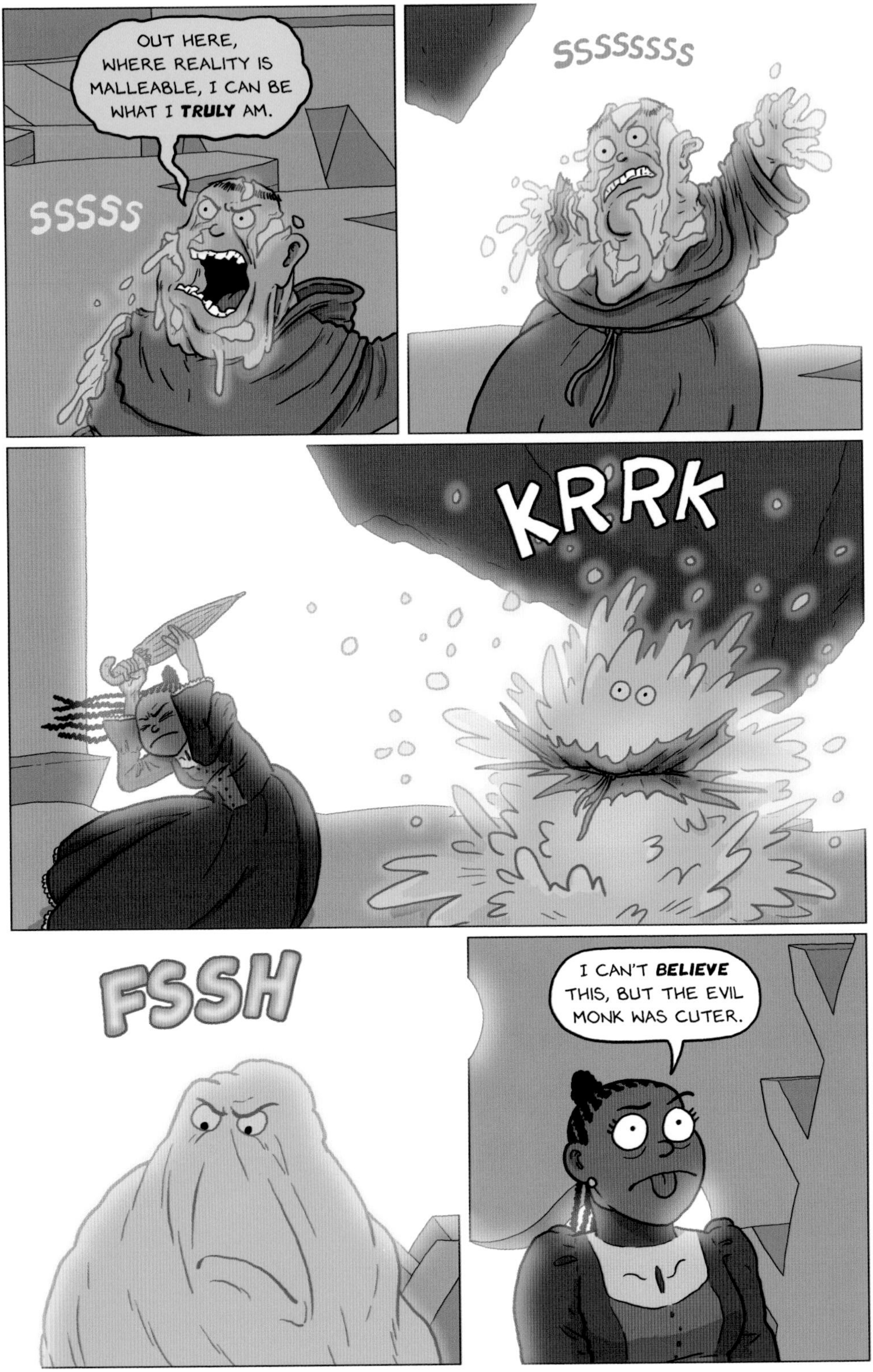
OUT HERE, WHERE REALITY IS MALLEABLE, I CAN BE WHAT I **TRULY** AM.
SSSSS
SSSSSSSS
KRRK
FSSH
I CAN'T **BELIEVE** THIS, BUT THE EVIL MONK WAS CUTER.

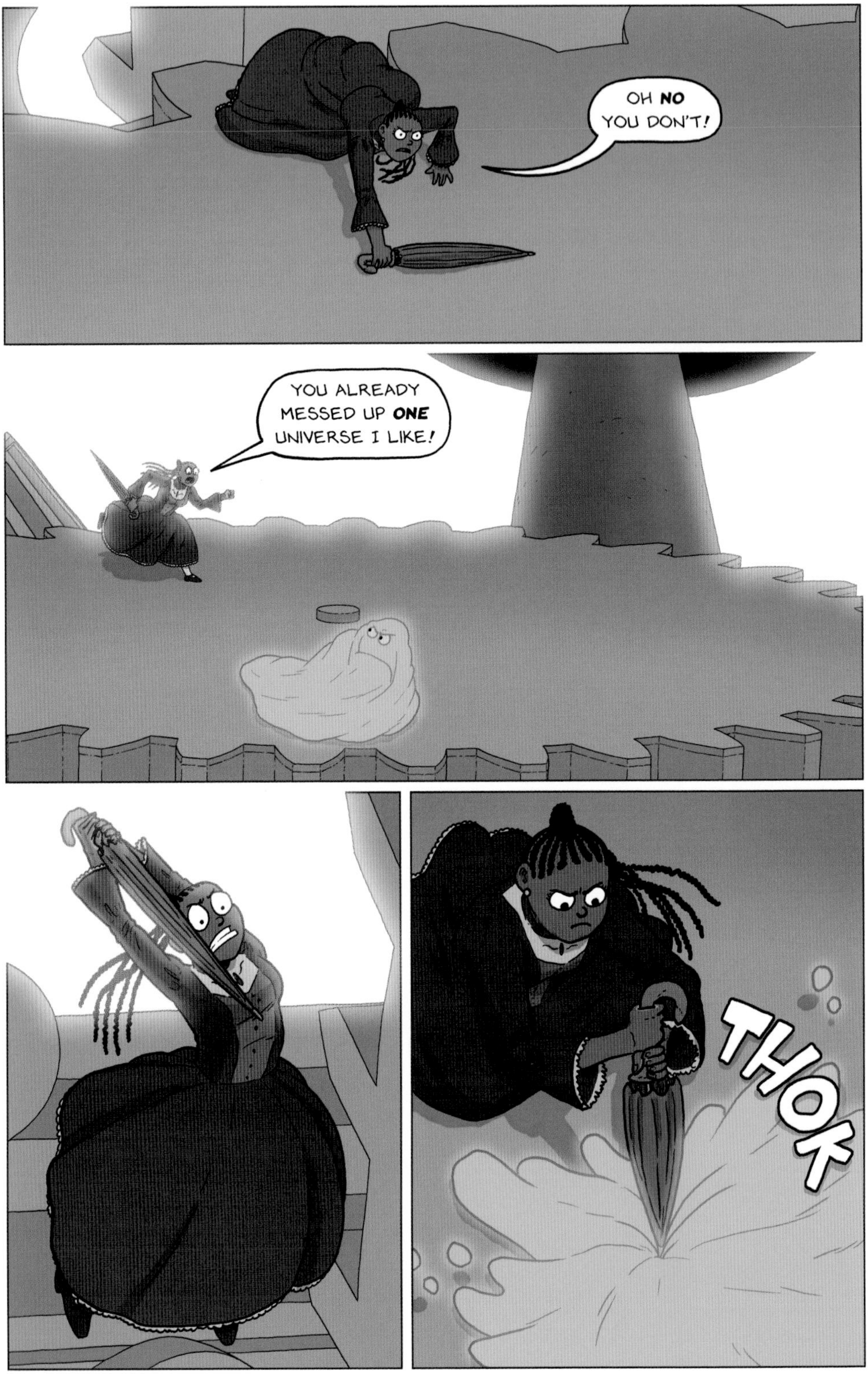
OH **NO** YOU DON'T!
YOU ALREADY MESSED UP **ONE** UNIVERSE I LIKE!
THOK

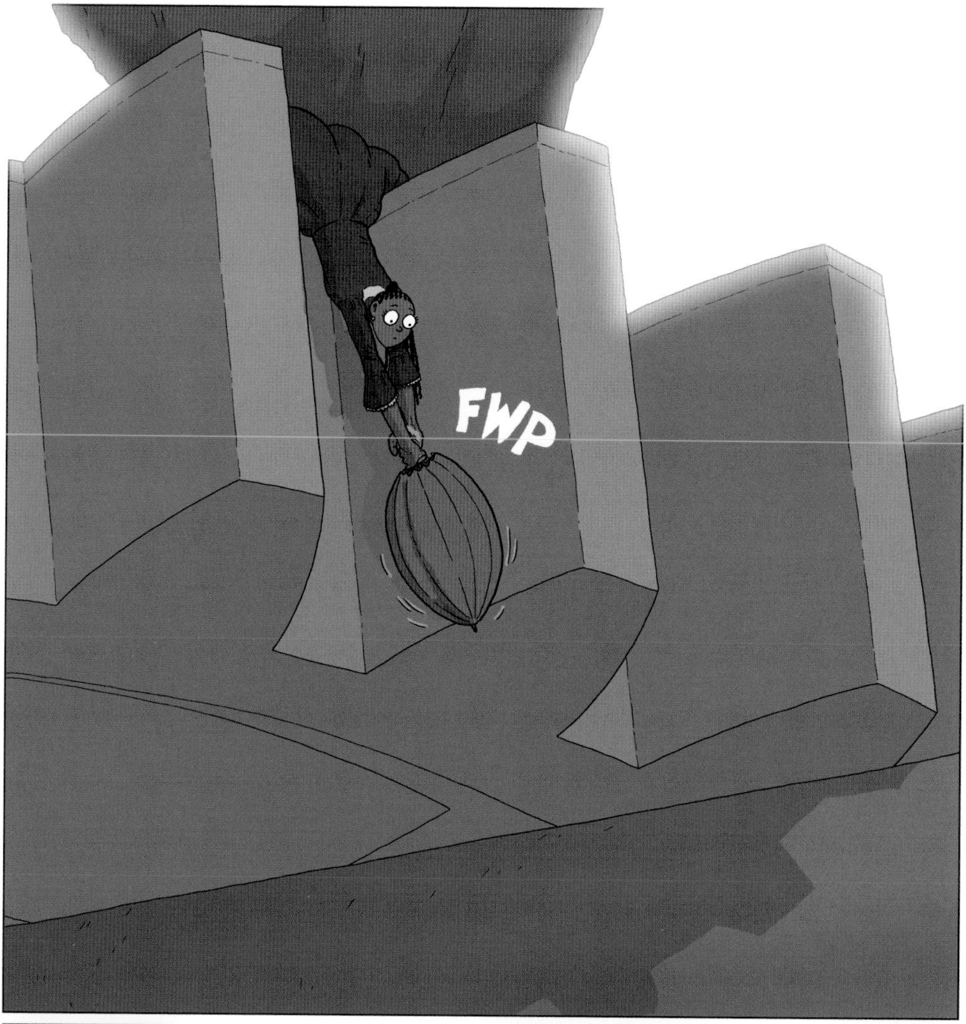
FWP

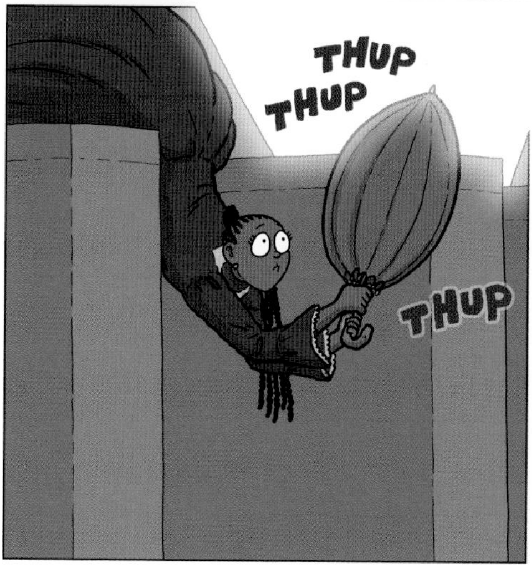
THUP
THUP
THUP

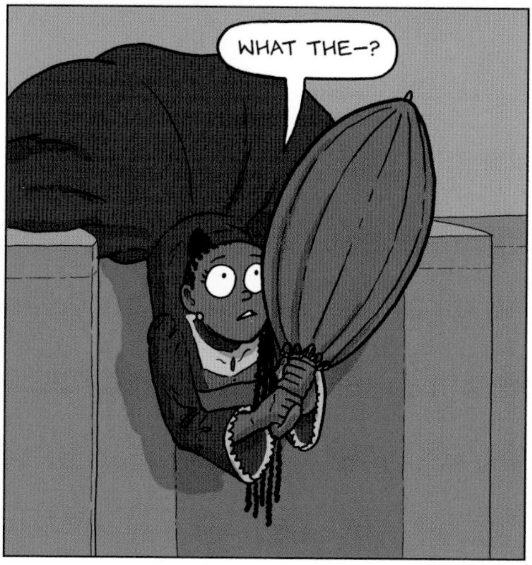
WHAT THE—?

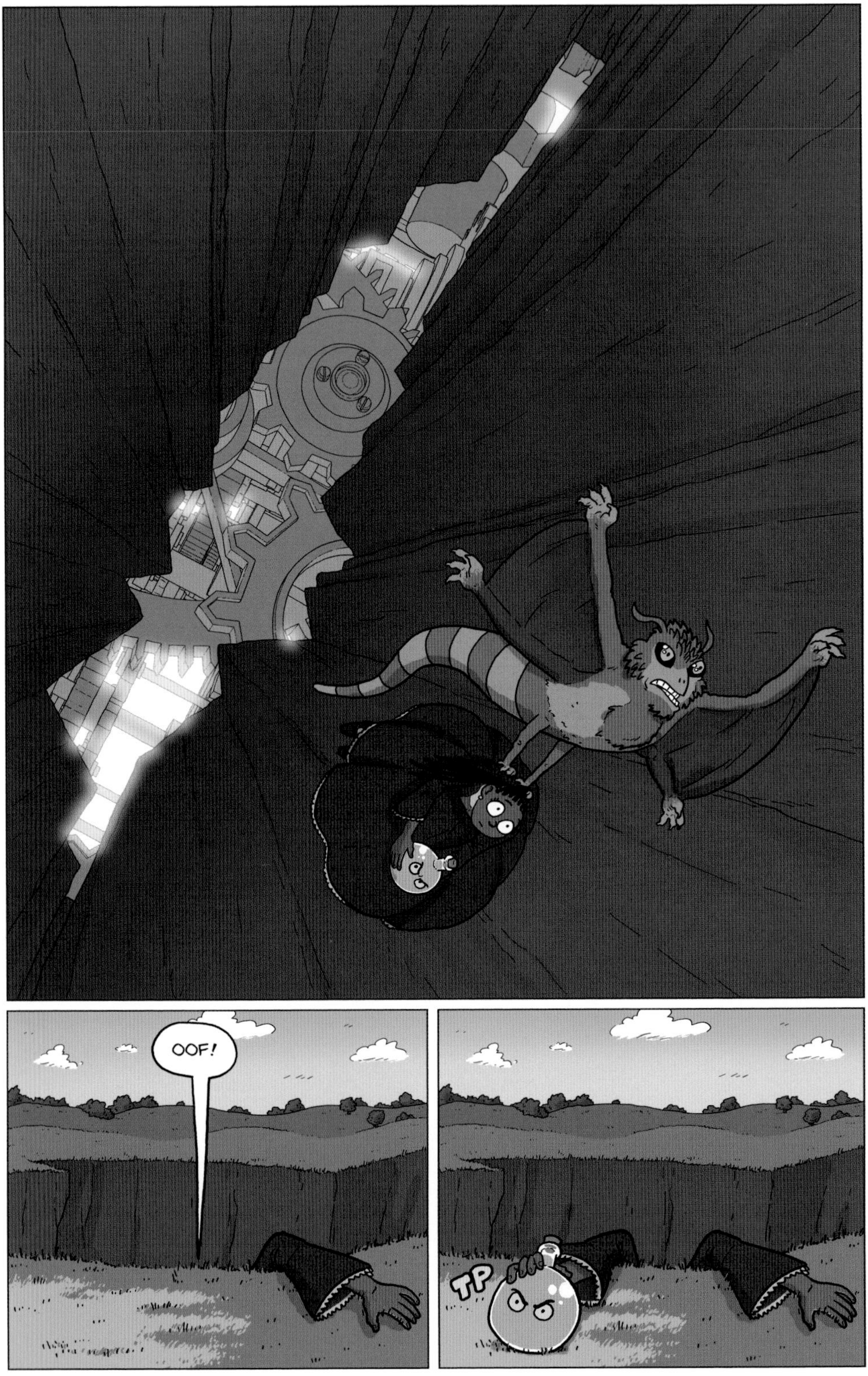
OOF!
TP

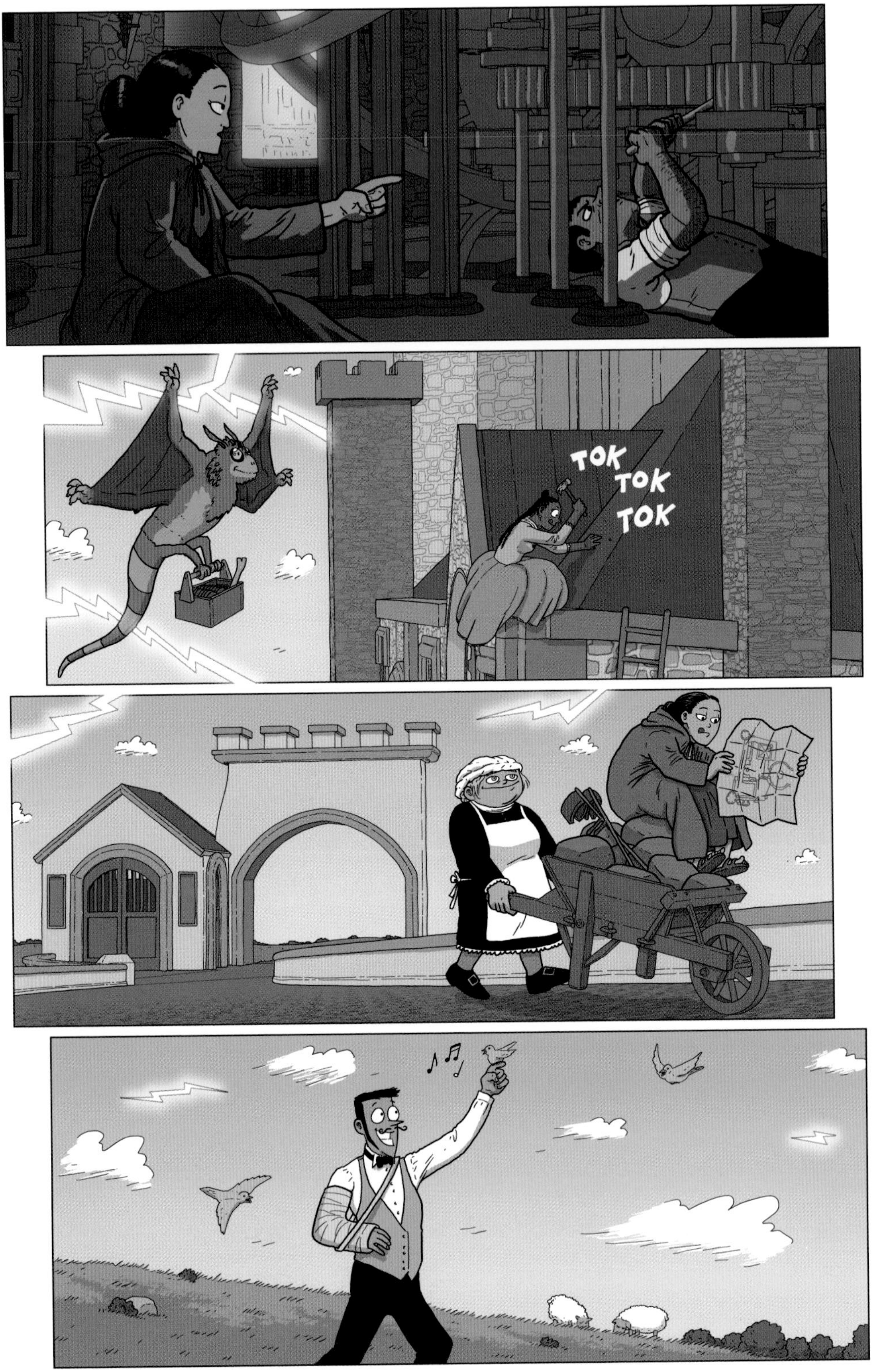
TOK
TOK
TOK

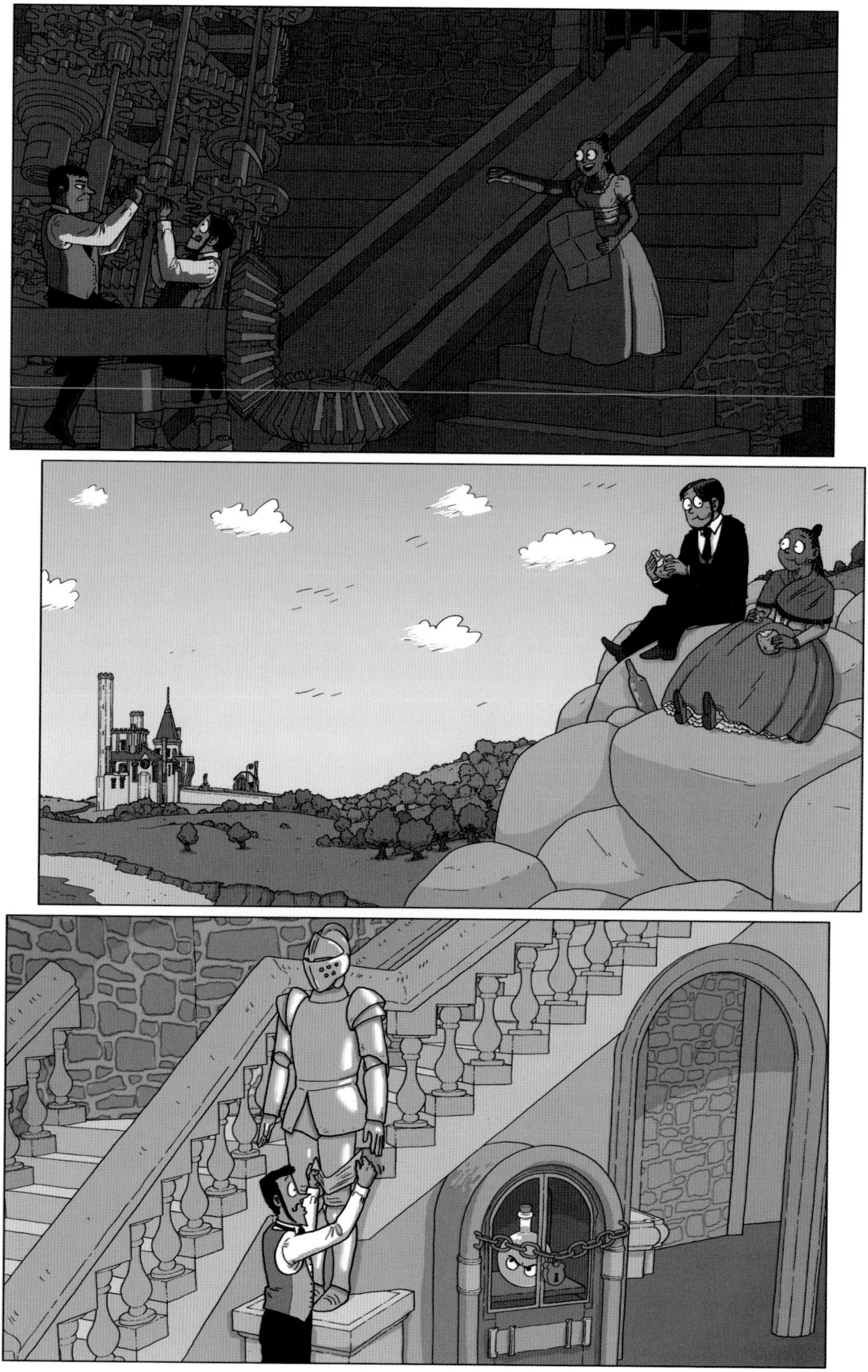

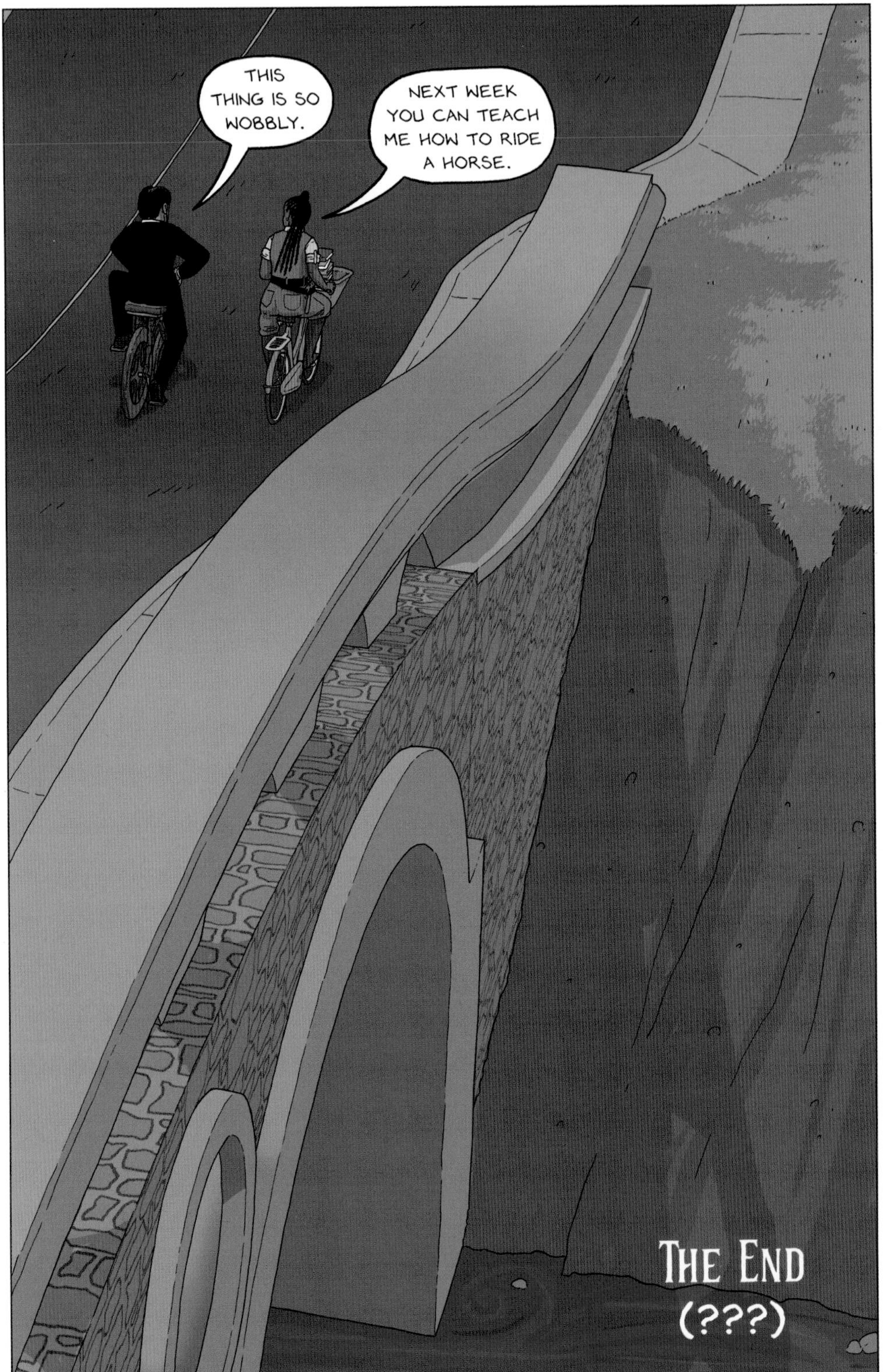
THIS THING IS SO WOBBLY.
NEXT WEEK YOU CAN TEACH ME HOW TO RIDE A HORSE.
THE END
(???)

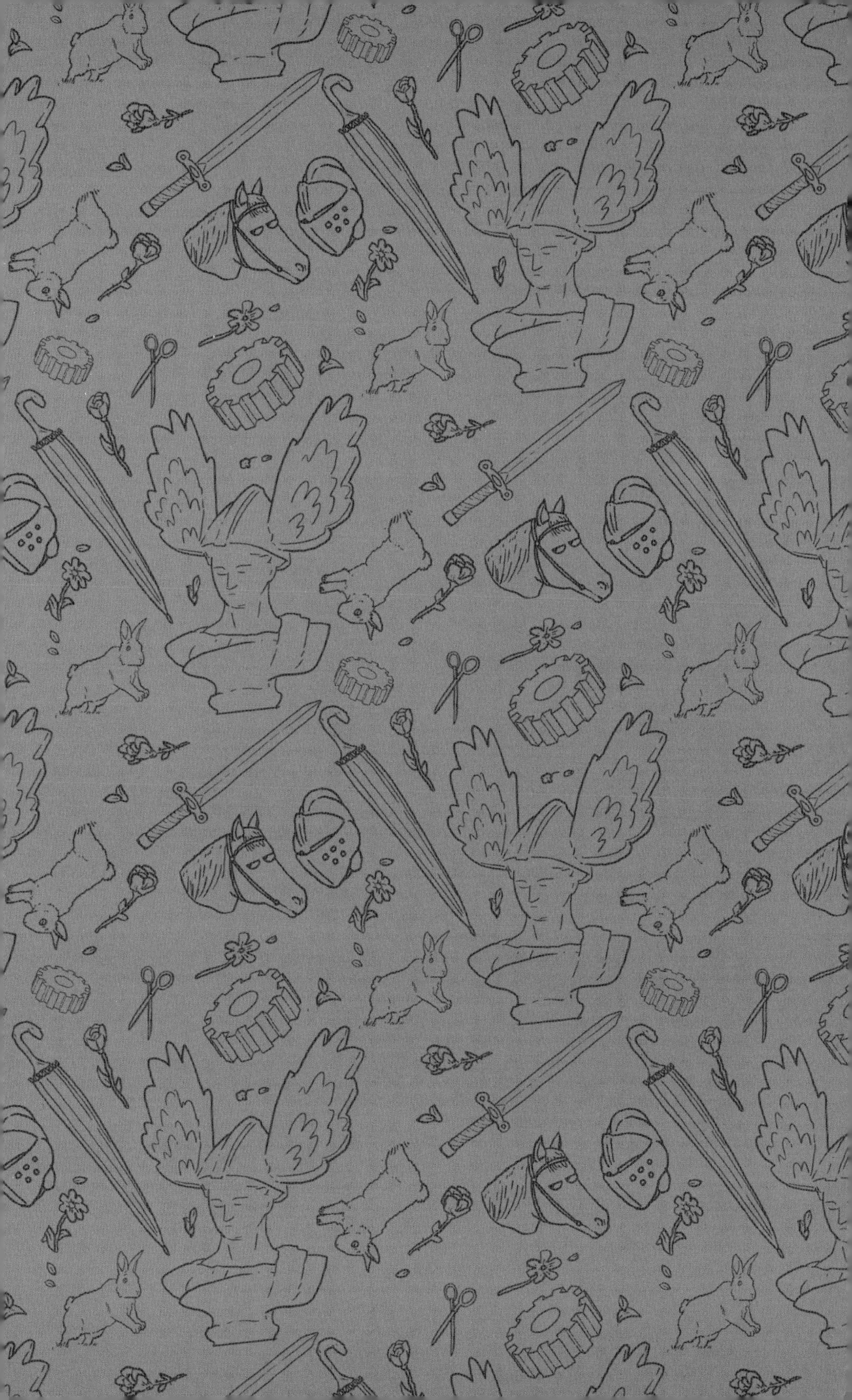

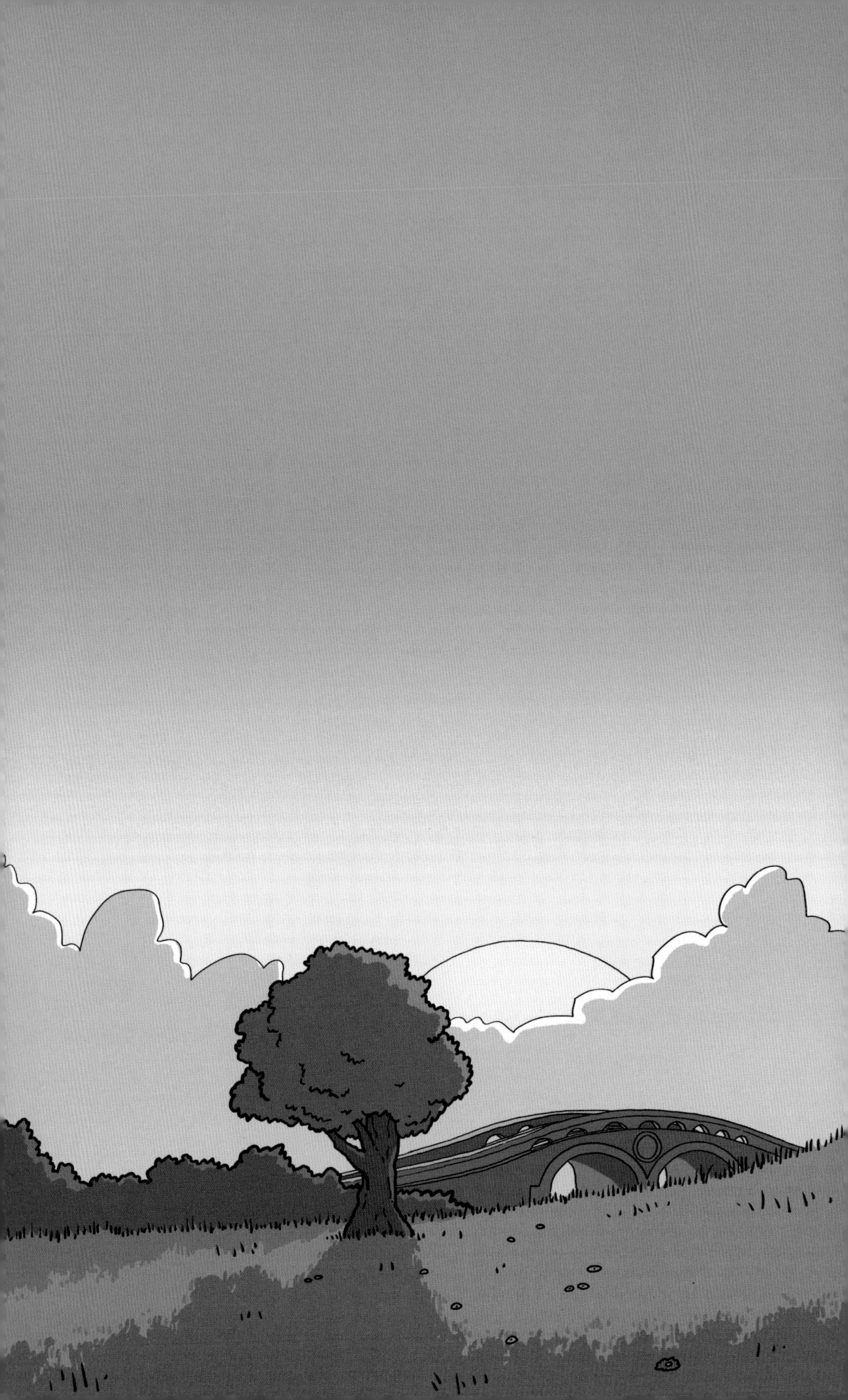

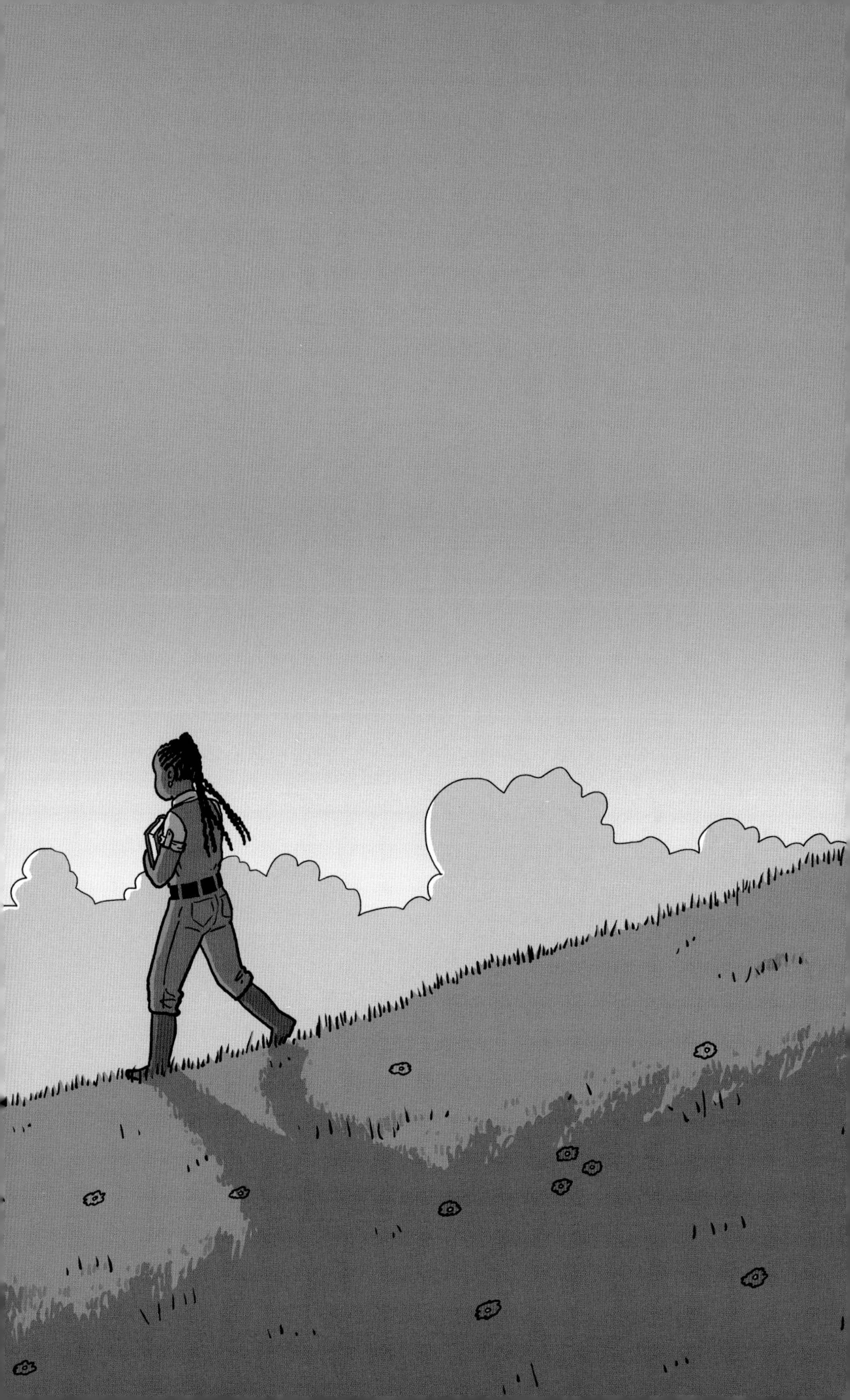

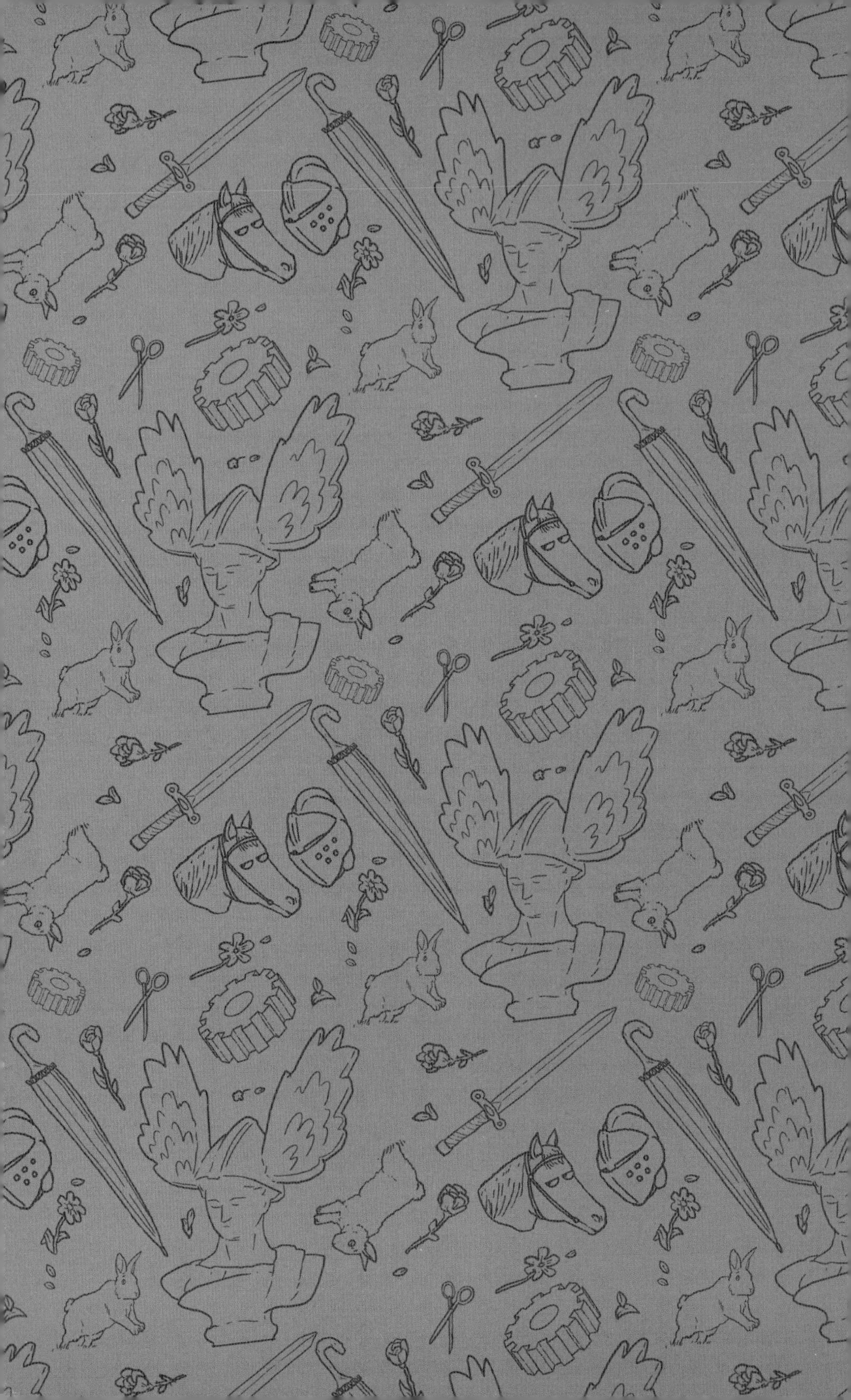